MYSTERIES OF

C🜨VE

MYSTERIES OF

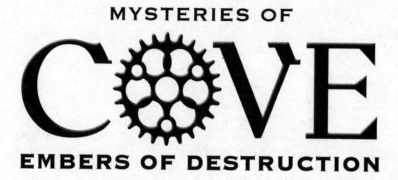

C**O**VE

EMBERS OF DESTRUCTION

J. SCOTT SAVAGE

SHADOW
MOUNTAIN

To Chris, Lisa, Heidi, Richard, Sarah, and the rest of
the staff at Shadow Mountain who believed

Visit us at ShadowMountain.com

First printing in hardbound 2017
First printing in paperbound 2018

Library of Congress Cataloging-in-Publication Data
Names: Savage, J. Scott (Jeffrey Scott), 1963– author. | Savage, J. Scott (Jeffrey Scott),
    1963–. Mysteries of Cove ; bk. 3.
Title: Embers of destruction / J. Scott Savage.
Description: Salt Lake City, Utah : Shadow Mountain, [2017] | Series: Mysteries of
    Cove ; book 3 | Summary: "Trenton, Kallista, and their friends from Discovery
    trace the origins of the dragons to San Francisco where they must battle a powerful
    white dragon in order to save the city and everyone who lives there"— Provided
    by publisher.
Identifiers: LCCN 2017021826 | ISBN 9781629723396 (hardbound : alk. paper) |
    ISBN 9781629724201 (paperbound)
Subjects: | CYAC: Dragons—Fiction. | Robots—Fiction. | Technology—Fiction. |
    San Francisco (Calif)—Fiction. | LCGFT: Fantasy fiction. | Steampunk fiction.
Classification: LCC PZ7.S25897 Em 2017 | DDC [Fic]—dc23
LC record available at https://lccn.loc.gov/2017021826

Printed in the United States of America
LSC Communications, Crawfordsville, IN

10 9 8 7 6 5 4 3 2 1

1

Angus was a stubborn, rust-brained know-it-all.

Kneeling on the floor of the long-abandoned building where they were spending the night, Trenton brushed away the drawings he'd made a few minutes earlier. "Let's try this again." Using a twig as a pencil, he sketched a square in the dirt. "This is where we are now." Several inches to the right, he added a sloping curve. "And this is the hill over there."

With shadows hiding Angus's eyes, Trenton couldn't tell if the muscular boy even glanced at the battle plans before muttering, "If you say so."

Unlike the others, Angus refused to wear a helmet when he flew the dragon he shared with Simoni, and his forehead had been sunburned so many times the skin had taken on a permanently gritty, reddish appearance, broken only by the large white circles left from his goggles.

Angus sat with his back propped against a vine-covered wall, picking his teeth with a pine needle. In front of him, a small cooking fire crackled and popped. Smoke drifted up through the rotting rafters and rusted beams of the building's three floors above them.

Although the concrete floor of the warehouse was still intact, more than a hundred years of neglect had buried it beneath a deep layer of soft soil covered with bushes, ferns, and other leafy plants. The only thing keeping it from being filled with trees like the rest of the forest was the fact that the upper floors blocked the sunlight during the day.

Ignoring Angus's obvious disinterest, Trenton drew a narrow valley beyond the hill, added a pile of leaves to represent what could have been houses in the past, and on the opposite side of the hill and valley, placed some pebbles to mark the rocky shore of the Pacific Ocean.

Trenton sucked in a deep breath of damp air, which had grown noticeably cooler since the sun went down. If tonight was anything like the last few nights, a thick fog would roll in from the ocean, masking everything more than a few dozen yards away in its glistening silver cloak and lingering until several hours after sunrise the next morning.

Trenton added a pair of circles on the other side of the hill. "Assuming the dragons go back to where we saw them this afternoon, they should be here and here. If Kallista and I circle around to the valley with Plucky and Clyde before the fog clears, we can set up an ambush." He drew a pair of triangles representing their dragons and an arrow going from the square to the hill. "You and Simoni fly over the hill, drive the dragons into the valley, and bam! They're trapped."

Angus curled one side of his mouth down and shook his head. "Nope."

Trenton flung the twig into the fire. "What's wrong with my strategy?"

"Don't know if your strategy's any good or not." Angus scratched above his right eyebrow, examined his fingernails, and flicked away a bit of dead skin. "We just don't need it. All those arrows and circles are a waste of time."

"A waste of time?" Trenton pictured Angus clenched firmly between the teeth of an acid-breathing red dragon. It was an image that helped keep him from exploding when the blowhard was being particularly obnoxious—which felt like all the time lately. "What's *your* plan?"

"Don't need a plan." Angus leaned forward to toss his pine needle into the flames where it flared then shriveled into blackened ash. He clasped his hands above his head and stretched his arms. Trenton noticed Angus's eyes flick toward Simoni, who'd been watching from her own shadowy corner. No doubt he was checking to see if she was impressed by his bulging biceps.

Not that Trenton cared or anything. He and Simoni had dated in the past. Okay, maybe *dated* was the wrong word. But they *had* been good friends. What she saw in Angus, he couldn't imagine.

Trenton turned to Simoni. "*You* think it's a good idea, right?"

Simoni wrapped a length of her long red hair around one finger and shrugged. Her green eyes glanced from the plans on the ground to Trenton. "Well . . ."

Angus smirked, and Trenton imagined how the yellow acid breath of the dragon would melt the cocky expression off his face. He didn't really want anything bad happen to Angus—at least not *that* bad—but even a pinecone falling on his head would do the trick.

"Clyde?" Trenton called. "Come look at this."

Clyde glanced up from the cook pot he'd recently removed from the fire. His pale, round face was normally split by a wide grin as he cracked jokes, but now he rubbed the back of his hand across his mouth and gestured with the metal spoon he was holding. "Love to, but I have to finish seasoning this soup before it gets cold."

Trenton didn't know why he'd bothered asking. Clyde had played the peacemaker of the group since they'd left their mountain home, Discovery, two months earlier. Not that Clyde wasn't a good fighter. He and Plucky had killed dragons. He just preferred cooking, drawing, and making people laugh to arguing.

Trenton glanced toward the three steam-powered dragons that loomed above them like great metal guardians. Clanks and clangs came from deep inside Ladon, the dragon Trenton and Kallista had built together. He couldn't ask Kallista and Plucky to back him up. They were working on a secret project.

He'd tried joining them once, hoping to get a peek at what they were working on, but as soon as he'd stuck his head through the access hatch on the dragon's back, they'd snapped their plans shut and told him to mind his own business.

"Let me guess," he said, turning to face Angus. "You want to go over the hill with no organization, shoot as many fireballs as fast as we can, and hope for the best?"

Angus held out his hands, palms up, and bared his teeth in a hungry grin. "See, you do understand me after all. Fly fast, shoot hard, and count the bodies later."

Trenton jumped to his feet and blew out an exasperated breath.

On the other side of a nearby hill were a pair of dragons. The first was a medium-sized blue, the kind of dragon that filled its belly with water and shot out clouds of scalding steam. The second—larger, its scales streaked black and red—had no breath weapon of any kind.

That didn't mean it wasn't dangerous, though. In fact, just the opposite.

Three weeks earlier, Trenton and his friends had been flying through a canyon searching for dragons. As always, Kallista was in the front seat of Ladon with Trenton behind her. Simoni and Angus were flying ahead of them, dodging in and out of the craggy openings in the cliff.

Clyde and Plucky were to his left. They had recently switched controls, with Clyde in the front seat steering and aiming their dragon's head. Plucky—who had a knack for sensing danger—was in the back, handling altitude and the dragon's fire attack.

Ladon was soaring close to the ground when a black dragon burst out from under a low rock shelf. Surprised by the creature's sudden appearance, Kallista turned sharply to the right as Trenton yanked back on the flight stick to take them higher.

Trenton glanced over his shoulder and noticed streaks of crimson against the black scales, as though someone had randomly brushed the dragon with red paint.

"What kind of dragon is that?" Kallista yelled.

"Not sure," he called. "Circle around."

They'd discovered several new kinds of dragons on their flight south, and Trenton had learned it was best to keep a safe distance until they could figure out what kind of weapons the dragon had.

Clyde, however, immediately began firing, and Simoni turned to give pursuit.

Banking away from the attack, the black-and-red dragon flew straight at Plucky and Clyde, who seemed unable to decide if they should break away after Kallista and Trenton or stay and fight with Simoni and Angus. By the time Clyde turned to flee, the dragon was on top of them.

"Get down there!" Kallista screamed.

Trenton was already moving the flight stick. They plunged back into the canyon, blasting flames before them.

Caught between the crossing lines of fire, the dragon snapped its glistening fangs at Plucky, then turned tail. Angus scored a direct hit on the back of its neck, and the monster dropped like a stone before crashing to the rocks below.

"Another kill!" Angus bellowed, waving his arms above his head.

It should have counted as a shared kill, but Trenton knew Angus wouldn't see it that way. Flying low over the canyon floor to make sure the dragon was dead, Trenton didn't realize anything was wrong until he heard Clyde's cry for help.

Trenton snapped his head around.

Their dragon, Rounder, bobbed up and down in the air as if caught in a storm, then dropped nearly a hundred feet, one wing brushing against the side of the cliff before Clyde could steer them away.

As Trenton watched, Rounder dove toward the jagged rocks below.

They were going down too fast.

"Pull up," Angus yelled.

"I can't!" Clyde turned in his seat to look back. "Something's wrong with Plucky."

The small figure seated behind Clyde was slumped to one side, her helmet-covered head bobbing loosely like a broken spring. The rear driver was the one who controlled the dragon's altitude. Without Plucky's help, Clyde had no way to stop Rounder's dive.

"We have to help them!" Kallista said, banking sharply toward Clyde.

Clyde leaned over the back of his seat, but he couldn't reach the flight stick.

Trenton watched helplessly as Rounder flew closer and closer to the ground. Coming up toward them, he could see the look of panic on Clyde's face. There was nothing Trenton and Kallista could do, unless . . .

"Take me under them," he yelled.

Kallista stepped on the pedal that steered them right; the

sun was blotted out by the shadow of the mechanical dragon above them. Hoping it wasn't a huge mistake, Trenton pulled back on the stick. Sparks shot out, and metal screeched as Ladon's head butted against Rounder's belly. Metal talons passed so close to their left Kallista had to dodge to avoid being gouged.

"Again!" she yelled.

Trenton smashed the dragons together again, and Rounder's angle of descent lessened.

It was working!

"Get under the wing," Simoni called from their right. She and Angus had positioned the left wing of their dragon, Devastation, under Rounder's right wing.

Kallista steered left, and Devastation and Ladon took up positions beneath Rounder's wings, bumping the dragon gently to keep its flight steady, until the mechanical dragon reached the ground.

It wasn't a pretty landing, but Clyde managed to come to a stop without smashing into the ground or hitting a tree. They had all been terrified that Plucky was dead. The cut on her shoulder wasn't deep, but she had flopped lifelessly as they carried her down from the dragon.

Fortunately, after a few hours, she was able to move again, and by that night, she was able to speak. That was how they'd discovered the black-and-red dragon's fangs carried a potent poison that caused nausea and paralysis with even a mild touch.

Now, standing in the abandoned warehouse near the warmth of the fire, Trenton glared at Angus.

With the knowledge of what they'd be fighting the following day and a good idea of the geography they'd be flying above, it was the perfect time to lay out a blueprint for the coming battle. Only instead of planning, Angus wanted to pick his teeth and flex his muscles. Not for the first time, Trenton wondered if the real reason Angus had come on this trip was to impress Simoni.

He pointed a finger at Angus. "Your shoot-first attitude is going to get you killed one of these days."

"You want to know who my attitude is killing?" Angus pushed himself to his feet with a grunt. "Take a good look up there," he said, jerking his chin to point past Ladon to Devastation, the dragon he and Simoni flew. "What do you see?"

Trenton didn't need to look to know what Angus was pointing at. Every time one of them killed a dragon, Clyde painted a dragon skull on the neck of that team's mount. Plucky and Clyde tended to be more cautious, working as scouts and driving the creatures into the open for the other teams to attack, but they still had three and a half trophies on Rounder's neck; shared kills earned half a skull.

Trenton and Kallista had eight full skulls, not including the dragon they'd killed in Cove.

Angus and Simoni had twelve and a half confirmed kills. Trenton thought they should have shared credit for at least two of their kills, but even taking those into account, they'd clearly taken down more of the scaled monsters than any other team. The two of them worked well together.

Simoni had picked up on the mechanical dragon's controls surprisingly quickly. She flew with a quiet precision, always finding the right angle of attack, shifting to counter a dragon's moves before the creature had even made them.

But a big part of their success was pure reckless aggression on Angus's part. He seemed to take every battle personally. Not content simply to win, he had to demolish whatever he was fighting against. On the few occasions when another team got the kill instead of him, he brooded about it for days. Sooner or later, though, that recklessness was going to get someone hurt.

Trenton kicked dirt into the fire. "You know it's not just you in the air."

Angus's grin slowly dissolved. "What are you saying?"

"I'm saying you aren't the only one flying. Risk your own life if you want. But there are six people up there counting on each other. Just the other day, you cut in front of Kallista and me and your fireball nearly hit Plucky and Clyde."

Angus stepped toward him. Trenton had grown nearly three inches over the last few months, and he now stood eye-to-eye with the boy who had bullied him every year they'd gone to school together. But Angus's shoulders were still broader than Trenton's, and he outweighed him by at least thirty pounds. "The reason we cut in front of you was because you and your girlfriend were too gutless to go for the kill yourselves. If anyone is a danger up there, it's you."

Trenton balled his hands into fists. Kallista wasn't his girlfriend, and to suggest that they were cowards . . . He tried picturing Angus getting ripped to pieces by a dragon, but it didn't help. "Don't you dare call—"

"Who's hungry?" Clyde asked, squeezing between them with a bowl of steaming soup. "You're going to love this. It's possibly my greatest creation yet. I call it Dragon Fire Delight. It's spicy but also, you know, delightful." He shoved the bowl into Angus's hands while pulling Trenton away by the elbow. "See if you can taste the secret ingredient. I'll give you a hint. It's crushed pumpkin seeds."

Angus lifted the bowl to his mouth and took a noisy slurp. "At least *somebody* around here is useful."

2

Trenton stomped deeper into the building, putting as much distance as he could between himself and the others.

As he left the fire behind, the darkness closed in around him, and he found it more and more difficult to keep from tripping over the roots and bushes. While the building made a good place to rest and recover, it let in precious little light from the sky overhead. After he narrowly missed running face-first into an exposed metal beam, he stopped to catch his breath.

Outside, the wind blew, making the building sway and creak. Trenton gripped the beam with one hand, craning his neck to study the floors above him. He could make out a small sliver of moonlight through the broken timbers. When he was fairly sure nothing was going to fall down on his head, he allowed himself to slump against a wall.

He and Kallista should have come here on their own. Maybe they hadn't killed as many dragons as Angus and Simoni had. But killing dragons hadn't been the point of leaving Discovery—at least not *all* of it. No matter how many of the creatures they killed, there were hundreds more ready to take their place. Maybe thousands. This trip was supposed to be about finding the source of the dragons, not seeing how many skulls they could collect along the way.

For a moment, he wondered how his mother and father were. He'd intentionally forced himself not to think about his family since leaving Discovery. Part of it was to avoid feeling homesick. When he and Kallista first left to search for her father, Trenton had been thrilled to explore a world he'd been told was destroyed. And it *had* been exciting, seeing sunlight for the first time, feeling rain, the trees, the ocean—being free to do whatever he wanted whenever he wanted.

Only the longer he was gone, the more he missed things he'd taken for granted: eating with his parents, hanging out at the park with friends, waiting for his father to come home from the mines. Although he wouldn't admit it to anyone, he even missed working on the farms of the food production level.

But there was another reason he'd been trying not to think about home. After Trenton and his friends left, the citizens of Discovery had sealed the entrance to the mountain using explosives and heavy equipment. They'd kept a small vent open in case any outside humans came looking for help, but they needed to protect themselves from the dragons outside.

Dragons had attacked Seattle, ripping the city to shreds and killing everyone. The only person who might have escaped was Kallista's father, Leo Babbage, and that wasn't a sure thing. The day they found Seattle in ruins, they'd also discovered that the charred remains of the Whipjack airship were gone. They hoped that meant Leo had managed to repair the ship enough to get it in the air and had escaped the city before the dragons attacked. Kallista firmly believed that if he had, he would have headed south in search of the origins of the dragons.

It was clear the attack on Seattle had involved several dragons working together. Had it been revenge for the dragons killed outside Discovery? For the weapons of war Trenton had helped the Whipjacks create? Or simply because the people were there and the dragons could kill them?

Ander, a friend of Trenton's who had been killed outside

Seattle, had been a member of the Order of the Beast, a group who believed dragons could talk to each other as well as to humans.

Trenton didn't accept that last idea at all. But what if dragons *could* communicate with each other?

At least a couple of the dragons they fought outside the entrance to Discovery had escaped. If the dragons attacked Seattle for revenge, wouldn't they attack Discovery as well?

If Trenton and his friends couldn't locate the source of the dragons and come up with a way to stop them, it might only be a matter of time until the dragons worked together to dig their way into the mountain and kill everyone like they did in Seattle.

The sound of shuffling footsteps came from the direction of the fire. Trenton could barely make out the figure walking toward him.

"I'm not hungry," Trenton said, assuming it was Clyde coming to smooth things over with a bowl of soup.

"I'm not surprised," Simoni said. She picked her way through the undergrowth until she'd reached Trenton. "Clyde mixes the weirdest things together. Yet everything he makes ends up tasting like squash."

Trenton struggled not to grin. Clyde viewed himself as a gourmet chef, but mostly he threw random things in a pot and picked some crazy name for whatever came out. Even Plucky, who'd lived on meager rations in Seattle, turned her nose up at a few of Clyde's creations.

Still, Trenton couldn't forget how Simoni had failed to back his attack plan.

"I'm surprised you didn't stay with Angus."

Simoni glanced around at the darkness. "I thought it would be more fun to come here and pout with you. It's the perfect place for it—dark, damp. It's got a very brooding, 'leave me alone so I can feel sorry for myself' atmosphere to it."

Trenton felt his ears grow hot and was glad she couldn't see his face. "I'm not pouting."

"Really? Because I was pretty sure you were feeling sorry for yourself." She held up her hands. "But, you know, if you came out here to commune with nature or something, I'll leave."

How did she manage to see through him so easily and point out how dumb he was behaving? It was aggravating sometimes. But he liked having someone to talk to who understood him so well. He grunted. "Angus is a jerk."

Simoni nodded. "He *is* a show-off. And he *does* take too many chances. The only reason I flew in front of you and Kallista the other day was because I knew Angus was going to take a shot and I wanted to make sure the two of you were out of the way."

Another gust blew through the open walls of the building, sending ghostly fingers of mist through the dark and ruffling Simoni's hair. Trenton tried to see her face, but it was too dark to read her expression. "If you know that, why didn't you tell him to go along with my plan?"

Before she could reply, he shook his head. "I mean, I know it's a complex strategy, and you haven't been flying nearly as long as I have—"

"So?" Simoni's voice had a clear edge to it.

"Well," Trenton said, "it's just that you're used to harvesting plants and milking cows, not flying a dragon. You don't—"

Simoni cut him off. "It wouldn't have worked."

"—understand," Trenton finished before he realized what she had said. "Wait, what?"

Simoni put her hands on her hips. "Your *complex* strategy wouldn't have worked. You had Angus and me flying over the hill to drive the dragons toward the four of you."

The sound of flapping wings came from over their heads, and Trenton jerked away from the wall before realizing it was only a large bird—an owl, maybe. "I should have known," he grumbled. "You want to make sure you and Angus get the first shot at the dragons. Another skull on the mighty *Devastation*."

Simoni stared at him, silver moonlight reflecting off her eyes. "You may not like it, but Angus is the best shot of all us. His natural aim is amazing. I move the head, but he knows exactly when to fire. I honestly think he could hit a squirrel on the run from two hundred feet away."

Trenton started to interrupt, but she held up a hand.

"That's not the problem, though," she continued. "You're assuming that when Angus and I roust the dragons they will fly toward the valley. But the first thing the blue dragon will do when it realizes it's under attack is head for the ocean."

"Of course." Trenton's shoulders slumped. Without water to make steam, a blue dragon was defenseless. How had he not thought of that? "If we'd gone with my plan . . ."

Simoni waited for him to finish.

"We'd have given the blue dragon the chance to prepare a steam attack." He rubbed a hand across his jaw. "If you knew that all along, why didn't you say something back there? Angus would've loved that."

"Maybe I was busy thinking about *milking cows* or *harvesting*." She rolled her eyes.

"Yeah, I guess that was a stupid thing for me to say," he admitted.

She'd known he was wrong, but she'd intentionally waited to tell him his mistake when they were alone, which meant she hadn't wanted to embarrass him. He shoved his hands in his pockets, feeling awkward and grateful at the same time.

He shuffled his feet. "Thanks."

In two quick steps, Simoni closed the distance between them. She reached toward him in the darkness, and he thought for a minute that she was going to . . . well, he didn't exactly know, but it wasn't the sharp jab in the chest she gave him.

"You have to stop trying to prove you're the best at everything."

Trenton took an involuntary step backward. "What are you talking about? I'm not trying to prove anything."

"From the day you decided you were going to be a mechanic, you couldn't stand anyone getting better math or science grades than you. You hated being assigned to food production, but you still had to get the highest score on the midyear tests. It kills you whenever anyone beats you at anything."

Trenton felt like Simoni had slugged him in the stomach. Of course he wanted to be the best at what he did. Who wouldn't? "It's not like it's a competition."

"Isn't it?" Simoni asked. She ticked off the points on her fingers one by one. "You hate that Angus and I have more kills than you. You can't stand that Kallista and Plucky haven't consulted with you about their project. You want to be the best mechanic. You have to be the best shot. You want to plan our attacks. It wouldn't surprise me if you've tried telling Clyde what to cook."

He didn't know what to say. Was that how everyone viewed him?

"You're a good mechanic," Simoni said, "but Kallista is better. You're a good shot, but Angus is more accurate. Clyde is funnier than you are. Plucky is better at sensing danger."

"So I'm mediocre at everything. What *am* I best at?" Trenton shouted, not caring who heard him.

"Maybe it's not about being the best. Maybe it's about

everyone doing what they can—working together. Give it time. I'm sure you'll find your role."

Before he could say anything, she leaned forward and kissed him on the cheek. "Let's get back to camp. Somebody needs to tell Clyde to keep the pumpkin seeds out of his soup."

3

Kallista raised her head the next morning, rubbing her eyes. She shifted in Ladon's front seat where she liked to sleep. It wasn't the most comfortable bed, but it gave her a sense of security she didn't feel on the ground. She glanced toward the sky. A glittering mist covered everything, just as it had the last few nights. She couldn't make out even the faintest trace of dawn. It would be at least another hour, maybe two, before the sun began to think about burning through the fog.

Tugging the blanket back over her head, she'd closed her eyes when she heard a soft *click-click-click*. That must have been what pulled her from a deep, and much needed, sleep.

The footsteps on the ladder to her left were so quiet she might not have noticed them if the clicking hadn't already awakened her. Shaking her head, she leaned over the side of the dragon in time to see a face emerge out of the fog.

"It's too early," she groaned. "Go back to bed."

The face broke into a guilty smile but continued to come closer. "Couldn't sleep, then, could I?" Plucky whispered. "Too rum excited. Figure I can have it done in another hour, two tops. Yeah, yeah?"

Kallista ran her fingers through her dark, spiky hair before wondering if she'd remembered to wash the grease off her hands before collapsing into bed the night before. Oh, well, it was too late to worry about it now. At least the grease and her hair were both the same color. "When you say *you* can have it done in an hour, you mean *we*."

"Right 'nuff." Plucky climbed the rest of the way up the ladder, bouncing in her mechanical leg braces when she reached the top. "Fair excited, ain't you? Run the plans through me head all last night. We can power it up in time to smash them beasts t'other side of the hill."

"We haven't even tested it," Kallista grumbled. Prior to meeting the Whipjack girl with the burned legs, Kallista wouldn't have believed anyone could be more stubborn than she was, but Plucky took persistence to a new level. "It will take at least two to three hours to finish the modifications, then we have to run tests. We don't even know if it will work, and if it does, we still have to decide whether to run the power to the wings or . . ."

Plucky grinned at her.

"What?" Kallista asked. "I'm not saying I'm going to . . ." But timelines were already running through her head—what pieces needed to be installed, how long it would take, what checks they'd need to make before starting Ladon up. The Whipjack girl had done it again. She threw her blanket aside, shivering in the cold air. "I can't believe you talked me into this."

"Plummy!" Before Kallista was out of her seat, Plucky was over the top of the dragon and opening the hatch. "Let's get cracking, yeah, yeah!"

• • •

A trickle of sweat ran down the side of Kallista's nose. With both her hands gripping the driveshaft for the new turbo fan, all she could do was puff out her lower lip and blow at the drip—which, of course, launched the salty bead of water directly into her left eye.

"Hurry up and tighten the last bolt," she said, trying to blink away the pain.

"Just a nudge more, and . . ." Plucky eased the wrench slightly forward and whistled softly through her teeth. "That's got it."

Kallista released her grip on the metal rod. It didn't move. It looked straight from what she could tell, too. "Give it a spin."

Plucky grabbed one of the fan blades and turned it. Not a single squeak or vibration came from the bearings. The rod held steady. "Plummy, huh?" she asked.

Kallista nodded. That was one of the things she liked about Plucky. When you showed her how to do something, she picked it up the first time. Plus, unlike some other people in the group, she didn't feel like she needed to talk all the time. The two of them could work for hours with only the occasional "Hand me that wrench" or "Have you seen the three-quarter-inch bolts?"

"That's it, then, yeah, yeah?" Plucky asked, wiping her hands on a rag. "It's finished, ain't it?"

"I guess it is." Kallista leaned against the inside wall of the dragon to admire her design. They hadn't powered it up yet, but already she knew it would work the way she'd imagined it would. She could see the pieces moving in her head as though watching a tiny operational model of what she'd built.

Kallista gathered up the tools and made sure everything was in place to fly. They'd need to put the turbo through a rigorous set of tests before trying it out, but if it worked, it could mean the difference between winning a battle and ending up as a dragon's lunch. She was proud of what she and Plucky had accomplished.

Along with the pride came a twinge of guilt. This wasn't the first change she'd made to her father's design. She and Trenton had modified the steam engine, discovered a metal fabric to use for the wings, and even switched the fuel source from coal to wood. But with each of those changes, she could tell from her father's plan that he'd expected her to make the modification—counted on it, in fact.

This was the first time she'd changed the dragon in a way he hadn't planned for. What would he think if he could see what she'd done? Would he approve or . . .

A howl from outside interrupted her thoughts. Clyde screamed.

Dragons!

Kallista was out of the hatch before the first scream died. Scanning the skies, she leaped over the seat and reached for Ladon's ignition.

"Where's the rusty buzzards?" Plucky shouted from Ladon's back.

"It's okay," Trenton called up from below, raising his hands. "It isn't a dragon."

"B-b-bees," Clyde said, his face white.

Kallista looked down and saw Clyde backing away from a large brown nest in a tree near where he'd been cooking. She shut Ladon's access hatch and climbed down the ladder.

By the time she'd reached the ground, Simoni had led Clyde away from the nest. "It's all right," Simoni said, holding Clyde by the arm. "They aren't bees. They're wasps. I'll take care of them, and you can sit over here while we finish packing."

Sweat covered Clyde's face, and his whole body shook. He opened and closed his hands, flexing his fingers, but his eyes never left the nest. How could someone who killed dragons be so terrified of something so small?

Simoni ripped a couple of green boughs from a small pine and tossed them into the morning fire. Immediately, the white smoke from the fire turned a smudgy black. Using her jacket,

Simoni fanned the dark smoke up into the nest. The buzzing coming from the brown oval died away, and the wasps that had been flying around crawled back inside.

"Impressive," Trenton said. "Where did you learn how to do that? And how did you know they were wasps?"

Simoni shrugged. "There were a couple of nests on the food production level. After the green dragon attacked the city, the nests had to be moved. Mr. Blanchard showed us how to put the wasps into a stupor using smoke."

Kallista looked up at the nest. Wasps were nasty creatures that stung over and over and needed almost no provocation to attack. A lot like dragons. She and Trenton had discovered a couple of wasp nests the first week after leaving Discovery in search of Seattle.

"Why would they keep wasps in Cove?" she asked.

"No idea," Simoni said. "I got the feeling we weren't supposed to know about them. They were in a small barn at the back of the level. I think Mr. Blanchard might have gotten rid of them after the attack because I never saw them again."

"I don't remember that," Trenton said.

Simoni shook her head. "You and Kallista were in the hospital at the time."

Clyde, who appeared to be feeling calmer, called out, "I left breakfast for you and Plucky on the rock over there. It's something new. I call it Asparagus Oatmeal a la Clyde."

Kallista tried to hide her disgust, but it must not have worked very well because Simoni said, "It really is delicious. You should try it."

"Feel free to have mine," Kallista snapped, unsure whether the girl was joking or not. Simoni bugged her. It wasn't just the fact that she had betrayed them to Cove's leaders, nearly dooming everyone in the city to destruction by the green dragon. It was that everything about her was so . . . *wonderful*. She was always cheerful and perky.

People were like machines. None of them were perfect. The more they appeared that way, the bigger their flaw was once it was discovered. She glared at Simoni until the girl flounced her perfect hair and turned away.

Angus, on the other hand, was a pain pretty much all the time. "Are we going to laze around all day or kill dragons?" he called from where he sat by a tree, doing nothing to help.

Still holding her wrench, Plucky called down from Ladon, "Ain't lazing, you birdbrained dandy prat! Some of us has been working all morning."

"You keep saying that, but I haven't seen any results," Angus said.

Plucky shouted back, and the two of them traded insults.

"Pleasant morning?" Trenton asked Kallista, gathering up the utensils Clyde had dropped.

"It *was*," Kallista said. "Are you going to tell me that green dreck is delicious too?"

Trenton laughed. "I'll tell you what it tastes like as soon as you tell me what the two of you are working on up there." He jerked a thumb toward Ladon. "You know, I helped build that. I'm risking my life as much as you are every time we go up. If you're making changes, don't you think you should let me in on them?"

The wind shifted, and Kallista moved to keep the smoke out of her eyes. "You don't trust me?"

"It's *you* who doesn't trust *me*." Trenton unscrewed the lid of his canteen and took a drink. "What happened to the days when we talked everything out?"

Kallista stared at the smoke before turning away. She refused to say it, but she missed the days when it was only the two of them—making plans, taking chances, testing theories. When they were building the dragon, they'd learned to depend on each other. Sure, they argued—at times agreeing on anything had been like trying to mix water and oil—but over time, they'd become like two pistons in the same engine, urging each other on when they needed it and easing back when they didn't.

In Seattle, they'd started to drift apart. Then Plucky entered the picture, and Simoni, and Angus. Even Clyde, who was probably the kindest person in the group, couldn't stand a minute of silence without cracking a joke or blurting out whatever he happened to be thinking at the time.

It was like shoving six pistons into the same engine. In theory, it should have made them stronger. Except each of the pistons was trying to go in its own direction. As soon as you figured out one, the others changed things up. The more time she spent around other people, the more she realized why her father preferred machines.

"You want to see what we've been working on?" she asked without looking at Trenton. "Go ahead and look. I won't stop you."

The canteen lid rattled as Trenton screwed it back on. "Not until you want me to. What I want to know is why you're keeping secrets."

Kallista sighed. Why hadn't she shown him? He *had* helped her build Ladon, and he was right about risking his life. It wasn't that she didn't trust him, because she *did*. It wasn't even that her project was such a big secret; she'd show it to everyone soon enough. It was just that she wasn't used to being around so many people all the time.

The hours she spent modifying the dragon, with only Plucky working wordlessly by her side, rejuvenated her. It was like the days she'd spent with her father. The two of them could work side by side, adjusting and repairing machines without saying a word, lost in their concentration of the work but comforted by each other's presence.

She knew that once she showed everyone her project, they'd all be asking questions and clamoring for more information. Angus would want his dragon modified immediately. Trenton would worry about safety. And Clyde . . . well, he had something to say about pretty much everything. Then what would she do for privacy?

"Just tell me you aren't building a giant chicken," Trenton said.

Kallista snorted and turned around. Before they'd found the plans for Ladon in the museum, they'd joked that the talon they'd built from the pieces her father had hidden looked like the foot of a giant chicken. "It's a new weapon," she said with a grin. "We're going to shoot humongous eggs at the dragons."

"If we time it right, we can shoot the eggs with fire and flash fry them over the dragons' eyes."

She clapped a hand to her mouth. Just like that, the two of them were laughing. It was almost like old times. Maybe people weren't completely awful. "Actually, we've been building—"

A blur of metal flew through the air. Angus ducked as Plucky's wrench barely missed his head.

"What are you doing, you crazy grease monkey?" Angus shouted. "You could have killed me!"

"Shame I didn't!" Plucky yelled back. "Call me a hog-grubber again and I'll bash you witless."

"I didn't call you a hog-whatever." Angus stepped back as Plucky searched for something else to throw at him. "I only said I don't believe you're actually building anything up there. You're using it as an excuse to sleep in late. You didn't have to—"

"Not building anything?" Plucky screeched. "You sorry, slug-a-bed, starched . . ." For once, Plucky couldn't come up with a strong enough insult.

"Maybe we should break this up," Trenton said to Kallista, starting toward them.

"I'll show you," Plucky yelled. She turned to the front of the dragon and started it up. Smoke belched from the exhaust as the engines roared to life.

Realizing what Plucky was about to do, Kallista raced toward the ladder. "Plucky, no!"

Still shouting, Plucky flicked the switch they'd added to the controls. The dragon that had been quietly vibrating before now, shook as though a fierce wind was pounding against it. All four clawed feet rattled in the dirt, digging small trenches.

"We need to test it first!" Kallista yelled. But it was too late. Flames flashed from Ladon's underbelly, and the smoke coming from the exhaust turned from gray to black. Steam hissed in the air as the turbo fans kicked in.

Plucky pounded the fire button, and a ball of flame burst from the dragon's mouth. It was so bright it made Kallista squint. The fireball—more than three times the normal size—blasted into the trunk of an oak fifty feet away. The tree exploded. Chunks of bark and wood shot in every direction.

Kallista dove to the ground as a flaming spear whizzed past her head.

It was nearly a full minute before pieces of the tree stopped thumping to the ground. Blinking against the bright orange afterimage, Kallista dared to look around. Where the oak had stood, there was nothing but a charred piece of trunk, maybe ten feet tall and slanted severely to the left. It was as if the rest of the tree had disappeared. A few pieces of burning wood littered the ground; they would need to put those out before the whole forest caught on fire.

One by one, Kallista and the others stood up, checking themselves and each other for injuries. Miraculously, none of them had been hit by the flying debris. Particles of dust and ash floated in a slowly descending cloud. Long green smears marked an area around the fire pit. It took Kallista a moment to realize they were the remains of Clyde's asparagus oatmeal.

Plucky, eyes wide and mouth slack, turned off Ladon's engine. Her pink tongue darted out across her teeth before disappearing. "Um, rum sorry about that."

Trenton looked at Kallista and pulled a single oak leaf from his hair. "So, I guess that's what . . . ?"

Kallista let out a long, slow breath. "That's what we've been working on."

4

"I can't believe you didn't tell me you turbocharged the engine," Trenton called from the backseat of their dragon. "That's amazing!"

"I was going to." Kallista directed an irritated glance to her left where Plucky and Clyde flew Rounder. "As soon as we had a chance to test it."

Clyde steered to the left, keeping the two dragons in tight formation. Behind him, Plucky hunched her shoulders. "Said I was sorry, didn't I? Lost my wool-brained temper, yeah, yeah."

With their steam engines running at minimal power, the three dragons glided almost silently through the air—Ladon in the middle with Rounder and Devastation to either side. Less than fifty feet below, the treetops formed a green canopy so thick Kallista couldn't see the ground. They were flying low, hoping the dragons hadn't heard the explosion. Although much of the fog had burned off, several thick pockets remained, especially to their right where ocean met land.

"I don't see what the problem is," Angus shouted. "My only question is how soon we can get *our* upgrade. With that kind of firepower, I could take down two dragons at the same time. Maybe even three."

"The *problem* is we could have started a forest fire. Or woken the dragons." Trenton adjusted his flight stick, and Ladon dropped a few feet closer to the treetops.

27

"Careful back there." Kallista glared at him. This was one of the things she'd been afraid of. He was a habitual worrier.

"Careful?" Trenton raised his eyebrows. "Maybe you should have thought about being careful when you decided shooting fireballs the size of houses was a good idea. Did it ever occur to you the boiler might not be able to handle that kind of pressure?"

"No, that never occurred to me," Kallista said, the blood in her temples pounding. "Maybe you could explain how steam engines work. It's not like I've been fixing them all my life or anything."

"Guys," Clyde said. One look from Kallista snapped his mouth shut.

Kallista twisted in her seat to look at Trenton. "First of all, it isn't just fire. The blowers provide a short burst of power that can be used to fly faster, turn sharper, smash a boulder with one talon, or, yes, shoot more fire than normal."

"That's all great," Trenton said. "But how's that going to keep the boiler from exploding? Have you even considered the increase in steam pressure? How long can you run the fans before the engine explodes?"

"Of course I considered the increase in steam pressure. Based on my math, we can run the turbos for a minute—two, tops—before they overheat. I'm going to add an override that turns them off automatically. I just haven't had the time yet." She stared at Trenton, waiting for him to argue. When he didn't, she released a slow breath. "You can double-check the numbers when we get on the ground."

She wasn't good at apologies, even when she knew she should make them. This was as close as she could come.

Trenton seemed to understand. He adjusted his goggles and looked toward the approaching hill. "Unless they've moved, the dragons should be on the other side of that rise." He paused for a moment before turning to Simoni. "How do you think we should approach them?"

Since when was Simoni in charge of the attack plan? Trenton always decided on their approach. Simoni looked at Trenton, and something passed silently between them. Kallista tugged at the strap of her helmet. Maybe she wasn't the only one keeping secrets.

Simoni pointed to the left. "Angus and I will fly around the hill and come in from the east. With the sun in the dragons' eyes, it will make it harder for them to see us. Clyde, you and Plucky wait for us to circle around, then come straight over the rise. You should be right on top of the dragons, forcing them to break cover."

She nodded toward the ocean, barely visible through the fog to their right. "The blue should go straight for the water. Kallista and Trenton, you will be waiting there. If the blue is on its own, go for the kill. If they both come your way, delay them until the two of us can close in on their flanks. As long as you keep the blue from filling its belly, it will be defenseless."

Kallista wiped her goggles with the sleeve of her jacket, clearing away the water that had beaded on the lenses. It was a good plan. A very good plan. How had someone who spent all her time planting seeds come up with it?

Simoni held up one hand. "On my count. Three—two—one." She and Angus banked right while Clyde and Plucky took their position.

Kallista veered toward the ocean as Trenton dropped Ladon closer to the treetops.

"Something you want to tell me?" she asked, angling her head to keep an eye on the other two dragons.

"About what?"

Kallista had spent enough time around Trenton to know when he was playing dumb. But did that mean he wanted her to push harder to learn the truth or would pushing only make him more stubborn about hiding it? If only people came with instruction manuals.

When Angus and Simoni disappeared from view, Kallista headed toward the mouth of the valley where they discovered a stream emptying into the ocean.

"That could be a problem," Trenton said.

Kallista nodded. "If the blue dragon gets water from the stream instead of the ocean, we'll be waiting here for nothing. But if we fly up and arrive too soon . . ."

Trenton bit his lower lip. "We could ruin the plan."

For the next several minutes they soared above the crashing waves while below them large white birds squawked as they searched the beach for food. Prior to leaving Discovery, Kallista had never seen a seagull. But the closer they got to the water, the more the creatures swarmed in noisy white packs.

She rose in her seat, straining for some sign of what was happening. A thick band of fog hugged the streambed, turning the far bank into a billowing white curtain. "I think we should go."

"Let's wait a little longer." Trenton pushed his goggles up on his head, searching the trees.

As seconds ticked by with no sign of the dragons or their friends, Kallista became more and more certain something had gone wrong.

She had nearly decided to go, no matter what Trenton thought, when a flash of blue scales burst from the trees.

"Go!" Trenton screamed, yanking his goggles back into place. He cranked the throttle to full power as Kallista angled to cut the blue dragon off. Kallista smiled. With the dragon's attention focused on Devastation's pursuit, it wouldn't see them until it was too late.

Trenton hit the fire button, and a gout of flames burst from Ladon's jaws. At the same time, a shadow fell over them.

Acting on pure instinct, Kallista pushed the foot pedals, turning hard to the left. The black-and-red dragon stretched its jaws and ripped a gouge along the shoulder of her leather jacket, and she looked up in time to see the beast scream with fury, fangs glistening with poison, and circle back around. Trenton dropped them into a dive. Trees raced toward them, and it took every bit of strength Kallista had to muscle the flight control hard enough to keep from crashing.

Once they had leveled out, Trenton leaned forward. "Did it get you?"

She ripped her jacket off over her head and checked her arm. Her shirt was untouched. "No, I'm—"

"Look out!" Trenton shouted.

The black-and-red dragon had returned, talons raised. With nowhere else to go, they dove into the opening above the stream. Trees blurred past on their left and right. The blue dragon appeared ahead of them. Steam swirled from its nostrils, and its belly was fully extended.

Kallista looked for somewhere to escape. They were too low to fly over the trees. The black-and-red dragon had forced them down toward the stream, and the blue had them cut off. Where were Rounder and Devastation?

Trenton shot a fireball toward the blue dragon, but its blast of water extinguished it before it could do any damage. Kallista eyed the trees to her right, wondering if she could make a turn, but it was no good. The stream was too narrow, the branches too close.

The blue raced straight toward them, steam billowing from

between its teeth as it opened its jaws. The black-and-red was right on top of them. The only way out was to crash into the shallow water below.

"The turbos!" Trenton yelled. "Fire the turbos."

Even as she reached for the switch, she knew it was too late. The dragons would be on them before the turbos had time to kick in. Ladon's talons brushed the surface of the stream, sending sprays of water to either side. Mere feet away, the black-and-red screamed.

Then it and the blue dragon pulled up and flew away.

Kallista looked left and right, trying to figure out where the dragons had gone.

Trenton pointed to the right. "They went into the fog." He pulled them up from the stream as Kallista banked left.

She circled slowly, waiting for the dragons to reappear. It had to be a trick. Only what was the point? The two dragons had Trenton and her trapped. In dozens of fights with dragons, she'd never seen them break off a battle when they had you outnumbered.

Two shapes appeared from upstream, and she was already turning Ladon, ready to flee, when she realized it was their friends.

"Where have you been?" Trenton yelled as the two mechanical dragons soared toward them.

Clyde flew Rounder over to join them, and Plucky shook her head. "Ruddy mud-crunchers wasn't where we expected."

"They were hiding in the fog on the other bank of the stream," Simoni said. "Almost like they knew we were coming. We didn't even realize where they were until we heard your shouts."

Trenton yanked off his helmet. "Something's wrong with this whole situation."

Kallista nodded. Dragons didn't set ambushes, and they didn't give up a fight when they had the advantage.

Angus slammed his fist against the side of Devastation, searching the air. "Which way did they go?"

Kallista pointed south. "That way, but—"

Before she could finish, Angus shouted, "Let's get them!"

Simoni gunned Devastation's throttle, sending their dragon darting into the fog bank.

"What are you doing?" Trenton yelled after them. "You won't be able to see a thing." But it was too late. They were gone.

Kallista clenched her jaw. Even she wasn't *that* crazy.

"Gots to go after 'em, yeah, yeah?" Plucky asked.

Clyde scratched the back of his neck, his dark eyes wide as he stared at the nearby dense gray wall.

"This doesn't feel right," Trenton said.

That was exactly what Kallista was thinking. She circled above the river, hoping Simoni and Angus would return. It was strange to be the cautious one; in the past, she'd always been the first to take chances. But this battle was nothing like the others they'd had with dragons. What happened to Simoni's carefully planned strategy?

After nearly a minute passed with no sign of their friends, Kallista blew out an exasperated breath. "We have to go after them."

Trenton looked at her and nodded. "Into the fog."

5

Cold, wet air blasted Trenton's face. He'd slowed Ladon's wings, but with the thick fog surrounding them, it was impossible to tell how fast they were moving.

Kallista kept wiping the moisture from her goggles, but Trenton knew there was nothing to see. Even the dragon's powerful headlights merely reflected off the fog. Less than fifty feet to their right, Clyde and Plucky were visible only as a faint silhouette marked by the twin glow of their dragon's eyes.

"Let's go a little higher," Trenton called, pulling back on the flight stick. The last thing they needed was to run into a hill.

"Sticking with you." Clyde's voice floated ghostlike through the mist as the shadow that was his dragon rose with them.

Kallista cupped her hands to her mouth. "Simoni! Angus!"

There was no answer. She glanced at the compass and steered more to the left.

"This is exactly what I was talking about," Trenton said. "Angus's stupid risks put all of us in danger. I can't believe Simoni flew right in."

"You agreed to bring them," Kallista said.

Trenton had no response to that. Instead, he flexed his gloved hands, trying to keep his fingers warm.

A few minutes later, Kallista scooted forward in her seat. "I see something."

Trenton leaned to the right to look around her. The fog appeared to be thinning, letting a few rays of sunlight push through. He thought he could make out shapes ahead. He eased the flight stick back, his right hand hovering above the fire button.

Then, as though a curtain had been whipped away, the fog disappeared, revealing what lay behind it.

"Oh," Kallista whispered.

Trenton's hand dropped from the fire button as he tried to comprehend what he was seeing. It was a city, though the word was completely inadequate. Calling this a city was like calling the mountain that housed Discovery a hill.

Thousands of glittering metal buildings of all shapes and sizes covered rolling hills. Interspersed among them were hundreds of towers that had to be at least four or five hundred feet tall. Each tower was covered with ornate copper, brass, and silver scrollwork that reflected the morning sunlight, and rows of arched, metal shutters circled level after level.

Machines and factories puffed steam into the air. Canals, elevated pipes, roads, and cables ran in so many directions it was like looking down on a maze.

"Look at that," Clyde said, pointing toward the ocean.

Trenton's jaw loosened at the sight of an enormous bridge spanning the blue-green bay. Twenty or more massive metal pillars rose hundreds of feet out of the water. Silver lines thicker than his leg supported three different levels.

Thick chains and gears lifted nets full of fish from boats that floated beneath the bridge, and mechanical arms moved the fish into rows of linked metal cars that waited on tracks that ran along the top-most level of the bridge. Trenton thought they might be called *trains*. Smaller vehicles trundled freely across the lower levels of the bridge.

Turning to the left, he saw what looked like enormous insects scuttling through rows of tall green plants.

"Are those spiders?" He shuddered. They had to be ten feet tall.

"I think they're machines," Kallista said. "People are sitting in them."

She was right. Hundreds of the round machines climbed about the fields on jointed metal legs. Some of the machines were outfitted with digging tools, while others had cutting blades. Men and women perched in raised seats controlled the machines.

Now that he realized there were people in the city, he noticed them everywhere: walking the streets, driving vehicles, operating machines. As he and Kallista glided by one of the towers, several men and women stopped their work to look up at them, shading their eyes with their hands.

The people appeared to be pushing a huge pile of what looked like slaughtered animals—cows, maybe, or sheep—down a street paved with large brass plates. But as he looked closer, he realized the huge plates were a conveyor belt, sliding everything forward with loud clanks and thumps.

Something flew toward them from the left, and Trenton spun around, sure it was the black-and-red dragon again, but it was only Simoni and Angus.

"Isn't this amazing?" Simoni asked, a wide smile splitting her face.

Trenton's mouth worked as he tried to find words. There was no way to explain this. What was this place? How was it even here? Where did all these people come from, and how had they survived?

He glanced at the fog they'd flown through. "Where did the

dragons go?" Was there something about the fog that kept them away from the city?

"Some of those machines down there must be weapons," Angus said.

Yes, that made more sense than the fog. Obviously, the people were able to defend themselves. What kind of weapons did they have that were so powerful?

"We've got to find out about their technology," he said. "How they've managed to fight off the dragons."

The six of them circled above the city, trying to take it all in.

"You there, in the air!" a voice boomed so loudly that Trenton jumped. "Welcome to our city." The voice seemed to come from everywhere at once, echoing off the buildings as if a hundred giants were shouting together. *Welcome-ome-ome to our city-ity-ity.*

Trenton cupped his hands to his mouth. "Who are you?" Compared to the giant's voice, his sounded puny. Could they even hear him?

"Please fly toward the flashing light," the voice boomed again.

Glancing down, Trenton spotted a brass horn mounted on the corner of one of the buildings. Down the street there was another just like it. A voice-amplification system, he thought. His hands itched to take it apart and get a better look at how it worked.

At the top of a silver tower, a light flashed so brightly it was easy to see even in full sunlight.

Clyde looked toward his friends. "Should we?"

Trenton remembered all too well what had happened the last time they'd found a new city. He could tell Kallista did as well. Her eyes scanned the ground below them. "It's too easy," she said at last. "A huge city with machines to fight off dragons has been here all along? And we've never heard of it?"

"Kind of hard to hear about anything when you're enclosed in a mountain," Trenton said. But he knew what she meant. This place was a like a huge plate of candy waiting for someone to come along and reach for it. He studied the buildings and streets. There wasn't a scorch mark to be seen. And it wasn't like something as big as a dragon could hide in the shadows of an alleyway. Either the dragons left this city alone or there was something he was missing.

"I want to see their weapons," Angus said with a grin.

Trenton did too. After all, they'd come looking for a way to keep the dragons away, and clearly these people had accomplished it. No matter the risk, they had to find out how they were doing it.

"Let's see what they want," Kallista said.

Only Plucky seemed uncomfortable with the decision. She looked left and right, one hand twisting the key on the side of her leg braces. "Feel like a clucker sitting down to dinner with the fox, yeah, yeah. Gingerly now."

Trenton nodded. "Be careful, and everyone keep a lookout."

Kallista circled Ladon toward the tower. Simoni and Clyde followed.

As they approached the tower, a circular stone plaza with a beautiful fountain in the center came into view. Standing near the fountain was a group of about twenty men and women. Each of them was dressed in identical off-white pants and shirts, although a few people had red or green sashes tied across their chests.

One of the men with a green sash waved a flag in their direction. Another held a small box up to his mouth and the voice-amplification system boomed again. "Welcome, welcome!

We haven't had any visitors in ages. And those machines of yours are amazing!"

Trenton searched for any sign of trickery or danger, but the people below appeared genuinely excited to meet them.

"Don't like it, yeah, yeah," Plucky muttered. "Looks like a wily tongue-pad if I ever seen one."

The man with the talking box put it to his mouth again. "You are safe here. We won't harm you. Land by the fountain."

For a moment, looking at the stone circle, Trenton remembered how the Order of the Beast in Seattle had taken him, Kallista, and Leo to be sacrificed to the dragons. Only these people looked nothing like the Order of the Beast, and they certainly didn't look like Cochrane and his band of Whipjacks.

Still, something about what he'd seen flying over the city stuck in the back of his mind. Something didn't add up.

"Careful," he whispered.

Kallista nodded. "Move to the edge of the circle!" she shouted down.

The figures below consulted with each other, then they all moved away, leaving the talking box on a wooden stand.

Trenton bit the inside of his cheek before nodding. "Guess we better go down."

Before he could touch the flight stick, though, Simoni and Angus dove toward the fountain. "Always have to be the hero, don't you?" Trenton muttered as he and Kallista followed.

Clyde and Plucky slipped in behind them.

As soon as Simoni and Angus landed, the people cheered and started forward. Something silver flashed at the corner of Trenton's vision, but when he turned for a closer look, there was nothing there.

Trenton glided to a spot a few feet to the left of Devastation. Kallista worked Ladon's legs to run as they hit the ground. No sooner had its talons touched the stones than Plucky gave a shriek behind them.

"Bolt, you gudgeons! It's a ruddy trap."

Trenton spun around to see another group of men and women running out of the alleys surrounding the plaza. Each person carried lengths of steel chains looped around their shoulders. At the same time, the people along the edge of the circle rushed forward, pulling long hooks out of their shirts.

A ball of fire shot past his head, and people scattered, some of them dropping their chains.

"Take that, you rusty bleaters!" Plucky howled.

Kallista rammed the throttle forward, and the engine howled in protest. Ladon's metal talons slipped on the smooth stone, and it was all they could do to keep the dragon from falling. Trenton pulled back on the flight stick, trying to get airborne. A couple of men with chains came up on his left, and Trenton swung Ladon's tail in an arc, sending them flying through the air.

They were coming up fast on one of the buildings surrounding the plaza. No wonder the people had urged them to land there. As soon as Ladon's feet left the ground, Kallista banked hard right. Metal screeched against metal as their wingtip scraped the side of a building. Then they were in the air.

"Help!" Simoni shouted.

Trenton looked back to see several chains wrapped around Devastation's legs and tail. A couple of men were climbing up the ladder as several others flung hooks at Simoni and Angus.

"Get me a clean shot!" he yelled.

Kallista pulled Ladon's head to the right, and Trenton smashed the fire button, hoping Kallista's aim was true. A second blast of fire came from above.

"Dance on embers, won't ya!" Plucky yelled, cackling with delight.

With flames raining down, the people fled the stone circle. Immediately, Simoni and Angus charged forward, blasting fire of their own as they circled the fountain, picking up speed. A moment later, they were in the air.

"What is wrong with you?" Trenton screamed at the people below.

"I don't think they're our problem," Kallista said, her voice low.

Trenton looked up from the plaza, and his anger turned to terror.

Throughout the city, the arched shutters on the tower walls were sliding open, revealing doorways. From every door, dragons emerged—each one flying directly toward Trenton and his friends.

6

"Fly!" Clyde screamed, red spots appearing on his cheeks as he darted Rounder first east, then cut sharply west. "We have to get away."

Plucky wasn't any more decisive, her head swiveling left and right as she pounded the fire button, sending fireballs randomly through the air.

The problem was, they had no path to escape. Dragons were coming from every direction.

Trenton's stomach twisted. Why hadn't he seen this sooner? This had been the dragon's plan all along. The two dragons had lured them into the city. The humans had gathered them in one place, and now Trenton and his friends were trapped.

All over the city, more and more tower doors were opening. What had been twenty or thirty dragons had grown to at least fifty, maybe more.

Simoni's long red hair snapped in the air behind her as she circled above the plaza, bobbing and weaving. "We're surrounded," she yelled, her voice carrying an edge of hysteria.

Fireballs and acid clouds filled the air as the creatures closed in. The sound of their screeches and roars was deafening. Trenton quickly realized his estimate of fifty dragons was low. There had to be at least a hundred, maybe two.

Angus was the only one who didn't seem terrified. Baring his teeth in a hungry snarl, he raised a fist. "This will be a day these monsters will never forget. There won't be enough room to paint their flaming skulls." He pointed toward the nearest dragon less than two hundred yards away and closing fast. "Attack!"

"Are you crazy?" Trenton yelled. "They'll slaughter us."

Kallista looked back at Trenton, her lips tight and gray. "Surrender or die?"

Trenton gripped the flight controller in his sweat-slick palm. Dragons were not simply dumb brutes. This was a sophisticated trap, set up in advance, which meant the dragons knew Trenton and his friends were coming. More, it meant that the humans and dragons were working together. How was that even possible?

If the dragons knew they were coming, they must also know what they'd done.

Except there was no way to survive a fight against two hundred dragons. If he pushed the stick forward, Kallista would land, but after all the dragons they'd killed, surrender wasn't an option. If he took them up, he knew she would fight to the end with him. His friends' lives were literally in his hands.

He searched the city. There had to be another way. His eye caught on the white tower to the west. Set high on a hill, it was at least twice as tall as any of the other towers. It was impossible to see what lay beyond it.

But maybe . . .

He put his hands to his mouth. "Form up!" he yelled.

As though he had been waiting for someone to tell him what to do, Clyde flew to Trenton and Kallista's left. Surprisingly, Simoni and Angus formed on the right without a word of complaint.

"Stick close, and lay down a steady stream of fire," Trenton called.

Angus and Simoni nodded.

"Like a gruntling on a sack of corn," Plucky yelled.

Trenton assumed that meant yes.

"Which way?" Kallista said.

Trenton pointed toward the white tower. "Go!"

Kallista gunned the thrust regulator, and they shot forward. She glanced over her shoulder just as a small silver dragon flew past, fast. Silvers couldn't breathe flame, but they could shoot spikes from their twin tails.

"I got it!" Angus shouted.

Flying close to Ladon's right wingtip, Simoni curled Devastation's neck around and back. With perfect timing, Angus blasted a single ball of flame straight into the silver's snout. The dragon screeched and veered away, but there was no time to celebrate. Two more dragons were coming in on the left, while another three closed on the right.

"Back off, you rusty buzzards!" Plucky screamed. Unlike Angus's precision shot, Plucky blasted a random cloud of fireballs that sometimes hit a target and sometimes missed by a hundred feet. A green dragon dodged an attack only to fly straight into one of Plucky's errant shots.

Trenton and Kallista alternated their attacks between left and right, focusing on whichever dragon was nearest. But even with the three of them firing constantly, it wasn't enough. Dragons closed in on them from every direction. Trying to avoid them all was like trying to avoid specific raindrops in a downpour.

Trenton spun around in time to see three small gold dragons approaching from the right. He swatted at them with Ladon's tail—hitting one with a bone-crushing thud—but the other two dodged nimbly and released a series of quick fireballs. Ladon shuddered under him.

"Look out!" Simoni yelled as a huge blue blasted them with a cloud of steam.

Trenton ducked his head, trying to protect his face from the hot vapor that scalded every inch of exposed skin.

Another blast of flames flared nearby.

"I'm hit!" Clyde screamed. Rounder rocked like a wheel on a bad set of bearings.

Dragons were all around them now, coming in from all sides, high and low. A red dragon appeared from below, shooting a stream of yellow metal-eating acid. Kallista veered right, narrowly missing Clyde and Plucky, but bits of Ladon's right wing melted away, burned by the acid.

Angus and Simoni were a machine, firing at everything in sight. But even they were taking heavy damage. There were too many dragons to fight, and more were arriving every second.

They were halfway to the white tower, though Trenton could barely see it through the cloud of dragons. It was now or never.

Trenton clutched Kallista's shoulder. "Hit the turbos."

Even with the roar of the battle all around them, she must have heard him because she reached for the controls and, a second later, clouds of black smoke poured out from their steam engine's exhaust.

Trenton's seat began to shake as the engine beneath him howled. He glanced toward the pressure gauge, where the needle was rising rapidly into the red. He hoped Kallista was right about the boiler handling the extra pressure. She glanced over her shoulder, and Trenton waved his arm in a wide arc from left to right.

She pointed Ladon's head as far to the right as it would go without endangering Simoni and Angus. Normally Trenton used the fire button in single bursts. This time, that wasn't going to work.

Trenton held his hand above the button until he could feel the turbo-charged engine rattling his teeth. "Now!" he shouted, slamming his hand down.

Fire jetted from Ladon's mouth in a cloud so hot Trenton could feel the air baking his face even from the backseat.

Kallista, using her feet to control the steering pedals and her hand to swing Ladon's head from side to side, laid down a stream of red-hot destruction.

The dragons in front of them dove out of the way, screeching in pain and fury. Some of them crashed to the ground—wings and bodies blackened by the powerful flames.

A narrow path opened in front of them for a few seconds, but unless they did something to keep it that way, it would close just as quickly.

Trenton pointed to the top of the tower. "Go!" he shouted to his friends.

Plucky and Clyde fled through the opening. Angus grimaced, blood streaming down the side of his face from a gash on his forehead, but he followed Simoni's lead as she flew after Rounder.

Kallista, however, banked hard left, heading straight into the swarm of dragons behind them.

Ladon's enhanced speed pushed Trenton deeper into his harness, the straps digging into his shoulders. For a brief moment, the dragons hesitated. That was all the break Trenton needed. With a scream of fury, he pounded the fire button. Dragons scattered as blasts of flame filled the air.

Working the controls with perfect teamwork, Trenton and Kallista slashed through the creatures' ranks, throwing the dragons into turmoil and turning their coordinated attack into chaos. Yellows dodged only to fly into the reds' acid clouds. Greens and golds were hit by silvers' spikes. Hit in the side by another dragon's fireball, a blue lashed out with a jet of steam.

Kallista looked back at Trenton. "We have to go."

Trenton nodded. Their surprise attack had created confusion, but already the dragons were beginning to regroup. Diving low over the buildings, they swooped Ladon around to the east.

On the ground, people cowered under any shelter they could find as fire, acid, and spikes rained down on them.

For a second, Trenton wondered why the people were still in the city. Why hadn't the dragons killed them?

He didn't have time to worry about the answer, though.

Up ahead, Simoni, Angus, Clyde, and Plucky were almost to the tower. But so were dozens of dragons. It was going to be close.

They were almost to the tower themselves, and Trenton saw what he'd hoped he would on the other side. A hundred feet beyond the great white spire, the ground abruptly fell away in a sheer cliff. Beyond it, blue water frothed and crashed against the rocks. And beyond that, the water disappeared in a wall of thick silver fog. All they had to do was make it to the fog and they'd have at least a small chance of escape.

Devastation and Rounder reached the cliff and dove over the edge, disappearing from view.

As Trenton and Kallista raced behind them, Ladon began to shake and bob. Fire belched from the dragon's furnace.

"I have to shut it down," Kallista yelled. She switched off the turbo, and the black smoke turned white. The roaring of the engine dropped, as did their speed.

Ladon dove nearly to the street, and Trenton and Kallista maneuvered their dragon around buildings, dodging the attacks.

The cliff approached agonizingly slowly as more and more dragons converged around them.

"Can you use the turbo again?" Trenton yelled. One boost would get them over the edge.

"Not for a couple of hours."

A fireball blasted their right rear leg, and it took every ounce of Trenton's control to keep Ladon from smashing into a raised pipe.

Eyes fixed on the water ahead, Trenton barely noticed the white tower sliding open until something launched itself out of the uppermost level.

Sun glinted off pearly scales and silver horns, and Trenton felt as though a physical force was forcing his head to turn. A *white* dragon. He'd never seen anything like it. The creature's wings unfurled as it flew from the window, spreading wider and wider, until they blotted out the sun.

No dragon could be that big.

The white dragon soared in his direction, and when its violet eyes met his, Trenton's blood turned to ice and, for a moment, his brain swam aimlessly. His fingers left the flight controls.

"What are you doing?" Kallista yelled.

Trenton's head snapped around, and he realized they'd reached the cliff. Blue-green waves rolled beneath them. Ramming the flight stick forward, he dove toward the water. Dragons screeched above, but already the icy-gray mist began to wrap itself around them.

Just before they disappeared into the fog completely, Trenton risked one last look back at the white dragon. It was strange—it was almost as if he'd heard it call out to him.

7

Kallista had no idea how long they'd flown or which direction they were going. The cold gray waves below them all looked the same. She could still hear dragons screeching and howling, and an occasional fireball lit up the clouds. She kept waiting for a dragon to burst out of the fog, talons bared, but the longer they flew, the fewer dragons she could hear, until at last there was nothing but the sound of the wind and the soft whoosh of the ocean below.

Had they lost them? Had the dragons turned back? Or were they silently stalking them, waiting for the right moment to attack out of the mist?

Somewhere in the distance seabirds cried. Did that mean they were heading toward land or away from it? Or did it mean nothing at all?

She assumed the others had escaped, but she hadn't seen or heard anything from them since they'd disappeared over the cliff.

"Did you see the dragon?" Trenton asked.

Kallista snorted. "Which ones? The dragons that *nearly* killed us, the ones that *almost* killed us, or the ones that *should have* killed us?"

Trenton slid forward in his seat, leaning toward her. "This one was pure white. You didn't see it?"

"I was sort of occupied." Kallista didn't understand why he

was all worked up. Since they'd left Discovery, they'd seen green dragons, red dragons, dragons with two sets of wings, dragons with stripes. What was another dragon? "I'll add it to the list."

"This one was different. For a second I . . ." He was silent so long Kallista glanced back to make sure he was okay.

"For a second, you what?"

Trenton swallowed, blinking behind his water-spotted goggles. "I don't know. Nothing, I guess." He shook his head. "Do you think the others made it out?"

"I hope so," Kallista said. "I saw them fly over the cliff." Now they just had to find each other in the middle of the ocean.

For the next ten minutes they flew in silence, then Trenton tapped her shoulder. "Do you hear that?"

Kallista tensed, searching the mist for a sign of scales or flames.

"It's not dragons," Trenton said. "Listen."

Kallista lifted the earflap of her helmet. "I don't hear anything except the waves."

"Exactly. Waves hitting land."

He was right. Since they'd left the cliff behind, the water had been a gentle murmur. Now she could hear a crashing.

"I think it's coming from that way," Trenton said, pointing to the left.

Kallista adjusted course, trying to steer toward the sound, but it was hard to tell exactly which direction it was coming from.

Slowly the mist cleared, and a bare expanse of rocky land came into view. It was an island, mostly flat but covered with a profusion of rocks and boulders. Except for clumps of grass and brush, there was no sign of life. Certainly no dragons.

"Over here!" Clyde shouted, waving from the seat of his dragon.

Kallista turned to see both Rounder and Devastation

crouched close to the ground. They were nearly hidden by a rocky outcropping, but as they flew closer, Kallista could see the heavy damage both dragons had taken.

Rounder's neck was bent at a strange angle, and several of its talons were cracked or missing. Scorch marks covered its body, and a trail of oil dripped down one leg.

Devastation was in even worse shape. It tilted too far to the left, leaning heavily on a damaged leg joint. The left wing was almost completely blackened and so shredded it was a wonder they'd been able to fly at all. Although the engine was off, a trail of dark smoke drifted up from the turbine.

Deep gouges in the dirt several hundred yards away made it clear how hard both of the dragons had landed. They must have walked Rounder and Devastation until they found a place to hide.

"They're lucky to be alive," Trenton said.

Kallista rubbed her face. "We're *all* lucky to be alive."

Ladon's right wing pulled strangely in the wind, and she leaned around to see how much damage their own dragon had taken. Two of the struts on the wing were broken, steam puffed out of a large gouge on the left side of the boiler, and the tail hung straight down as though every one of its joints had been snapped.

"This is going to be a rough landing," Trenton said.

"Come in low and slow." She searched for a stretch of smooth sand to cushion the blow, but the entire island was nothing but rock.

"Hold on," Trenton said as he brought them down.

Ladon's tail hit the ground first, throwing them hard to the right.

Kallista tried to correct, but the leg controls were sluggish in her hand.

"Pressure's dropping!" Trenton yelled.

They began to tilt. Rocks blurred by as they tried to slow down. Kallista fought the controls, leaning to her left as if her weight could keep them from going over. "Use the wings as brakes."

Trenton spread their wings, titling them back. They caught a gust of air, lifted, bounced hard on the ground, and came down with a loud crash.

Kallista dug Ladon's talons into the rocky earth, grinding the machine to a stop less than fifty feet from the other two dragons.

Clyde, who had ducked down, both arms thrown over his head, slowly uncovered his face. He looked like someone had pounded him with a mallet. Both eyes were blackened, and blood tricked from a gash on his chin. His helmet was twisted sideways, and his jacket looked like an animal had chewed it up and spit it out.

But he was grinning as he sat up. "Hey, you two, I missed that landing. Think you could try it again?"

"We were afraid you didn't make it," Simoni called as Kallista walked Ladon toward them. For once, she didn't look like she'd just attended a fancy luncheon. Her face was covered with smudges that could have been grease but were more likely bruises. Her hair was a rat's nest of snarls and knots. The ends were frizzled as if they'd been scorched.

"Not me." Plucky grinned, revealing a split lip and a missing tooth. "Knew you was right as wrenches, I did. Did you see them rusty dragons running for cover, yeah, yeah?"

"If we'd had a turbo on Devastation we'd probably have killed twice as many dragons," Angus said before seeming to hear what he'd said. He shook his head. "You know what? I don't even care about painting skulls anymore."

The right sleeve of his jacket was gone, and he stuck his tongue out, touching the blood that coated his cheek. "To be honest, I thought we were goners." His arm hung limply at his side as he nodded toward Trenton. "That was smart thinking going for the ocean. You probably saved our lives."

"Well, um, th-thanks," Trenton stuttered. "I didn't think about it. It was just instinct."

Kallista noticed his face turning red. Was this the first time Angus had paid him a compliment?

She studied the three heavily battered dragons and sighed. "We have a lot of repairs to do."

Trenton patted her shoulder. "The dragons can wait. Right now, we need to take care of ourselves."

Simoni pulled open the storage hatch on the back of Devastation. Luckily the storage compartments of all three dragons had taken minimal damage so their food, maps, and other supplies were mostly okay. "I'll get the first-aid supplies."

"I'll get some food cooking," Clyde said. He looked up and down the shoreline. "Do you think we can find enough wood to start a fire?"

Angus winced as he climbed out of his seat. "There should be some on the beach."

"You aren't in any condition to gather wood," Kallista said. "You need someone to look at your arm."

Angus snorted and climbed down the ladder one-handed. "I can carry more wood in one arm than the rest of you combined."

"Let him," Simoni said.

"I'll help," Trenton said. His pant leg was torn, and he limped as he climbed to the ground, but Kallista guessed that after surviving such a close call, maybe they all needed to prove to themselves that they were okay.

"Got any idea where we are?" Plucky asked.

"I'm not sure," Kallista said. "I'll have to look through my father's maps."

Plucky fiddled with the key on her mechanical leg braces. "What are we going to do now?"

"I have no idea," Kallista said.

8

The sun was edging toward the western horizon before they finally felt safe. At least for one night. Most of the fog had burned away that afternoon, and there had been no sign of dragons. Kallista thought the smudge she could see in the distance might be the mainland.

If she could see it, could the dragons see her? The thought wasn't comforting.

Now, as the evening air began to cool, the fog was rolling back in.

"Any idea where we are?" Trenton asked, gnawing on the edge of a hard biscuit. He and Angus had managed to bring back enough bits of driftwood and brush to get a fire started.

Kallista shuffled through her father's maps before finding the one she was looking for. "It's hard to tell because my father didn't have the best maps of this area, but I think we're here." She tapped a series of small dots about thirty miles off the coast of a place labeled San Francisco.

Plucky leaned over Kallista's shoulder. She'd cleaned up her cuts, but unless they could find a dentist, she would always have a gap where one of her teeth had been knocked out. "Looks too rusty close to them dragons for my liking."

Trenton nodded. "Once we get back in flying condition, we should find somewhere safer to hide."

Clyde looked up from the cook pot hanging over the fire. "Discovery's safe."

When no one else responded, Kallista set down her map. "You want to go back?"

Plucky exchanged a glance with Clyde. "Can't rightly stay, can we? Dragons is hunting us now. We was plum lucky to get out'a there with our lives." She tried to take a bite of her biscuit, grimaced, and dunked it in a cup of water.

Kallista's head hurt. She didn't want to go back to Discovery, but she also didn't want to fight a hundred dragons again. No matter where she looked, she couldn't see a good solution to their problems. Her stomach rumbled, and she nearly sighed in relief. *That* was a problem she could solve. "I can't believe I'm saying this, Clyde, but whatever you're cooking smells pretty good. Is it ready?"

"As ready as it will ever be." He grabbed a metal ladle and spooned stew into a bowl.

Kallista crumbled her biscuit into the bowl and tasted it. "This isn't bad," she admitted. Although the dried meat was stringy and hard, Clyde had added something sweet.

"It's the dried apples," Clyde said proudly. "They give it a certain zing." He stirred the last of the stew and glanced at the others from under lowered brows. "The truth is, we're completely out of onions, potatoes, and dried carrots. Other than the apples and jerky, we only have a few questionable turnips left, some flour and rice, and several dried tomatoes. Oh, and the rest of the bulbs Simoni dug up last week."

"How long will that last us?" Trenton asked.

"Depends how much weight you want to lose," Clyde said. When no one laughed, he shrugged and said, "A couple of weeks. Three, tops."

Angus, leaning against a boulder, picked up a rock with his

right hand. His left arm was in a sling. He claimed he didn't need it, but Kallista noticed he didn't move that arm any more than he had to. He hefted the rock, eyeing the seagulls that hopped about in the shallow water. "I might be able to get us some meat."

Simoni looked down from the top of the outcropping. "It doesn't look like there's any better cover than where we are. We should set guards through the night to watch for dragons."

Kallista studied the horizon, wondering what good it would do. They'd been lucky to escape the city. If the dragons found them out here, there was nowhere to go, nowhere to hide.

Trenton rubbed his jaw. "Once the fog comes in, whoever is on guard will be lucky not to fall off a rock and break an ankle."

Simoni climbed down from the rock and moved closer to the fire. "You want to sleep without a guard and hope no dragons find us?"

Trenton shuddered. "I'll take the first shift."

Simoni nodded. She tried to brush her fingers through her knotted hair, realized it was impossible, and took a bowl of stew from Clyde. "What's the plan?"

"Clyde tells us we have three weeks of food left," Trenton said.

"Three weeks, *tops*," Clyde corrected.

Trenton sketched a salute toward his friend. "And we still have to get the dragons in flying condition."

"How long will that take?" Angus asked.

"Reckon we could have 'em ready by tomorrow?" Plucky asked.

Kallista shook her head. "There are hardly any resources on this island. It'll take at least two days, but more likely three."

"And what will we do once the dragons *can* fly?" Clyde said.

Trenton tossed a rock from hand to hand. "I guess we could

go back to Discovery, let them know what we've found, and refill our supplies."

"You want to run?" Angus slapped the ground next to him with a beefy smack. "We came here to kill dragons."

Clyde curled his fist around his ladle. "You want to fly back into the city and blast away? You're going to get us killed," he said, his voice rising.

Angus sat partway up. "You have a better idea?"

"Stop bossing people around," Kallista said to Angus. "No one put you in charge."

"No one put anyone in charge," Angus fired back. "I can do what I want."

Simoni, who'd been scooping up handfuls of sand and letting it trickle between her fingers, shook her head and said, quietly, "No. You can't."

Everyone went quiet. Angus plopped back, a stunned expression on his face. "What?"

"You can't fly a dragon unless I go with you. You aren't the one deciding what we're going to do."

So this was her plan. Start by convincing Trenton to let her make the attack plans, then twist Angus around her finger. "Let me guess," Kallista said, "*you* want to be in charge."

Simoni ignored her and turned to Clyde. "When the dragons attacked, you were flying around like a baby calf out of the barn for the first time."

Clyde blushed. "I was just trying to come up with a plan."

Angus cracked his knuckles. "Maybe you should stick to cooking and painting pictures."

Simoni glared at him. "You should talk. Your decision was to attack head-on. If we'd done that, we'd all be dead."

That quieted Angus. Simoni looked at each of them, one by one. "None of us had any idea what to do. We were all flying in different directions, panicking, and with good cause. The only reason we're here, and alive, is because one person came up with a plan and led us to safety."

Every set of eyes turned to Trenton.

"Wily shaver you was," Plucky said. "Quick as a whip, yeah, yeah."

Trenton twisted his hands together, looking like he wanted to disappear into the fog. "It wasn't like that. I just thought if we could make it to the ocean . . ."

Simoni waved away his protest. "Last night you asked me what you were best at. The truth is, I'm not sure you're the best at anything."

Angus guffawed, but one look from Simoni and his mouth shut with a snap.

She looked back at Trenton. "We might not be willing to admit it, but right now all of us are trying to prove we belong out here. We're all hiding how terrified we are; Angus maybe most of all. We need someone to pull us together, to make us believe. Maybe your job on the team isn't to be the best at any one thing but to make the rest of us better. A leader doesn't lead by proving how great he is—he leads by making the people around him great. I think you're that person, Trenton. If you're willing to lead, I'm willing to follow you."

"So am I," Clyde said at once.

Plucky nodded. "Yeah, yeah."

Angus dug the heels of his boots in the dirt, but when Simoni said, "Angus will follow you, too," he didn't argue.

Trenton looked at Kallista. "It was your father's dragons that got us here in the first place, so if you—"

Kallista shook her head. "I'm not a people person." The last thing she needed was everyone wanting her to settle their arguments. But if anyone, even Trenton, thought they could tell her what to do, they were mistaken.

Simoni clapped her hands. "Then it's decided. You tell us what to do, and we'll follow you."

"Okay, well . . ." Trenton ducked his head and rubbed his hands on his pant legs. "I guess I'd like to sleep on it."

Simoni stood up and began kicking sand onto the fire. "Great idea. Let's all get some sleep. I'll take the second watch."

"I'll take third," Kallista said. When she was a little girl, her father had introduced her to a woman who was one of the most skilled mechanics in the city. Kallista had watched in amazement as the woman took apart, then reassembled, a steam engine with her eyes blindfolded. What she had witnessed tonight was no less amazing.

The others might not realize it, but they'd just been taken apart and reassembled like pieces of a machine. And Simoni was the skilled mechanic who had done it. Apparently she was full of surprises.

9

After his shift, Trenton thought he would fall asleep as soon as he wrapped his blanket around himself. Instead, he found himself shifting from one position to another on the rocky ground. In the past, he'd complained about sleeping on roots or the occasional pinecone. Now he'd give anything for a pile of leaves and pine needles to curl into.

What really kept him awake, though, was the thought that his friends had willingly placed their lives in his hands. Was he worthy of that trust? He didn't feel like it. What had he accomplished that made him worth following?

He'd helped build the dragon, but only because he was the one who'd found the part in the mine. He'd discovered the truth about Cove, but only because Kallista had helped him. Everything in Seattle had happened because Plucky shot him and Kallista down.

Simoni wanted the others to believe that he'd been so smart ordering everyone to fly toward the ocean when the dragons attacked. But how much of that had been an actual decision and how much had been pure instinct? You get chased, you run. Thinking back to that moment now, everything felt like a blur.

Still, there was a big decision to make, and they'd asked him to make it. Wrapping his blanket around his shoulders, he got up and walked through the dense fog. Boulders appeared like ghosts out of the mist, and after banging his shins on them twice, he slowed his pace.

The city they'd found had to be San Francisco, although the people living there might have another name for it by now. Had he expected to find a secret message like the ones Leo Babbage left in the games he'd played with Kallista? *Here is where the dragons came from, and here is how you can defeat them.* Had he expected to find a group of people ready to follow him, like the Whipjacks? Look how that had turned out.

For years, the people of Cove had locked themselves away from the dangers of the outside world. Trenton had been incensed to discover the leaders of his city had lied, not just to him but to everyone. Now, seeing what the outside world was really like, he wondered if maybe the leaders of Cove had been right all along.

Was it better to live in ignorance of the dangers around you or to realize you were nothing more than an ant crawling on top of a log poised to crash into the fire at any minute?

How could he go back to the people who'd trusted him and explain that no matter what they did, no matter how hard they fought, they would never defeat the countless dragons who would root them out sooner or later?

On the other hand, now that they knew what was here, didn't they have to do something about it? He and the others had been so proud of the dragons they'd killed—painting skulls like trophies. How insignificant that looked when compared to the fact that dragons had nearly wiped out the whole human race and driven human technology almost back to the Dark Ages. Except for here, in a city run by dragons.

Looking back on it now, he and his friends had been incredibly naïve to think six kids could change the world. How could they possibly stop a race of creatures so powerful they had destroyed human civilization?

Or had they?

San Francisco appeared to be the dragons' headquarters. There had to be at least three hundred of them living in the city, with far more humans than that. Why were the dragons allowing people to live among them? He doubted it was generosity or mercy keeping the humans alive.

A face appeared out of the fog, and Trenton stumbled backward before realizing it was Angus. "What are you doing out here?" he asked. "Simoni has the second shift."

If Angus was surprised to run into Trenton, he didn't show it. Then again, he didn't show many emotions other than anger or frustration. He'd probably learned it from his father. Marshal Darrow, who had been the head of Cove's security forces, wasn't exactly known for his winning smile.

Angus picked up a rock and bounced in his palm. "Took her shift so she could sleep. I wanted to check on things. Make sure everyone's okay."

That was about as likely as him asking to take over cooking duties. What did he really want?

Angus tossed the rock into the fog where it made a soft *bloop* as it fell into the water. "Guess you're deciding what to do once our dragons are fixed, huh?"

"I assume you have an opinion," Trenton said.

"I have lots of them," Angus said. "Not sure which one is right."

Well, that was a first. Trenton felt unexpectedly awkward. It wasn't like he and Angus had a lot of discussions. Mostly they either argued or ignored each other. "Do you, um, want to talk about it?"

Angus glanced up into the night sky as though searching for

dragons, although the odds of seeing anything in the fog were pretty much zero. "You know why I agreed to come with you guys?"

"To impress Simoni?" Trenton suggested, and Angus actually laughed. Trenton grinned. "I assumed it was to kill dragons."

"Yeah, those are both true. But mostly it was because my dad told me to."

Trenton nearly stuck his finger in his ears to clean them out. He couldn't have heard that right. "Your *father* wanted you to fly with us?"

"Don't look so surprised," Angus said. "I know most people don't like my dad." Trenton started to disagree, but Angus shook him off. "He can be kind of tough, and there's only one thing he cares about more than himself."

"Bossing people around?" Trenton suggested. Mr. Darrow was a loudmouth, a jerk, and a bully—a lot like his son.

"Okay, *two* things. He cares about keeping the city safe. He talks about it all the time. He said dragons are the biggest threat to Cove—he refuses to call it Discovery—and if I was any kind of son at all, I'd go out and kill so many of them that our city would never be in danger again."

"You want to go back to San Francisco and kill more dragons?"

Angus rubbed his arm in the sling and winced. "To be honest, I'm not sure. If this trip is all about killing dragons, then yes. We might as well go out in a blaze of glory, right?"

Trenton thought there would probably be a lot more blaze than glory.

"On the other hand," Angus said, "if this is about keeping Discovery safe, shouldn't we go back and warn them of what's out here?"

Trenton wasn't used to hearing Angus say so much at one time. How long had he been thinking about it? "What would your father say if you went back?"

"That I'm a coward," Angus said immediately. "But, honestly, after what we faced in the city today, nothing else is all that scary."

That was a point they could both agree on. Which brought him back to what he'd been considering before Angus showed up. Even if they managed to get their dragons in perfect working order, there was no way the six of them could even make a dent in the number of dragons in a head-to-head fight. Clyde was right about that. All they'd accomplish would be getting themselves killed.

"What if there was another way to fight the dragons?" he said, not realizing what he'd been thinking until the words came out of his mouth.

Angus's eyebrows rose. "Your girlfriend has another secret weapon no one's told me about?"

Ignoring the girlfriend jab, Trenton frowned. "Not a weapon, exactly. There are too many dragons to fight, and they're too powerful. But what if we could find a way to, I don't know, maybe poke around the city and look for weaknesses—use our brains instead of our muscles."

"Thinking's your department. But if you figure out a way to kill more dragons without us getting killed at the same time, I'm in." Angus sniffed and wiped his nose with the back of his hand. "Guess I better finish my shift before Kallista wakes up." He nodded to Trenton and walked away into the fog.

Trenton thought back to what he'd seen in San Francisco and how much of it had been centered around the humans. The dragons lived in the towers, but most of the buildings were designed for people. Dragons didn't need bridges or roads or the spiderlike vehicles that crawled through the fields. And even if they had wanted them, they couldn't have built them. Talons were great for ripping and tearing but not much else.

After the dragons had sprung their trap, Trenton remembered wondering what the humans were doing there. Why had the dragons let the humans live? The answer was obvious. The train cars of fish, the piles of food on the conveyor belts. Even for a city of that size, there was way more food than necessary. San Francisco wasn't a city of a humans fighting against dragons; it was city of dragons being fed by humans. It was the Order of the Beast all over again.

Was it possible the dragons *needed* the humans? That they'd become dependent on them? And if so, was there a way to use that dependency against them?

He wasn't sure. And he didn't know how the knowledge could help him and his friends in their current situation, but at least it was a start.

With that in mind, he went back to camp and was finally able to drift to sleep.

10

The next morning, after breakfast, he presented his thoughts to the rest of the group.

By the time he finished, Kallista was nodding. "I bet almost all of those machines were built by humans specifically for the purpose of feeding the dragons."

"You think the dragons are using people as slaves?" Simoni asked.

"They have to be," Angus said. "I mean, no one would willingly serve those monsters."

"Order of the Beast did, yeah, yeah," Plucky said quietly.

Trenton nodded. The Order of the Beast not only willingly served the dragons but actually worshipped them. But the people in Seattle were living in a hole in the ground, looking for any help they could get. The people in San Francisco weren't that desperate.

"I'll bet they don't see a lot of outsiders," Simoni said. "If we could find a way to talk to them, we could tell them what we know and find out what they know. Maybe we could even help some of them escape."

Trenton was relieved that they'd come to the same conclusion he had. "If we could get a few people out of the city, we could ask them about the city's weaknesses. They live with the dragons. They have to have some ideas."

Angus stripped the sling from his arm and tossed it away.

"That sounds exciting and all, but do you think we can just stroll into a city full of dragons and ask the people, 'Hey, how's it going?' without someone noticing?"

"We won't know for sure until we go back and have a look around," Trenton said. "It's better than running away. And it's *much* better than launching a full-scale attack."

"Catch a look, yeah, yeah?" Plucky seemed excited by the idea. "I'll sneak a peek. See what's what, won't I?"

"What do you think, Clyde?" Trenton asked.

"Would this look-see be from a distance or would we actually be going in the city?" Clyde asked.

"Definitely from a distance. I'm thinking we fly by just after twilight when the dragons aren't so active. Do you think you could draw a map of what you remember of the city's layout?"

Clyde nodded. "I'll get on it."

Trenton took a deep breath. Just like that, they'd agreed to go back to a place where they should have died the day before. It felt like the right thing to do, but he hadn't been prepared for the weight it put on his shoulders. "All right, then. We get the dragons fixed today and tomorrow morning. Then, tomorrow night, an hour before sunset, we head out."

That next afternoon, Kallista and Plucky stayed busy cannibalizing materials from nonessential parts of the dragons and using them to repair the wings and legs. It left some odd-looking holes in the dragons' bodies, but Kallista said they'd be airworthy by that evening.

Simoni was on guard duty, and Angus was out gathering more wood. Realizing no one really needed his help, Trenton wandered down the shoreline to where Clyde was sitting on a rock with a pad of paper on his lap and a pencil in one hand.

He held the pencil poised over the tablet, poked it toward

the paper, paused, pulled back, and tried again. When the pencil tip touched the sheet, he winced as if in pain.

"Is everything all right?" Trenton asked.

"What?" Clyde's head jerked up before he realized it was only Trenton. He set down the pencil and gave a weak smile. "Just trying to make the map. Some days drawing is harder than others."

"You don't remember the city?" Trenton asked. "It doesn't have to be perfect. Do the best you can."

"It's not that." Clyde flexed his fingers before picking up the pencil as though it were a poisonous snake. "I know art isn't bad, but . . ."

All at once Trenton understood. "The retraining?"

Clyde hesitated before nodding. "Most of the time I'm all right. But every now and then it's like trying to punch my way through a brick wall."

Back when creativity had been against the law in Cove, Trenton had constantly found himself risking punishment by building new things, but it was Clyde who had been caught sketching on his chalkboard.

Clyde had returned a day after being seized by the guards and put into retraining. After that, it had been months before he could even look at a piece of chalk without trembling. He'd never discussed what happened that day.

Trenton traced a line in the sand with his foot. "Do you want to talk about it?"

Clyde sighed. "No. I'm fine."

"Okay. If there's anything I can do . . ." As Trenton turned away, Clyde spoke up.

"What do you love most in the world?"

"Building things," Trenton said at once. "I mean, you know, after my parents and all that."

Clyde nodded. "Imagine if building things made you so sick you felt like you were going to barf. If even the thought of it gave you stomach cramps and cold sweats. You still loved it, but you also hated it."

Trenton rubbed the back of his neck. "I don't understand. How can you love something and hate it at the same time?"

"I don't understand either. Not really. That's why I've never told anyone about it." He ran a finger down one edge of the tablet and shivered. "The day the guards took me for retraining, they questioned me all afternoon. Why was I drawing? What was I drawing? Did anyone else know? How long had I been drawing? It was the same questions over and over, only asked different ways in different order."

"What did you say?"

"What *could* I say?" Clyde gave a shaky laugh. "It was a mistake. I didn't know what I was thinking. I'd never done it before, and I'd never do it again. I was terrified. When they finally threw me into a cell, it was after midnight. I would have said anything to get some sleep. It must have been an hour or two later when they woke me up and put me in the . . ." He swallowed and nearly gagged. Sweat beaded on his forehead and his upper lip.

Trenton placed a hand on Clyde's shoulder. "You don't have do this. Don't put yourself through it all over again."

Clyde wiped his forehead. "No. I need to tell someone. Maybe getting it out will help." He took a long breath and released it with a slow *whoosh.* "After they woke me up, they put me in this room. They made me put my hands into . . ." He gulped hard. "At the time I thought it was a jar of bees, but they were shiny, like green jewels, and now I know they were—"

"Wasps," Trenton said. "That's why you were so terrified of them back at the campsite." He remembered Clyde's fingers and hands had been swollen when he returned from the retraining. He'd been stung by wasps. "Why would they do that?"

"I don't know." Clyde wiped his face again, his eyes staring out to sea. "Afterwards, they handed me a slate and told me to start drawing. I didn't want to, you know, because it was wrong. But they made me. At first it was all right. I drew pictures of little things—tools and plants.

"Then something changed. I started to itch, like I was allergic to the chalk. My fingers began to swell, and I had a hard time breathing. The guards were whispering something to me, but I couldn't hear what they were saying. My head was swimming, and the room kept going in and out of focus. I wanted to stop drawing, but my hand wouldn't obey. And then it was like my hand was burning. The chalk was on fire, but I couldn't let go. I couldn't—" Clyde's lower lip trembled.

"Stop," Trenton said. "Don't relive it."

Clyde hiccupped and took a gasping breath. His face was scarlet. A tear leaked from one eye. "I could live with the pain. Only it's like they stole the best part of me and replaced it with something horrible."

"I'm so sorry. I had no idea," Trenton said, thinking of how close he'd come to being sent to retraining himself. Would he have come out shaking every time he thought of building something? "You never have to draw anything again."

"No." Clyde wiped the tears from his cheeks. "It would be so easy to give up. I've thought about it every day since I got out. Each time I start shaking, I ask myself why I'm putting myself through this. Is drawing worth it? But the day I quit drawing is the day I give up that part of me for good. If I stop, it means they won. I won't let them take my art. I won't."

Trenton had never heard his friend speak so forcefully about anything.

Clyde seemed to realize the same thing. He shook his head, the fierce scowl on his face replaced by an embarrassed grin. He looked down at the pencil in his hand. "Get out of here and stop bugging me. I have a map to draw."

"Sure." Trenton took one more look at his friend before heading back to the campsite. To think he'd believed Clyde just liked to tell jokes, draw pictures, and cook weird stuff. You never really knew what was inside people.

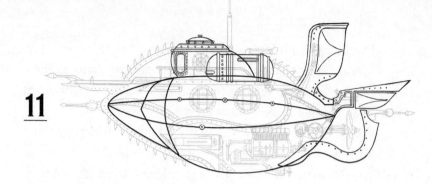

11

Kallista had hoped the fog would roll in with the setting sun. But other than a few stray clouds, there was nothing to hide their approach as they neared land—except for the darkness, and the darkness was about to disappear. Lights were coming on in buildings and towers and along streets until the sky above the city was nearly as bright as day.

"Do you think we should call off the plan?" she asked, scanning the sky for dragons.

Trenton hesitated, and she didn't have to see him to know he was struggling with the pressure of his new leadership role. She didn't envy that. On the one hand, she didn't want anyone telling her what to do. On the other hand, Simoni was right. There were too many of them in the group to have everyone going their own direction. She was okay with one person running things, as long as she wasn't the one.

"What do you think, Plucky?" Trenton asked, keeping his voice low.

"Right bright for a proper look-see, ain't it now?" Plucky called. "Might be all right to take a peek through the window, see if the latch is ajar, yeah, yeah? As long as we keeps an eyes out for them rusty dragons."

Kallista had spent enough time around Plucky that she barely noticed the Whipjack slang anymore. "You want to fly around the edges of the city and check the security?"

Plucky tapped her nose. "Plummy."

"Okay," Trenton said. "But keep your engines running slow. No talking unless you have to. And absolutely no fighting. If you even think a dragon might see you, head out to sea."

"Gingerly as a clucker among the tabbies," Plucky agreed.

Trenton waved one hand in a straight line above his head, and the three dragons formed a single-file column with Ladon in the lead, Rounder second, and Devastation taking up the rear.

Kallista glanced toward Angus, wondering how long he'd keep taking orders. She assumed the only reason he'd agreed to let Trenton lead the team in the first place was because Simoni had pushed it. Angus didn't like people telling him what to do either.

As they reached the edge of the cliffs, Trenton gave Kallista's left shoulder a firm tap, and she turned north to follow the edge of the coast. Even from a distance, the bright lights of the city made it easy to make out what was going on.

At this time of night in Discovery, all of the businesses would be shut down while people went home to eat dinner or go to bed. Here, though, trains loaded with coal, ore, and grains continued to run across the city. Most of the buildings appeared closed for the night, but fires glowed in a few factory windows, and trails of gray steam issued from a few smokestacks.

Outside one of the buildings, she saw at least a hundred of the strange spiderlike vehicles parked side by side. It looked as though some of them had trailers hooked to the back, and a few had cutting or digging implements on the front or sides.

For the most part, the streets were empty. But why keep them so brightly lit? Then she looked closer and realized at least some of the people walking outside were guards. Another thing to keep an eye on.

The dragon towers were illuminated as well, but the arched doorways were all closed.

"You think the dragons are asleep?" Trenton asked.

"Not all of them," she answered, pointing out a dark shape to the north gliding along the edge of the city lights. It was a dragon—although in the darkness she couldn't tell what kind— and it was flying in their direction. She scanned the skies for somewhere to hide. The bridge would hide them nicely, but they couldn't reach it in time without increasing their speed and making more noise.

"Let's get out of here," Trenton said.

Simoni whistled twice softly. To anyone else, it would sound like a birdcall, if they could hear it at all. To the six dragon riders, though, it was the signal for something coming up on the left.

Kallista looked over her shoulder to where a second dragon flew behind them over the water. That ruled out heading back to sea.

"Rusty galoots," Plucky muttered. "Keeping a right tight watch on the nest."

She reminded herself that tonight's mission was about gathering information, not fighting dragons. If they kept their heads down, they should be fine. "Which way?" she asked. When Trenton didn't respond, she pushed the right foot pedal, sending them sailing past the cliff into the city.

"What are you doing?" Trenton demanded.

"Keeping us from being spotted." She waited for him to argue.

Instead, he pushed the flight stick forward, sending them into the shadow of a nearby tower. "Good call," he said. "Our best chance to avoid being spotted is to stay near the light without actually going into the light."

Flying along the edges of the light was like a game—swoop low between a pair of houses, follow the shadow of a tower, swoop beneath a factory wall, come out under an elevated pipe. Except in this game, the consequence of losing was death.

As they darted from one building to another, she began noticing things about the city she hadn't before.

Along the outside edges of the city were rows and rows of small, square buildings that had to be houses. There were hundreds of them, and every single house looked exactly the same. Farther to the north, on the hills overlooking the bay, were other buildings that also looked like houses, but those were much bigger.

The best spots around the city were reserved for the magnificent towers she now knew were home to the dragons. Each tower stood away from the other buildings, and she thought she could make out people standing guard at the base of each one. She would need to keep an eye on the shuttered archways. If they began to open, it'd be time to get out fast.

The center of the city appeared to be composed almost entirely of factories and industrial plants. They soared above a large building that reeked of fish. In front of another plant were tall stacks of something vile that gave off a horrid stink like rotting meat.

"Cowhides," Trenton whispered.

How many cows must have been killed recently to leave that many skins? How many dragons fed?

The gleaming metal train tracks crisscrossing the city looked like a mixed-up puzzle at first. But now she could see a pattern. Tracks came from outside the city directly to the factories. To bring in coal and food? Another set of tracks ran out of the factories toward huge open spaces and several other large buildings.

"That's where they feed them," Trenton said from behind her, his voice far too loud.

"Shh," she hissed. "What are you talking about?"

"That was a fish-processing plant back there. We had one almost exactly like it back in Discovery—well, a smaller one, obviously. And did you see that pile of animal bones? That must be what the fields are for, and the machines with the claws. I'll bet if we look around, we'll find ranches with cows and sheep. The dragons are using the humans to provide them with food. Those empty courtyards and factories are where the humans feed the dragons."

No wonder the city was so big. The ranches alone had to be massive.

He pointed to the right. "I want to get a closer look at that building over there. The one with the people in front of it."

Unlike the beautiful dragon towers, the factories were un-impressive buildings, three stories of dull concrete. The one Trenton was pointing at had its lights on and steam coming out of its smokestacks. Where the towers were clean and sparkling, this factory was covered with soot. Copper pipes ran up the out-side of the walls, and metal grates covered most of the windows. Pieces of rusty ladders hung outside of a few windows. Whatever they'd been used for in the past, the ladders were nothing but leftover junk now.

Groups of men and women walked out of the large open doors on one end of the building, loaded down with bags and boxes that they dumped into trailers hooked up to the spiderlike vehicles parked outside.

Bright lights illuminated the building from all angles. Fortunately, the lights were all focused toward the building, leaving the sky overhead somewhat dark. Still, it would be tricky getting close enough to see anything useful without being heard.

She twirled her hand in the air, signaling for the three drag-ons to fly high above the building. Several hundred feet up, she stopped twirling her hand and made a fist. Behind her, Trenton shut off Ladon's engine. The others did the same.

Flying silently, they could use their broad wings to glide through the night. They wouldn't be able to stay airborne long, but if they were quiet, no one would be able to see or hear them.

Keeping far enough away to avoid the building's lights, Kallista banked around to get a better look. Trenton brought them even with the top of the building, and she could see through the windows running along the side of the factory.

The top floor appeared to be empty, but the bottom two floors were an open warehouse filled with conveyer belts and a large machine that chunked, cut, and ground. A processing plant.

Clusters of people worked along the line of moving belts and pulled levers on the machines. There were a few men, but it was mostly women with their hair tucked up in caps and stained aprons covering them from their necks to their knees.

Trenton leaned close and whispered, "Everyone's wearing the same gray clothes. You think it's some kind of uniform?"

Kallista shook her head. "Not all of them. A few are wearing gray pants and white shirts. I'll bet those are the bosses."

A woman stepped out of the building, and Plucky gave a surprised squawk. It wasn't much, but in the silence of the night, it sounded like a siren.

The woman put a hand to her eyes, searching the sky in their direction. "Who's there?" she called. "Is someone out there?" The woman's voice carried through the nearby streets, and several other women came to see what she was yelling about.

Kallista cut hard the other direction, but it was too late.

Angus gave a single whistle as a dragon approached from the right.

"We have to find a place to hide," Kallista whispered.

Trenton started the engine, and they rose back into the sky. "There." He pointed to one of the fields where the people had been driving the spiderlike machines. It was the only area nearby that wasn't brightly lit. It would be a difficult landing in the dark, but it looked like the only option.

Kallista steered toward the field, staying as close to the edge of the light as she could before darting into the darkness. Trenton dropped them into a steep dive. Tall plants slapped at Ladon's feet. They hit the ground with a clunk. Dirt exploded around them.

Two thuds sounded behind them as Rounder and Devastation landed.

Digging Ladon's talons into the ground, Kallista came to a sliding halt and cut the engine. She whipped her head around, studying the sky to see if they'd been spotted.

It was easy to make out the shapes of two large dragons outlined against the city lights. They circled in the air, screeching, then flew toward the building, making ever larger loops. It would only be a matter of time before they reached the fields.

Had the dragons seen them land or were they simply patrolling the area? Either way, it wasn't going to matter if they kept coming in this direction.

Hands on their dragons' controls, the six riders kept the engines running. The creatures were getting closer and closer. Any minute they would fly directly overhead.

"Get ready to take off," Trenton whispered.

The two dragons were nearly on top of them when something exploded inside the city. A white ball of flame lit the night, and shouting echoed in the distance.

Immediately the dragons flew away to investigate.

Kallista held her breath, afraid to make a single noise, until the dragons were finally out of sight.

"What was that?" Simoni asked.

"No idea," Kallista whispered. "But it couldn't have been more convenient."

Trenton turned to Plucky. "What were you doing back there over the factory? You almost gave us away."

Plucky hunched her shoulders. "Couldn't help me'self, could I? Saw someone I recognized out front of that building."

Kallista tilted her head. "How could you possibly know anyone here?"

Plucky set her jaw. "Don't know what she's doing here, but I know her, all right, yeah. Known her since I was a chit."

Kallista frowned. "Are you telling me that you saw someone you recognized from . . . ?"

Plucky nodded vigorously. "From Seattle."

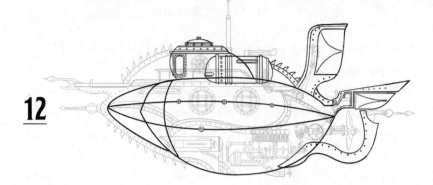

12

With their mechanical dragons hunched as low as possible to avoid being seen, Trenton and his friends stood in the dark cornfield, trying to figure out what Plucky had actually seen and what they should do about it.

Trenton stripped a leaf from the cornstalk beside him and twisted it between his fingers. "I'm telling you it's not possible," he said in a hushed voice.

"I seen what I seen." Plucky's hands were fists against the sides of her leg braces. "Her name is Talysa Sainz. Lived no more'n three houses down from us. Played the fiddle and sang me ditties when I was just a chit, before . . ." She shrugged. "Before the fire."

Angus kicked a clod of dirt. "You saw her for a second—two at the most—in the dark, while we were flying. How can you be sure it was the same person?"

"Wasn't just when I was a chit," Plucky said. "Seen her lots of times, I have. Her was sitting not five rows away in the city meeting after Trenton and Kallista was captured."

Trenton held up his hand. "Okay. She looked like someone you knew in Seattle. But you saw what happened to the city. No one survived."

Clyde spoke up. "What if she left before the attack?"

Trenton balled the leaf in his hand. "It wouldn't matter. Seattle is at least a month or two away by land. Even if she left a week before the dragons attacked, there's no way she could have arrived here before us."

Kallista pushed her goggles up on her forehead. "Unless . . ."

Everyone looked at her. Since the day they'd discovered the remains of the airship missing from the charred ruins of Seattle, Trenton knew Kallista had hoped her father had somehow managed to repair the ship and leave the city before the dragons attacked. Kallista hadn't talked about it, but it wouldn't be the first time her father had escaped death.

More than once as they flew south, Trenton had seen her scanning the skies with a hopeful look on her face. She claimed she was watching for dragons, but he'd known what she was really searching for.

Kallista ran a hand across her mouth. "My father must have escaped from Seattle before the dragons attacked. He would have needed a crew to operate the ship, wouldn't he?"

It was possible. "Did this woman, Talysa, have a mechanical background?" Trenton asked Plucky. "Is she someone Leo would have recruited for help with the ship?"

"Maybe." Plucky fiddled with the key on her leg brace. She glanced at Kallista. "Mostly she worked in the city center. Keeping track of books and papers."

"That doesn't mean she couldn't have joined his crew," Kallista said. "My father could train anyone."

Simoni moved closer, cornstalks rattling as she shoved past them. A pair of birds cawed at each other. "If Talysa did come from Seattle with your father, and if she's in the city now—"

"I know what it means," Kallista snapped. "They've been captured. I have to go talk to her. She'll know what happened to him."

For a moment, everyone looked anywhere but at Kallista.

It was one thing to check things out from a distance, but going into the city itself, on foot, was risky.

"Too dangerous," Trenton said. "We can't just rush into the city without more information. Let's find one of those cattle ranches—somewhere out of the way—and talk to the people there first. We'll fly back to the island, make a plan, and—"

"I'm going in tonight," Kallista said. "Now. The rest of you can wait here or return to the island if you want, I don't care."

Angus chuckled. "So much for Trenton being in charge."

Simoni pushed past him until she and Kallista were face-to-face. "We agreed to have one person lead the group. *You* agreed. I know you want to find your father. But this is exactly what we can't do, each go running off in our own direction."

Even in the moonlight, Trenton could see Kallista's face darken. "If it wasn't for my father, we'd all have been killed by the dragon that attacked Cove."

Trenton had been the leader of the group for only one day and already things were falling apart. "I'm not saying we won't look for your father. But why rush into it?" He was sure Kallista would tell him that she was going and he could do whatever he wanted, the way she had so many times in Cove.

Instead she took a deep breath, held it for a moment, and bobbed her head. "All right. I'll do it your way. We'll come back."

Looking like he was stepping on hot coals, Clyde approached them. "Not to make things worse, but maybe Kallista is right. Maybe now is the *best* time to go into the city."

Trenton looked at him in disbelief. "What are you talking about?"

Clyde rubbed the back of his neck. "Dragons sleep at night, right? And hunt during the day?"

"Most of them," Kallista said slowly, clearly uncertain of Clyde's point.

Still looking uncomfortable at interrupting, Clyde said, "I just think that maybe tonight might be our best chance to look around. We made it here without being spotted. Since we *are* here, and since we know where this woman is *right now*, why not talk to her now? Who knows if she'll be in the same factory tomorrow?" He pulled a piece of paper from his pocket. "This is the map I drew. It's not perfect, but it should get you to the factory."

Trenton was silent for a moment. He looked at each of his friends in turn. Kallista and Clyde had made good points. But so had Simoni. Making a decision that was best for everyone was hard.

"Okay," Trenton finally said. "Kallista and I will go in together. The rest of you stay here and watch the dragons." He checked his pocket watch. If we're not back in two hours, or if you get discovered, fly back to the island."

Plucky gave her leg braces one final twist. "How you going to know who to talk to, yeah, yeah? What this plan calls for is a regular sneak thief. I'm coming with you."

• • •

Standing in the doorway of a small shop, Trenton turned the map first one direction, then another. He was impressed by how much detail Clyde had managed to put into it from one rushed visit. But his viewpoint had been from up above. The city looked very different once they were on the ground.

Kallista pulled the map out of his hands. "You have it upside down."

"I know I have it upside down. I'm trying to line it up with the city."

Kallista studied the map, then poked her head out of the doorway, looking both ways. "I think maybe we need to go . . ." She scratched her head, turned the map around, and gave Trenton a warning look. "Don't say it."

Together, the three of them studied the map.

"The bridge is that way," Trenton said. "Which means the white tower is over there, and—"

Kallista tapped a series of squares. "We came from the fields here, which means we need to go that way. I *think*."

Plucky rubbed the side of her nose. "Reckon I could shimmy up one's these walls and case the place."

With her twisted legs, it was hard to believe Plucky could climb a brick wall or shimmy up a pipe. But Trenton had seen her do it more than once. She managed to use the metal braces as a tool, prying them into notches and levering her small body into spaces that appeared impossible to reach.

"We might have to," Trenton said. "But let's head to the next cross street. We should be able to see the lights of the factory."

Sticking close to the walls, they crept through the shadows to where the street they were on intersected with a much bigger boulevard. Trenton noticed a gleaming metal walkway on the other side, and after checking to make sure there were no guards in the area, he and the others hurried across to get a better look.

"It's a mechanical sidewalk," Kallista said, running her hands over steel plates that connected to each other with metal nubs like tiny, interlocking fingers. Powerful engines at each end of the walkway turned gears connected to chains that disappeared under the plates. "I saw people riding these the day we flew in."

Trenton examined the tracks on the left and right sides of

the walkway. "Along with a huge pile of meat. The factories have to be somewhere near where this starts."

He wanted to find the controls that started and stopped the walkway, but just then a small figure moved in the shadows and a voice hissed, "Get out of the street."

The three of them spun around.

"Dodge it!" Plucky said. "Couple of beefeaters up ahead."

Trenton turned to see a pair of uniformed men round the corner. The one on the right carried a lantern, while the one on the left held a long rod that narrowed to a point.

Trenton looked for whoever had warned him, but the stranger was gone.

Plucky tugged Trenton and Kallista into a narrow opening between two buildings. "Don't think they laid peeps on us yet. But best we give 'em the dodge before they has a chance to."

Moving with only a faint clicking, Plucky hurried down the alley. At the far end, it opened into a square where several sets of train tracks met and crossed.

"Did you hear that back there?" Trenton said. "Somebody warned us about the guards."

Kallista turned to Plucky. "Was that you?"

Plucky shook her head.

Had one of the others followed them into the city? If so, how did they get ahead of them? And why hide?

"There's the factory," Kallista said, looking to the left. "I recognize the barred windows and rusty ladders from when we flew over it before. Let's go."

She started down the tracks, but Plucky grabbed her sleeve, pulling her back to the alley.

"What's wrong?" Trenton asked, looking for more guards.

Plucky held her head angled to the left and sniffed. "Me

whiskers is tingling." She glanced around, then peered carefully into the square, sniffing again. "You two get a whiff a that?"

Kallista inhaled slowly, nostrils flaring. "I don't smell anything."

Trenton didn't either. But he heard something: a faint clicking sound, like fingernails tapping on a desk, coming from the direction of the factory.

Plucky yanked her head back from the wall. "Cripes! It's a dragon."

Trenton and Kallista looked up, but Plucky shook her head. "Not up there. Down there in the street."

Carefully, Trenton peeked around the corner. Waddling purposefully up the middle of the tracks was what looked like an underdeveloped dragon. It was at least thirty feet long and nearly half that wide, and it lumbered up the street on four clawed feet. A ridged spine ran down the center of its back.

As Trenton watched, the strange-looking dragon paused, spread a pair of stubby, dark-green wings, and managed to fly a few feet through the air before thumping back to the ground. It twisted its flat head from side to side, opened a mouth filled with needle-sharp fangs, and flicked its tongue as if tasting the air.

The creature's head turned toward Trenton, its black eyes gleaming in the moonlight. Although it had been walking slowly before, now it broke into a quick trot. It flapped its wings, moving in a kind of half-flying, half-running waddle that would have been funny if it wasn't so terrifying.

"It smells us," Trenton said.

Quickly the three of them turned back the way they'd come, racing down the alley. At that moment, the two guards they'd seen earlier appeared at the other end. Trenton spun around in time to see the strange dragon squeeze its thick body in after them.

He searched the alley for doors or windows but saw nothing. The walls would be impossible to climb.

A large, dark shape soared over the opening, blocking out the stars and enveloping the alleyway in total darkness.

They were trapped.

13

Kallista stared at the unfamiliar dragon plodding toward her. Even with its stubby wings tucked against its body, the creature filled the alley from wall to wall. The dark-green scales covering it rasped like sandpaper as it scraped against the brick. Ten feet into the alley, it opened its mouth, uttered a wet hiss, and flicked its tongue.

Turning the other direction, she saw the two guards standing at the end of the alley. Had the men seen the three of them yet? If not, they would soon enough. If she charged the men, Trenton and Plucky might be able to get away. She was channeling her inner courage when a dark shape soared over the rectangle of sky above her.

That was it, then. They were surrounded. Even if one or two of them managed to get past the guards, there was no way they'd escape the city.

Something fell from the sky and slapped the back of her head. She whirled around to find a length of rope dangling behind her. No, not one length of rope but two.

Looking up, she couldn't see anything. It was as if the rope rose into a complete void.

"Hurry," a familiar voice whispered down.

She stared up into the darkness. "Dad?"

She grabbed the rope and realized it was a ladder. It wasn't a dragon overhead. It was an airship! But why couldn't she see it?

"Trenton, Plucky, it's my father."

Trenton stared at the rope in Kallista's hands as if she'd conjured it from thin air. Plucky didn't pause a beat before grabbing the first rung and pulling herself up the ladder like a squirrel up a tree.

Kallista elbowed Trenton. "Climb."

It took him longer to get his hands and feet set on the swaying ladder. By the time he'd climbed far enough for Kallista to follow him, the lumbering dragon was almost to her. Its black eyes gleamed like glass beads. Mewling hungrily, it forced itself through the alley toward her.

The guard at the other end held his lantern above his head. "Who's there?"

Kallista tightened her grip on the ropes and yelled "Go!"

Immediately, the ladder yanked upward. The ship moved forward with a whir of fans, and Kallista flew with it. Her ascent was so rapid that the guards were still staring into the alley by the time she zipped over their heads. If they did look up, what would they see? A girl appearing to fly? Throwing a glance over her shoulder, she saw the guards heading deeper into the alley. Wouldn't they be surprised when they found themselves face-to-face with a hungry dragon?

In nearly complete silence, she floated above the buildings and past towers toward the edge of the city.

A soft rumbling sound came from above her, and the ladder began to rise. She stared upward, trying to see the airship. Even knowing what was above her, all she could discern was an oval shadow. Holding tight to the ropes, she watched the shadow grow bigger and bigger.

It wasn't until she was nearly inside that she could make out a pitch-black hull that was only a little lighter than the open hatch above her. Hands grabbed her, pulled her up, and helped her stand on a wooden deck that swayed gently beneath her feet.

"Step this way," Trenton said. "Careful of the winch."

She blinked her eyes. "I can't see anything."

"Give it a tick," Plucky said. "Your eyes will adjust."

Kallista allowed Trenton to guide her forward and found she could see a slightly less-dark square above and ahead of her.

"Step up," Trenton said.

As she climbed the stairs, her eyes began to adjust. Or maybe it was because of the stars she could see shining above her. By the time she reached the last step, she knew where she was: the captain's quarters of the airship from Seattle. And there, standing at the wheel, was her father.

"Dad!" she shouted, running across the cabin and throwing her arms around him.

He stumbled, but a smile spread across his face. "You look surprised to see me."

"I'm surprised to see you floating above us at the exact moment we were about to be captured by guards or eaten by a dragon."

"How did you find us?" Trenton asked. "It was a miracle you arrived when you did."

Kallista caught the quickest hint of guilt cross her father's face. She folded her arms across her chest. "It was no miracle. How long have you been spying on us?"

Leo rubbed a hand across his stubbly cheek. "I'd hardly call it spying. I've been here for less than a week. After witnessing your hasty departure two days ago, I knew you'd be back. If there's one thing I can count on, it's my daughter's curiosity."

"You saw us fly into the city?" Trenton asked. "How? Where were you?"

"All in good time," Leo said.

Kallista ground her teeth. "If you saw us getting attacked by the dragons, why didn't you help us?"

"What do you think the dragons would have done if I'd sailed over the city in a slow-moving airship? Who would I have helped?" Leo released the wheel to wave his hands in a gesture that included all of them. "Besides, I knew you'd escape. I did design your dragons, after all."

He took the wheel again and narrowed his eyes. "I was, however, more than a little surprised to see your sudden burst of speed, and those flames. If I didn't know better, I'd think someone modified my design. I want to hear all about it."

Kallista wasn't about to let her father off that easily. Maybe he couldn't have helped them or warned them, but she wouldn't put it past him if he'd intentionally held off to see his machines in action.

At that moment, though, Plucky burst forward with a grin. "Added a turbo booster to the engine, now didn't we? Fire the plummy thing up, and she flies like a rum prancer with its tail a'fire."

Leo lowered his eyes to study Plucky. "And who is this? You look familiar."

"Plucky, at your service," she said. "Triggest Whipjack in all of Seattle, and a bit of a plummy mechanic, if I do say myself. O'course nothing the likes of you or your daughter." She shot out her hand, grabbed his, and pumped up and down briskly. "How dost do, my buff?"

Leo gave her a knowing grin. "Ah, of course. One of Cochrane's crew."

Kallista, who still had her arms folded across her chest, waited for Plucky to finish gushing before fixing her father with a stern glower. "How long were you following us tonight?"

"The whole time, of course," he said without even trying to

look abashed. "I watched you enter the city, fly by the factory, and land in the field. When I observed you entering the city on foot, I thought you might need some assistance. So, yes, I was following you."

"Did you create the explosion that drew the dragons away?" Trenton asked. "Did you warn us about the guards?"

"I'm afraid I don't know anything about either of those," Leo said.

Kallista narrowed her eyes. "How did you follow us all that time without us or the dragons seeing you?"

Her father raised an eyebrow. "I'm surprised you didn't figure it out for yourself. I have the benefit of being able to fly without an engine, making me silent as a gliding hawk. And I found a large supply of black paint in Seattle when I was repairing the airship, so it's all but invisible at night—which is the only time I fly."

Kallista frowned in frustration. "Nice to see you care, Dad. Did it ever occur to you to let me know you were here? Maybe let me know you were alive?"

Leo frowned. "Why would you believe anything else? I assumed that once you went to Seattle and found me and the airship gone, you would travel here next. This was the most obvious place to meet up."

"We found empty holes and charred wood in Seattle. The dragons killed everyone in the city. What did you expect me to think? You didn't even leave me a note."

Her father dropped his head until his chin pressed against his chest. "I'm sorry for worrying you. You're right—I should have left a note. But you are wrong about the dragons. They didn't kill the inhabitants of Seattle. As best I can tell, the people are all here."

"I knew it!" Plucky shouted.

"She saw someone she thought she recognized," Trenton explained.

"Quite likely," Leo said. "A few days after I left the city, I witnessed a horde of dragons flying north. The next day, they returned with men, women, and children clutched in their talons. It was remarkable. Of course, they were able to fly much faster than I could in the airship."

"Remarkable?" Kallista gripped a handful of her hair, tugging until her scalp burned. "Dad, isn't it obvious these people are being forced to serve the dragons? That's why we were going into the city. To contact them and see if we could find a way to help."

"And to look for your father," Plucky added.

"You were looking for me?" Leo asked.

Kallista gave Plucky a searing gaze. "Yes, Dad. That's what people do when they care about someone. They look for them. We thought the woman Plucky recognized might have been helping you fly the airship. If she'd been captured, we thought it was possible she might know where you were."

"I have no need for a crew," Leo said. "I modified the controls so one person can fly it easily. Every night, as I traveled south from Seattle, I set the automatic flight controls and made excellent time."

"That's how you beat us here," Trenton said.

Leo nodded. "That, and I had a head start. Let me show you around."

With Plucky close on his heels, he gave them a tour of the airship, pointing out each of the changes he'd made. As he'd said, he'd painted the ship black and automated nearly every aspect of flight. Due to the fire damage that had nearly destroyed the airship, the rebuilt version was only half the size of the original. But what Leo had accomplished was impressive enough that Kallista wondered how he'd managed to finish it all before the dragons arrived in Seattle.

Trenton dropped back to walk next to Kallista. "He loves you," he said quietly. "He just doesn't know how to say it. That's the real reason he followed you tonight."

Kallista sniffed. "He'd follow a cockroach around if he thought it was going to do something interesting." She caught up with her father. "Fascinating as this tour is, we need to find a way to destroy the dragons and free the people they've captured."

He rubbed the top of his head. "Of course, of course. Defeat the dragons. Free the people."

He sounded convinced, but she wondered how much his coming to San Francisco had to do with stopping the dragons and how much of it was to study them. Did he even see a difference?

She shook her head. "The first thing we need to do is get back to Simoni, Clyde, and Angus and let them know what's happening."

Her father shrugged. "Here we are."

Kallista looked over the rail of the airship and saw that they were hovering directly above their three mechanical dragons still hidden in the cornfield.

14

Thirty minutes later, they were on their dragons again, following the airship as Leo led them across the bay. Trenton spotted several guard towers located along the edge of the water, but no one seemed to notice the midnight black airship as they flew overhead.

Leo had said he was leading them to a secret hiding place. A mile or so north of the city, the airship turned toward a small island in the center of the bay. Unlike the rocky island where they'd spent the previous night, this one was lush with trees and brush.

True to his word, Leo easily maneuvered the airship by himself, circling past a grove of thick-trunked oaks before easing toward the ground.

Trenton glanced south at the city lights, which appeared precariously close, and west to the bridge, which was even closer. "This doesn't seem very safe."

No sooner were the words of out his mouth than a crumbling three-story building came into view. Covered with vines and surrounded by trees, the structure couldn't have been any better camouflaged if someone had done it on purpose. Nearby, a tall, thin building rose above the trees.

Dropping neatly toward the ground, Leo sailed the airship between a pair of trees and through a ragged opening where one of the walls of the building had given way. By the time he landed, the ship was completely hidden from view.

Kallista shook her head. "He never does anything without a reason," she said before flying in after him.

Once they were settled into the building, Leo offered Clyde the use of his airship to prepare dinner. It turned out he had a surprisingly full pantry, including wild potatoes he'd found on his way from Seattle and a chicken he'd caught on the island.

While Clyde cooked, Leo took the rest of the group on a brief tour. "This was originally built as a military garrison," he said, walking them through the building. "Fortress Alcatraz. You can still see some of the cannons outside, although they are nearly rusted through now."

"What are those?" Angus asked as they passed a row of small cells covered with rusty bars that ran floor to ceiling.

"Several years after the garrison was built, a portion of the fort was turned into a military prison." Leo gestured to the last cell where a steam generator was connected to a pair of wires running into a vat of water. "I imagine you know what that is," he said to Trenton.

"A hydrogen-producing tank," Trenton said. It was a smaller version of the rig he'd set up in Seattle. A hose mounted to the tank would allow the hydrogen to be pumped out of the cell into the airship's envelope, giving it the lift it needed to float. "Where did you get the parts for this?"

Leo shrugged. "I brought some from Seattle. Others I've managed to scavenge here and there."

Trenton wanted to ask more about where parts could be scavenged—they'd had a hard time finding enough resources to repair their dragons after the battle—but the inventor was already leading them onward.

By the time they returned to the airship, dinner was nearly

ready. The meal was the best they'd eaten in weeks. Clyde had mashed the potatoes and roasted the chicken with the last of their turnips.

"This is delicious," Angus said, crunching a leg bone between his teeth. Except for a few rabbits they'd managed to snare, it was the first fresh meat they'd had since leaving Discovery.

"There are a surprising number of chickens wandering the island," Leo said. "The cats hunt them, of course, but the fowl are plentiful. Perhaps you can help me snare a couple of chickens for our dinner tomorrow."

"Cats?" Plucky asked, looking around. "There's tibbies here?"

"Nasty, feral things." Leo wrinkled his nose. "Stay away from them. Who knows what sorts of infection they might have?"

Plucky stared down at her empty plate. "My mum had a tibby when she was a chit, but food got tight and they ate it."

Trenton had never seen a cat. He guessed Discovery's founders had been more focused on bringing in animals they could use for food than ones that needed to be fed.

"If we're done talking about cats," Kallista said, "can we discuss the plan?"

Trenton nodded. "Good idea. How do we get into the city?"

Leo placed a hand over his mouth, hiding a yawn. "Plenty of time to discuss that tomorrow after a good night's rest."

"Shouldn't we set out guards?" Trenton asked.

Leo shrugged. "We're quite safe here. But it might not hurt."

"I'll take first watch," Angus said.

"Very well. You can sleep in the airship tonight if you'd like."

Kallista was the only one who didn't take him up on his offer. She said she preferred to sleep on Ladon, but Trenton suspected it was her way of showing her father she still hadn't forgiven him for his behavior.

Early the next morning, Leo took them outside to show them the tower Trenton had noticed the night before.

The wind blowing off the ocean was so bitterly cold it cut through Trenton's leather jacket. Rubbing his hands together to warm them, Trenton searched the sky. This close to the city there had to be plenty of dragons nearby. He needn't have worried. The thick woods provided a perfect canopy all the way from the garrison to the small house near the southern tip of the island.

Trenton sniffed the air. There was a strong scent that was both minty and sweet. "What's that smell?"

"Eucalyptus trees," Leo said. "The distinctive aroma comes from eucalyptol, an oil in the plant's leaves. I rather like it, don't you?"

Trenton sniffed again and decided he did.

It turned out that the building *was* a tower, built on top of the house. Inside, the tower was mostly hollow except for a spiral staircase that wound around the wall.

"Watch your step," Leo said. "The building appears to have survived the great earthquake of 1906 with minimal damage, but the stairs have deteriorated over time."

"What is this place?" Simoni asked, craning her neck to look toward the top. "I've never seen anything like it."

"Not surprised," Leo said with a laugh. "Living inside a mountain, there's not much need for nautical history. You are inside a lighthouse. Using lamps, reflectors, and a powerful lens, lighthouses used to send out a piercing beam of light, which gave sailors a landmark to navigate by and a warning to avoid the island. Not much need for that now, but as you will soon see, this building will suit our purposes quite well."

As they reached the top of the stairs, Plucky gasped. "Rust and cinders, look at that view!"

Trenton felt the same way. Taller than the three-story building beside it, the tower offered a magnificent 360-degree view of the ocean and the city across the bay. Large windows on all sides had once been covered with glass, though now only a few shards remained. Open to the elements, the floor was covered with bird droppings, and the remnants of several nests still clung to the ceiling.

"Have a look," Leo said, pointing to a telescope mounted on a tripod. "But don't step into the sunlight. As long as you remain in the shadows, the dragons can't see you."

Trenton leaned toward the eyepiece and found he had a perfect view of the city.

Carefully moving the telescope, he watched as people walked or rode vehicles through the streets. The image was so sharp he could see the faces of individual people. Overhead, hundreds of dragons filled the air.

"This is amazing," he said. "How does it work?" He started trying to unscrew the front lens, but Leo stopped him with a laugh.

"I like the way you think, son. I'd be happy to let you take it apart later. Maybe we can even build one together. But first let's give the others a chance, shall we?"

One by one, each of them looked through the eyepiece.

"I could map the city perfectly with this," Clyde exclaimed. "I can actually read the signs on the front of buildings."

"Is this how you saw what we were doing?" Trenton asked.

Leo nodded. "I designed it myself. It's more powerful than the ones the Whipjacks built in Seattle."

Kallista went last, moving the telescope slowly left and right before stopping for a moment. She stared toward the city for several minutes, then took a piece of folded paper out of her pocket and jotted down some notes.

"This place is perfect," Trenton said. "What are the chances you could find a hideout this well-hidden with such an ideal spot for studying the city?"

Leo's mouth quirked up for a moment. "Actually, the odds were quite good."

"You knew about this island before you came here, didn't you?" Trenton asked, wondering why he was still surprised by such revelations. "Did you read about it in a book or something?"

"I like to do my research before making any decision," Leo said. "Let's go back to the garrison and plan our next move. You may return anytime you like."

As they started back down the stairs, Kallista's mouth moved silently. Trenton didn't need to read her lips to know what she was saying: *Always a reason.*

• • •

They gathered together on the deck of the airship. Clyde and Angus stretched out on the floor, leaning against the railing, Simoni and Trenton sat cross-legged, and Plucky perched expectantly on the stairs leading up into the ship's envelope. Only Kallista and Leo remained standing.

"So, how we are going to get the people out of the city?" Kallista said.

"Are you sure that's wise?" Leo asked. "How would you get them out? And where would you take them? It's not like we could hide thousands of people here. And even if you could hide them, how would you feed them?"

Everyone looked at Trenton, and he felt the weight of leadership on his shoulders. "We weren't actually planning on bringing everyone out. Only a few. Last night, Plucky saw a woman she recognized. We were hoping she could give us some clues about how to stop the dragons."

"Talysa," Plucky murmured.

"Right." Trenton shoved his hands into his coat pockets, trying to gather his thoughts. "I guess we should try to focus on finding her. Find out what she knows. Tell the others we're out here. Once we have more information, we can come up with our next step."

Leo pinched his chin. "How were you planning to avoid the security lights outside the factory? And the patrols? I've counted six separate guards making a circuit around the building, several of those nasty dragons you encountered last night, and even the occasional dragon flying above."

"I, um . . ." Trenton paused. He should have realized there would be guards around the building. Even if they made it to the building, they'd probably be caught right away. Maybe he wasn't such a good leader after all.

"We could land on the roof," Simoni suggested, covering for him. "All the lights point downward, so it's dark up above."

"Excellent strategy." Leo grinned and nodded. "But how do we get inside the building once we're on the roof?"

"Bombs," Angus said. "Do you have any more of that gunpowder from Seattle?"

Kallista rolled her eyes. "We aren't blowing anything up." She pulled out the piece of paper she'd taken notes on after looking through the telescope. "There's a small structure with a single door on the roof. Maybe some kind of maintenance access. It's probably locked, but I'm sure I could pick it open."

Plucky turned around with a quick grin. "If it's a dub lay you wants, I'm your girl. You may be able to pick the lock, but I'm a whiz at the black art."

Leo raised an eyebrow.

"She knows what she's doing," Kallista said.

"What do you think?" Simoni asked Trenton. "You're the leader."

Some leader. He hadn't come up with a single idea. He shrugged. "Sure. Let's do it."

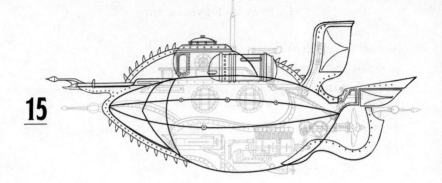

15

Kallista examined the improvements her father had made to the airship as they pulled it carefully out of the building that night. Instruments and levers had been moved to a single panel within easy reach of the wheel in order to control speed, altitude, winches, hatches—everything the crew had been responsible for previously. The entire craft could be operated with only small adjustments.

He must have been working day and night to get everything done before the dragons arrived. Even then it was likely he'd finished many of the modifications after leaving Seattle. He was a genius when it came to building things.

If only he was half as good with people as he was with machines.

"Is there anything we can do to help?" Trenton asked.

Leo pointed out the window. "Keep an eye out for rare, night-hunting dragons. Wouldn't want to have this go down in flames again."

Kallista rolled her eyes. Where had his concern been when they had been flying into the dragons' ambush?

She shook herself, trying to push the angry thoughts from her head. Her father couldn't help it if he was better at fixing machines than he was at raising a daughter. She should know. She'd inherited many of the same traits from him. The difference was, she recognized it as a weakness—reminding herself that those around her were human beings with feelings, not pieces of a machine to be rearranged and bolted together.

Honestly, her father probably had no idea she was angry at him. Or why.

She walked out onto the deck where Plucky was looking at the automated rigging. "Right trig bit of inventing, yeah?"

"He's very good at getting things to work the way he wants," Kallista said.

Something moved beneath Plucky's jacket, and she shifted quickly, turning her body so her front was shielded from view.

"What do you have there?" Kallista asked, coming around for a better look.

"Ain't got nothing." Plucky walked toward the stern of the ship. A hiss came from inside her jacket, and she jerked.

Kallista hurried after her. "What's in your jacket?"

"Nuffin, I tell ya." A muffled cry came from under the leather, and Plucky stopped. Refusing to meet Kallista's gaze, she unzipped her coat and pulled out a white-and-brown ball of fur. The ball shifted in her grip, and a pair of blue eyes blinked at Kallista.

"What is that?" Kallista demanded.

Plucky gave a quick nod. "A tibby—a cat. Only a bit of a thing." She held the creature toward her, and Kallista took a step back. The last thing she wanted to do was touch an animal that could be dangerous.

"Where did you get it?"

"Found her curled up under a bush outside the building. She looked practically starved. Didn't have no mum or sisters to care for her, so I give her a bit to eat." She rubbed the top of the fur-ball's head, and it gave a small *mew* before rumbling like a tiny steam engine.

Kallista flapped her hands. "I can't believe you wasted food on a wild animal. And what made you think it was a good idea to bring it with you tonight? We're trying to be quiet, and you've got a mewling, growling, hissing—"

"Couldn't leave it back in that cold, empty building, could I?" Plucky tucked the rumbling ball inside her jacket and stepped back as though afraid Kallista would try to take it from her. "She's got no family. Like me."

Kallista could only imagine what the others would say if they discovered Plucky had an animal onboard. Getting in and out of the city was going to be hard enough under the best conditions. If her father knew, he would undoubtedly land the ship and make Plucky get rid of it.

Maybe it was the thought of her father that made the decision. It certainly wasn't common sense. "Okay. You can keep her with you. But don't let it interfere with the mission."

Plucky grinned. "I can pick a lock with one hand tied behind me back. With two even. Once cracked a door holding the picks in me teeth."

Kallista didn't know if that was true or not, but she wouldn't put anything past the girl. "Try not to let anyone else see."

Plucky patted the front of her jacket. "Plummy."

The flight into the city went much more smoothly than Kallista had expected. Using the wind to push the airship's fins and rudders, they were able to glide silently over the bay and above the brightly lit buildings. The black paint made them all but invisible, and as it turned out, her father had another trick up his sleeve. When the skies above them cleared, Leo flicked a switch, and tiny pins of light appeared at random spots on the sides of the envelope, making it look like stars shining in the darkness.

A dragon glided past them no more five hundred yards away without a single glance in their direction.

Trenton joined her at the railing. "I've been wondering. Why don't all the dragons live here? It seems like a much better place for them than being in the wild. I mean, here they don't have to hunt; the people feed them and take care of them."

Kallista shrugged. "Maybe some of them like it better in the wild."

"Maybe." Trenton ran a hand along the smooth wood of the rail. "Have you ever considered . . ." He pressed his lips together as if afraid to speak the words he was thinking.

"Giving up?" Kallista asked.

"No." Trenton blew out a pent-up breath, his shoulders sagging. "Not if there's still a chance of defeating the dragons. But what if we bring these people back and discover there is no weakness?"

"Then we come up with another plan. Try a new direction."

"What if there *are* no more plans?" He spread his arms as though reaching out to the city. "All these dragons. This city. It's too much. It was one thing to hunt dragons one or two at a time—to have this vague idea that one day we'd find the source of the dragons and find a way to stop them. Only now that I see what's here, can the six of us—seven, with your father—even dream of defeating a city full of dragons?"

Kallista didn't have an answer. She'd never played a game she couldn't win, never found a puzzle she couldn't solve or a machine she couldn't fix. That didn't mean there wouldn't be a first, but she wasn't there yet. "My father hasn't given up yet. Neither have I."

"Yeah." Trenton shifted from one foot to the other. "Maybe I'm overthinking things. Being the leader makes me nervous. I'm afraid I'll mess things up."

Kallista patted him on the shoulder. "Don't worry. If you

mess things up badly enough, we'll dump you. I don't think Simoni would do much worse than you."

Trenton snorted a laugh. "Thanks for the confidence."

Clyde hurried to join them, his footsteps echoing loudly on the deck.

"Could you make any more noise?" Kallista asked. "I'm not sure *all* the dragons in the city heard you yet."

"Sorry," he puffed. "Your dad sent me to get everyone. He says we're about to land."

Kallista looked down to see they were nearly to the factory. The building's bright lights and puffing smokestacks made it easy to spot. The three of them rounded up the others and joined her father in the captain's cabin.

Leo looked through the front ports of the airship and began angling the craft downward. "I could lower you to the building through the hatch, but I think it'll be safer if we land in the shadows on the roof and have you go over the side. I'll stay with the ship in case we need to make a quick departure. How long do you think you'll be?"

"Not long," Trenton said. "If things go well, we can arrange a longer meeting somewhere safer."

Kallista wet her lips. She'd been considering something, but she wasn't sure how the others would take it. "I think just the girls should go." Before anyone could interrupt, she hurried on. "I noticed most of the workers in this factory are women, which doesn't mean much by itself, but since it's a woman we're trying to talk to . . . I think we'd have a better chance of gaining her confidence if Plucky, Simoni, and I contact her first."

"Who's going to protect you if you get attacked?" Angus asked.

Kallista rolled her eyes, Simoni put her hands on her hips,

and Plucky flicked her wrist, displaying a gleaming blade in her hand.

"Think we can protect ourselves if any ruffians tries to put the pinch on us," Plucky said.

Simoni eyed the wicked-looking knife. "Where did you get that?"

Plucky flexed her fingers, and the blade disappeared. "Lady gots to take care of herself, now don't she? Keeps a couple of shivs on me at all times. Never knows when something, or someone, might needs cutting."

Trenton nodded. "All right. But be careful. We know there are guards outside the building, but there could be more inside, too. If you get in trouble, shout and we'll come for you."

The deck thumped softly beneath their feet, and Kallista's father released a silver lever to his right. "We're here."

16

As Kallista slipped over the side of the airship, she had a strong sense that she wouldn't be back. The feeling was so powerful she nearly turned to look at the others watching silently from the deck. But that felt too much like inviting bad luck. Instead, she watched her footing and hurried to the door that was set into a steeply angled structure at the center of the building.

The surface of the roof was covered with pea gravel that crunched with each step the three of them took.

Plucky's brace creaked as she knelt before the door and studied the lock. "Gots the keys?" she asked, holding out one hand.

Kallista placed the lock picks in her palm, and Plucky slipped them into the slot. Her fingers manipulated the picks with the same confidence Kallista felt handling a wrench or adjusting a piston. As she worked, she whispered something under her breath. It took Kallista a moment to realize she was singing.

"If old Mr. Grim should come tonight," Plucky sang, "duck me head and take the bite. Sell me teeth and keep the gain, but never sells me watch and chain."

It didn't exactly inspire confidence.

"Do you want me to do it?" Kallista asked.

"Tich," Plucky snapped. With the tip of her tongue poking out from the corner of her mouth, she lifted the pick in her left hand, and there was an audible snap.

Kallista was afraid one of the picks had broken, but when Plucky stood up with a grin and turned the knob, the door swung open.

"It was a bubble. An infant with his mouth full of pap could'a done it."

As she handed the picks to Kallista, a soft *mew* came from inside her jacket. Plucky gave Simoni a worried look. But Simoni only reached into her pocket and handed her a sliver of meat. "The poor thing's probably hungry."

"You knew?" Kallista asked.

"Please." Simoni flipped her hair. "She's spent every spare minute creeping around that old building, holding out scraps of food and calling. What did you think she was doing?"

Kallista raised her chin. "I thought it wasn't any of my business." She wasn't about to admit she hadn't been paying attention. "Are we going in or are we going to stand around all day jabbering?"

With no light inside the door, all they could see were the first two steps going down, which didn't look as though they had been used much, if at all. Many of the structures in the city were obviously new, but from the looks of it, this one might have been around since the original dragon attacks.

Plucky pressed her back against one of the walls and eased down sideways, one splintered wooden step at a time. "Sticks close to the side to avoid squeaks, yeah, yeah."

Following her example, Simoni and Kallista stayed on the side of the stairs. There was a door at the first landing of the staircase, but Kallista led them past that, remembering that the top floor of the building was empty. They continued down until they reached the first floor.

Kallista gripped the doorknob. She wondered if it might be locked, but it turned easily in her hand.

"Hold up," Plucky whispered. She spit on the hinges, rubbing the moisture in with her fingers before carefully easing the door open.

As soon as she did, the smell of cooking fish drifted through the opening, along with the sound of women's voices.

"Must be a kitchen," Simoni whispered.

"It's making my mouth water," Kallista said.

Careful to make as little noise as possible, the three of them edged around the corner, leaving the door open in case they needed to make a quick escape. They stood at the end of a dark hallway. Buckets, mops, and other cleaning supplies stacked on a shelf along one wall gave off a faint scent of ammonia.

Outside the hall, a group of women stood beside a large vat, shoveling steaming piles of cooked fish onto silver trays. Another group of women placed the trays on a conveyer belt where they were whisked into the dark mouth of a machine that made a constant *chunk-chunk-chunk* sound.

From the greasy stains on their aprons and gloves, Kallista could tell they'd been working for a while.

"I wish we'd thought to wear clothes that matched theirs," Simoni said.

Plucky put a hand to her forehead. "Never thought'a donning no disguise."

Neither had Kallista, and it was obvious she should have. As she and Trenton had noticed the night before, all of the workers wore gray pants and either gray or white shirts that buttoned up the front. She, Plucky, and Simoni were going to stand out immediately.

There wasn't anything they could do about it now. Grabbing a broom from the shelf, she walked forward briskly. Plucky and Simoni did the same.

As soon as the three of them stepped into the room, the conversation stopped.

A woman with a shovelful of fish stared at them. "Are you new here?" She looked them up and down, glancing toward the hallway. She didn't appear alarmed, just surprised.

"Um, yes. New," Kallista said, wishing she'd given more thought to a cover story. In her mind they'd simply found the woman Plucky knew, told her they were planning a rescue, and gotten her out of there. Another reminder that maybe she was as bad with people as her father was.

A tall woman with wiry gray hair and a face that looked like it had been pressed with a hot iron until it was nothing but planes and sharp angles walked over from the other side of the room. "Where did you come from, and what are you wearing?"

Simoni stepped forward, all smiles. "We've just arrived, so we don't have our uniforms yet," she said in a voice that was even more sugar-sweet than normal. "It's all a little confusing."

The woman glanced toward the hallway behind them with a frown. "Who is your supervisor?"

"We was told to ask for Talysa Sainz," Plucky said, holding up a bucket as if that explained everything.

A small woman with rosy cheeks hurried over from the conveyor belt and bobbed her head at the sharp-faced women. "She's one of the new ones from Seattle. I think she's in packaging. I'll go get her, Lenora."

Several of the other women in the room moved closer to see what was going on, but at the mention of a name they knew, most returned to what they'd been doing. But Lenora, who was either the leader or just very nosy, wasn't going away. "When did you get in? I haven't heard anything about the dragons bringing anyone new. And I would have."

Kallista forced herself not to look toward the door that was their escape. "A few hours ago. We were brought in by a blue and a red."

Simoni reached out and touched Lenora's hair. "This is such a beautiful shade of silver. It looks like my mother's."

Sure that Lenora would realize what Simoni was up to, Kallista was amazed when the woman's hard face softened. "Thank you, dear. But I am sure I am far older than your mother. I'm old enough to be your grandmother."

"Oh, you are not!" Simoni gushed. She squinted her eyes, studying the woman from one side and then the other. "I don't see a single wrinkle."

"Stop it," Lenora said and actually giggled. "Possibly a very young grandmother." She put a hand on Simoni's head. "You might not believe this, but when I was a girl, my hair was almost the exact color as yours."

Kallista glanced toward Plucky, who gave her a knowing grin. True, you could catch more flies with honey, but this was pouring the honey on pretty thick. She couldn't be that charming if she practiced for a hundred years.

"Here she is!" The woman with the rosy cheeks rushed into the room, leading a second woman Kallista assumed must be Talysa.

"Plucky!" Talysa's brown eyes flashed, and her reddish-brown hair flew back from her shoulders as she ran across the room and threw her arms around Plucky. "When did you get here?"

For the first time all night, Kallista allowed herself to relax. A part of her had been afraid Plucky had been wrong or that if the woman did exist she wouldn't remember Plucky. Clearly that was not the case.

She squeezed Plucky's shoulders. "You've gained some weight. You look good. After you left with Cochrane and the rest of the Whipjacks, I was afraid . . ." She pursed her lips. "I'm glad you're all right." She turned to Simoni and Kallista. "Who are your friends?"

"I'm Sarah, and this is Heather," Kallista said, not sure why she was lying, but looking around at the women watching her, she felt uncomfortable providing their real names.

Talysa's eyes flickered between the three of them, taking in their mismatched clothes. "How did you get here?"

"Can we talk privately?" Kallista asked. She nodded toward the hallway, but Talysa must not have taken the hint because she led them farther down the room.

Everyone on the floor watched as Talysa led them to an area of the warehouse where the machinery wasn't so noisy. She sat on a wooden chair and nodded at them to do the same. "Is everything all right? I can't tell you how happy I am that the dragons finally found you."

Kallista felt the hairs along the backs of her arms tingle. The tone of this conversation felt wrong.

Plucky eyed the rest of the women in the room before saying in a hushed voice, "We didn't exactly come in with dragons, yeah, yeah? Sort of pussyfooted around them, if you get my meaning."

Talysa frowned. "You're saying the dragons *didn't* rescue you? But they know you're here, of course."

Rescue? Kallista looked around the room. There were too many eyes watching them, expressions ranging from concern to suspicion. What if Talysa couldn't speak freely here? She leaned close, whispering low and quick. "We know the dragons captured you from Seattle. We've come to help you escape. You don't have to say a word. Just nod your head, and we'll get you out of the building and away from the city."

Talysa's frown disappeared, replaced with an uncertain

smile. "Why would we want to escape? We aren't the dragons' prisoners." Her voice began to rise. "We serve the most powerful creatures on earth. Gladly."

"Please," Kallista said. "Not so loud. We're here to help you, but—"

Talysa stood. "You don't understand," she said, speaking louder than ever. "The dragons are the rulers of all. To feed them, to bathe them, to help them in any way is the greatest honor any human can aspire to. I'm only sorry they didn't bring me here sooner."

Around the room, women left their machines, coming toward them, each one smiling like a true believer. Talysa turned to the women and gestured to Kallista, Simoni, and Plucky. "They haven't met the dragons. They don't understand how glorious it is here. We must take them to meet the dragons."

One of the women grabbed Kallista by the elbow. She yanked away, holding her broom in front of her like a spear.

"It's all right," Lenora said. Instead of being angry, she looked sad. "You poor, poor things. You've lived so long with fear. Don't worry, as soon as I saw you, I sent a messenger to let the dragons know you are here. Soon you will meet them and bathe in their glory." She reached toward them, but Plucky's knife was suddenly waving back and forth her front of her face.

"Back off, gudgeons, or I'll gut you like a grunter." She gripped the knife tightly in one hand and the bucket in the other. "You ain't keeping us here."

Lenora backed away, her hands in the air. Still, there was no sign of anger. If anything, her expression looked like pity. "No one will keep you here against your will, child. Only—"

"Good," Kallista said. "Then we're leaving."

Pushing the women aside, the three of them ran across the room. True to their word, none of the women tried to stop them. On every face was a look of profound sadness, as if Kallista and her friends had rejected a wonderful gift.

Kallista flung the broom behind her as she approached the open door that led to the roof. Feet pounding, they raced up the stairs. She glanced over her shoulder to see if Plucky was falling behind, but the girl was almost tripping on Simoni's heels.

"Take off!" she screamed toward the airship, lunging through the door to the roof. "Get the ship in—"

The words died on her tongue as she saw Trenton, Clyde, Angus, and her father standing beside the ship—their hands in the air—surrounded by three black dragons.

17

Let go of me!" Kallista twisted out of the grip of the guard holding her right wrist.

"Gladly." The woman pulled open a door, and the guard holding Kallista's left wrist shoved her through.

Kallista stumbled across the concrete floor, hitting her head against the far wall and landing in a heap.

Plucky and Simoni rushed to her side.

"Are you okay?" Plucky asked, helping her into one of three chairs set behind a small metal table.

Kallista pulled at her chair, wondering if she could use it as a weapon. It was connected to the floor, as was the table.

"Are you bleeding?" Simoni asked, parting Kallista's hair.

Kallista could already feel a lump forming on the crown of her head. "I'm fine." She brushed Simoni's hand away. It had been a long night, and she didn't think it was close to being over. After they had been captured, she, Simoni, and Plucky had been taken to a building where they were fingerprinted, washed, and dressed in gray pajamas.

Following that, the three of them were separated. Kallista had spent the last two hours lying to one question after another.

"What is your real name?"

"Flossie."

"Where did you come from?"

"A city deep beneath the ocean where everyone eats sand cakes and wears sharkskin boots."

"How did you get here?"

"By slingshot."

"What is your real name?"

"Flossie."

Eventually they'd given up and brought her here. She assumed Simoni and Plucky had gone through the same thing.

"You didn't tell them where we came from, did you?" she whispered, wondering if anyone might be listening.

"Of course not," Simoni said.

Sitting in front of the table, Plucky swung her feet. "They took me knives. Even the small one I keep hidden in my braces. They took Allie, too. That's what I was calling the tibby. Said I'd only get her back if I behaved."

Simoni dropped into her chair. "You didn't see the boys, did you?"

Kallista shook her head. "They wouldn't tell me where they'd taken my father, either."

"Dirty gudgeons wouldn't tell me anything," Plucky said. "Just kept repeating 'You'll learn what you need to know once you answer our questions.'" She folded her arms on the table, resting her head on them. "I'm so tired I can barely keep my eyes open."

"Do you think they know who we are?" Simoni asked. "What we've done?"

Kallista knew what she was asking. Did they know that they'd killed dragons?

She studied the small, white-walled room. There were no windows, no fixtures or holes in the walls, and only the one door, but that didn't mean they couldn't still be listening.

"I don't imagine it's that hard to put two and two together

and figure out that we were the ones who flew into their city on mechanical dragons. As for the rest of it? I honestly don't know."

Plucky looked at Kallista out of one eye. "We should never have come. Did you hear what Talysa said? They don't want to escape. They *like* it here."

Kallista got up from her chair, pacing back and forth across the room. Six steps, turn. Six steps, turn. "You don't really believe that, do you?"

Simoni fiddled with the hem of her gray shirt. "They sounded sincere."

"All the best liars do."

"I don't know," Simoni said. "What reason do they have to lie?"

"To keep us here until they could get the dragons." Kallista slapped the wall. "Don't you get it? After you told that nasty old woman how pretty she looked, she called the dragons to come and get us. She probably earns extra dessert for every person she catches."

"What do you think they'll do to us?" Plucky asked.

Kallista shook her head. In Seattle, even attempting to kill a dragon was enough to earn a death sentence from the Order of the Beast. Here, in a city run by dragons, the punishment had to be at least as bad.

A moment later, the door opened, and a woman stepped inside. She looked to be in her late thirties or early forties, with long, silky black hair and a quick smile. She took the three of them in and clapped her hands. "Three new girls! How exciting is this?" She held out her hand. "My name is Trina."

"You can quit the act," Kallista said. "We know you aren't our friend."

Trina's smile disappeared. "Of course I'm your friend. How

can you say such a thing? I'm here to welcome you on what will be the best day of your life."

"You clanker-telling witch," Plucky snarled.

"If you want to make it the best day of our lives, let us go," Kallista said.

"You'll be out of here in no time and snuggled tight in your warm beds. First, though, I need to ask you a few questions, then I can assign you a job and a place to live. After that, you can come and go as you please." Trina's perky smile returned. "Other than caring for the dragons themselves, I have the best job in the whole city." She noticed the lump on Kallista's head. "Oh, my! How did that happen?"

"It happened when the guards threw her into the room," Simoni said. "You say you want to help us, but no one here has been very nice."

"You poor dear, you must be exhausted. I remember my first night here. Such a difficult time adjusting to a new place, new clothes, new food. Can I get you something to eat? A glass of water?"

Simoni gave Trina a smile that turned adults to butter. "Thank you for asking. I'm fine."

Kallista glared at both of them.

"Very well." Trina opened a folder. "This won't take long at all. Would you please take your seats?"

"I'll stand," Kallista said.

Still smiling, Trina riffled through her papers. How could anyone bear to smile that long?

"You are Plucky and Kallista, of course." She turned to Simoni. "But I don't know who you are."

Kallista felt a shock race up her spine at hearing Trina say her name, but she refused to show any sign that the woman was right.

Who had told her? Was it one of the boys? What if they were harder on them, torturing them until they told the truth?

She felt a second shock when Simoni said in her sweet voice, "My name is Simoni."

Why was she telling this woman anything?

"Excellent," Trina said. "I'll put that right here in my notes." She flipped through her papers again. "It says here you three haven't been as cooperative as you could have been. The people whose job it is to process you into the city are very nice. It isn't necessary to fight, I assure you. You're going to love it here, once you adjust."

"We don't *want* to adjust," Kallista growled.

Simoni leaned across the table, her face a mask of sincere interest. "We want to help," she said, and Kallista could have smacked her. "But I don't understand what's happening here."

"Of course," Trina said. "This is quite a change, I imagine. Perhaps I can answer some of your questions."

"Thank you," Simoni said, sounding like she was going to give the woman a big hug and bake cupcakes with her. "First of all, I'm worried about the boys."

Trina tapped her folder. "They're fine. I saw them not fifteen minutes ago. All three are being processed exactly as you are, only in a different building. You'll be able to see them soon, I promise."

Three—not four. Kallista desperately wanted to ask about her father. She knew Trina had intentionally not mentioned him because she wanted to draw her into the conversation. Kallista refused to give her the satisfaction.

"Thank you," Simoni said. If Kallista hadn't known better she would have sworn the girl was buying Trina's lies. "I'm not sure if I should even bring this up, but you mentioned we could come and go as we please."

Yes, Kallista thought. *At last we're finally getting somewhere. Put her on the spot. How do we get out of here?*

"I'd love to see more of your wonderful city," Simoni said. "The bridges, the moving walkways, the farms. I'd love to get a closer look at everything, but so far, no one has been willing to let us go outside."

"You want a tour?" Trina said, and Simoni gave out what could only be described as a squeal of excitement.

A tour? Really? That's what you're going for?

"As soon as you've had a day to rest, I'll take you to see all the sights," Trina said. "Unfortunately going outside right now would not be wise."

"Afraid we'd bolt?" Plucky asked.

"Of course they are," Kallista spat.

"Not at all," Trina said. "As I told you before, you are free to leave the city anytime you like. But once you see what we have to offer, I don't think you'll want to. There is no place you'll find that offers more than we have here. Safety, food, recreation, learning." She looked at Kallista. "I understand you enjoy reading. We have the best library in the world. This city is the most wonderful place. Once you talk to the dragons, you'll understand."

Kallista froze. "*Talk?*"

Simoni shook her head. "Dragons *can't* talk."

"Not *all* of them." Trina laughed. "But a few. How else could we communicate with them?"

"You mean sign language," Kallista said. "Gestures or signals. They don't actually speak human words."

Trina frowned. "Not all dragons choose to use the human tongue, but those that do most certainly speak words."

"That's impossible," Kallista said. "In millions of years only a few species of animals have learned to mimic human speech.

123

And none can use more than a few words in a meaningful way. My father and I discussed it over and over in Seattle."

Simoni tugged at her hair. "Maybe they learned how from being around humans here?"

"In less than two hundred years?" Kallista clenched her hands. "First an entirely new species appears without any warning, then they learn to do something no other animal besides humans have done in all of history? No. Something's happening here that we don't understand."

"How do we know you ain't feeding us a bunch of clankers?" Plucky asked.

Either Trina had heard Whipjack slang before or she understood Plucky's meaning by the context. "Once you meet the monarch, it will all come clear." She clucked her tongue. "What can I do to show you I'm on your side?"

"Give me my tibby back," Plucky said at once. "And my knives and my clothes."

"We all get rid of our old clothes as a sign of unity and togetherness," Trina said. "And I'm afraid we don't allow weapons. But I'll get your cat right away. Wait here."

As if they had any choice.

Trina got up and walked through the door.

As soon as they were alone, Kallista glared at Simoni. "Why are you being so sweet with that woman? Tell me you don't believe her lies."

Simoni shook her head. "I don't think she *is* lying."

Kallista couldn't believe what she was hearing.

Simoni turned in her chair. "What does she have to gain by lying? What did the women in the factory have to gain? They didn't seem scared or stressed. I honestly believe they like it here. And they think we will, too."

Kallista felt her face heat up. "Do *you* think you'll like it here?"

"Of course not," Simoni said. "But not everyone came from a city like Discovery. This may be the best they've ever had. We came here to find out what's happening in the city, to look for weaknesses. You aren't helping our chances with your attitude. Do you think you could try to be at least a little nice for a change?"

"Fine." Kallista dropped in the chair. It was bad enough that Simoni was so nice. Did she have to be right, too? "If this city is so great, why are they keeping us locked up?"

"That's what we have to find out," Simoni said.

"Here you go," Trina said, bustling back into the room. She handed Allie to Plucky. "Is there anything else I can help you with before we finish our questions and get you to bed?"

Kallista tried to force her lips into a smile. It seemed to physically hurt her cheeks. "You offered us a tour, but couldn't we look around on our own?"

Trina shook her head. "If you were to go outside by yourselves right now, you would become a meal for the Ninki Nankas."

"Ninki whats?" Plucky asked.

"Ninki Nankas. You may have seen them on your way in. Long, squat things with flickering tongues. They are distant cousins to our magnificent dragons, as you can tell by their wings, but that's where the resemblance ends. They patrol our streets, protecting us from the wildlife that would otherwise enter our city."

"You get a lot of wild animal attacks in your city? Packs of wolves and rabid bears?" Kallista scoffed.

"You're making a joke because you don't believe it's possible. But trust me, there are more dangerous animals out there than you might think. The Ninki Nankas leave us alone but attack any creatures they don't recognize."

"If they leave humans alone, why do we need to worry about them?" Kallista asked.

Trina touched the tip of her nose. "They hunt by smell. Part of your processing is to introduce them to your scent. Once one of them has it, they all have it. From that moment on, they know who you are and where you are. As long as you stay where you belong, they leave you alone."

They know who you are and where you are. The message couldn't have been any clearer.

"Now then," Trina said, putting a note in her folder. "Only one more thing, and we'll be done. Everyone in our city has a job. We all take great pride in giving back to the mighty dragons who give us so much. What talents do you bring with you?"

Kallista folded her arms across her chest. "I don't have any talents." Simoni glared at her, and she sighed. "I'm a mechanic."

"Very good," Trina said, making a check mark on her paper.

"Plucky is great at building things," Simoni said. "I'm good with numbers. I used to order parts and do inventory for my father's business."

Kallista was so shocked she couldn't speak. That was a lie! Simoni had never worked with numbers. She was farmer.

Simoni glanced at Kallista and casually brushed a finger across her lips.

"Wonderful," Trina said. "I'll assign you to our supply department, and Plucky can work in the machine shop. Kallista, I'll need to see what openings we might have in the mechanic shops. Until then, you'll start working on one of our ranches. Shoveling manure isn't the most exciting job, but it is an honor for us all to do our part."

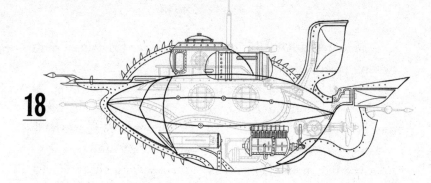

18

Working his way down a row of tomatoes, hacking weeds with a long-handled hoe, Trenton wondered where the cold air had gone that had chilled him to the bones a few days earlier. The morning had been cool, and tonight the temperature would drop, but now, with the sun beating down on his head, it felt like a hundred degrees. At least his small straw hat offered some shade. As if the heat wasn't bad enough, the field was thick with the stench of fertilizer.

"Why can't we use a quadracrus?" Clyde asked. After three days in the fields, they'd learned the official name for the spiderlike vehicles, but most people simply referred to them as "quads," for their four legs.

"Because these people hate us," Angus said. "They'll torture us for a week or two, wait until our hands our covered with blisters and we can no longer straighten our backs, then they'll execute us for murdering dragons."

"Or maybe we're stuck working in the fields instead or cooking or fixing things because you mouth off to everyone you meet," Clyde said.

"Quiet," Trenton said, looking around to make sure no one had overheard them. Garvin, their field supervisor, was a bully who delighted in punishing the smallest infractions. But he was a few hundred feet away, and the next set of workers was well ahead of them. "If they knew we'd killed dragons, they would have done something about it by now. The fact that they haven't means they don't know. I'd like to keep it that way."

"Oh, they know," Angus said. "They know everything."

As if to emphasize his point, a long, dark-green shape waddled down the row ahead of them, flicking its tongue in and out as it moved. With its blunt, arrow-shaped head and tiny wings, it looked like it should be clumsy and awkward, but it managed to walk almost daintily through the field of tomatoes without damaging a single plant.

The people who had captured Trenton and the others had warned them that the Ninki Nankas could be dangerous, but Trenton hadn't believed them. Until yesterday, when he'd seen one attack.

Trenton had been exploring the edge of the field where it met the forest surrounding the city—gauging how hard it would be to escape—when a small, striped, furry creature appeared out of the trees. For a moment, he and the creature stared at each other, both surprised by the sudden appearance of the other. He didn't think the creature was a threat, and he certainly had no plans to attack it.

He'd had no idea the Ninki Nanka was behind him until a green blur raced past him, snatched up the animal in its sharp teeth, and . . .

He didn't want to think about what the guard-dragon had done, or what was left of the furry creature when it was over. Afterwards, he'd thrown up for nearly ten minutes. That night at dinner, he hadn't been able to eat a thing.

Now, he, Clyde, and Angus stood frozen in place, hoes held out before them as if the blunt tools would have the least impact on something as powerful as one of those killing machines. Ten feet away, the Ninki Nanka raised its snout, flicked its tongue, and fixed each of them with its glassy-eyed stare.

Trenton didn't know what he would do if the creature decided to attack. Even at a trot, the beast moved faster than he could sprint. If it really wanted to catch something, that something would be caught. The only reason they'd avoided being caught by one when they'd been trapped in the alley was because the dragon had been too fat to squeeze between the buildings. And then Leo had shown up.

"Skat! Go find some rodent to eat," a boy shouted from behind Trenton.

He turned around and saw a tall, thin boy with dark hair that fell over his pale face, nearly down to his chin. The boy stepped in front of the Ninki Nanka and snapped his fingers.

The Ninki Nanka bared its fangs and flicked its tongue. For a moment, Trenton thought the creature was going to attack. Then it shook its head, appeared to sneeze, and shuffled away.

"How did you do that?" Clyde asked.

"Trade secret," the newcomer said with a grin.

"Exactly what trade are you in?" Trenton asked. The boy's skin wasn't tanned from constant toil outside like the other farmworkers. And the black grease on his knuckles and under his fingernails was an even bigger giveaway. "Are you a mechanic? What are you doing out here?"

The boy's grin widened even more. "You're sharp. I like that." He studied the other workers, then dropped his voice. "Do you still want to kill dragons?"

Angus scowled. "What are you, some kind of spy?"

The stranger ignored him. "I hear you lost something. Three somethings to be exact. If you get them back, are you going to run away?"

Trenton shook his head. "If we'd wanted to run away, we wouldn't be here now. We're trying to help the people of the city. Only, it turns out they don't want our help."

"Some of them do," the boy said.

Trenton shook his head. He remembered trying to talk to the men who had "processed" him and his friends into the city and how they had laughed at him when he brought up the idea of rescue.

In the distance, Garvin began heading in their direction.

The boy spoke quickly. "Sometime today you're going to meet with the monarch. I think you'll be okay; you all look younger than me. Assuming you still want to fight after that meeting, and assuming those three machines of yours might help in the battle, I can help you get them back."

"The monarch?" Trenton asked. "And why does it matter if we're younger than you?"

But the boy was already walking away.

"How do we know we can trust you?" Angus growled.

"Because I've already kept you from being caught twice," the boy said over his shoulder.

Clyde started after him. "You didn't tell us your name or how to—"

His breath cut off with a grunt as Garvin's heavy club hit his spine with a sickening crack. Clyde collapsed like a puppet whose strings had been cut. He lay on the ground, mouth gaping as he tried to suck air back into his lungs.

Garvin, six feet two inches of solid muscle, was a good ten years older than Trenton and tanned almost to the color of tree bark from working in the sun all day. He looked down at Clyde and spat on the ground. "Catch you slacking on the job like that again and it will be your head next time." He spun toward Trenton and Angus. "Who was that you were jawing with?"

"None of your business," Trenton growled. He started to help Clyde up, but Garvin stepped in front of him, a sadistic grin on his face.

He twirled his club on its leather string. "You want some of this, too? Come and get it."

"I'll take some," Angus said. Before Garvin could turn, Angus knocked him across the arm with the handle of his hoe. The club fell from his grip, and his arm dropped limply to his side. Angus swung again, catching the man in the gut hard enough to drive the air of him.

"Nobody picks on my friends," Angus said as Garvin bent over, gasping.

"Get . . . you," Garvin grunted. His eyes went to his club lying several feet away.

Angus grinned. "Go ahead and pick it up. As soon as you do, I'll break your arm."

"You wouldn't talk so big if you weren't the only one holding a weapon," Garvin said, slowly straightening.

"Look who's talking," Trenton said. "You used your club on a kid half your size when he wasn't even looking."

"Tell you what," Angus said. "We'll make it even." He tossed his hoe aside. "In fact, just to be fair, I'll only use one arm."

In a flash, Garvin leaped for his club. Angus stuck out a foot, and the man went sprawling to the ground. Angus stalked after him, every bit as deadly as one of the guard dragons.

Abandoning his club, Garvin leaped to his feet. He feinted right, then threw a roundhouse punch with his left hand.

Angus avoided the punch easily, jabbed an elbow into the man's ribs, then smashed his fist into Garvin's left shoulder.

"Want to go for just feet?" Angus asked.

Garvin shook his head, his hands hanging uselessly at his sides.

"Good idea to stop while you can still walk."

Trenton felt sick to his stomach. "Did you really have to do that?" he asked Angus.

Angus rolled his eyes. "A bully doesn't stop until somebody makes them. Trust me, I should know."

While Trenton helped Clyde to his feet, Angus picked up his hoe. He glared at Garvin. "In case you're thinking about coming for us later on, maybe with a couple of your friends, or telling anyone what happened here, know that I'll be happy to teach you this same lesson again," Angus said, tapping the wooden handle against one palm. "Any questions?"

Garvin shook his head again, this time much more vigorously.

The whirring of gears and clicking of mechanical legs came from behind them, and they all turned in time to see a quad racing toward them. This one used all four legs for movement and had a broad metal shield on the front and a seat in the back. The man driving it was a city guard.

"What's going on here?" the guard demanded.

"My friend had a little farming accident," Angus said, gesturing to Clyde. "Our supervisor came to make sure he was okay."

"Is that true?" the guard asked.

"Yes," Clyde said, stifling a moan as he put his hand to his back.

Trenton grabbed Clyde's hoe and handed it to him.

Angus gave Garvin a sharklike grin, and the man quickly nodded. "That's how it happened all right." Wincing, he bent down and barely managed to raise his arm enough to pick up his club.

"Clumsy farmers," the guard muttered. He shook his head. "Well, what are you waiting for? Get in."

Clyde wiped mud from his cheek. "Me? Get in that? With you?"

"All three of you," the guard snapped. "And be quick about it. You don't want to be late."

"Late for what?" Trenton asked.

The guard looked at him as if he was an idiot. "For your appointment, you slow-witted dirt-diggers. You're meeting the monarch."

The monarch. Trenton didn't know who that was, but he had a pretty good idea.

The three of them quickly climbed into the backseat of the quad, and the guard set off, racing his quad across the field in jerking leaps and bounds, the machine smashing the tomato plants in the process.

Holding on for dear life, Clyde turned to Angus. "Since when am I your friend?"

Angus spat over the side of the quad as carelessly as if they were going to lunch. "Don't let it go to your head."

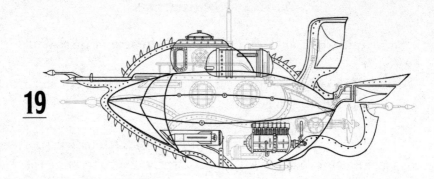

19

Long before they reached their destination, Trenton knew where they were headed. The white tower stood over the city like a fang pushing up into the sky. Twelve rows of arched windows stretched from nearly the base of the building to the golden spire at the top, looking like a giant crown.

People jumped aside as the quad charged along the wide, winding boulevard that led to the tower.

"This is it," Angus said, his words mostly covered by the clacking of the quad's metal legs on the cobblestone street. "They'll take us to the headman, and he'll sentence us to death. Then they'll chop off our heads and put them on the spikes of that golden crown."

"I always pictured a crown on *my* head, not the other way around," Clyde said with a sickly smile.

"They're not going to execute us, and the monarch isn't a man," Trenton said. He hoped the first part was true, but he was sure of the second part. He thought back to the gleaming white dragon that had stared out of the tower at him the day they barely escaped from the city, and a fiery fist clenched in his belly. "It's not even human."

As they neared the tower, he could see it was surrounded by a white stone wall that might have been marble or polished granite. Surrounding the wall was a circular courtyard with stones that sparkled in the sunlight. The guard stopped the quad just outside the courtyard. As Trenton looked down, he realized why. Each brick glimmered a deep yellow.

Angus leaned out of his seat. "I think that's real gold."

"Look," Clyde said. "It's the girls."

Before the boys had climbed out of their seats, Simoni and Plucky ran to the side of the vehicle, the two groups greeting each other as if it had been years instead of days.

"How have you been?"

"We were so worried about you."

"They wouldn't let us see you."

Clyde groaned as he stepped down to the golden bricks.

Plucky was immediately at his side. "If them bird-witted cullies laid a hand on you, I'll—"

"I'm fine." Clyde wrapped his arms around Plucky. "It's good to see you."

Plucky stared at Trenton over Clyde's shoulder, her brown eyes wide. "Yeah, yeah," she murmured before slowly raising her arms to hug him back.

Simoni examined the backs of Angus's hands, which were covered with scrapes and beginning to bruise. "Did the other guy get the worst of it?"

Angus flexed his fingers. "Always."

Kallista stood slightly apart from the other girls. Trenton walked across the courtyard to join her. She looked across at the quad, which was turning to leave. "Where's my father?" she asked quietly.

Trenton shook his head. "I haven't seen him since they took us in for processing."

She scowled as though she didn't believe him. "You must see him at night in the dorm."

"He's not in our building," Trenton said. "I've checked

every floor. I thought since you're his daughter, they might have . . ."

Kallista folded her arms tightly across her chest, cupping her elbows in her hands. "They told me I'd be allowed to see him, but they lied. Like they have about everything else."

Tension was thick between her and the other two girls. Trenton noticed that they were wearing different clothes. Kallista had on gray pants and a shirt similar to what he, Clyde, and Angus were wearing, while Simoni and Plucky wore white.

"Is everything okay?"

The muscles along the sides of Kallista's jaws jumped. "*Nothing* is okay. We have to get out of here."

"I know," Trenton said. "I've been searching for a way to leave the city, but the Ninki Nankas are everywhere."

Kallista shook her head. "We have to find a way to get our dragons."

"I know," Trenton said again. "Hiding them on the island seemed like a good idea at the time, but maybe we should have left them somewhere more accessible."

"I don't care if we have to swim." She squeezed her fingers around her elbows until her knuckles turned white. "Have you listened to the people in this city? They *want* to be here. It's like they think serving dragons is some big honor. They don't even realize they are all slaves."

Deep chimes sounded, and the gates swung open. Kallista looked around one last time as the guards motioned them to come forward.

"I'm sure he's fine," Trenton said, hoping that was the case. He tilted his head back to look at the tower as he walked through the gate. This close it was even more impressive. Fanciful designs ran up the outside walls, which were inset with silver and gold scrollwork. Gems bigger than his knuckles glimmered around the outside of each arched window. He estimated the tower was nearly five hundred feet from the base to the tip of the crown and wider across than ten men standing side-by-side with their arms outstretched.

Plucky rubbed her hands together. "Like to do a snatch-and-grab on that, wouldn't I now?"

"Don't even think about it," Clyde whispered.

There was a commotion back at the gate. When Trenton turned, he saw Kallista standing outside the entrance, her feet set wide as if daring anyone to try to move her.

"The monarch awaits your presence. Now!" the larger of the two guards said.

"I'm not going anywhere until I see my father."

The second guard lowered the tip of his spear. "Get in the tower."

Trenton ran back toward Kallista. "Maybe someone inside can tell us where he is."

She narrowed her eyes and set her feet more firmly.

The big guard stepped toward her. "You *will* go to the monarch if I have to carry you."

"Go ahead." Kallista balled her fists. "But I promise you won't like it any better than I do."

Angus grinned as though enjoying the standoff, but Trenton knew that drawing attention to themselves wasn't going to help their chances of escape. Just as the first guard handed his spear to the second and reached for Kallista, Leo Babbage came running out of the tower entrance.

"It's all right, Kallista. I'm here. I'm fine. They brought me in a few minutes ago. I've been waiting for you."

Kallista ran to her father. "Are you okay?"

"I'm fine," he said.

She looked him over carefully.

"Really," he said with a smile. "They've treated me surprisingly well." Not only did he look well, he actually looked more excited than Trenton had ever seen him. Like Simoni and Plucky, he wore white pants and a shirt. But his shirt had a red sash running diagonally across his chest. Trenton wanted to ask what it meant, but Leo wouldn't stop talking.

"Have you seen the workings of that bridge of theirs?" he asked, waving his hands in the air. "It's remarkable. And I had a chance to go under the mechanical walkways. An amazing feat of engineering, although I noticed right away how it could be improved."

"The monarch awaits you," the guard told Leo in a much more respectful tone than he'd used before.

"Yes, yes." Kallista's father walked through the entryway, twisting his head to look at the walls and ceiling. "Fascinating architecture."

Inside the tower, they took a sharp right, passing a plain metal door that looked out of place compared to the rest of the tower. A deep thrumming vibrated up through the floor. Trenton placed his hand on the door; he could feel it there, too. It had an odd rhythmic pattern to it: *grum-rum-rum-bump, grum-rum-rum-bump.*

"What do you think that is?" he asked.

"An engine, I would imagine," Leo said. "Or perhaps a generator."

"Move along," the guard said, nudging Trenton in the back with the shaft of his spear.

"Where have you been?" Kallista asked her father, hurrying to keep up with him.

"What did you say?" Leo turned his head to admire a metal air vent.

Kallista grabbed his arm. "Trenton says you aren't sleeping in his dorm."

"No. They gave me a house of my own."

A deep line creased the center of Kallista's brow. "Why would they do that?"

But Leo was already moving to examine a spiral brass staircase that ran up the side of one wall, reaching halfway to a hole in the ceiling. "What's this?" he asked, kneeling to get a better look at the base.

"I'm sorry, sir," the guard said, "but I need you to step onto the stairs."

One by one they climbed the steps. The staircase was so narrow that no more than one person at a time could stand on a single step. Simoni went first, then Plucky, followed by Clyde, Trenton, Leo, Kallista, and the two guards.

Trenton looked up through the hole. Past the opening, he could see another level with a hole in that ceiling as well. The openings seemed to continue level after level, maybe all the way to the top of the tower. Unfortunately, the stairs stopped well short of the first hole. He looked back at the guards. "Hate to tell you, but unless you've got some extra steps in your pocket, this is going to be a very short trip."

No sooner had the words left his mouth than the stairs began to vibrate.

"Hold on to the railing," the guard said.

Slowly the staircase began to turn. As it did, the stairs rose into the air like a giant corkscrew. As they rose, the speed increased.

"Like a drill bit," Leo said, twirling his finger in the air.

They were moving so quickly Trenton's hair blew back from his forehead.

"Whoa," Clyde said, turning his face toward his shoulder. His skin was an alarming shade of green.

Kallista was the only one who didn't seem affected by the surprising mode of transportation. She put her foot on the step her father was standing on, pulling herself up so she could speak into his ear. Trenton leaned back to catch what they were saying. "What does your sash mean?"

So she had noticed it, too.

Leo looked down at his chest, running a finger along the red cloth. "Who knows? Some kind of identification, I suppose."

Kallista glanced at the guards standing behind them. "We're planning an escape. You *do* want to escape, don't you?"

Leo's face grew serious. "Of course. When?"

"I don't know," Kallista said. "I'll send you a message. Where can I find you?"

Leo glanced at the guards as well before whispering, "The main manufacturing building in the center of town."

Spinning so quickly the levels they passed were nothing but a blur, they shot through an opening to the next level. Then, without warning, the stairs clunked to a stop. Leo fell forward, knocking his head into Trenton's hip. Plucky slipped and would have fallen if Clyde hadn't reached out to catch her.

Feeling dizzy, Trenton looked around him. They were standing on a crystal floor that ran from one side of the tower to the other. The arched windows were open, giving them a view of clear blue sky in every direction. It reminded him of standing in the island lighthouse, only on a scale much grander than he could have imagined.

The guards immediately stepped off the staircase and dropped to one knee. One of the guards placed a fist to his forehead and shouted, "Behold the monarch!"

Trenton turned slowly. Although he knew what he was

going to see, he still felt his breath catch in his lungs at the sight of the huge white dragon that filled the room from floor to ceiling. It was looking out the window that faced the sea.

Trenton had no idea what the dragon's powers might be, but he instinctively understood that this was the most powerful creature he'd ever seen. The most powerful he ever would see, even if he lived to be a hundred.

20

"What is it?" Kallista whispered, hands clamped to the staircase railing.

"It's the dragon I told you about," Trenton said. "The one I saw right before we escaped into the fog."

Clearly it was a dragon. But like none she'd ever seen before. For one thing, it was huge, nearly twice as large as the black dragon they'd shot down outside Discovery with the laser cannon. Most dragons' scales were rough, like chunks of armor, but the ones running down this creature's back were a glassy white. They reflected the sunlight coming through the windows into tiny starbursts of color that bounced off the ceiling and floor.

Its broad wings were divided into five distinct sections with a sharp point at the top of each segment. Its horns were silver spirals so straight and uniform they appeared to be metal sculptures. The tail curving around its hindquarters looked like a rope woven out of diamonds.

As though waiting for them to finish admiring it, the creature stared out to sea for a full minute.

At last it turned, spreading its wings until they stretched from one side of the room to the other. Glimmering white plates of armor encircled its face and head, creating a halo effect, and a snowy beard sprouted beneath its chin.

Its violet eyes glittered, and for a moment Kallista wanted to worship at its feet. The only word she could think of to describe what she was seeing was *majestic*. Then the dragon turned its gaze to meet hers, and her guts twisted in a painful knot.

This wasn't a creature to be worshiped; it was the essence of nightmares. Death served cold on a crystal platter with no conscience or remorse. It glared down at her with an expression both cruel and amused. She could imagine the beast slicing her open with one of its ice-white talons and grinning while it watched her bleed to death.

"It has six legs," Trenton whispered.

For a moment, Kallista didn't understand what he was talking about. The creature stood on four massive scaled legs like every other dragon they'd seen. Then she realized it was holding a golden goblet in a smaller set of legs that jutted out from under its wings, almost like human arms.

After looking them each in the eye, the dragon wrinkled its snout, baring dozens of icicle-like fangs. "Are you afraid? Do I terrify you?"

One of the guards looked up and rushed toward them, pushing Trenton to his knees. "All kneel before His Majesty."

The white dragon laughed. "They are newcomers. I think we can do without the formalities today."

"It *can* talk," Kallista murmured. Trina had been telling the truth. The Order of the Beast had been right all along.

"You said that was impossible," Trenton hissed.

Kallista shook her head. This wasn't simple mimicry— repeating a word or phrase. The white dragon spoke perfectly, as if it had been speaking English its whole life.

She glanced toward her father, but his eyes were locked on the dragon's.

A guard raised his spear over his head. "No one talks to the monarch without permission!"

"Hold," the dragon said, stroking its beard with the talons not holding the goblet. "This group is special. Do you know what makes them unique?"

The guard lowered his eyes. "No, my lord."

The creature's violet eyes flashed, and Kallista felt her legs wobble. "These humans have killed dragons."

The knot in her stomach turned to ice. It *knew*.

The dragon lifted the golden goblet, and a red liquid that looked suspiciously like blood ran into its mouth. "These boys and girls before you, these *children*," it roared, rattling the tower walls, "have killed not one, not two, but more than twenty of my brothers and sisters."

Still looking at the floor, the guard gripped his spear in both hands. "Allow me to avenge the death of the chosen, my lord."

Angus grabbed the stair railing and vaulted over it to land on the crystal floor. "You want to kill me?" He spread his arms wide, pushing out his chest. "Go ahead. Because if I have the chance, I'll kill another twenty of you."

"No!" Kallista yelled, shoving her way past her father on the stairs. She was sure the guard would launch his spear through Angus's chest. His arm was drawn back, muscles quivering, but he only stood there, fingers tight on the shaft, waiting to be commanded.

Instead, the dragon's expression shifted in a way Kallista couldn't understand. It wasn't like reading a human face, but somehow she knew that, for the moment at least, the threat of death didn't feel as near. The creature laughed until its beard shook. It threw the goblet at the wall, mashing it into a gold-and-red lump. "I'm not going to kill you. I brought you here to congratulate you."

For a moment, there was silence. Then the dragon waved them forward with one of its legs. "You're confused. Come down and let's talk." It motioned to the guards. "You two, fetch me another drink. I'm parched."

Trenton leaned toward Kallista. "Do you hear an echo in your head when it talks?"

Kallista nodded. It was like she could see the words coming from the dragon's mouth while hearing its words in her head an instant later. It was an odd, disorienting feeling. Could it have something to do with how easily they understood the creature's words?

Slowly, as though still fearing an attack, Trenton and the others stepped onto the crystal floor. Kallista was positive it was a trap. The only question was when and how it would be sprung. Her father was the only member of the group who didn't seem terrified. He studied the white dragon like a man seeing stars for the first time.

Once all of them were off the staircase, the guards moved onto the steps and the machinery whirled them down out of sight.

"I'd offer you a chair," the dragon said in a magnanimous tone, "but I'm afraid my kind doesn't use them. Although, to be honest, I wouldn't mind a throne if someone could design one that fit my proportions. Who knows? Maybe one of you will invent it."

"I don't think so," Trenton said.

The dragon raised its wings in a gesture that looked surprisingly like a human shrug. "Feel free to stand or sit on the floor. Whatever makes you comfortable." As if taking its own advice, it curled its front and rear legs beneath it and lowered its massive body to the floor.

"You're wondering why I don't punish you for killing my brothers and sisters. To answer that, you must first understand the history of this city, which is really the history of the world as it has now become and ever will be." It flicked a wing tip toward one of the windows. "Look outside."

Kallista glanced at Trenton, then walked close enough to the edge of the room to look over the city. She angled herself so she could see out while still keeping a wary eye on the creature behind her.

"Two hundred years ago, humans ruled everything you see below you. Of course, it was a pale shadow of what it is now, but you get the idea. Humans weren't the strongest species; they weren't the fastest. Please don't take offense, but they definitely weren't the most attractive. Do you know why they ruled?"

"Because they were the smartest," Kallista said. The answer was obvious.

"Perhaps. Although, based on my experience, humans are rather stupid. No, it's because they were the most effective killers. Now and then, one of them was slain by a lesser predator—a bear, a large cat, perhaps a sea creature—but most of that goes back to the stupidity. By and large, they took what they wanted and destroyed anything that got in their way. Thus, they were the rulers. Until one day they weren't."

"You're talking about the arrival of dragons," Trenton said.

"I'm talking about the birth of a new ruling species. Stronger, faster, smarter, yes, even better looking. But most importantly, more effective killers. I suppose you've read the stories. If not, feel free to visit the library. There are some lovely photographs of the carnage that took place once humans realized they were no longer at the top of the food chain."

"But where did you come from?" Simoni asked.

"Where does any advancement come from?" the dragon asked. "You may as well ask where the wind comes from when it blows away the fog. Where the sun comes from that swallows the darkness."

It was avoiding the question, but Kallista sensed there was a hint of truth in its words. Did the dragon not know how its species had come to be? Or was it hiding something?

The dragon stretched all six of its legs, flicking the talons out like crystal daggers. "What matters is that our arrival marked the beginning of a new day. Humans' time at the top of the heap was over."

She was sure the creature was avoiding something, but she didn't know what. "If you're all-powerful, why bother to let humans live at all?"

For an instant the dragon's eyes flared, and a purplish-blue light filled the room. Kallista felt as though the tower had briefly been turned upside down. Her legs wobbled, and she would have fallen if Trenton hadn't grabbed her hand.

"I think you know the answer," the dragon said.

Kallista's father, who had been silent up until that point, stepped forward. "You need us."

The creature chuckled. "*Need?* Do humans *need* pigs or chickens or"—it glanced toward Plucky—"or noisy little balls of fur? No. We don't need you. But we can make use of you. The same way humans make use of chickens to get eggs."

"Or pigs to make sausage," Trenton added.

The dragon burst into startled laughter, its back talons gouging the crystal floor. "If I wanted to eat you, I'd have you on a spit now."

"Is being forced to serve you any better? Should we be pleased that you view us as pigs instead of sausage?"

"Yes, well, that's what it really comes down to, isn't it?" The dragon flashed its wide grin, composure regained. "The history of humans is filled with tales of encountering lesser animals. Some they domesticated: the sheep, the cow, the dog. Others— too dangerous to be trusted or trained—they destroyed, occasionally going so far as to wipe them completely from the face of the earth."

The dragon stood and walked toward them until it was so close a single flap of its wings would send them hurtling through the arched opening to the ground below. "You wonder why I do not begrudge the fact that you dared to murder dragons. What would be the point? Can you blame a wolf for biting? A snake for striking? It is the nature of humans to kill. To be perfectly honest, I blame the dragons you killed for their weakness."

It moved its wings slightly, and Kallista leaned forward to keep from sliding across the floor toward the window behind her.

"I admire your ingenuity. I know about your mechanical flying machines and find it a touching attempt to be like those you admire. At this very moment, they are being transported from the island for disassembly and inspection. I'm sure there's much to be learned from them. Perhaps we can use some of your technology in our machines here. Flying vehicles might speed up certain operations."

Trenton's shoulders slumped, and Kallista felt what little optimism she'd had for escape begin to fade. Clearly they knew about the dragons, but she'd hoped for a few more days before they discovered their hiding place.

Clyde moved closer toward Plucky. "What are you going to do to us?" he asked the white dragon.

"That is up to you. For a time, it seemed your species was destined for the same fate your kind inflicted on so many other species. Extinction. I changed that. The humans we find useful, we save. The others, well, when the chicken stops laying eggs . . . The seven of you appear smart, talented, resourceful, even. But you also bite. The question is, can you be domesticated or must you be destroyed?"

"What if we don't want either choice?" Kallista demanded. "We were told we were free to leave the city."

The dragon grinned, exposing every fang in its mouth. "Every human in this city is free to come and go as they like. Of course, if you stay, you will be expected to contribute. In exchange, you will be provided with food, safety, lodging, entertainment, and most important of all, protection. Should you choose to leave, I can promise you none of that."

"You're saying if we try to leave you will kill us?"

"I'm saying that if you stop being useful to the city, I can no longer offer you protection. Not from wild animals outside the city, and not from the tribes of feral humans living in the woods. Not even from the Ninki Nankas; it's in their nature to kill as well."

Across the room, the stairs spun up through the hole and clanked to a halt as the guards returned with a huge pitcher and another goblet.

"Time for you to go," the dragon said. "Consider your next decisions carefully. Your lives may depend upon it."

As they started toward the stairs, the dragon held out one leg to block Kallista's father. "I'd like you to stay awhile longer. I have a few more questions for you."

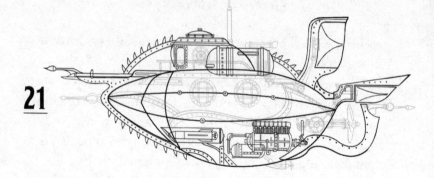

21

The next few days stretched out until Trenton had to remind himself it had been less than a week since they'd been captured and not months. Every time a dragon flew overhead, he flinched. How could anyone ever get used to the creatures watching you everywhere you went? Eyeing you like a spider considering a fly.

The worst were the ones that spoke. At first, he'd assumed it was only the white dragon, but he quickly realized many of them could speak at least a few words. You might be walking along and a red dragon would drop to the ground in front of you, point a talon, and grunt "Go" or "Food." If you didn't figure out what it wanted quickly enough, it would knock you down or singe your clothing with flames.

Every time he heard footsteps behind him or caught a flash of motion from the corner of his eye, his heart raced, sure that the monarch had decided Trenton and his friends should die for their crimes after all.

The day after they'd met the monarch, a group of men had stopped them on their way to the fields. Angus had balled his fists, ready for a fight, while Trenton searched for a way to escape. Neither were necessary. It turned out Clyde was being given a new job. Apparently his artistic talents qualified him to be an apprentice in the building-and-community design department.

That night, he came back to the dormitory wearing a white shirt and pants.

"Look who's all fancy," Angus said, plucking a clod of dirt from the knee of his pants and smearing it down one of Clyde's sleeves.

Clyde brushed at the dirt, trying to laugh off the comment. "It doesn't mean anything."

But it did. There were hundreds of rules governing the city. Every day, Trenton picked up a few more. Gray clothes identified humans who performed manual labor. White was for the professional class. Those who fell somewhere in between wore white pants and gray shirts. A band of color across the chest marked people deemed most valuable to the city. The thicker the band, the higher the rank.

Other rules were more obvious. Work was from eight until five, with an hour for lunch. Breakfast and dinner were served in the dormitories—or cooked in private homes for those who had them. Although, those granted clearance could eat dinner at designated restaurants spread through the city. Since Trenton and his friends didn't have clearance, they were required to go straight from the dormitory to work and back again. Exploring was limited to within a single block of those two places; the Ninki Nankas, with their beady black eyes, made sure of that.

Unless they were required to work together, men and women living in the dormitories were only allowed to mingle on Rest Day—the last day of the week—which nearly everyone had off.

Trenton was surprised at how few children he saw. Maybe they were assigned to a different area of the city.

A little past noon on the day before Rest Day, Trenton and Angus stood on a hill overlooking the bay. Toiling in the fields was backbreaking work, but at least the breeze coming off the water kept them cool.

Angus yanked a beet out of the ground, wrinkled his nose, and tossed it into the basket strapped to his back. "Surprised you haven't been put in charge of oiling squeaky wheels or something."

Trenton yanked a plant free of the rich soil and banged it against his leg to knock off the dirt. "Surprised you haven't been put in charge of roughing up prisoners or something."

Angus nodded as though the idea had merit. "Maybe they heard about your excellent grades in food production class."

"Maybe they heard your dad was a bully who forced everyone to follow a chancellor who nearly got us all killed."

Insults finished, they went back to picking. They'd have to stay late if they didn't finish their quota on time.

Garvin hadn't bothered them again since the day Angus beat him up. In fact, Trenton hadn't seen him at all. Maybe he'd been transferred to another field where the workers he picked on didn't fight back.

Although he wouldn't say it to Angus, Trenton was surprised he *hadn't* been transferred out of the fields. Clyde had been promoted to a job that took advantage of his talents. Although he didn't know where they'd been assigned, Simoni and Plucky were both wearing white. That left only Angus, Kallista, and himself stuck doing manual labor.

"Maybe it's because they want to keep an eye on us," he muttered.

Angus snapped a beet plant, showering Trenton with dirt. "What are you talking about?"

"Maybe they're keeping us out of the city because it's easier to keep track of what we're doing here. They know as long as we're spending every day in the fields, we can't get into any trouble." If that was the case, did it mean someone in authority had decided Simoni, Plucky, and Clyde could be trusted? By that reasoning, someone must have decided Trenton, Kallista, and Angus were a risk.

"If that's the plan, it's working," Angus said. "By the time I get done working out here, the only thing I want to do is eat and fall into bed. Almost makes me wish Garvin would come back to break up the boredom."

From the other side of the field, a quad came trundling toward them. It was outfitted with a pair of metal rakes on the front and a two-legged trailer on the back. The trailer was filled to overflowing with fertilizer.

Trenton placed a sleeve over his face. "I hate when they bring those carts by. It makes the fields stink for the rest of the day."

The quad angled across the field, and Trenton realized it was coming straight toward him. "Watch out!" he shouted, diving to the side as one of the metal legs stabbed the ground inches from where he'd been standing.

The quad cut sharply to the right, and the trailer swung wildly, going up on a single leg for a moment. Dirt and fertilizer spilled over the side, covering Trenton from head to foot. The quad turned again, the driver heading in another direction.

Angus howled with laughter, clutching his stomach, as Trenton wiped the dirt from his face. "It was like the driver did that on purpose," he said. At least three feet of the row he'd been picking was now covered. He'd have to dig out the plants again before the sun went down.

Looking down, he saw something white sticking out of the dirt. He pulled it loose. It was a folded piece of paper. Quickly he opened the note.

Meet tomorrow at noon. Zoo south of city center. Look for the bear cage. Do not tell anyone. Destroy this note after reading it.

He looked around for the quad, but it had already disappeared into the next field over. He tried to recall the image of the driver's face. The quad had gone by fast, and the driver had been wearing a scarf that covered his face up to his nose, but Trenton was almost sure the skin between the scarf and the floppy dark hair had been pale white.

. . .

Rest Day was like a mini carnival. Except for the people running the food stands and exhibits, everyone was off work. Men, women, and children crowded together, eating, laughing, and playing games.

All of the food was free, and what few guards there were stayed out of the way. Trenton didn't even see any Ninki Nankas lurking about, although he was sure they were there somewhere.

South of the city center, twenty or thirty cages contained a variety of animals, many of which Trenton had never seen before: monkeys, brightly colored birds, a horse with black-and-white stripes.

"They all look so sad," Clyde said.

Trenton agreed. When he'd realized he'd have a chance to see an actual bear, he'd been excited. But almost all of the animals lay on the floors of their concrete cages, watching the people going by with listless eyes. Only the large brown bear paced back and forth in its cage, its wicked-looking claws clicking with each step.

"I'll bet that guy could do some damage if he got out," Angus said.

On the other side of the bear cage, a woman with long

brownish-red hair was playing a violin. A brightly colored bird on her shoulder bobbed back and forth to the music.

A dark-haired boy appeared out of the crowd and called to the woman, "Sounding good, Talysa," before continuing by.

Talysa nodded without stopping her music.

"That's the kid from the field," Clyde said.

"Come on," Trenton said, hurrying after the boy before he could get lost in the crowd.

The boy continued past several cages before ducking behind a food cart.

Trenton, Angus, and Clyde followed, darting through the opening to find Kallista, Simoni, and Plucky waiting in a small alcove filled with pipes and cords. It was the first time the six of them had seen each other since their meeting with the monarch.

Angus raced forward and pulled Simoni into a hug. "How are you?" He looked her up and down as though checking for damage.

"I'm fine," Simoni said.

Standing off to the side was the dark-haired boy along with three other kids. "About time," the boy said with a grin.

"What's this all about?" Trenton demanded. He turned to Kallista. "Who are these kids?"

Kallista's eyes narrowed. "I thought you knew them."

The boy stuck out his hand. "Alex Vaughn. These are my coworkers."

A tall boy with lots of freckles eyed them up and down. "They don't look that special to me."

"They built those mechanical dragons? I doubt it," said a skinny boy with lots of red hair.

A girl with a long dark ponytail offered a cheerful smile. "Forgive their rudeness. We don't see new kids here a lot—especially not kids who fly into our city on mechanical dragons." She stuck out her hand encased in a leather work glove. "I'm Hallie Meredith, the tall one is Michael Whitlock, and the one with all the red hair is Joey Moore."

The redhead gave a quick nod. "People call me JoeBob on account of I bob my head a lot when I talk."

Kallista gave Hallie's gloved hand a brief shake, and Trenton did the same.

"I got a note saying these guys know where our dragons are," Kallista said.

Trenton frowned. "Same here. Although mine came covered in a pile of dirt that got dumped on me."

"That was my fault," Alex said. "I didn't mean to actually dump it on you."

Hallie tugged at her ponytail. "Alex has an odd sense of humor."

Michael chuffed. "You can say that again. He's pulled way too many pranks on me since I've known him."

"Is that what this is?" Trenton asked. "Some kind of prank? Or do you really know where our dragons are?"

"We know," Alex said. "But before we take you there, we have to make sure you're on our side."

"Your side of what?" Clyde asked.

"'Side of what.'" JoeBob snickered. "I like that."

Alex gave him a warning look. He studied Trenton, Kallista, and the others. "Why did you come here?"

Even though he'd just learned the boy's name, Trenton felt like he could trust him. Maybe it was because he was one of the few people who didn't seem in awe of the dragons, or maybe it was because they were both about the same age and there didn't seem to be a lot of kids in this city. Whatever the reason, he found himself giving a completely honest answer.

"We've been hunting dragons for the last eight weeks, looking for their source."

Michael folded his arms across his chest. "Well, you found it."

"And now that you have?" Alex said. "Now that you've seen what the city is like, what will you do if you get your dragons back?"

"What would you do?" Kallista asked.

"I'd leave," Michael said. "No question. Get out of this dragon-stinking city and never come back."

"You seem to be the only ones who feel that way," Trenton said. "Everyone else loves it here."

"You mean the adults," Hallie said, rolling her eyes.

Alex nodded. "All the adults think the dragons are the source of everything good. But us kids don't. We do everything we can to sabotage things for the dragons. We call ourselves the Runt Patrol."

"You created the explosion the night we were in the field," Trenton said.

"And the warning about the guards," JoeBob added. "That was me."

Alex nodded. "The Runt Patrol is committed to doing whatever it takes to free our city—and our parents—from the dragons. For some reason, kids change when they get older here. It's like they start believing everything the dragons say. They go from hating the dragons to practically worshipping them."

Trenton remembered what Alex had said before they had been taken to meet the monarch. "That's what you meant about us being younger than you."

"Right," Alex said. "Michael and I are getting older. We've been planning to escape before we become like the rest of them, but then you guys arrived."

"The woman who processed us claimed we could leave anytime we wanted," Kallista said.

Michael guffawed. "They'll let you leave all right. But as soon as you do, they'll kill you."

"Why?" Trenton asked. "What's the point of keeping us here?"

Alex tilted his head. "You built those mechanical dragons, and you managed to kill over a dozen real dragons, from what I've heard. That makes you both a resource and a threat. As long as they can keep you here, using your mechanical talents for them, they'll let you live. But the day you try to leave, you're a threat."

"I'm still planning on escaping," Michael said.

Alex scuffed the toe of his right shoe in the dirt. "Up until we saw you fly into the city, we'd assumed it was impossible to kill dragons. We did what we could to harass them, but we figured eventually we'd have to leave the city before we started being mindless slaves like our parents." He looked from Trenton to Kallista. "Do you think . . . If we got your dragons back, could we find a way to stop the dragons for good?"

"Not in a straight-up battle," Trenton said. "But if we knew more about the city, we might be able to find a way to outthink them."

"Oh, we know everything about the city," Hallie said.

JoeBob shook his hair out of his eyes. *"Everything."*

"All right," Alex said. "Let's go get them."

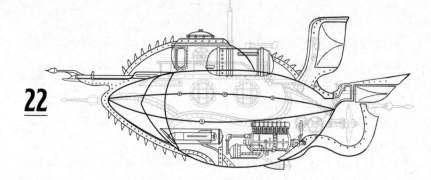

22

Stick close to me," Alex said. "You've been spied on ever since you got here. And I don't just mean by the Ninki Nankas."

"Spied on?" Plucky asked. "By rusty who?"

"Adults," Michael said. "They don't trust kids." He gave a lopsided grin. "Not that they should."

Alex stepped around the side of the food cart, peeked in both directions, then ducked back. "Okay, we have to make this quick. We know where your dragons are. The mechanics have only been testing them so far, but Lizzy says they could start taking them apart as early as tomorrow."

"Who's Lizzy?" Angus asked. "And how does she know all this?"

"We get around," was all Alex said. "The building where they are is locked, but no one will be working there tonight. The dragons are lazy, and the guards are minimal on Rest Day."

Clyde ran his fingers through his hair. "If it's locked, how do we get in?"

Alex reached into his pocket and flashed a shiny key. "Freshly minted. It pays to have friends in small spaces."

He dropped to one knee and sketched a map in the dirt, while the others crowded around him. "We can't all go together or people will get suspicious. Head out from here in groups of two so you can look out for each other. I'll meet you at the southeast corner of the library in thirty minutes. From there, it's only a couple of blocks to the building where they're keeping the dragons."

"Aren't you forgetting the Ninki Nankas?" Angus asked. "I don't think they're going to like us nosing around where we don't belong."

"Leave the Ninkis to me," Alex said. "If we split up now and everyone goes in different directions, it will make it harder for them to keep track of us and less likely that they'll suspect we're up to anything. Do your best to make sure you aren't followed, but don't be late."

Trenton looked around, realizing Hallie, JoeBob, and Michael were no longer with them. "Were did your friends go?"

"To scout out trouble." He brushed the dirt until there was no sign of the map. "You didn't tell anyone else about the notes, right?"

"Right," Trenton said.

He noticed Kallista avert her eyes before saying, "Of course."

"Okay," Alex said, "see you in thirty minutes."

• • •

"You told your father, didn't you?" Trenton said as he and Kallista approached the library.

"He's one of us," Kallista said.

"Why didn't you explain that to the Runt Patrol?"

Kallista chewed her lower lip. "They might not understand. He's not gullible like the other adults here. Besides, I had to tell him. We're going to need him to help us plan our next move against the dragons."

Simoni and Angus were already at the library when Trenton and Kallista arrived. Plucky and Clyde showed up a minute later.

"Plum exciting, yeah, yeah?" she asked, bouncing on the balls of her feet.

"Plummy terrifying," Clyde said, trying to catch his breath. "We must have passed at least six of those Ninki Noonkis."

"Ninki *Nankas*," Alex said, coming around the corner with Michael and JoeBob behind him. "Named after mythical creatures from Africa." He looked back at the two boys. "Were any of them followed?"

JoeBob shook his head while Michael chuckled. "Great idea to try this on Rest Day."

"We aren't *trying*," Alex said. "We're doing."

"Where's Hallie?" Kallista asked.

A metal plate in the street popped up almost under her feet. "Taking a nap while I waited for the rest of you to show up."

"The sewers," Trenton said, his eyes lighting up. "Why didn't I think of that? The Ninki Nankas will never find us down there."

"Think again," Hallie said. "The pipes are filled with them. If you listen, you can hear them splashing."

"That's probably how they manage to get around without being seen," Angus said.

Clyde sighed. "Then we're sunk."

Alex opened his hand. "Plucky, can I borrow a knife?"

"Right you are," Plucky said, pulling a silver blade with a burnished metal handle out of her shirtsleeve.

Simoni stared at her. "I thought they took your knives."

"Dirty bleaters did," Plucky said. "Made these m'self in the machine shop."

Alex took the blade from her and, without a word of warning, pulled at the hem of Clyde's shirt and cut off a slice near the bottom.

"What are you doing?" Clyde asked, staring at the ragged cloth.

"You next," Alex said to Trenton. He quickly cut a slice from everyone's shirt, including his own, and tied them into a ball.

Hallie took the ball from Alex and dropped it into the sewer opening. "The water should carry that at least a couple of blocks," she said, leading them down the side of the building.

Trenton glanced back at the open hole. "Aren't you going to close the cover?"

"Nope," Alex said. "If anyone sees the plate, they'll think we went underground."

"Until they find the ball of our shirts," Simoni said.

"By that time it will be too late." Alex stopped halfway to the corner of the building. "JoeBob?"

The redheaded boy knelt by the far corner of the library. He pulled a screwdriver out of his pants pocket and opened a small panel in the wall. "Everyone inside," he said.

Each of them dropped to their hands and knees and crawled into the dark opening. Michael was last, pulling the panel closed behind him and jamming it in place.

It was pitch-black.

"Where are we?" Clyde asked.

"A maintenance shaft," Alex said. "There's a ladder to your left that leads all the way to the roof. Everybody up."

Kallista was first, and five minutes later, she reached the top of the ladder. Feeling blindly above her, she found a metal lever, twisted it, and opened the door to the roof. Afternoon light flooded through the opening, along with blessedly cool air.

Clyde popped out behind her. "Let me out. I hate the dark."

Trenton looked around the roof. "What now? There isn't anywhere to go."

Alex turned to Hallie. "How much time?"

Hallie pulled out a pocket watch. "Less than a minute. We're running late."

"Let's go," Alex said. He kicked the hatch shut and jogged to the north end of the building. They arrived at the edge at the same time as a steam engine sounded below.

Kallista peeked over the side. "A train?"

"We jump when the last car comes by," Alex said.

Kallista leaned over to study the tracks. The library wasn't a tall building, and the train tracks were raised. It was no more than a five-foot drop, but the distance between the building and the tracks was nearly eight feet. She was concerned about Plucky.

She needn't have worried. As the last car came by, Plucky backed up, shouted, "Bung your eye," and leaped over the side.

The rest of them quickly followed. Clyde was the only one who nearly didn't make it, but when he hit the edge of the train car, Plucky grabbed his hand and pulled him up.

From there on out, it was simple. Clearly the Runt Patrol had done their homework. Five minutes later, the train slowed as it approached a long row of warehouses. Alex led the others down a ladder on the back of the train, waiting for the right building before jumping off.

"This is it," Alex said, pointing to a warehouse that looked no different from any of the others.

They approached the building carefully, searching for any sign of a guard. A figure stepped out of the shadows, and Alex pulled them back out of sight.

"It's okay," Kallista said. "It's just my father."

"Your *father?*" Alex's mouth drew into a tight line. "What's he doing here? You said you didn't tell anyone." For the first time, color seemed to come into his pale face.

"He's not like other adults," Trenton said, trying to calm him down.

It didn't work. Alex withdrew the silver key from his pocket with a shaking hand. "You've made a huge mistake." He threw the key to the ground and ran back toward the train tracks with the other Runt Patrol members.

"Come back," Kallista called. "Just talk to him."

But it was too late. They were gone.

Trenton picked up the key. "Don't worry about it. It will be all right."

But Kallista wasn't so sure.

The Runt Patrol had taken some huge risks to get them there, and she had betrayed that trust. Even if they got the mechanical dragons, without the Runt Patrol's knowledge of the city, they'd be right back where they started. Maybe even worse.

"I need to go after them," she said. "Apologize."

"There's no time," Simoni said. "Rest Day will be over soon, and if we're not back by curfew, the Ninki Nankas will hunt us down. If we're going, we have to go now."

Trenton shrugged. "We'll find a way to make it up to them."

Plucky patted her shoulder. "Can't rusty blame you for saving your own da, now can they?"

Kallista could see her father standing in the shadows near the warehouse door. Why did everything feel so terribly wrong?

When they stepped into the street and her father came running toward her and wrapped her in his arms, she felt some of her dread fade. She wouldn't say it, but a part of her had been afraid he wouldn't show up at all or that he'd try to talk them out of leaving. She knew how much he loved to learn new things, and this city was brimming with new technology—not to mention a completely new species of animal.

He reached out and gently gripped her elbow. "You're safe. I was afraid something might have happened to you."

"We're fine," Kallista said, her voice shaky. "But we need to hurry. It's getting late."

"Yes. Of course." He glanced around. "Didn't you say there were going to be more than six of you? That we would need to make two trips?"

The muscles of her jaw twitched. "No. Just the six of us. And you, of course. I think we can use the turbo to carry you on the back of Ladon if Trenton squeezes into the front seat with me. At least long enough to get us out of the city."

"Are you sure you'll be able to carry me?" her father asked. "I could always go later."

"I'm not leaving you behind again," Kallista said. Even though her palms were slick with sweat, she grabbed his hand and closed it in her fingers. She'd lost him two different times. She was not going to lose him again.

"Right." Leo turned to the warehouse. "So this is where they're keeping them."

Trenton slid the key into the lock.

Kallista held her breath as he twisted the key, sure it wouldn't work. But the lock clicked, and the door swung open smoothly.

"Inside, quick," Kallista said. She checked the street in both directions before hurrying inside and pulling the door shut behind her. "Find the light switch," she said, still holding her father's hand.

"I've got it," Clyde said. There was a click, and bright lights flickered on, illuminating the large room.

Kallista blinked. The building was empty. "Where are the dragons?" Something was wrong.

"Are we sure this is the right place?" Clyde asked.

"It has to be," Simoni said. "The key fit the door."

Trenton turned around slowly, as if three, thirty-foot mechanical dragons might be hiding in the rafters. "Maybe they're in the next warehouse over."

That was it. They simply had the wrong building. The key probably fit all the other doors on this row. They'd try each one until they found the right building.

Her father squeezed her hand, then turned to face her, eyes filled with sorrow. "They aren't in any of the warehouses. I'm sorry, I couldn't let you take them."

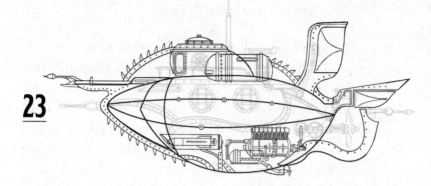

23

Kallista released her father's hand. "What are you saying?"

Leo wiped his palm across his forehead. "I had the dragons moved yesterday. After you told me what you were planning."

Icy fingers reached down her throat into her chest and closed around her heart. "Someone else found out? You moved the dragons so we could try the plan again when the time is right."

"I'm sorry." He reached for her, but she backed away. "I can't let you have them."

"No," she whispered. Then repeated it louder. "No. I don't believe it. You're lying." She stared into her father's eyes as if they were alone in the room. "Tell me where you took our dragons."

"They aren't here anymore." He rubbed his hands together. "I wasn't completely honest with you before, but I am telling the truth now. Will you let me explain?"

She searched his face for some clue. Some hint that this was another one of his games. He'd done many things she didn't agree with, and more than once he'd let her think he was dead. He'd deserted her, manipulated her, failed to express his emotions. But she truly believed to the center of her heart that he would never intentionally hurt her.

Even when she didn't agree with his approach, she knew

there was always a reason for what he did. If there was one thing she knew about her father, it was that. He did nothing without a good reason.

She took a deep breath, then another, trying to slow her galloping heart. A reason. There *was* a reason. "Tell me."

Her father met her eyes for a moment, then spread his hands to take in all the others, and she remembered they weren't alone. "I told you I had left the city of Seattle before it was attacked. That wasn't true. I *had* repaired the ship before I left, but I couldn't get anyone to join my crew. I was in the process of modifying the controls so I could fly it myself when the dragons arrived."

Kallista remembered thinking he hadn't had time to make all the repairs and changes before he left, but she'd assumed he'd continued to work on the ship as he flew south.

"I was sure they would kill me along with all the others," he continued. "But they didn't. None of the other dragons speak English as clearly as the monarch, but they were able to make themselves understood. I was shocked, of course, but I quickly realized the dragons are unlike any creatures the world has known. They assured us that as long as we didn't fight back they would take us to their home. To San Francisco."

"That's why you didn't leave a note."

He nodded. "I didn't have the chance."

"But if they captured you, how did you get away?" Trenton asked. "How did you hide on the island?"

"I wasn't hiding," Kallista's father said. "The dragons have known about Alcatraz for years. I was waiting there for you. I was supposed to intercept you before you entered the city. Only I didn't have a chance. Later, when you returned, the dragons allowed you to land in the field. The night I brought you to the factory everything was arranged. The dragons were waiting."

"You set us up?" Angus said, his face turning red. "It was a trap?"

The reason, the reason, Kallista repeated inside her head to the beating of her heart. "Did they threaten you? Were they going to hurt you? Is that why you cooperated with them?"

"No," he said. "That wasn't it. As soon as I saw the city, I realized how much things have changed. I'd been imagining the dragons were a plague on the world. Something to be fought, like locusts or famine. A pestilence. But once I met them, once I understood who they are and what they've done, I realized the dragons aren't something to fight against. They are the next rung in the evolutionary ladder."

"Let me get this right," Angus said. "You joined the dragons voluntarily. You're on their side?"

Kallista's father laughed. "You don't understand. There *are* no sides. There are no battles. The war was fought before any of us were even born, and we lost. We should no more fight against what has happened to the world than a flock of sheep should fight against their shepherd."

Kallista paced back and forth, wringing her hands. "No. No. I don't believe that. *You* don't believe that. This is another one of your games. What am I supposed to do? What are you trying to teach me?"

"There are no more tests. No more games. It isn't easy, but it's time to admit that everything has changed. This city, serving the dragons—it's our future."

"Maybe it's *your* future," Trenton said. "But we aren't giving up. We're going to fight. Tell us where our dragons are so we can leave."

Kallista's father shook his head. "I can't do that."

"Please," Kallista said. "Dad. I don't understand why you want to stay, but it's your choice. But you have to give us *our* choice, and we choose to fight the dragons. Don't do this to my friends. Don't do this to me. We still have time to go."

He wiped tears away from his eyes. "I've always tried to protect you. Don't you see that's what I'm doing now? If I let you leave here—if I let you try to destroy these creatures who are so much wiser and more powerful than we are—I'd be condemning you to death. The dragons will not allow anyone to stand against them. They will destroy you."

"Let them try," Angus growled. "I'd rather die fighting than live as a coward like you."

Simoni, who had remained silent, stepped forward.

"Mr. Babbage, my mother and father are back in Discovery. Trenton's are, too. And Angus's and Clyde's. We all love them as much as you love your daughter. Maybe we can't defeat the dragons. But if we don't try, it'll only be a matter of time before the dragons find them."

Kallista's father raised his chin. "Maybe that's for the best. Discovery wasn't built to last forever. Its resources are limited. But here, everyone will be able to experience the outside world. To live full and useful lives, serving the dragons."

Angus charged forward, slamming a fist into Kallista's father's stomach, knocking him to the ground, and wrapping his hands around his neck.

"Stop it!" Kallista screamed, grabbing Angus's arms. He was too strong. She couldn't budge him. Her father's face turned purple as he gasped for breath. His mouth opened and closed like a fish flopping about on land.

Then Trenton was at her side, bringing his hand under Angus's arm, and pushing against the back of his neck. Clyde and Simoni grabbed his other arm. Plucky jumped on his back, pulling his head up, and they all tumbled to the ground.

Kallista's father rubbed his throat, gasping for air. "No," he croaked. "When the dragons find Discovery, they'll let everyone live, let them serve."

Kallista sat with her arms around her knees. Tears dripped down her cheeks. What happened to the father who taught her to play patty-cake? Where was the man who read fantasy stories to her even though they were against the law? *That* man had risked his life more than once to save everyone in Discovery. She didn't know who *this* man was.

"What happens now?" she asked. "Do we wait here for the guards to show up?"

Her father coughed, swallowing until he could speak. "No one knows you're here. They think I moved the dragons back because I needed more room. They want to build more of them." He rubbed his throat again. "I know it's hard for you to understand right now, but I considered every possibility before making this decision. It is the best for everyone. You'll be happy here. Get better jobs. Move out of the dormitories. Soon, you'll have freedom to go anywhere in the city. Just promise me you won't try to escape."

Kallista rubbed her forehead. It felt like a stake had been driven into her brain. "Tell me one thing. Why are you *really* doing this?"

He stepped forward and, before she could stop him, took her face in his hands. He leaned toward her until they were almost nose to nose. He'd lost weight, and several days' worth of stubble covered his cheeks and chin. When had all those specks of gray appeared in his hair?

In his dark eyes she saw pain, but also the expression he wore whenever he was teaching her something new. "The day your mother died, I swore I'd take care of you. Since the day she died, I've tried to do what was best for you."

She pulled away from his grip. "The monarch said we could leave."

Leo sighed. "It doesn't matter what they say. The dragons will not allow anyone to escape the city. They would view it as an insult to their dominance. If you try to go, they will kill you."

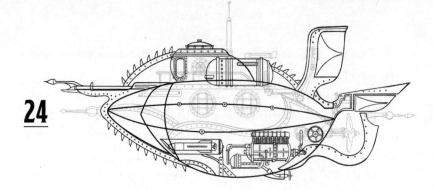

24

The next morning, two men with wide, green, diagonal sashes across their shirts showed up at the dormitory. They pulled Trenton, Clyde, and Angus out of their rooms before breakfast and told them to pack their things. Not that there was a lot to pack; they didn't have much in the way of personal belongings.

"You think Mr. Babbage told the guards about last night?" Clyde whispered.

"He said he wouldn't," Trenton whispered back. But if he'd lied about everything else, what were the chances he'd lied about that as well?

Angus eyed the two men who followed them out of the building. "If those guys try anything, I think I can take them."

There were no guards waiting for them in the street, though. Instead, parked at the curb was a deep silver quad with gold piping. Unlike the utilitarian quads used in the field, or even the upgraded versions used by the guards, this vehicle was obviously built with nothing but luxury in mind. Two doors on either side of the vehicle opened onto leather seats so soft and supple that sitting on them felt like climbing into a feather bed.

As one of the men slid into the driver's seat, the other loaded their meager belongings in a small compartment at the back of the vehicle.

The driver started the quad, and it walked smoothly down the street.

Trenton leaned forward. "Where are we going?"

"The Seven Hills," the man in the passenger's seat said. He glanced at the three of them with obvious curiosity. "It's quite an honor. I suppose you three must have unique talents."

"I guess," Trenton said. But he knew this wasn't about his talents. It was Leo's way of rewarding them for giving in and agreeing not to try to escape again.

As the quad began climbing a steep hill, Trenton realized they were heading away from the uniform block houses and toward the nicer homes with lots of windows. Squat buildings were replaced by more dragon towers and individual houses that grew bigger and bigger the higher they went.

"Fancy," Angus said as they drove past a tall house with domed towers and a spire.

"I've never seen a house so big in my life. It looks like a castle," Clyde said, pointing to a massive stone edifice with stained-glass windows, wrought-iron balconies, and a porch that wrapped around the front and sides. Trenton imagined five families could live in such a house without seeing each other for days.

The driver pulled up in front of another large house and stopped. Trenton glanced at his friends. "Are we picking someone up?" he asked.

"We're dropping you off," the driver said, ushering them out of the quad. "This is where you live now."

"That can't be right," Clyde said.

"No mistake," the driver said.

Still sure they were at the wrong place, Trenton followed Clyde and Angus up the porch to the front door. Feeling like an intruder, he pushed the door open. "Hello? Is anyone here?"

Simoni poked her head out of a door at the top of the stairs. "Plucky, Kallista," she called. "The boys are here."

Plucky and Simoni ran out of their rooms.

"Allie and me has our own room," Plucky called, happily holding her squirming, white-and-brown cat to her chest.

Kallista came out a moment later, a deep vertical line running down the center of her forehead.

"How are you?" Trenton asked.

She tried to smile but failed. Tears leaked from the corners of her downcast eyes.

They walked into a sunny kitchen where a polished wooden table was set with six plates and platters of eggs, bacon, and buttered toast.

"Look at this kitchen," Clyde said, giving a low whistle of appreciation.

Angus sniffed the bacon and stuck a piece in his mouth. "Where did this come from?"

"Didn't think Clyde was the only one who could cook, did'ja?" Plucky asked.

A beautiful brass telescope stood in front of one of the windows.

"Look at that view," Simoni marveled, staring out to where the ocean crashed against a rocky beach.

Trenton dropped into a seat at the end of the table. He hadn't eaten since lunch the day before, but he knew if he put anything in his mouth right now he'd choke on it. "This is wrong."

Plucky broke off a piece of bacon and fed it to the kitten in her lap. "Feels like a rusty dawb, it does."

"A what?" Clyde asked, taking a piece of toast from the platter.

"A bribe," Plucky said. "A sop, greased palm, yeah, yeah?"

"For what?" Simoni asked.

Trenton drummed his fingers on the table. "Kallista's father said we could get better jobs and move out of the dorms. Do you think he could have arranged this?"

Simoni nodded. "There was an envelope on each of our beds upstairs. You'll probably find new assignments on yours as well."

Angus filled his plate until the food threatened to overflow the edges. "If Kallista's father wants to give us better food and better jobs, who am I to say no? Not like he left us a lot of choice."

Trenton shook his head. "If we were moved to a better location in the dorm, maybe given an extra change of clothes or a better work shift, I could accept that. But look at this place. Leo's been here, what—a few weeks longer than us? Do you really think he has that kind of clout?"

"If he didn't do this for us, who did?" Clyde asked.

Trenton looked at Kallista sitting on the other side of the table, her eyes locked on the empty plate in front of her. "What if it's not a bribe?" he said, his thoughts slowly coming together. "What if it's a distraction?"

For the first time Kallista looked up. "What are you saying?"

"I'm not sure. Back in the tower, the monarch seemed awfully interested in your father. What if he's doing something for the dragons? Something they don't want us interfering with?"

Kallista pressed her hands to the sides of her head. "He wouldn't do something like that."

Angus stopped eating. "Really? You heard him. You think there's anything he wouldn't do for the dragons?"

Kallista squeezed her mouth shut, and for a moment, Trenton thought she was going to cry. Then she lifted her chin.

"Maybe he was right. Maybe we should just accept everything."
She waved her hands. "Is this really all so terrible?"

Trenton couldn't believe what he was hearing. "You want
to accept that fact that we'd all be servants to the dragons?"

Kallista shook her head, her eyes glistening. "I don't know!"
she shouted. "All right? I just don't know." With that, she
jumped up from the table and ran out of the room.

25

Kallista was lying on a bed large enough to sleep three, her face buried in her arms, when she heard a knock at the door.

"Go away," she called without looking up.

The knock came again.

"I said, go away!"

The door swung open, and she sat up. "Don't you listen?"

"Not very well," Trenton said, standing just outside her room. "I thought that was one of the things you liked about me."

"It's one of the things I hate about you."

"Right. I keep getting those mixed up."

"I know why you're here," Kallista said, wiping her eyes. "And I don't want to talk about it."

"I know you don't," Trenton said. "But I think I need to hear what you have to say."

She was sure her eyes were bright red. She hated to cry worse than almost anything. "Since when do you listen to me?"

Trenton leaned against the doorjamb. "Remember that time in Seattle when I volunteered to take part in the joust? I about got my head knocked off. Then you tricked the guy with the bolt in his ear and coldcocked him."

"Weasel," Kallista said. "His name was Weasel." She couldn't help smiling at the memory. "What's your point?"

"No point," Trenton said. "I just thought that story would cheer you up. Now will you come talk to me?"

Kallista swung her legs over the side of the bed. "You're a jerk." She climbed down and followed him to the staircase where they sat side-by-side on a dark wooden step.

"I'm sorry," Trenton said. "I didn't have any right to talk about your father."

"You had *every* right." She clasped her hands in her lap and looked at the ragged edges of her thumbnails. When had she started biting them again? She hadn't done that since she was seven or eight. She thought maybe her father had put some nasty-tasting solution on them to break her of the habit, but she couldn't remember.

She raised her thumb to her mouth, realized what she was doing, and pulled it away. "I spent all last night replaying what happened in the warehouse over and over in my head. I've thought about it so many times I can repeat every word he said. Do you want to hear it?"

"I heard what your father thinks," Trenton said. "I want to hear what you think."

"That's the problem. I don't know what *I* think. Do you ever hear yourself talking and realize you're repeating word-for-word something your father told you?"

Trenton laughed. "Just the opposite. For years, my mother would tell me how bad technology was, so, of course, I'd think the exact opposite. I wonder sometimes if the reason I grew up determined to be a mechanic is because she was so against it. How crazy is that? To spend your whole life trying to prove your mother wrong."

Kallista shook her head. "No crazier than spending your whole life trying to prove your father right."

"So is he?" Trenton asked. "Is your father right?"

Kallista could hear the murmur of voices coming from the kitchen downstairs. Were the others talking about her? "Last night I was positive he wasn't. But something occurred to me this morning. What if there's nothing to fight for anymore?"

Trenton opened his mouth, but she held up her hand. "I'm not talking about quitting. If there's something to fight for, I'll fight. Only . . . were the people in Seattle happier there than they are now?"

"They were free."

"Right. But free to do what? Starve? Fight for who got the best hole in the ground? What did their freedom buy them? The Whipjacks hated the dragons. The Order of the Beast served the dragons, only without all the benefits they have here. And the people in the middle tried not to get trampled by either one. I talked to some of the people in the dorms, and not one of them wanted to go back. Have you actually met anyone who's unhappy—other than the Runt Patrol?"

"Well, there was this guy who worked in the fields with us. But I don't think he was unhappy. He just liked to beat people up."

Kallista snickered. "Sounds like Angus."

Trenton grinned. "It kind of does." Then he turned serious. "What about our friends and families back home? Are we supposed to turn our backs on them?"

"Absolutely not. But you heard what my father said. There are some good things about this place. Maybe it would be okay if our friends and families came here, too."

"That's easy for you to say. Your family is already here."

"Yes, my father is here. And look how much he's been able to help us." She waved her hands at the lush carpet, the polished stairs, the grandfather clock with the mechanical bears that marched out and played drums every hour. "You said yourself that the reason we have all this is because my father is valuable to the city. So why not make ourselves valuable, too?"

She tried to drive home the point. "Let's say we *do* fight. Without our dragons, our chances of surviving a battle are nearly zero. So *when* we fail, and *when* the dragons end up finding Discovery, what do you think they'll do to the families of the kids who attacked them? Your mother and father. Angus's family, Simoni's, Clyde's."

"So you're saying we just do everything the dragons want?"

"I'm saying the people of Discovery are probably going to end up here one way or another. You have to ask yourself what will help them most. Us trying to fight? Or us trying to make ourselves valuable enough that they are treated the way we'd want them to be?"

Trenton tapped his hands on his knees. She could see him turning the idea over in his head. "Let me ask you one question," he said at last. "If your father was out there instead of in here, would you be saying the same thing?"

She stuck her thumbnail in her mouth, chewing on the ragged edge. "I think so. But I don't know for sure."

Trenton got up. "You've given me a lot to think about," he said before going downstairs to join the others.

Kallista looked at her thumbnail. She'd chewed it so far down it was starting to bleed. Everything she'd said made sense. It was completely logical. Without their dragons, their chances of escape were next to zero. And this house was much better than the dormitory. It was where she'd want her mother to be living, if her mother were still alive.

So why did she feel like what she'd just done was every bit as wrong as what her father had done the night before?

26

When Trenton came into the kitchen, the rest of the group was standing around the table, waiting for him.

"So?" Angus asked. "Is she cracked?"

Trenton scowled. "She made some good points. If we fight the dragons and fail, what happens to our families? You know, if the dragons capture them."

It had sounded more intelligent the way Kallista put it.

"We should go for a ride," Simoni said.

Clearly, she wanted to leave the house to get him away from Kallista. Was that fair, though? Wasn't Simoni the one who said they were in this together? Weren't they were supposed to be a team?

But she was already leading the others down the front hall. They walked out the front door and around the corner of the house.

"Don't we have to go to work?" Trenton asked.

"No work." Clyde grinned. "The letters said we get today off."

On the side of the house was what looked like a fancy shed, or maybe a place to keep horses. Simoni swung open the wide double doors, revealing a shiny quad.

"Wow!" Trenton said, forgetting about his problems for a moment. "This is ours?" Ever since he'd seen the quads, he'd wanted to get a closer look at them. He poked his head under one side to see how the hydraulics worked.

"You can take it apart later," Simoni said, tugging his sleeve.

"Fine," Trenton said with a longing look at the vehicle's complex drive mechanism. "I can't wait to get my hands on the controls."

But Angus was already in the driver's seat. "Hop in back and hold on," he said. "Let's see how fast this thing can go."

Trenton thought it was more likely they'd find out how hard it could crash.

Plucky sat up front next to Angus, poking at the controls and wiggling the levers. The kitten looked around with wide blue eyes. "Never been on a ride before, have you, Allie?" she cooed.

Trenton squeezed into the back between Clyde and Simoni.

Angus pushed a button, and the engine cranked to life. It rattled and chopped, spitting out a cloud of coal-colored, dust-smelling smoke. "Something's wrong with this thing!"

Plucky fiddled with a couple of the controls, and the engine smoothed to a purr.

Trenton leaned toward Simoni. "Something's wrong with the driver."

Angus tugged a lever toward him, and the quad leaped backward, smashing into the wooden wall. "Oops."

"Try this way," Plucky said. She pushed the lever forward, and the quad scuttled out the door like a giant metal insect.

It turned out that the quad wasn't really all that difficult to control once it got going. Even with no practice, Angus was able to pull out of the driveway and head down the middle of the street without running into anything else.

"Kallista wants to give up," Simoni said as they drove over the hill and down the other side.

"It's not giving up," Trenton said. "We have to think about the future. Is this a battle we can win?"

"Your father worked in the mines for years. If he was here, would he tell you to fight the dragons or quit?"

Angus steered too far left, overcorrected, and went up on the sidewalk for a moment before clattering back into the street. "My old man wouldn't take anything from no dragons, and neither will I. I'll die before I bow down to those fire-breathers."

Trenton shook his head. "I'm not taking about bowing down to anyone or anything. Kallista was just—I mean, I was just thinking that if our families get captured, it would be better for them if the dragons thought we were valuable. You've seen my mom. Who's going to take care of her if she gets stuck in one of those dormitories or sent to work on the farms?"

Simoni tugged on a strand of hair. "Is that *you* talking, or Kallista?"

Trenton shrugged. "It was her idea, but that doesn't mean it's wrong."

Clyde scratched his cheek. "Do we really know for sure that Discovery *will* be taken by the dragons? They've been attacked twice. I don't think they're going to be fooled that easily."

"Yeah, yeah," Plucky said. "Discovery ain't no hole in the ground, like Seattle."

Simoni pushed back her hair. "It doesn't matter if we're in a big house or the dorms. As long as we're forced to stay here, we might as well be locked in one of those barred rooms on Alcatraz. It's just a fancier cell. And what about the people here? We keep talking about protecting our own families, but don't the people of San Francisco deserve the right to be free?"

"It doesn't seem like they want to be free," Trenton said.

"Or maybe they just don't believe that freedom is possible."

Simoni set her jaw. "What do you think the Runt Patrol would say if you tell them we're giving up after one failure?"

Trenton didn't have to think twice. He knew the answer. And he knew it was the *right* answer. "We have to find our dragons and fight."

Plucky petted her kitten, who seemed to be enjoying the jerky ride. "Rusty things could be anywhere in the city, couldn't they?"

"I don't think so," Simoni said. "Last night, in the warehouse, Kallista's father let something slip that I don't think he meant to. The first time he mentioned our dragons, he said he'd had them moved. That could mean anywhere. But the second time he said they been moved *back*."

"Back?" Trenton repeated. "As in, back to the island?"

"It's the perfect place to keep them out of our reach," Clyde said.

Trenton looked across the bay. From where they were, Alcatraz looked so close. But he had no illusions any of them could swim so far.

Angus pulled the quad to the side of the road, and they all the studied the scene below them. Along the docks below were twenty or thirty boats of all sizes, sailing in and out of the bay. Some were obviously fishing boats, their decks covered with nets and crates. Others looked like they were transporting cargo, and there were even a few barges covered with piles of inky-black coal.

"We could snatch one of them boats," Plucky said. "Get back to the island snip-snap."

"Good luck with that," Angus said. "Look at the security around that place."

He was right. More than a dozen dragons soared above the

bay, and he could see at least twenty towers dotting the coast. "They're watching the water like hawks," Trenton said.

"And look at all the guards checking everyone going in or out of the docks," Clyde said. "Obviously they've thought about this before."

Trenton shook his head. "The thing I don't understand is why they even need to guard the city if everyone is so happy to be here."

"Maybe they aren't all as happy as they seem," Simoni said. She tapped her finger to her lower lip. "Do you think we could build a boat ourselves and sneak across to the island at night?"

Angus shaded his eyes with one hand. "Those look like spotlights on the towers."

"Wasn't no spotlights the night we come in on the balloon, yeah, yeah?"

"That's because it was a trap," Simoni said. "They made it easy on purpose."

"We'd never make it to the island without being spotted," Trenton said. "Anything moving across the water would be obvious." The thought triggered a memory. Back in Seattle, when he'd been working on the machines for Cochrane, he'd studied some books on warships. He'd never had time to build one of his own, but he remembered seeing a picture in one of the books.

He smacked a fist into his palm. "I have an idea."

Simoni raised an eyebrow.

"I like the look on your face," Clyde said.

Trenton nodded slowly. He thought it could work. "The dragons and guards would spot anything moving *across* the water. But they wouldn't see a ship that moved *under* the water."

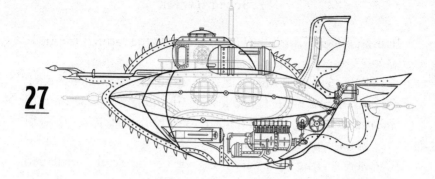

27

The next morning, Trenton and Kallista reported to their new jobs at the address provided on their letters to find a group of twenty or so kids strapping on tool belts and headlamps like the kind Trenton's father had used in the mines. None of the kids looked any older than fifteen.

When Leo had promised them better jobs, Trenton assumed it would be an administrative position like what Simoni had or designing things like what Clyde did, but this was even better. It felt good to smell grease and strap on a tool belt.

Trenton looked around and recognized a familiar redheaded kid. "Hey, JoeBob," Trenton said. "And Hallie," he added, noticing the girl behind him.

Both kids exchanged an uncomfortable glance, and then looked away.

"Tool belts and work gloves are in the cubbies," Hallie said.

Kallista looked at Trenton, her eyebrows drawn down in a question. "I'm sorry I lied to you guys. And if you see Alex—"

"You must have us confused with someone else," JoeBob said before tossing his belt over his shoulder and walking away.

Hallie looked embarrassed as she added with a pointed look, "We've never seen you before."

Trenton sighed. "I guess we deserve that." He looked around. "Are all the mechanics in the city children?"

"Only in the Runt Patrol," a small boy with spiky blond

hair answered instead of Hallie. "This is the land of the little people."

Hallie wrinkled her nose. "What he means is that the job we do requires people who are small enough to squeeze into tight spaces." She eyed Trenton. "You're definitely on the tall side, but at least you're skinny."

Were all the kids here members of the Runt Patrol? No wonder Alex knew all about the city. With so many mechanics sticking their noses into the machinery, they had to be aware of everything that happened. He had to find a way to get them back on his side.

"I haven't seen so many kids in one place since we got here," Trenton said.

A tall figure standing in the corner shook back his dark bangs and said, "People see what they're looking for."

Trenton blinked in surprise. Alex had been there all along, listening and watching silently. Trenton started toward him, but Alex shook his head.

"You're working with Michael," he told Trenton. "Grab your tools and get out there."

The kids weren't joking about tight spaces. The first job Trenton was assigned to was greasing one of the moving walkways. The job required him to lie on his back, slide through an access hatch, and scoot along a metal surface while a moving chain rumbled by six inches from his nose.

"The lube joints are every three feet," Michael said, scooting along the other side of the walkway. "Don't miss any or we'll have to do it all over again tomorrow. And don't let the chain touch your nose. The other kids'll make fun of your scabbed face for weeks." He sniffed and spat down the opening beneath them. "Not that it's ever happened to me."

"Of course not," Trenton said with a grin, hoping an

attempt at humor would help him get back on the Runt Patrol's good side.

They worked in silence for a while. Trenton fell into an easy rhythm. Scoot, scoot, scoot, squirt grease. Scoot, scoot, scoot, squirt. Even though it was tight and stuffy, Trenton found he enjoyed the work. He'd missed being around the sound of heavy machinery, the smell of oil, and the humidity the steam engines inevitably produced.

More than once, Trenton considered mentioning the mechanical dragons, but Alex and the others had made it clear they weren't ready to talk. Maybe if he did his job, they'd open up to him.

"You're not too bad at this," Michael said. "Takes most newbies a couple of weeks before they can keep up. Assuming they stick it out that long. Most of 'em can't take the tight spaces."

"This is nothing when you've nearly been crushed in a mineshaft coal feeder," Trenton said. "Have you been working as a mechanic for long?"

"Almost two years. Pretty soon I'll be too big, and they'll reassign me. Started out working in the fields. This beats that job by a mile."

"Tell me about it," Trenton said. "I'm glad I left the fields behind."

Something banged against the top of the walkway, and a cloud of grit fell into Trenton's eyes.

"Need to get yourself a pair of goggles," Michael said.

Trenton looked over to see that Michael was wearing a leather strap around his head with a pair of glass lenses on the front. Trenton's flight goggles had been taken away with the rest of his possessions, but Michael's rig was sturdier, designed for work, with different lenses that could be swung in and out for greater magnification.

"Where did you get those?" Trenton asked, trying to blow the grit off his face. "I didn't see any goggles with the gloves and tools."

"None of the adults listen when we tell them what we need," Michael said. "So we make them ourselves. Alex might be able to hook you up if you get back on his good side."

Trenton shifted around to pull out a rock that had slipped down the back of his shirt. "Speaking of Alex, what would it take to get back on his good side? I've been considering a project that might be of interest to someone looking to . . . make a change."

"You and the girl?"

Trenton considered the question for a moment. Kallista would be a huge help building the submarine, but after what she'd said at the house the day before, he didn't know if he could trust her. It was a terrible feeling.

"Just me," Trenton said at last. "Kallista is trying to figure some things out for herself."

Michael grunted. He shot grease into a joint and looked at Trenton out of the corner of his eyes. "Stick around long enough and maybe you'll get a chance to prove you can be trusted."

Trenton glanced over his head. Only a few more joints to go before they could climb out the other side. "What do you want to do when you stop working with the Runt Patrol?"

Michael snorted. "Whatever it is, it won't be here."

"You're still planning on leaving?"

Michael gave him a silent look and continued working. After a moment, he said, "Maybe."

Worried he was pushing his luck but needing the information, Trenton said, "It seems like you've figured out a way to get around the Ninki Nankas, so what's holding you back?"

"It's not that easy," Michael said. "There are ways of going anywhere you want without the Ninki Nankas stopping you. But that only works *inside* the city. Any of the dragons—and I mean *any*—see you trying to leave . . . might as well throw yourself off the cliff into the sea."

Trenton had more questions, but once they were out from under the walkway, Michael stopped talking.

At lunch, Trenton looked for Kallista but learned she was working with a crew on the other side of the city. Michael was hanging out with another group of boys and was pointedly ignoring Trenton.

Instead, Trenton took his food and approached Hallie and JoeBob. They didn't look happy to see him, but they made room for him at their table.

"How did you like the walkways?" JoeBob asked with a sneer.

What was that expression for? Had he done something to offend the boy? "It was fine," Trenton said. "Nice to get to work with my hands again on some heavy machinery."

JoeBob muttered under his breath and handed Hallie his fruit tart.

Hallie smiled in triumph. "JoeBob heard you and your friends live up in the Seven Hills in one of those big fancy houses. He bet me you wouldn't last the morning."

"How do you know where I live?" Trenton asked, taking a bite of his fish salad.

JoeBob shook his mop of red hair out of his face. "We know everything that goes on in this city. Thought you'd have figured that out by now."

Hallie's fruit tart was halfway to her mouth when she stopped. "You mean you *do* live in the Seven Hills?"

"I do now. Is that bad?"

Hallie and JoeBob looked at each other. JoeBob shrugged. "It's just that most of the people who live up there work in fancy jobs. Not tightening chains and replacing bearings."

"Guess I must be lucky." Trenton glanced at the two of them, hoping he might be able to get them to elaborate on what Michael had told him. "I was talking to someone earlier who said he wanted to leave the city."

"Michael," Hallie said at once. "He has a big mouth."

JoeBob shook his head, a clump of hair falling over his right eye. "You must have heard him wrong. There's no way out."

"What if I knew of a way?" Trenton said. "Do you think Alex would be willing to talk to me?"

"Alex speaks for himself," JoeBob said. He and Hallie gathered up their lunches and left without giving Trenton a second look.

That afternoon, Trenton joined five other kids in the back of a large quad headed for the bridge. It was the first time Trenton had been to the structure, and he was anxious to get a closer look at how it worked.

Once they reached it, the workers divided into two groups of three. Trenton was grouped with a pair of brothers—Jack and Cameron. The other three—a joke-cracking boy named Graysen, a small but determined girl named Lizzy, and a curly-haired boy named Asher—were put in the second group.

It was a good thing Trenton wasn't afraid of heights because their job was to inspect the huge cables that supported the bridge. The first person on the team searched for loose metal strands in the cables and noted them in a small book. The second person checked the bolts of the huge metal clamps, and the third person greased the fittings.

As they neared the top of one of the highest girders, wind slapped at Trenton's face, and the cables thrummed with a deep moaning sound. The view was great, though. He looked toward Alcatraz and saw a boat anchored at the south end of the island. It was probably just wishful thinking, but for a moment, he could have sworn he saw a flash of gold-colored metal.

"Hear that's where you and your friends came from," Cameron said, studying Trenton with curious eyes that looked too big for his face.

"How did you know that?" Trenton asked.

Jack tucked his wrench in his belt. "Is it true you were hunting dragons?"

Trenton wasn't sure what to say. He wanted to gain the Runt Patrol's trust, but it seemed like most people in the city liked the dragons, or at least put up with them. It was like the Order of the Beast all over again.

The two brothers watched Trenton intently.

"What did you hear?" Trenton asked, hedging his answer.

"I heard you killed a lot of them," Jack said. His little brother nodded, eyes still wide. They didn't seem angry, only curious.

"Yeah," Trenton said, hoping it wouldn't turn the brothers against him. "We did."

They worked the rest of the day in silence. Trenton didn't know if that was a good sign or a bad one.

When he returned to the shop, he found Kallista putting away her tools. "How was your day?" he asked.

"Long," she said, pulling off her gloves. "It's nice to be working with machines again, though."

Trenton looked around to make sure no one was listening. "Some of the kids were surprised that we were assigned here since we live up on the hill."

"If you don't like it, you can probably ask to be transferred," she said with a shrug.

He leaned closer. "It's just that Angus and Simoni and Plucky got, you know, white-shirt jobs. Clyde even has one of those little sashes now. Why do you think your father sent us *here?*"

Kallista's face tightened. "We don't know that my father sent us here. And if he did, it was probably because he knew we liked to work with machines." With that, she turned and marched out of the building.

Trenton was one of the last kids to put away his tools. As he was tucking his hard hat and gloves into a bin, he saw Alex step through the door. "Everything okay with your friend?"

Trenton unbuckled his tool belt and put it away. "She's just stressed out about some things."

Alex flipped back his dark bangs. "Heard her father's in tight with the dragons."

Trenton narrowed his eyes. Where were these kids getting their information? "What do you know about Kallista's father?"

"Not much," Alex admitted. "Only that he's been spending a lot of time around the white tower. Guess he's been keeping secrets." He tilted his head and gave Trenton a sardonic smile. "The first rule of living with dragons is that no one gets something for nothing. You start living in fancy houses and people start to wonder if you and your friends made a deal with those scaled devils."

"Hardly," Trenton said. "In case you didn't hear, we were captured by them. They nearly killed us. Listen," he whispered, moving closer, "I know you don't want to talk about what happened at the warehouse, and I don't blame you. What Kallista did—no matter her reasons—was a complete betrayal. But I think I know where they took our dragons."

"Do you?" Alex arched an eyebrow, and Trenton realized Alex had probably known where they were before he did.

"I've got an idea of how to get them back," Trenton said. "But first I need to find a place to build something—something pretty *big*. Do you have any idea where I could get access to a private building and machining tools?"

Alex laughed. "I know everything about this town."

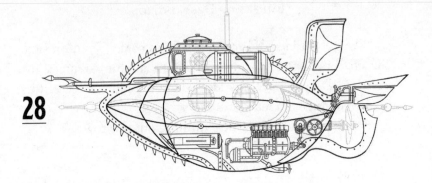

28

Outside, the streets were filled with people getting off work. Hundreds of dragons flew back and forth over the city, snapping at humans who weren't moving fast enough or didn't appear to be doing their jobs. Trenton couldn't help flinching every time one of their shadows dropped over him. But Alex and the rest of the Runt Patrol treated the city like a giant playground, ducking into pipes, scrambling over walls, and generally staying out of sight.

Alex pulled him into a doorway as a dark-green shape soared slowly overhead, its golden eyes studying the people moving below it like bugs. Once the dragon was past, Alex pushed under a loose piece of fence and climbed beneath a row of metal trailers. Now and then, Trenton caught sight of other small figures ducking and dodging their way through the city.

There could have been as many as ten kids or as few as five. He thought he recognized most of them, but with the way they moved from one shadow to the next, it was hard to tell for sure.

"What happens if a dragon catches you somewhere you shouldn't be?" Trenton asked.

"First offense is usually three days with no food and only a cup of water a day. Second offense can be anything from a beating to losing a hand or a foot. The dragons themselves don't do that, of course. They've got plenty of sadistic guards waiting to take orders."

Trenton shuddered, remembering how Angus had protected Clyde from Garvin. "What happens after that?"

Alex led him to a partially covered canal where they splashed through a few inches of mossy green water. "Ever notice how well fed the Ninki Nankas look?"

Trenton's throat went dry. "They wouldn't."

"They *would*, and they do," Alex said. "The guards even take bets on how long it takes a Ninki Nanka to finish eating its victim. I've seen it happen."

It was all Trenton could do to keep from throwing up. "Why do they do it? Why do so many people willingly serve the dragons? If they all revolted at once, refused to feed the creatures or . . . ?"

Alex gave his quirky grin.

"Okay, yeah, I mean I know the dragons would kill anyone who refused to obey. But most of the people in this city seem happy to be here. Like it's a privilege."

"A lot of people think it is," Alex said. "I don't understand it myself. It's like they get used to it until they can't imagine any other way."

Trenton walked through the water behind him, feet soaking wet. "But not the Runt Patrol?"

Alex turned to look at him, his face more pale than normal. "Most of the kids want to fight. Not all of them, but most. Only something happens to you when you reach a certain age. It's like the fight gets sucked out of you little by little until you completely give in. One day you're talking about doing whatever it takes to get away, and the next, the only thing you care about is serving the dragons. I've seen it happen to friends of mine." He wiped a shaking hand across his face. "And I can feel it happening to me. Some mornings, lately, I go outside and see the dragons coming out of their towers. I see people marching to their jobs, laughing and smiling, and I think, 'It wouldn't be all bad.' That's why I have to get out—soon—before it's too late."

"That's your secret," Trenton said. "You and the others. Why you want to escape the city."

Alex set his jaw. "One of them. Prove to us that we can trust you and maybe we'll show you more."

They peeked out from under the cover of the canal. Less than twenty feet away, a Ninki Nanka waddled down the street.

"Stay here," Alex said, pressing Trenton back with one arm. He lifted his fingers to his mouth, and a sharp whistle split the air. Instantly, five kids—Graysen, Lizzy, Asher, Hallie, and JoeBob—darted out of their hiding places and into the street.

"Tell them to stop," Trenton said. "That thing will rip them to pieces."

Alex held a finger to his lips. "Watch."

The Ninki Nanka hissed at the sudden appearance of the kids, opening its mouth to reveal sharp fangs. It flicked its tongue, tasting the scents in the air, but instead of charging, the beast shook its head, sneezed, and then flicked its tongue one more time before wandering away.

"What just happened?" Trenton asked.

"Earn our trust first," Alex said.

Once the Ninki Nanka was gone, Alex led Trenton out of the canal to a line of factories and warehouses. A few of them had smoke coming from the vents, but most looked like they hadn't been used in a long time.

Alex stopped outside one of the abandoned buildings. The windows were covered with dust, and the front gate was chained closed. He shot a quick look in both directions before peeling up a section of fence. "Follow me," he said, ducking through the opening.

Once they were inside the fence, he hurried to a four-inch

metal drainpipe on one of the corners and began shimmying up. Alex moved quickly, and it was all Trenton could do to keep up. By the time he'd climbed through a window twenty feet above the ground, the other kids were right behind him.

Inside, he could see right away that the building had once been a machine shop. The tools and machinery were coated with a thick layer of dirt, but they looked like they might be operable once they were cleaned up.

Trenton bent forward, his hands on his knees, trying to catch his breath. "Does this stuff work?"

"Most of it," Michael said, walking up beside him.

"And the ones that don't we can get working," Asher said, shaking back his blond curls.

Trenton followed the others down a set of splintery steps to where a metal table was covered with large sheets of paper and design equipment that looked much newer and cleaner than anything else in the room.

"Had a couple of the kids borrow a few supplies from the design shop on the way," Alex said, nodding to Jack and Cameron, who were lounging on a stack of pallets across the room.

JoeBob folded his arms across his skinny chest. "Now it's your turn. Tell us what you want this place for and how it's going to get us out of the city."

"You could ask a little nicer," Hallie said.

Alex brushed his hair out of his face. "No. JoeBob is right. We took a big risk bringing you here. It's time for you to open up. What's the plan?"

Trenton took a deep breath. Technically the plan wasn't only his, and he hadn't had a chance to make sure the others were okay with him telling the Runt Patrol their secret. But these kids were right. They'd told him at least some of their secrets, not to mention they'd found this amazing building. He knew that without their help, building a submarine would be impossible.

"They took our dragons after we were captured," he said.

JoeBob snorted. "Of course they did."

"But we think we know where they are," Trenton said. "They're in an old fort called Alcatraz."

"The island?" Lizzy asked. "There's no way you can reach that without the dragons seeing you."

The light that had been in Alex's eyes went out. "She's right. The dragons watch the harbor like hawks, and if they don't spot you, the guards in the towers will. You might as well kiss those mechanical dragons of yours good-bye."

Trenton reached into his pocket and pulled out a folded piece of paper. He'd been working on the drawing every spare chance he got. "They can watch the top of the water," he said as he unfolded the sheet, "but not underneath."

The Runt Patrol gathered around him as he spread the paper out on the table.

It was a set of designs for a completely enclosed, underwater vehicle. The ship was more than ten feet long with a pair of tall, matching rudders on the back and narrowing to a point on the front. Scalloped fins angling down from the sides made it look like a metal fish.

Twin glass domes on the top covered a pair of seats inside where drivers could control the underwater ship with pedals and levers. With all the machinery they'd need to make the ship run, it would be a tight fit, but he thought two people could squeeze in.

"It's called a submarine," he said.

The kids around him gathered closer.

"What's this?" Graysen asked, pointing to a brass tube rising out of the top.

"It's an underwater telescope," Trenton said. "It uses lenses and mirrors to see above the water while the rest of the ship remains out of sight below."

JoeBob gaped. "You designed this yourself?"

Trenton felt himself blush. It wasn't anything like what Leo Babbage could do, but he was proud of his work. "I saw something like it in a book, and I came up with the rest myself. I'm pretty good at inventing things." He tapped the paper on the table. "There's still a lot of work still to do. I have to figure out how to store enough oxygen to stay underwater, and some way to keep from crashing into unseen obstacles, but I have some ideas."

Michael ran a finger across the design. "You think it will work? I mean, an underwater boat is crazy."

"We won't know until we test it," Trenton said. "But, yeah, I think I can build it, and I think it will work."

"We," Hallie said. "We'll build it."

Alex studied the plans. "It only carries two people. How are we all going to escape?"

Up until that afternoon, Trenton had only been planning to get him and his five friends out of the city. Well, four, if Kallista refused to leave. But if the Runt Patrol was going to help him, they deserved the chance to escape too.

"Maybe we'll build more than one," he said. "Or maybe we'll take multiple trips back and forth. The submarine can only hold two people at a time, and the dragons can only carry two, but I promise we'll find a way to take anyone who works on this."

A bang sounded from up on the platform where they'd climbed through the window. Trenton looked up to see a girl staring down at him.

Alex started forward, but Trenton put a hand on his shoulder. "It's okay. She's with me."

Somehow, even with her leg braces, Plucky had followed them all the way to the warehouse and climbed up the pipe and through the window without anyone hearing her.

She wound the key on her braces with a soft *click-click-click* and grinned. "Looks plummy. When do we start building it, yeah, yeah?"

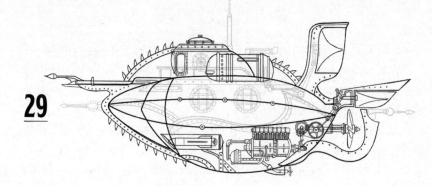

29

I demand to know where my father is, and I'm not leaving until I see him." Kallista planted herself in front of the bored-looking woman behind the counter, refusing to break eye contact.

It had been a week since Kallista and the others had moved out of the dormitory and into the house on the hill, and she hadn't seen her father since the night in the warehouse. She'd tried the city design office, engineering, the central mechanic shop, even food processing—anywhere the greatest inventor in the city might be, and yet every single person claimed to have no record of him.

And now she was at the city housing department getting the same story.

The woman dropped her gaze. "I don't know what you want me to do," she said, shuffling a stack of papers in front of her.

"I want you to find him," Kallista said.

Maybe he'd realized he'd made a mistake. Maybe he was trying to find a way to fix it right this minute. Or maybe not. It was possible he still felt that the dragons were the next rung on the evolutionary ladder and there was no point in fighting against them. But no matter what he had done or how he felt about it, he would not go this long without talking to his own daughter.

Would he?

He *had* left her alone in Cove, and he *had* left Seattle

without her. But the first time was because his life had been in danger, and the second time was because the dragons had captured him. Now that they were in the same city, he wouldn't ignore her. He couldn't.

She tried to convince herself he was caught up in a big project and had lost track of time, but she was beginning to fear more and more that the dragons had done something to him. What if he'd done something to anger the dragons? What if he was locked up somewhere—or worse?

Kallista clenched her hands in front of her until her knuckles turned white. "You say you have a record of every person living in the city, correct?"

The woman set her mouth in a frown before muttering, "I only have what I've been given, and I have no record of a Leo Babbage. There's nothing more I can tell you."

The line behind Kallista was growing longer by the minute, the people grumbling, but she didn't care. She'd been pushed around from one spot to another long enough.

"Then get someone who *can* help me," Kallista said.

"I'm sorry." The woman placed her hands flat on the counter. "I need you to step aside so I can help the next person in line."

The man behind Kallista tried to step around her, but she moved to block him. "I'm not leaving until you get someone who can tell me why my father, who has been in the city longer than I have, has no record of living here."

The woman stood up, her bored expression replaced by an angry scowl. "Leave this building at once or I'll have security take you away. Trust me, little girl, you do not want that."

Kallista's tongue stuck to the roof of her suddenly dry mouth, but she refused to back down. "Do it. Maybe *they* can tell me where my father is."

The people behind her gasped, but the woman reached to the side of the counter and turned a crank. A moment later, a click and a hiss came from a small metal horn and a man's voice asked, "What is it?"

The woman looked at Kallista as if giving her one last chance, but when Kallista didn't move, the woman sighed. "I have a citizen who refuses to obey the rules."

A moment later, the door swung open and a man and a woman in uniform marched to the front of the line, grabbed Kallista by her elbows, and pulled her away from the counter.

Kallista didn't struggle. If this was the only way she could get answers about her father, so be it. She squinted at the bright sunlight as she was pulled outside.

"Shouldn't you be at work?" the woman asked.

"I want to see my father," Kallista said. "No one has a record of him anywhere."

"Maybe he's no longer in the city," the man said, his voice gruff.

Was that supposed to be some kind of joke? No one left the city. Unless . . . Her breath caught in her throat. "Do you know where he is? Did something happen to him?" Surely if he'd been hurt, someone would have told her.

Before either of the guards could answer, a shadow passed overhead. Kallista looked up to see a massive black-and-red dragon touch down in front of them. Both guards dropped to their knees, pulling Kallista down with them.

"How can we serve you?" the female guard asked without looking up.

"I take girl," the dragon said in a gravelly voice.

Kallista looked up in surprise. What would the dragon want with her?

The male guard yanked her up from her knees and shoved her forward. "As you command."

Kallista stumbled toward the black-and-red dragon, and it reached out to grip her in its talons. Sweat ran down the back of her neck, and her muscles turned to liquid. The only time she'd felt a dragon's talons had been in battle. She glanced up and saw the dragon open its mouth. Venom glistened on its long fangs.

Was this how she would die? Had the dragons decided her questions about her father were worth killing over? Without another word, the dragon spread its wings and rose into the air. Its talons closed tighter and tighter around Kallista's chest until she worried her ribs were going to snap.

"I can't breathe," she tried to shout, but all that came from her lips was a croak.

Looking around, she saw where they were headed, and what little breath she'd had left whooshed from her lungs.

The dragon flew to the top level of the white tower and through the open window, where it tossed her roughly to the floor and bowed to the white dragon sitting regally before them. "As requested, Majesty."

The monarch nodded, and the black-and-red dragon flew away.

Kallista got to her feet and rubbed her bruised ribs. "Why am I here?"

"Bow before me, human," the monarch snarled.

"Not until you tell—" Kallista began. Before the words were completely out of her mouth, the white dragon spread its wings and gave a mighty flap at her. A hurricane-like blast of wind lifted her up and threw her fifteen feet across the room, where she smashed against the wall. Her ribs screamed in agony as she crumbled to the ground.

The dragon spread its jaws, and a blast of purple energy

smashed into the wall above her. Although the sky outside was clear, a bolt of lightning struck just outside the window, filling the air with the smell of an overheated engine.

Before she could even think about getting up again, the monarch was across the room, picking her up and slamming her face-first to the ground. Colored spots flashed in front of her eyes, and blood leaked from her nose.

The dragon flipped her over so she was looking directly into its purple eyes. "You will speak only when invited to, you will refer to me as 'Your Majesty,' and you will kneel unless I give you permission to stand. Is that clear?"

"Yes," she whispered. "Your Majesty."

The white dragon released her and strode back across the room. "That wasn't so hard, was it?"

Kallista shook her head, too scared to speak.

The monarch sat back down, picked up a golden goblet, and took a long drink. "Stand up. You look silly there on the floor."

Kallista rose cautiously, afraid it was another trick and that the white dragon would throw her across the room again, this time maybe cracking her skull or breaking her neck.

"I understand you've been traipsing across the city, making a nuisance of yourself," the monarch said in a jovial tone of voice.

"I—" Kallista began, before realizing she hadn't actually been asked a question.

The monarch waved his goblet. "You may speak."

"I'm looking for my father, Your Majesty," Kallista said. Blood dripped down the back of her throat, and she tried not to choke on it. "No one seems to know where he is, and I'm afraid something's happened to him."

"Why didn't you say so?" The monarch laughed. "You should have come to me first."

"You know where he is?" Kallista blurted, unable to help herself, then added, "Your Majesty."

The white dragon spread his wings, and Kallista ducked, but it was only a stretch. "Of course I do. I've been keeping him busy. In fact, he is here right now."

Kallista turned and saw her father standing at the back of the room. "Dad," she shouted, running to give him a hug.

He put his arms around her stiffly and patted her back. "Your nose is bleeding."

Kallista stepped away. She touched her nose and glanced at the white dragon. How long had her father been there? Had he seen what the monarch had done to her and simply let it happen?

"Where have you been?"

"I've been working on a project," he said in an almost mechanical voice.

She shook her head. "What kind of project? Where?"

For a quick second his gaze dropped to the floor, then he looked back at her. "I'm afraid I can't say." His eyes flickered to the monarch, then down to the floor again. "I've been spending very long hours in my . . ." His lips started to form a *W*, and she was sure he was going to say *workshop*, but after the slightest hesitation, he said ". . . laboratory."

Why did he call it that? She'd never heard her father refer to where he worked as a laboratory.

She glanced toward the monarch, who was watching them closely. Did his violet eyes flicker for a moment?

"I want to come with you," she said, turning back to her father. "Whatever you're doing, I can help. You know I'm good with projects." She turned from her father to the white dragon. "Please, Your Majesty, can you transfer me to wherever my father is working?"

"That isn't a good idea," her father said.

She turned back to him. "Why not?"

He studied her closely, his eyes so intent they nearly gleamed. "Do you trust your friends?"

"Of course," she said at once.

He shook his head. "I'm afraid I don't. What I'm working on is secret. I'm afraid no one must know about it."

"I won't tell them," she said. "I promise."

He gave her a sad smile. "I wish I could believe that. I really do. But if you want to know my secrets, you must first tell me yours."

She shook her head, confused. "What secrets? I don't have any secrets."

He leaned toward her and whispered so quietly only the two of them could hear. "I think your friends are up to something. Find out what it is, come and tell me, and then I'll know I can trust you."

She stared at him. What had happened to her father? This wasn't like him at all. "You want me to spy on my friends?"

He nodded vigorously. "Find out what they are doing, and come to one of the dragon towers—any tower will do. The dragons will know how to find me. Once I'm sure I can trust you, the two of us can work on my project together. It will be wonderful."

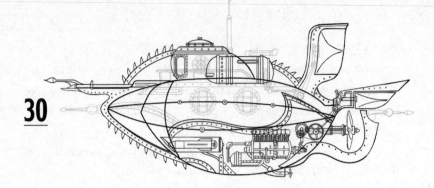

30

"O kay, listen up," Trenton called. "I've got assignments for each of you." He pointed to Michael, JoeBob, and Hallie. "I want the three of you to work on the rudder controls. They still aren't sturdy enough to handle the pounding we're going to get in the ocean. Michael, see if you and Alex can get the pump to work any more efficiently. Plucky, can you check the seals for leaks again? I think we're still getting water through a couple of the ports."

Each of them nodded and went to work. Trenton was worried that after a full day of working as mechanics, everyone would be too tired to come here and do more of the same type of work, but they actually pushed him to give them jobs.

Watching everyone work, he inhaled the sweet smell of freshly varnished wood, greased pistons, and the faint aroma of coal smoke. Combined with the sound of mechanics hard at work, he felt right at home.

It had been almost two weeks since they'd started on the project, and the submarine was nearly halfway complete, which made him proud. And in another couple of weeks, they'd be ready for their first test in the actual ocean, which made him worried.

The pounding the ship would take would probably reveal twenty new problems he hadn't thought of. But that wasn't what had him worried. They'd solved most of the issues so far; they'd figure out how to fix the new ones as well. His concern was how they were going to get the submarine to the ocean and back without getting caught—and killed—by the Ninki Nankas.

Trenton tapped Alex on the shoulder and pulled him aside. "You promised you'd tell me how you manage to keep the Ninki Nankas from tracking you."

Alex had been extremely helpful in keeping the dragon guards away when he was around. But when Trenton or Plucky tried to walk anywhere on their own, they had to hope none of the Ninki Nankas caught their scent. More than once, Trenton had been forced to run back to where he belonged, using every trick he knew to keep the creatures off his trail.

None of the Runt Patrol had that problem, and Trenton was dying to know how they did it.

Alex grinned. "Asking me to give up another secret, huh? What's it worth to you?"

"Copilot seat in the first ocean test run?"

"Deal." Alex put a hand on Trenton's shoulder. "Friday night, we'll be holding a ceremony for new Runt Patrol members. You and Plucky are officially invited."

Trenton noticed he didn't mention Kallista. Not that he could blame him. As far as Trenton knew, she was still backing her father's ideas. Trenton was pretty sure she knew he was working on something—he disappeared after work every night—but so far, she hadn't asked him what he was up to, and he hadn't volunteered the information. He wasn't sure what he'd say if she did ask.

He was positive she was keeping secrets as well. A couple of days earlier, she'd showed up at the house, her face and arms covered with bruises. She'd claimed it was a work accident, although she couldn't provide any details about where the "accident" had happened or anyone who'd witnessed it.

It was a terrible feeling not being able to confide in his best friend, and he wasn't sure how long he'd be able to keep it up.

"Well, I better get back to work on the pump," Alex said. "I'd hate to have her sink like a stone on the first run, especially if I'm inside."

Trenton nodded. "Trust me, I'm not taking it out any deeper than I have to on the first run. If she sinks, I want to be able to make it back to shore. It's not like we did a lot of swimming in Discovery."

As Alex went back to work, Trenton climbed up the rickety wooden stairs to get a better look at how the submarine was coming along. He thought it might be the most beautiful invention he'd ever designed. One of the first problems he'd faced was how to keep the craft from sinking to the bottom of the ocean or bobbing to the top.

Their first attempt, made completely out of metal, sank to the bottom of a large tank he and the others had built. No matter how much propulsion he created, the vessel was too heavy. There was no way to get it to come up out of the water under its own power.

The second attempt had gone much better. Using the same tools boatbuilders did, he crafted the hull of the submarine out of wooden planks held together with brass fittings. With metal fins underneath, a pointed metal nose on the front, and a gleaming rudder on the back, it looked like a large wooden fish. By the time they varnished the planks and sealed the whole thing, it gleamed a golden brown.

That version had easily stayed up in the water. In fact, it was too buoyant. Even after adding the steam engine, seats, and controls, he couldn't get it to stay underwater. He'd figured out a solution by putting more metal fittings on the outside, including a second set of fins on either side to increase stability, brass and glass portals on the sides and over the seats, and, of course, the underwater telescope and a small anchor.

The thing that brought it all together was the ballast tank connected to a pump. The tank was filled with air to start. When they needed to go down, air was pumped out of the tank and replaced with water. When they wanted to come back up, the water was pumped out again. It was an elegant plan that Plucky had helped him come up with that worked well.

The second problem had been much more difficult to solve. The submarine was powered by a steam engine, and since the city had a ready supply of coal the Runt Patrol could raid at will, fuel wasn't an issue. And the size of the engine was just right to fit in the back of the sub.

The problem was that as soon as they submerged, the engine used up all the available oxygen. They found that out the hard way. Trenton had been running the submarine's first extended underwater test and had started to feel light-headed. Before he could signal anyone, he passed out. If Plucky hadn't noticed the problem and ordered the sub pulled from the tank, Trenton might have died.

They'd been able to solve part of the problem by pumping oxygen into a tank and slowly releasing it when they went underwater. But that only allowed them to remain submerged a maximum of fifteen minutes. Not nearly long enough. He solved the rest of the problem by creating a backup engine powered by electricity stored in a bank of batteries under the seats.

He knew there had to be a better way of doing it. Maybe a chemical reaction like they'd used to make hydrogen for the airship. Only chemicals weren't his area of expertise. That had always been . . . No, he wasn't going there.

Something clanked against the outside wall, and he turned

to see Angus climbing through the window. He jumped to the floor, turned, and pulled Simoni through behind him.

"Hey," Clyde called from outside. "Can you give me a hand?"

"Sure," Angus said. He leaned through the window and clapped his hands. "Good job."

"Stop being a jerk," Simoni said.

"Fine," Angus grumbled good-naturedly. He bent down and pulled Clyde up and through the window with a single yank.

"What are you doing here?" Trenton asked. He'd kept them up-to-date on how the submarine was coming along, but they'd never actually come to see it.

"Thought we'd check on our ticket out of here," Angus said.

Clyde braced his arms on his thighs, puffing air. "Isn't there . . . an easier . . . way in?" He blew air out of his lungs like a runner at the end of a race. "Like, maybe a front door?"

"Can't risk it," Trenton said. "The guards come around every so often to make sure the doors are locked and sealed. We can't afford for them to notice any tampering."

He led his friends down to get a firsthand look at the submarine, beaming over how impressed they seemed with everything.

"Who's this?" Alex asked, wiping his hands on his overalls.

"These are my friends I was telling you about," Trenton said. He introduced everyone to the Runt Patrol.

JoeBob eyed Simoni, who was probably five years older than he was, and nudged Trenton. "Does she have a boyfriend?"

"Get out of here," Trenton said, pushing him back to his work.

Plucky's head popped out of the submarine, a smear of oil on one cheek. "Thought I heard a lot of clucking out here." She held up a wrench. "Make yourself useful, you lazy gudgeons."

"I don't know much about tools," Clyde said, "but I'm not bad at designs. Mind if I take a look inside?"

Plucky grinned and waved him over. "Suit yourself, yeah, yeah."

Angus ran a hand along the wooden hull and whistled. "Nice work, Trenton."

Trenton looked at his friends, both old and new, working on the submarine. His smile faded to a frown.

"Is everything all right?" Simoni asked.

Trenton swallowed. How did she know? Everything was nearly perfect—but one of them was missing, and he couldn't ignore that. "You told me back on the island that a leader's job is to bring people together. To use their strengths."

Simoni nodded.

"I feel like Kallista needs to be a part of this. Only, I don't know if I can trust her," Trenton said. "What if I tell her what we're up to and she tells someone?"

"Like when I told the chancellor about your dragon?" Simoni asked.

Trenton felt himself blush. He'd never been good at hiding his feelings. "I didn't mean it like that."

"I know," Simoni said. "You told me about your dragon because you trusted me. Do you trust Kallista?"

Trenton thought about it. Despite their disagreements, he wanted to trust her. The team didn't feel whole without her. *He* didn't feel whole.

The answer must have been clear on his face because Simoni smiled and patted him on the arm.

"You should tell her."

"Angus will be furious," Trenton said.

Simoni shook her head. "He's not the leader of our group."

He nodded. "I'll do it. First thing tomorrow." Just making the decision felt like a huge weight had been lifted off his shoulders.

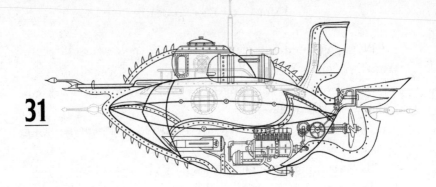

31

Kallista couldn't remember feeling this alone since a boy with a crooked smile and a bad haircut had come into the shop where she worked, looking for a tool only her father had ever used. Back then, she hadn't known she was lonely. Being raised by a single father with terrible social skills, she'd never known any kids she could call friends.

Her father had taught her at home, explaining that the city schools would not only stunt her growth and slow her learning but that half of what the teachers in Cove told her would be lies. She'd never questioned the fact that she didn't play with other children. Her father's lessons and games kept her busy, challenging her mentally and physically.

Usually, when she saw kids playing in the parks or going to school, she'd felt sorry for them. Their parents didn't love them enough to keep them out of the schools that rotted their minds.

Then one day, her father was gone, and she realized she had no one to talk to, no one to help her study or to laugh with. Her work in the mechanic shop did nothing to challenge her. For the first time, she'd wondered what it would be like to have someone her own age to talk to.

So, of course, the first thing she'd done after the boy came into her shop was follow him into an alley, knock him to the ground, and beat him up. It wasn't the most auspicious start to a friendship. And each time they'd gotten close to solving a riddle together, her jealousy flared up. Her father had left the clues for *her*, not some random wannabe mechanic. Even though she realized she needed him to help build the dragon, part of her resented the fact that he was playing her father's game.

It was only after months of working together, solving problems together, that she'd realized games were more fun when played with someone else. Solving mysteries were more satisfying when you had someone to compare notes with. She'd finally opened up and allowed herself to trust someone other than her father.

For the first time, she'd understood what it meant to have a friend.

And now she'd ruined that.

It wasn't that Trenton was mean to her. She thought she would have preferred that. None of them were unkind. Simoni still had dinner with her. Plucky discussed work over breakfast. Clyde cracked jokes. Angus . . . Well, Angus was Angus.

In the past, she might not have recognized the divide that had opened between them. But she'd spent enough time with the others to recognize there was something the others shared which she wasn't a part of. A gulf separated them, and it was getting wider every day.

It wasn't just the project that Trenton and Plucky, and maybe some of the kids in the Runt Patrol, were working on without her. No one had mentioned it, and she'd never let on that she knew, but she saw the way Plucky and Trenton disappeared right after work. The way they whispered together and glanced at drawings they didn't think she'd seen.

She couldn't blame Trenton. After all, hadn't she done the same thing when she and Plucky were working on the turbo booster? Even when Trenton had asked to help them, or even simply to know what they were working on, she'd refused.

It had been her private project.

How could she demand to know what he was working on now?

If that was all there was, she could have lived with it. Eventually they would tell her what they were working on, right?

But what then? She couldn't betray her friends, could she?

But could she turn her back on the man who raised her, who'd taught her everything she knew, who'd loved her the best he knew how?

The day she'd come back from the white tower, Trenton had seen the bruises on her face from the monarch's attack. She should have admitted then what had happened, told him what her father had asked her to do. Instead she'd come up with a lame story about injuring herself at work. She knew Trenton didn't believe her, but he'd pretended to accept her explanation.

She'd lied to her friends. She'd let her father think she might be willing to spy for him. She was caught in the middle of a chasm so deep and wide she couldn't see either side.

When she arrived at work, she found Trenton waiting for her.

He jumped up from where he'd been sitting with some of the kids from the shop. He shifted from one foot to the other, and she realized he was as nervous as she was.

"Is something wrong?" she asked.

"No. I mean . . ." He met her eyes for a moment before looking away. "There's a new job today. A transportation system they're putting in by Nob Hill. They want a couple of people to look at the chain drive, and I was wondering if you wanted to go with me?"

That was new. Trenton had only worked on the same crew with her a couple of times since they'd started in the shop. And he'd never asked her to go anywhere with him. She bit her lip. "Sure."

"Great." He grabbed his tools. "Let me get a quad, and we'll drive up together."

That afternoon ended up being the best time she'd had in weeks. The project was intriguing. Huge drums were connected to underground chains at the top and bottom of the hill. Six-person trams would be hooked to the chains through metal slots in the street. The cars would run slowly up the hill, turn around, and come back down. Then they'd repeat the process all over again. People could get on and off the trams at several stops.

If the project went well, the city planned on adding more trams with more stops.

The work crew was returning to the shop at the end of the day when Trenton abruptly pulled the quad to the side of the road and stopped.

He rubbed his hands against the legs of his pants, bouncing one knee up and down. "Kallista, there's something I need to tell you."

She thought he'd been trying to work up to this all day. "All right."

He took a deep breath, then let the words spill out of his mouth like water flowing over a dam. "I know you agree with your father. You want to stay here. And, you know, maybe you're right. Maybe the dragons are the next rung on the evolutionary ladder like your father says, but the thing is, we—that is me and Simoni, and well, the rest of us—we don't agree. And we're going to try to escape from the city."

He leaned back as though afraid she might hit him.

She waited a minute, trying to decide how she felt. Surprised? Hurt that they'd been planning this without her? Betrayed? No. She didn't feel any of those things. She thought she'd known all along that this was coming. It was a relief to get it out in the open at last. "When are you going?"

He bit his bottom lip. "Soon."

She nodded. "How are you leaving?"

His knee started bouncing again. "It might be better if you didn't know the details. In case anyone asks. But I will tell you that we know where the dragons are, and since Ladon is at least half yours, maybe completely yours, I felt like I needed to ask your permission before I took him."

She'd thought she was past feeling pain. Trenton leaving without her was bad enough, but the idea of him taking Ladon burned like fire in her chest. Her vision blurred, and she had to blink back tears to see clearly.

"Who will fly with you?"

"We haven't decided yet. Probably one of the kids from the shop. It turns out that most of the kids in the city feel differently than the adults. A lot of them don't want to serve the dragons."

She ran her fingers through her hair. Pain throbbed from her chest, through her throat, and into her brain. For the first time since she'd argued with her father, she was really and truly angry.

She slammed her hands against the quad's control panel, and Trenton jerked back. "Why are you telling me this?"

He ran a hand across his mouth, eyes darting left and right. "I wanted to ask your permission to take—"

"No!" She slammed her fist against the metal panel again, sending a sharp pain shooting from her wrist to her elbow. "You didn't have to ask me to take Ladon. I gave him up the day I tried to talk you into staying here. You didn't bring me here to work on the trams. You didn't even come here to tell me you were leaving." She clutched her hands together, trying to keep them from shaking. "Why did you bring me here? What do you want?" Tears streamed down her face.

"Okay," he said quietly. "You're right. I brought you here because I think—no, I *know*—what your father said is wrong. I know you love him, and you believe in him, and that he never does anything without a reason." Trenton swiped a hand across his eyes. "But I couldn't leave without asking you, if for once, you'd disagree with your father. I had to ask if you'd come with me."

Her heart pounded against her ribs. Her fingers felt numb. A wave of nausea raced through her, and she felt like she might throw up. This was the one thing she'd been too afraid to consider. The thing that terrified her so badly she forced it from her mind every time it tried to sneak in.

For her entire life, no matter how bad things got, there was one pillar of strength she'd been able to hold on to. One truth she could carry with her anywhere she went. The one and only solid thing in her life. And now her best friend was asking her to abandon it.

She finally allowed herself to ask the questions she had never dared to ask in her entire life. Was she willing to admit that her father was wrong? Was she willing to go against something he believed in so completely? Was she willing to leave him behind and never look back?

Blinking away the tears in her eyes, she nodded. "Yes. I'll go with you."

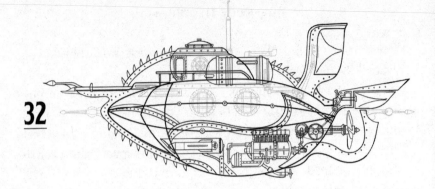

32

Trenton watched Kallista all through dinner, wondering if he'd made a mistake. The others had told him what they thought of his plan to tell her their secret, and it wasn't a universal agreement, to say the least.

Even after she'd agreed to go with them, the others didn't feel they could trust her. She'd always believed in her father but look what he had done. Was it a stretch to believe she might betray them as well?

What he didn't tell them was that when he'd been sitting on the side of the hill in the quad, he hadn't been sure what he'd do if she said no. He told himself he'd go without her—that he'd fly Ladon with someone else—but after all they'd been through, after all they'd sacrificed for each other, the truth was, he didn't know if he *could* leave her. If she'd told him she was staying, there was a good chance he might have told the others to leave without him.

But she'd agreed to go with him, and they were a team again.

"Are you taking me to see your secret submarine?" she asked as they climbed into the quad and pulled out onto the street.

"No," he said. "I mean, I can, if you want, but that's not where we're going now."

"I can't believe you built it without me," she said.

"It wasn't like you gave me much choice. You said you didn't want to be a part of escaping. What was I supposed to do?"

Instead of answering him, Kallista stared down the street.

"What's wrong?" Trenton asked.

She stood up in the quad. "Did you see someone? By the house on the corner?"

Trenton looked in the direction she was facing. The street was empty. They drove to the corner, but there was no one in sight.

"Who was it?" he asked. "Do you think someone's spying on us?"

Her forehead wrinkled. "It was probably just someone who lives in the area." She shook her head and checked her pocket watch. "Whatever we're doing, it better be quick. It's almost curfew."

Anyone out after nine on a work night would be taken into custody by the guards, assuming the Ninki Nankas didn't get them first.

"Actually," he said, "that's what we're going to test. Ever since we decided to escape, I've known we'd have to do it at night."

Kallista nodded. "Too many watching eyes during the day."

"Right. But the Ninki Nankas are everywhere at night and would track us down in a heartbeat."

"So how do we get past them?" Kallista asked.

As Trenton turned into the entrance to the mechanic shop where they reported for work every day, all the clocks around the city began to chime the nine o'clock hour. "That's what I'm hoping to find out."

As Trenton shut down the quad, a group of black shapes began to appear out of the shadows. He knew all of them on sight, but Kallista frowned in confusion.

"The kids from work?" she asked. "What are they doing here?"

A little blonde girl, who didn't look like she could be any older than nine, raised her fist in the air. "Night games!"

• • •

"You were supposed to bring Plucky," Alex said, folding his arms across his chest. He pinned Kallista with his gaze. "Not her."

"Kallista's decided to escape with us," Trenton said. "We can trust her."

Alex looked at the other members of the Runt Patrol and then at Trenton. "We couldn't before. She told her father about us."

"I made a mistake," Kallista said. "I'm sorry. Please give me another chance."

Trenton pulled Alex aside, but even though they kept their voices low, Kallista could still hear them.

"We need her," Trenton said. "She can help us with both the dragons and the submarine. I promise."

Alex still looked unconvinced.

"Okay," Trenton said, "if you can't trust her yet, trust me. She's my friend."

"I'll do whatever you ask," Kallista said to Alex.

Alex straightened his back. "Whatever I ask?"

"Just say the word."

Alex paused in thought for a moment, then finally nodded. "Pass our initiation—both of you—and then we'll talk."

Kallista and Trenton exchanged a glance. "What do we have to do?" she asked.

Alex grinned and pulled a white cloth from his pocket. "Easy. Just swipe this across the nose of a Ninki Nanka and don't get bit."

She looked at Trenton. "Please tell me this is a joke."

He raised his hands. "I thought it was too. But they say every member of the Runt Patrol has done it, and so far no one has been eaten. Not so much as a scratch."

Alex gave them a slight bow. "No one knows exactly who figured it out, but kids have been doing it since before I was born. It's pretty much a requirement if you want to go anywhere in the city at night." He pulled several clay balls out of the bag by his feet. He handed them to Trenton and Kallista. A funnel stuck out of one end of the ball and a candlewick poked out of the other.

Trenton turned the balls over in his hand and sniffed the clay. "What are these for?"

"Put them in your pocket for now." Alex pulled a pair of white cloth strips from the bag. "Rub these across your skin. Arms, face, the back of your neck. Anywhere you sweat. You want the cloth to smell as much like you as possible."

"What now?" Trenton asked once they'd finished.

Alex handed Trenton a small glass bottle. "Careful with this stuff. It's powerful. Only put a drop or two on the cloth."

Trenton unscrewed the cap, and an overpowering aroma drifted out.

"I've smelled this before," Kallista said.

Alex nodded. "Eucalyptus oil. Highly concentrated. Do not get it on your skin or in your mouth or eyes. If you do, you'll be burning for hours."

Carefully, Trenton added two drops on his cloth and two drops on Kallista's, then put the bottle in his pocket.

She took a whiff of the cloth, and the smell seemed to penetrate straight through her sinuses into her brain. Even such a small amount made her eyes water. "Wow, that's strong stuff. What now?"

Alex grinned. "Now the fun starts."

Footsteps echoed out of the darkness, and a skinny girl with wild yellow hair ran into the circle of light in front of the building. "It's coming. It's coming."

"She's about to become our newest member," Alex said.

The girl held out one of the clay balls, and Alex lit the wick with a glowing stick. The string hissed and spit sparks.

"It's called a punk," Alex said with a grin. "You actually don't need the smoke bombs, but they make it more exciting, and the littler kids think it's funny."

The click of talons on stones drew closer, followed by a loud hiss. Out of the darkness waddled a massive, dark-green Ninki Nanka. It stopped in front of the little girl, stared at her with emotionless black eyes, and opened its fang-filled mouth.

"Ninki Nanka!" the little girl called. She tossed the clay ball in front of the beast. There was a soft *pop*, and smoke billowed out around the Ninki Nanka's head. It jerked back for a minute as if confused, and the kids howled with laughter.

The smoke didn't stop the creature, though. If anything, it appeared to have made it angrier. It growled and lunged toward the girl.

Kallista put her hand to her eyes, sure she was about to see the child get devoured. Instead, the girl reached out and slapped a white cloth on the Ninki Nanka's horned snout.

The dragon pulled back with a hiss. Its dark eyes narrowed. It shook its head, sniffed, and let out a huge sneeze.

"Ninki Nanka, Ninki Nanka," the girl sang, taunting the creature and waving her hands in its face. Incredibly, the dragon only stared at her with a dazed look on its face.

"What's happening?" Kallista asked. "Why isn't it attacking?"

"The concentrated eucalyptus oil combined with the person's individual scent short-circuits something in the Ninki Nanka's memory," Alex said. "And since their memory is tied to their sense of smell through their rudimentary hive mind, once you short out one of them, your scent is removed from all the Ninki Nankas' memories."

"Capture the flag. Capture the flag," the Runt Patrol kids chanted.

The yellow-haired girl danced in front of the dazed beast before snatching the cloth off the end of its nose. Turning to the others, she took a deep bow, and everyone cheered.

"Okay," Alex said, turning to Kallista. "She's next."

Her heart was racing, but she managed to nod. She'd promised she'd do whatever it took to get the Runt Patrol to trust her. She couldn't let them down again. She couldn't let Trenton down. "Okay, what do I do?"

Alex pointed to the spot where the little girl had stood. "Wait right there, and we'll lure in another Ninki Nanka."

She walked to the spot by the building and stared out into the fog. She tried to tell herself she wasn't afraid. She'd faced bigger, more dangerous dragons than these Ninki Nankas. But it was one thing to fight a dragon when you were flying your own mechanical dragon and had fireballs at your fingertips and a friend at your back to help you. Coming face-to-face with one on your own was a different thing altogether.

The sound of nails clicking on the street floated out of the darkness, and it was all she could do not to run.

A curly-haired boy she thought might be named Asher came running out of the fog, and all the children began to shout, "Ninki Nanka, Ninki Nanka."

Kallista dug one of her smoke bombs out of her pocket. She turned around so Trenton could light the wick for her. When she turned back, a giant Ninki Nanka was less than twenty feet in front of her. Somehow, she managed to toss the smoke bomb in the beast's general vicinity.

She nearly froze when the huge creature hissed and lunged at her, but she forced herself forward and slapped the cloth on the creature's snout.

Just like the other one had before, the Ninki Nanka reared back, sneezed, and then lumbered away into the shadows.

Kallista sighed in relief. She looked at Alex, wondering if she had done enough to earn his trust.

"Congratulations," Alex said, patting her on the back. "Welcome to the Runt Patrol."

After Trenton tagged his Ninki Nanka, Alex shook his hand and said, "We're still testing the submarine in the ocean next week?"

"Absolutely." Trenton tried to hand his extra smoke bombs, punk, and the bottle of eucalyptus oil back to Alex, but he shook his head.

"Keep them. They might come in handy. Don't forget, the Ninki Nankas won't bother you now, but you still have to avoid the guards."

"Thanks," Trenton said. "We won't forget."

As they walked back to their quad, Kallista noticed a figure walking across the street. At first she thought it was one of the kids, but the shadow was too tall. She pulled on Trenton's arm.

"What's wrong?" he asked.

The figure stopped, seemed to look straight at her, then walked past the building to a dragon tower. He said something to the guard in front of the tower, and the man stepped aside.

"Who was that?" Trenton asked as the door to the dragon tower closed behind the shadowy figure.

Kallista clenched a hand in front of her chest. "I think that was my father."

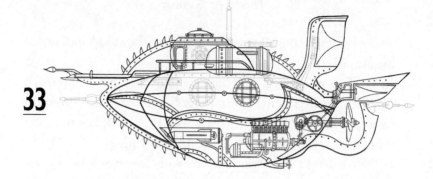

33

"A re you sure?" Trenton asked. "What would he be doing out
at night?"

"It's him," Kallista said. She'd only seen the figure in the
shadows, but she knew his walk. "I thought I saw him earlier,
when we left the house. I wasn't sure then, but I'm almost
positive."

Trenton peered into the darkness. "What would he be doing
out at this time of night?"

"I've searched the city for him for days. And now I see him
twice in two hours?" It didn't make any sense, unless . . . She
grabbed Trenton's arm. "I think he wants us to follow him."

"Into a dragon tower?" Trenton rolled his eyes. "Sure, we'll
just stroll up to the guard and say, 'Excuse me, but my friend's
dad went through that door, and we'd like to follow him.' We
aren't even supposed to be outside."

"A dragon tower," Kallista repeated thoughtfully. When
she'd been in front of the white dragon, she'd asked her father
where he was working, and he'd said . . . What was it? "He said
that if I needed him I should go to a dragon tower, that the
dragons would know how to find him."

"*Who* said that?"

"My father. I think he was trying to tell me something."

Trenton frowned. "You've talked to your father? When?

You've been looking all over for him since they moved us out of the dorms."

Kallista swallowed. She hadn't mentioned what happened with the monarch in the white tower because she didn't want to tell Trenton what her father had asked her to do, but the time had come to tell the truth—the complete truth.

"What I told you about the bruises before was a lie. I went to the city offices demanding they tell me where my father was. A dragon took me to the white tower. Once I got there, the monarch threw me around and threatened me."

"Why didn't you tell me?" Trenton asked.

She dropped her eyes. "My father was there. He asked me to spy on you. But I swear, I wouldn't. I didn't."

She could see the pain of her betrayal on Trenton's face. "I told the Runt Patrol they could trust you," he whispered.

"They can," Kallista said. "You can. I won't blame you if you don't come with me tonight, but I have to go. There's something my father is trying to tell me."

"What can he tell you that he hasn't already said?"

Kallista shook her head. "I don't know any more than I know why he came here tonight. But I have to go after him."

Trenton folded his arms. "I'm not letting you go alone. But whether you think your father is trying to tell you something or not, I won't let this jeopardize our plans. He's not going to stop our plans for the submarine the way he stopped us leaving on our dragons."

"I won't let him," Kallista said. "I swear."

Trenton didn't seem completely convinced, but at last he nodded. "All right. How do we get in the tower?"

Kallista looked around. They needed a distraction. Her eyes stopped on the guard's quad parked only a few feet away from him, and a plan came together in her head. She turned to three of the Runt Patrol kids still standing nearby. "What are your names again?"

"Hallie Meredith," said a girl with long brown hair and blue eyes.

A tall boy with freckles across his nose said, "I'm Michael. And this is JoeBob."

"You were the ones who took us to the warehouse to get our dragons?"

JoeBob smirked. "Fat lot of good it did."

"Maybe I can make it up to you," she said. "Teasing Ninki Nankas is fun. But how would you like to tease an actual city guard?"

Trenton frowned. "You really think it's a good idea to get them involved?"

"We need their help,"

"We want to help," Hallie said. "Guards are the worst."

Trenton shrugged, and Kallista pulled the three Runt Patrol kids close, giving them specific instructions on what to do and when. She turned to Trenton. "Now we need to find a way to get the guard away from his quad."

"Let me take care of that," Trenton said. He took one of the extra smoke bombs out of his pocket and pried open the top. He poured a measure of eucalyptus oil around the inside of the funnel, careful not to wet the material as well.

Kallista squinted her eyes. "Ouch! That's going to sting."

"That's the idea," Trenton said. He licked his finger and held it up to check which direction the wind was blowing. "This way."

Keeping a close eye out for any additional guards, they crept upwind of the tower. Trenton used the punk, which had burned almost to the end, to light the smoke bomb. The fuse sizzled, then hissed, turning a bright orange. He tossed the clay ball into the street, waited until a steady stream of smoke was pouring out of the funnel tip, and then shouted, "Fire!"

The guard outside the tower turned and ran toward the cloud billowing up from the street. Pushed by the breeze, the smoke floated into his face a few feet before he reached the bomb. The results were nothing short of spectacular.

As soon as the smoke made contact with the guard's eyes, he screamed and coughed. He tried to wipe his eyes, but that only made things worse. He tried to back away, but the wind had picked up and the cloud followed him.

One arm covering his face, he turned to run. At that moment, his quad roared to life. "Hey!" he screamed, tears dripping down his face. "You kids get off that!"

"Come get us!" Hallie shouted, waving her hands in the air.

Michael rammed the throttle all the way forward just as JoeBob yelled "Look out!" and pointed to the right. With a clash of gears and metal legs, the quad raced down the middle of the street.

"Come back here!" The guard ran after them, but by the way he was coughing and spitting, Kallista suspected he wouldn't make it a block before giving up. She hoped the Runt Patrol had a good ride and didn't crash into anything.

"Let's go," she said to Trenton. Sticking close to the buildings, they trotted down to the tower.

"You're sure you want to do this?" Trenton asked. "I mean, I bet the penalty for breaking into one of these places is pretty severe."

She nodded. She had to know what was going on. What if her father was in trouble? What if she was the only one who could help him? She tugged at the door, afraid it might be locked, but it swung open without any resistance. They quickly stepped through and pulled it shut behind them.

The tower was lit by flickering gas lamps. A walkway curved along the inside wall. She led the way, and twenty feet or so later, she saw a metal staircase spiraling up through the roof. Unlike the automatic stairs in the white tower, they would have to walk up these one by one.

Trenton had placed his foot on the first step when Kallista held up one hand. She tilted her head to listen for the sound of footsteps clanging against metal stairs. She heard nothing. By now, her father could have reached wherever he was going, but she had a feeling he hadn't taken the stairs. "Let's keep going."

They left the staircase behind and continued to follow the curving walkway. The narrow corridor was thick with the smell of the dragons living overhead. Trenton's and Kallista's shadows grew then disappeared as they passed each of the wall-mounted lamps. Almost exactly halfway around the tower, she saw a plain metal door set into the wall. There was a lock on the door, but the door itself was hanging open a few inches, as though the last person to go through had neglected to pull it shut.

Trenton looked at Kallista. "You think he went in there?"

She was sure of it.

Behind the door was another staircase. Unlike the fancy, wrought-iron one going up the center of the tower, this one was plain stone, the steps worn with usage. And instead of going up, they went down. There were no lights on the wall, so when Trenton pulled the door shut behind them, they were plunged into complete darkness.

Reaching out, she found Trenton's hand, and the two of them followed the staircase around and around. Soon, the air began to feel damp, and the smell of sulfur was replaced by a dank, mossy scent.

Kallista stopped. "Do you hear that?"

They stood silently for a moment, and she heard the sound again. *Clank, clank, clank.* Like metal banging against stone.

"Come on," she said, pulling Trenton behind her as she charged down the stairs.

A moment later, her knee buckled as she went to take another step down and instead found smooth floor beneath her. Trenton stumbled over her foot, and the two of them crashed into the far wall.

Kallista shook her head and tried to get back to her feet.

"Look," Trenton said, and Kallista found there was a faint light filling the area, enough that she could make out Trenton's silhouette in the darkness. Behind him, a lantern moved down the passage.

For a moment, she almost called out. But what if it wasn't her father? Or what if it was and he was upset that she had followed him?

Staying far enough back to avoid being seen, they followed the lantern through an array of twisting and turning passages. Several times they noticed staircases disappearing into openings in the stone walls.

At one of the openings, Kallista caught the distinct scent of dragons. "I think these passages connect all the city towers," she said.

Trenton looked at the narrow staircase. "There's no way a dragon could fit down that. Unless it was one of the smaller ones."

"No. But servants could, bringing food and whatever else the dragons might need."

Up ahead, the lantern went out, and Kallista feared they had lost the trail. Then she realized the hallway widened ahead with lights fixed to the walls again. They crept forward until they could make out a small alcove. Unlike the rest of the tunnels, this hallway was lit by electric bulbs.

Why? What was different about this area?

A figure stood facing a door on the other side of the alcove. As they watched, the man pulled out a pocket watch, glancing briefly at it. The electric lights lit the man's face, and Kallista set her mouth in a grim line. It was her father. But what was he doing here? And where was he going?

He tapped a metal panel beside the door, and four clear beeps sounded. He pulled the door open and disappeared inside.

"Let's go," Trenton said as the door began to swing shut.

"Wait," Kallista said, staying in the darkness until the door closed with a heavy metal thunk.

Trenton groaned. "How are we supposed to get in now? Those beeps were a code. Now it's locked."

Kallista chewed on her thumbnail, thinking. "He led us here on purpose."

"What are you talking about?" Trenton asked.

"Think about it. What are the chances he would conveniently show up where we were tonight? The unlocked tower, the metal banging sound, the lantern that waited until we saw it?" *Had* her father followed them from the house? Had he let them see him on purpose?

"This doesn't make any sense," Trenton said. "Your father had a chance to help us the night we tried to get our dragons back, and he betrayed us. How can we possibly trust him now?"

"I don't know," she said, wishing she had a better answer. "I know I shouldn't trust him. He's been lying to us ever since we got to the city. But why? He's never lied to me in my life. Why start now?"

Trenton pressed his palm against his forehead like he was

trying to stop a headache. "You think someone is forcing him to lie? Like blackmailing him or something?"

Kallista nodded. "I don't know how or why, but I think he's been trying to give me clues."

Trenton stared at her, and she hurried on. "The day I saw my father in the white tower, he said a bunch of weird things. Like that he was working in a laboratory. Not a workshop—a laboratory. That's also when he said the thing about me coming to the dragon towers."

He studied her eyes. He wanted to believe her, but she'd been keeping so many secrets. They both had.

"You could be leading me into a trap. You and your father could have set this up together."

She took his hands in hers. "I know you have no reason to believe me, but I'm telling the truth. I swear it." She thought for a moment. "I swear as a mechanic, and even more, as your friend."

Trenton nodded. That's what it came down to, really. They may not have been friends when they first started building Ladon together, but after everything they'd been through, he couldn't think of anyone he was closer to, anyone he wanted to believe as much. "All right. I trust you."

Kallista threw her arms around him. "Thank you! I swear I'll never keep another secret from you again."

He looked across the alcove. "We should go through the door, right?"

She shook her head. That moment when her father pulled out his pocket watch felt too intentional. A signal? Maybe it was a charade. Maybe there was something he wanted her to know. Something that, for some reason, he couldn't say out loud. "Let's wait a minute."

The beeping sound came from the door again, and Kallista

pulled Trenton back. As the door swung open, she glanced down the hallway, trying to remember how far back the nearest staircase was. Would they be able to find it in the dark?

It didn't matter because her father walked through the door, waited for it to swing shut, then turned down a different hallway without even a glance in their direction.

As soon as he was out of sight, they hurried to the door. Trenton tried the handle. It was locked. He glanced at the metal keypad set into the wall. "Any idea what the code might be?"

If her father wanted her to see what was behind the door, it would be a code she would know. If not, she'd made a huge mistake.

She tried her father's birthday, her birthday. Simple combinations like 1-2-3-5—the first four prime numbers—and more complex ones like 3-1-4-1—the first four digits of pi. Had he used any other four number combinations in any of the games they'd played?

"Maybe it's something as easy as 1-2-3-4," Trenton said. "Or four random numbers."

She shook her head. "He doesn't do anything without a reason." But *was* there a reason this time? Did he intend for her to discover what he'd been working on? Or was she simply trying to convince herself of something that wasn't true?

She thought back to the last two times he'd spoken to her. In the white tower and that night in the warehouse. She'd tried to push it out of her mind, but now she closed her eyes and remembered the feel of his hands on her face.

She'd asked him, "Why are you doing this?"

He pulled her close and . . .

Her eyes popped open.

"I know the code." With shaking fingers, she punched in four numbers: 1-2-2-4. "Please be right. Please be—

The locked clicked. The latch swung open.

He did want her to know. He did. His last words to her had been a clue. *The day your mother died, I swore I'd take care of you. Since the day she died, I've tried to do what was best for you.*

The day she died.

Her mother had died the day before Christmas.

She gripped the handle and looked at Trenton. "Let's find out what's inside."

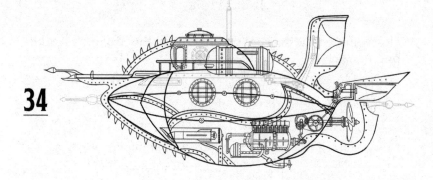

34

The first thing Trenton noticed when they walked through the door was the buzzing sound that cycled up and down like waves crashing against a beach. The room appeared to be round, but it was so large the far side was lost in shadows. Green light pulsed in time with the buzzing, starting at the center of the room and moving outward in flickering circles.

He reached toward Kallista, and she closed her fingers around his.

Even from a distance, he could see the source of the light was a large metal console at the center of the room. It was covered with hundreds of dials and gauges and flashing lights. Tubes ran up the console to a copper ball suspended from the ceiling. Porcelain conductors bigger around than his waist and five or six feet long stuck out all over the ball, making it look like a strange undersea animal.

As they watched, bolts of electricity ran up the tubes, out the conductors, and across bare metal cables that stretched to the ends of the room.

"What is it?" he asked. Although they seemed to be alone in the room, he kept his voice to a whisper.

"I don't know. I've never seen anything like it."

Hands clasped tightly together, they walked across the room. "Do you feel that?" Kallista asked. The floor was rumbling beneath their feet, along with the buzzing and the lights. The closer they got to the center of the room, the stronger the rumbling grew.

Trenton paused. There was a pattern to both the rumbling and the flashing lights that felt familiar. *Grum-rum-rum-bump.* "I know where we are," he said, looking at the ceiling. "I felt this vibration the day we met with the monarch. We're somewhere under the white tower. But this room is much too big to be a part of the tower itself. It must be in a cavern underneath it."

As they neared the console, the stone floor was a replaced with a metal grate. Kallista sniffed. "It smells like saltwater."

Kneeling on the grate, they heard the sound of rushing water and breathed in the unmistakable smell of the ocean. Trenton tilted his head to try to get a better view. Twenty feet beneath the grate there were two large tanks separated by a sheet of gray material. The same kinds of tubes going into the copper ball were connected to the gray material as well.

"Is it possible there's a steam engine down there?" he asked.

Kallista shook her head. "You can't run a steam engine on saltwater without corroding the tank."

It was a mystery, but they didn't have time to worry about it. The room was obviously a laboratory, and even though it was after work hours, Kallista's father or someone else could come in at any time.

They walked across the grate, footsteps echoing in the darkness below.

Drawing closer to the console, Trenton saw a series of metal plates that ran the length of a panel on one side. The plates were numbered from one to seventy-two. Beneath each plate was a column of gauges. Some were easy to understand, like pressure and temperature, but most of the others made no sense.

"What does Ca stand for? Or NaCl?" he asked, tapping one of the needles.

"They're abbreviations for chemical elements," Kallista said. "Ca is calcium. Na is sodium and Cl is chlorine, which you combine to make salt."

Why would dragons be measuring salt and calcium?

As he moved to get a better look, his shin banged against a drawer that had been left a few inches open.

Kallista pulled out the drawer all the way, revealing stacks of notebooks. She grabbed the one on top and flipped it open. It was filled with columns of scientific notations with a number on each side and the current date at the top.

Trenton studied the numbers. He'd been the best math student in his class, but this was pretty advanced. "These look like lab results. They must be running some kind of experiment."

Kallista ran her finger down one of the columns. "This is my father's handwriting."

Trenton dug through the piles to see if there was anything else beneath them. Halfway down the stack, the covers changed from paper to leather. The deeper he dug, the older the leather looked. He pulled one out and checked the date. "Look at this—1945."

"Let me see." Kallista took the notebook from him. "It's the same type of notations. Whatever they've been doing down here, it's been going on for a long time." She dug to the bottom of the pile and pulled out a book whose cover was almost in shreds. Trenton feared it would fall apart if he breathed on it wrong.

Holding the book gently in both hands, Kallista tweezed open the cover. The date at the top of the page was March 13, 1903. "Three years before the San Francisco earthquake," she muttered.

Trenton stepped closer to the console. He noticed there were switches above each of the plates. "What were they doing here?" he asked, studying the dials and buttons. As he took another step closer, his foot caught on the metal grate and he stumbled forward. As he reached for the console to steady himself, his hand knocked against one of the switches.

Kallista dropped the book she was holding. "No!"

Trenton reached to turn off the switch, but it was too late.

On the other side of the room, a light turned on, revealing a large glass cylinder running from the floor to the ceiling. The tube, which was at least twenty feet across, was filled with a dark, bubbling liquid. It looked like something was suspended inside.

Kallista put a hand to her mouth. "No. Oh, no."

"What's wrong?" Trenton asked. But she kept staring at the glass cylinder, her face ghostlike beneath the flickering green lights.

Trenton approached the tube. The closer he got, the clearer it became that there were wires and tubes running from whatever was inside to the top of the cylinder. Still twenty feet away, he realized what he was looking at. It was small, barely the size of a young pig, but he already could make out the wings, tail, and the hint of a snout.

"They're experimenting on dragons?"

Kallista rushed forward and grabbed his arm, her fingers sinking deep in the muscle of his bicep as she squeezed.

"Ow," he said, trying to pull away. "Ease up."

But she squeezed tighter. "They aren't *experimenting* on dragons. They're *growing* them."

"That's ridiculous. How could a person *grow* a dragon?"

Kallista placed her hands against the glass tube. "They're

growing embryos. The tube must be filled with nutrients. That's what they're measuring with the gauges."

Trenton walked up behind her and studied the creature floating in the murky, brownish-yellow liquid. It was definitely a tiny dragon. Scales as small and pink as his little fingernail were just beginning to appear on skin so thin he could see the creature's internal organs. A tiny heart pumped like a fist, opening and closing as it pushed fluid through the creature's veins.

"Why are they doing this?" he asked. "Can't the dragons just have babies like every other animal?"

"I don't know," Kallista said. "And I don't know why they need my father's help with it now. This has been going on for years."

Trenton looked more closely at the tube. At the base was a metal plate marked with the number seventeen. Below that was a bunch of writing that was hard to make out. "It looks like the kind with poison fangs. See the black-and-red stripes?"

Kallista leaned over the small writing. She gasped.

"What's wrong?" he asked.

She pointed to a line of text. "This is DNA sequencing information."

He felt a shiver run along the base of his skull. "Deoxyribonucleic acid," he whispered. "The building block of nearly every living organism. In my food production class, I learned that the founders of Discovery modified the DNA of some of the farm animals to help them survive better inside the mountain." He brushed away dust from farther down the plate. "Look, this says it's the DNA for a Gila monster. And this is for a snake." He ran his finger down the list. "Bat. Frog. I don't understand. What do bats and snakes and lizards have to do with dragons?"

She grabbed both his arms, shaking him. "*Everything.* Don't you see? I thought they were growing dragons down here, but they're *making* them."

"*Making* them? Like inventing a machine or something?"

"Yes, only they are using biology instead of machinery." She hurried to the next cylinder several feet down. Although it was still dark, there was enough light to see the panel at the tube's base. "This has whale DNA. I'll bet it's the blue dragon."

She looked around the room. "Turn on all the switches. Especially the ones toward the end."

Trenton ran back to the console and began flipping switches. With each switch, another cylinder lit up. Each one had a dragon inside. Some were as small as the black-and-red, but others were almost full-size.

Thoughts raced through his head. This had to be what Kallista's father was working on. But who would want to make dragons? And why? How long how it been going on? He glanced at the notebook Kallista had dropped, and his hand froze above switch number sixty.

The lab results had gone back to 1903. Three years before the San Francisco earthquake. One year before the dragons appeared. This was what he and Kallista had been searching for. This room was the origin of the dragons. But if they came from here . . .

He'd always assumed the dragons were something terrible that had *happened* to humans, like an earthquake or a flood. He'd imagined the dragons as a disease and the humans as heroic doctors trying to find a cure. He thought that if he and Kallista could track down where the disease came from, they could figure out a cure.

But the dragons hadn't *happened* to humans; humans had created the dragons. They had done this to themselves.

Trenton turned back to Kallista. "Why would they do it? Why would humans create something as terrible as a dragon?"

"Because that's what we do." Kallista laughed wildly, sounding slightly crazy. But why shouldn't she? This was crazier than anything Trenton had ever imagined.

Kallista paced back and forth in front of the control panel. "Everyone knew war was coming, right? So they gathered the greatest minds in science, brought them here, and told them to build the biggest, strongest weapons they could imagine." She gave the closest tube a sharp rap with her knuckle. "The deadliest weapons they could."

"You're saying they intentionally released dragons into the world?" Trenton asked.

"Who knows? Maybe they released one or two as a test. Maybe the earthquake broke open some of the cylinders. Or maybe the earthquake was a result of what they were working on. It doesn't matter now."

Trenton walked from one cylinder to another. He'd seen most of the dragons before, but some were completely unfamiliar to him, like a silver dragon with wings so wispy they looked like tissue paper and a crimson one with pincers like a crab.

Since the day he and Kallista had first read the newspaper articles her father had hidden for her, they'd asked the same question over and over. Where had the dragons come from? Now that he finally knew the answer, he wished he didn't.

He looked at a dragon with a birdlike beak, long legs covered with tiny barbs, and wings that looked like fins. "When we were in Seattle, you and your father said creating a new species was impossible."

Kallista spread her arms. "It takes centuries, even millennia, for a new species to come about. But the dragons aren't a new species. They're simply a mishmash of species that have always been here. All it took was a bunch of scientists to put them together in different ways. They created monsters."

Trenton shook his head. "The leaders of Cove said the outside world was destroyed by technology. They said creativity was evil. They were right all along. I wish my mother was here so she could say I told you so."

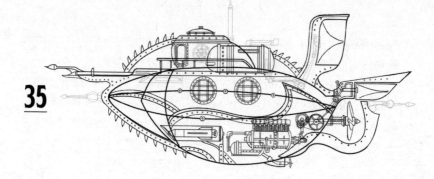

35

Trenton turned on the switches from sixty through seventy-two. The last two cylinders were empty. At first, he thought the five before that were also empty, but as he got closer, he saw something tiny—not much bigger than the tip of his pinky finger—floating inside. Each speck was white with a pair of tiny silver horns.

"Five white dragons," Trenton said, his voice trembling.

Kallista touched the plate at the bottom of one of the cylinders. Unlike the other plates, which were old and dusty, these looked as bright as if they'd been installed yesterday. "Bat. Parrot—that explains how the monarch speaks so well. But what's a jewel wasp?"

"Jewel wasp?" Trenton repeated. Why did that mean something to him?

Kallista looked up at him, her hands clenching and unclenching.

Someone had told him something about wasps not too long ago. About being stung by them . . .

"Clyde!" he shouted. "Clyde said that when they sent him to retraining they made him stick his hand in a jar full of wasps. He said they were shiny green, like jewels."

Kallista shook her head. "Why would they have done that?"

Trenton racked his brain. "Clyde said after he got stung by the wasps, his mind started acting funny. The guards talked to him, said strange things to him while he was drawing, and after they were done, he didn't want to draw anymore."

"You think the wasps they used on Clyde might be the same jewel wasps they're using to create the white dragons? But why?"

He studied the tiny white shape floating in the liquid. "I don't know. Wasps are dangerous but not exactly deadly."

Kallista pressed her clenched fist to her mouth. "Tell me again what happened to Clyde."

Trenton tapped his foot, trying to remember exactly what Clyde had said. "They didn't let him sleep, then they stung him with the wasps, and then they made him draw while they whispered things to him. After awhile, his hand started to burn and his brain felt strange. When the retraining was done, he didn't want to draw anymore. He's just now getting back to being able draw again without getting sick."

"Maybe the wasp's sting was the trigger. Like it poisoned his mind or something."

"Or changed it." Trenton ran his hand across the plaque. "But could a bite or a sting like that really change the way you think? Is that even possible?"

Kallista gestured to the laboratory surrounding them. "At the moment, I think *anything* is possible."

Trenton rubbed his forehead. He felt like he was close to figuring out something important. Like he had all the pieces of a machine working except for one last piece and no matter how he tried, he couldn't get it to fit with the rest of the parts.

"Let's say we're right. That there *is* something about a jewel wasp that can—I don't know—override a person's mind. Like an extra cog in a machine that makes it turn a different direction. The venom can make a person think something they didn't really believe, do something they didn't really want to do."

"Like Clyde thinking drawing was bad even though he used to love it."

"Exactly."

Kallista's brow furrowed. "Maybe. But what you're talking about is—"

"Mind control," Trenton finished. He slammed his palm against the cylinder in front of him, and the tiny white dragon wobbled in its liquid cocoon. "If the jewel wasp DNA can be used to control people's minds, then that's how the monarch is forcing everyone to obey it. The white dragon's power is mind control."

The color drained from Kallista's face. "That's why my father has been acting the way he is. He didn't betray us. The monarch is controlling his mind."

Trenton nodded grimly. "And not just his. I think the monarch is controlling all the adults in San Francisco."

• • •

Kallista ran back to the console and pulled out one of the earliest notebooks. "Look at these results," she said. "It says here they only had two dragon types at first. The Ninki Nankas— which seem to be kind of a trial run—and reds, which were the first real dragons." She tossed the notebook aside, thumbing through a few more until she found the first mention of a third dragon type. "The black dragons didn't arrive until 1955."

Trenton looked over her shoulder. "The dragons had already attacked the humans by then. Why would scientists keep creating new types of dragons after knowing what they'd unleashed?"

"They wouldn't. It doesn't make any sense." Kallista continued to flip through the notebooks, tossing each successive one onto the floor in a growing stack of horror.

Trenton picked up the earliest notebooks, moving from one to another. "1903. 1904. 1906." He stopped. "Where's 1905?"

Kallista looked down at the notebooks she'd dropped on the floor. They went through them again, one by one. The one for 1905 was definitely missing.

"Hang on," Trenton said. "Where's the book for the white dragon?"

They searched each of the notebooks from beginning to the end. There was no mention of a white dragon. It was like the white dragon didn't exist.

"What if the black dragon *wasn't* the third dragon?" Trenton said. "What if the third dragon was created in 1905? The year with the missing book."

"The white dragon," Kallista said. Suddenly it all made sense. "What if, after creating the Ninki Nankas and the red dragons, they created the white dragon? Maybe they didn't realize what the jewel wasp venom would do. Or maybe they created the dragon, intending to keep it controlled, but—" She dropped the notebook she was holding. "What if the earthquake released the white dragon before they were ready for it?"

"And it took control of their minds," Trenton said. "It could have forced the scientists to release the dragons they already had into the world."

"It could have forced them to make *more* dragons," Kallista said. "That could have been how it all went wrong."

Trenton nodded. "That would also explain why there weren't any new dragons until 1955. By then, the dragons had finished taking over the world. Then they came back here and forced the scientists to invent new dragons. But how did the dragons spread so quickly?"

"There could have been other labs," Kallista said. "Other scientists working on the same weapons in different locations.

All the original white dragon would have to do would be to force one scientist to free all the others."

"But where does your father come in?" Trenton asked. "If they've been making dragons here for a hundred and fifty years, why do they need him now?"

Slowly they both turned to look at the five cylinders numbered sixty-six through seventy. The cylinders with the new white dragons in them. The cylinders with the brand-new plaques.

"Maybe they lost the plans for white dragons in the earthquake," Kallista said quietly. "Maybe they needed someone to . . . to figure how to make copies of the monarch."

She picked up the last book, the one with her father's handwriting in it. She read through the pages more carefully now, paying special attention to the handwritten notes. She finally found what she was looking for scribbled in a margin.

"*Improved effects appear to work best on mature prefrontal cortexes. Subjects younger than twenty years of age show minimal control with new formula.*"

"It doesn't work well on kids," she said, holding the notebook up for him to see. "The part of the brain it controls doesn't develop in humans until they are older."

Trenton nodded. "Alex and Michael both said that when members of the Runt Patrol got older, they changed their minds about wanting to escape the city."

Kallista remembered how the monarch had stared at her with its purple eyes and she'd felt dizzy for a minute. Like it was trying to hypnotize her, but its power wasn't strong enough. "Maybe the jewel wasps in Discovery have a slightly different strain of venom—one that works better on kids. Maybe that's why the retraining didn't work perfectly on Clyde and how he's been able to fight it off."

Something still bothered her, though. "If the monarch can control all the adults in the city, then why have guards at all? It can't be just to keep an eye on the kids."

"This might explain it." Trenton pointed to a series of hastily sketched lines and numbers at the back of the notebook. It was a graph comparing the monarch's mind-control power to the number of people affected. "It looks like the more people it tries to control, the weaker its power gets. According to this, the monarch is already over the limit of what it can handle."

Is that why her father had been able to give her just enough clues to lead her here? Was he fighting against the dragon's control?

Trenton squeezed her shoulder. "I think there's more to it than that. The white dragon controls people, but some people have a stronger reason than others to fight against it. Alex and Michael have the Runt Patrol. Your father has you. He must have been fighting the monarch's control like crazy to drop those clues you followed."

Kallista looked at the tiny white dragons floating in their tubes and felt anger rise up inside of her. Her father was the most brilliant person in the world, and to know that some terrible creature and stolen his ability to think and forced him to do something he never would have done otherwise made her vision crinkle around the edges.

"No," she said. "I won't let them control my father anymore." She kicked a pipe connected to the console, knocking it from its bracket. She kicked it again, and one end of the pipe snapped loose. Air hissed from the broken end as she grabbed the pipe, bending it back and forth until the other end broke loose.

"What are you doing?" Trenton asked.

She grabbed the pipe and ran toward the nearest cylinder containing a white dragon.

The things her father had said were so unlike him, but she'd been too scared to question his decision until it was too late.

"Stop!" Trenton yelled. "We don't know what will happen if you—"

She raised the pipe over her head and smashed the side of the cylinder. A small crack formed in the glass. She knew that these white dragons were not the ones controlling her father, but she had to do something.

Trenton ran toward Kallista, screaming for her to stop. But she raised the pipe again and again, slamming the glass until she smashed a hole in the cylinder. A stream of brown liquid shot from the opening.

Instantly, alarms blared around the room. Thick metal covers slammed down over every cylinder. Red lights flashed.

"We have to get out of here," Trenton yelled.

Kallista stared at the puddle of liquid at her feet, the pipe hanging limply in her hand. The room swayed around her; she wasn't sure where she was.

Trenton grabbed her by the arm. "People will be here any minute. We can't let them find us."

Kallista shook her head, her senses returning. "Right," she said. "You're right." But when she tried to open the door, the lever wouldn't turn. She pressed the keypad, but the buttons didn't beep. "We're locked in."

Footsteps sounded outside the door. She looked around wildly. There was no other way out.

"I'm sorry," Kallista said. She let go of the pipe, and it clanged to the ground.

Voices yelled outside. The door lock clicked, but before it could swing open, Trenton grabbed the pipe from the floor and jammed it under the handle. The lever rattled up and down, and a voice said, "It's stuck."

The door rattled again. The pipe wouldn't stop them for long.

She searched for some place to hide, but except for the console and the cylinders, the room was bare. If they tried to climb up the copper ball, the electricity would kill them, and they couldn't go under—

Her eyes stopped on the metal grate in the floor.

"Come on!" she yelled, pulling Trenton after her. She grabbed the metal grate, sliding her fingers through the holes. "Help me."

Trenton grabbed the other side of the grate, and they both tugged.

With a screech, a section of the floor lifted up. She stared down into the water below. All she could see were two large tanks with a metal wheel on one wall. There was no door or even a ladder, but she could hear water rushing somewhere in the darkness.

Behind them, something heavy slammed against the door, and the pipe fell with a clang. She flipped the section of grate aside. "Take a deep breath!"

At the same time, both she and Trenton filled their lungs with air. She closed her eyes, grabbed Trenton's hand, and jumped.

"Stop!" a voice yelled, but they were already falling.

They hit the water and plunged into icy darkness. She tried to swim back up, but if felt as if something had hold of her legs, pulling her down. Her shoulder hit hard against the side of the tank, and for a moment she thought she felt Trenton grab at her.

Then she was hurtling through darkness. Her body banked

left and right, smashed like a rag doll against rocks and pipes. She fought her way to the surface, gasped for air, was pulled back down, and felt herself slammed against something sharp. Pain flared in her shoulder.

She felt her head starting to spin just as a pair of hands grabbed her, pulling her out of the water.

"It's okay," Trenton said, breathing heavily. "We made it."

Slowly she sat up. They were on a rocky shore near the entrance to a dark cave cut into the side of a cliff. She looked up and saw the top of the white tower high above.

Lightning flashed over the water, and a cold drop of rain splashed against her face.

Trenton grabbed her hand. "We have to stop them."

A second cold drop hit her face, and a wave crashed over her legs.

"We will," she said. "I don't know how, but we will."

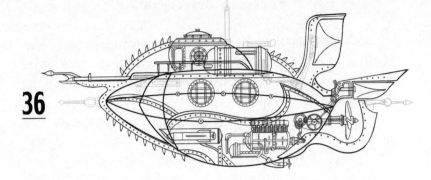

36

By the time they returned to the Seven Hills, it was after midnight. Rain slashed from the sky, and the wind coming off the water cut like an icy blade. There were guards on nearly every corner, and dragons soared overhead. It took them more than an hour to get back to their quad and another hour to make it to the neighborhood without being seen.

Although everyone should have been in bed, lights were on in buildings all over the city.

"You think this is because of us?" Trenton asked, turning the quad to avoid a pair of guards at the end of the street. The monarch would be angry that someone had broken into the lab. He'd be furious that one of tanks containing a white dragon had been damaged.

"I don't know," Kallista said. "Probably."

A quad loaded with boxes and crates raced by in the other direction without slowing down. "What's that all about?" Trenton asked.

They had barely parked when Simoni ran out of the house. "Where have you two been?"

"We have to talk," Trenton said.

They ran into the house. Simoni led them to the living room where the other kids were gathered and pulled the door shut behind them.

Angus leaned against the windowsill. "When the alarms went off, I figured you guys were the reason."

Clyde sat cross-legged on the floor. His eyes were bloodshot, and his cheeks looked flushed. "We've been looking for you everywhere."

"This is bad, you guys," Trenton said. He and Kallista sat on a flowered sofa and told the others everything that had happened. By the time they were finished, silence filled the room.

"Do you think you killed the white dragon in the tank?" Simoni asked.

"I don't know," Trenton admitted. "And even if we did, there were four others."

Plucky sat in a high-backed armchair, her braces lying on the floor and her feet tucked under her. She clutched Allie to her chest. "Them white dragons were itty-bitties, but how close do you think them other dragons is to coming outta the tanks?"

"Some of them looked pretty close," Kallista said. "They might be ready now for all we know."

Angus jumped up from the sill. "I told you we should have left as soon as the submarine was ready."

"We don't even know if the submarine *is* ready," Trenton said. "We haven't tested it."

Angus held up his fists. "Then we fight. We get our dragons, and we kill every dragon we can find."

"We can't get to our dragons without the submarine—" Trenton started.

"So we're just going to wait around and do nothing?" Angus interrupted.

Trenton leaped from the couch and squared off against Angus. "I didn't say that. You have no idea what you're talking about."

Simoni pushed between them. "This isn't helping any-thing."

"Attacking random dragons isn't going to help," Trenton said. "We need to stop the white dragon—the monarch. And we need to find a way to destroy the lab." He dropped back onto the couch. Outside, rain splattered against the windowpanes. "But I don't have any idea how to do that. Unless . . . what if we could overload the generator?"

Kallista nodded. "Those tanks under the grate generate electricity to run the lab. If we modified the wiring going up through the grid and increased the resistance to overload the circuits, then opened that waterwheel—"

"It would explode," Trenton said.

Simoni smiled. "So what if we destroyed the lab *and* killed the white dragon at the same time? Where did you say the lab was located?"

Trenton blinked. "Underneath the white tower."

Everyone began talking at the same time.

"If the explosion is big enough . . ."

" . . . it could take out the whole cliff . . ."

"And the tower with it."

Trenton tried to see it in his head. "We overload the gener-ator, blow up the lab, destroy the cliff, and take down the white tower. But we'd have to make sure the monarch is in the tower when the lab explodes. We couldn't risk having him fly out be-fore the tower falls."

"Couldn't fly if the shutters was nailed closed now, could he?" Plucky said. "If I was to crawl into the power conduit, I could shut the windows and keep 'em shut when everything goes boom."

"You could do that?" Clyde asked, obviously impressed.

Plucky tilted her head and ran a hand down her cat's tail. "Done harder when I was thievin' with Cochrane, yeah, yeah."

"This could work," Trenton said, feeling a thread of hope for the first time that night.

"Except how are you going to get back in the lab?" Angus said. "I bet that place is crawling with guards now."

Simoni tugged at her hair. "Couldn't you go back in the way you came out? Through the waterway in the cave?"

"The current's too strong," Kallista said. "We'd never make it through."

Trenton grinned. "We could if we were in a submarine."

They spent the next half hour hammering out the details. Trenton would operate the submarine since he was the most familiar with it. Simoni would go with him because her job gave her access to a cargo quad with a trailer big enough to get the submarine down to the water.

Kallista and Plucky would find the power conduit closest to the white tower and locate the circuits that opened and closed the windows. Clyde would act as a lookout, and Angus would handle any guards they ran into.

"What about them twisted piston Ninki Nankas?" Plucky asked.

"Do you have enough eucalyptus oil for four more cloths?" Kallista asked Trenton.

He checked the bottle. It would be close, but he thought there was enough. He handed her the vial and cloths, then fished the last of his smoke bombs out of his pocket. "You think you'll have time to use them?"

"We'll be fast," Kallista said.

Simoni checked her pocket watch. "We have to coordinate this just right. If you close the windows too early, the dragons will realize something is wrong. It will be light at six. Can everyone be in place by, say, five a.m.?"

Kallista looked at Trenton. "With this storm, the waves are going to be bad. Are you sure you want to take the submarine?"

"It will be fine," he said. It had to be. "You lock the tower down at five, and we'll blow up the lab."

"What then?" Clyde asked. "Where do we meet after the explosion?"

"I know a place by the docks," Simoni said. "It's far enough to the east that the guards don't patrol it much. There's a rock that looks like a bird's head. We'll land the submarine there. Then we can figure out what to do next." She glanced toward Kallista, who was staring out the windows. "Is that all right?"

"What?" Kallista shook her head, then nodded. "Yeah, the rock that looks like a dog east of the docks."

"Like a bird," Trenton said. "Are you all right?"

"I'm fine," she said. But her expression was strange.

As they prepared to leave, Angus pulled Trenton aside. "Don't let anything happen to Simoni. Except for my family, I care about her more than anything. If something happened to her . . ." He bunched his fists at his side.

Trenton nodded. "I'll take care of her. I promise."

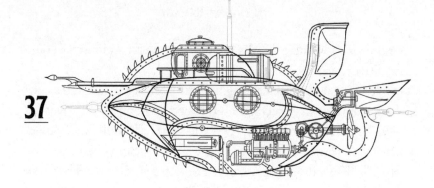

37

Lightning slashed the sky again and again, a silver-blue blade looking for a target to strike. Kallista didn't know if it was because of the storm or because of the alarm that had been triggered, but, for the moment at least, the sky was empty of dragons.

As Angus drove the quad slowly up one street and down another in the vicinity of the white tower, Kallista leaned over the side of the vehicle. "There's another one," she said, waving her hand.

Angus stopped the quad, grimacing up at the rain that was coming down so fast the streets looked like rivers. "You'd think that whoever invented a car on legs would have also considered putting a top on them."

"They probably have tops somewhere," Kallista said. "We just don't have time to look for them."

Plucky jumped out of the quad and hurried over to a metal plate set in the street. She studied the plate, then opened it and stuck her head into the dark hole. A few minutes later, she ran back to the quad and shook her head. "Keep going!"

Allie poked her head out of Plucky's jacket, hissed at the rain, and disappeared from view.

They didn't have time for this. It had taken much longer than she'd expected to use the eucalyptus oil on the Ninki Nankas. If they didn't find the right access port soon, Trenton and Simoni would blow the lab before Kallista and Plucky could seal the tower.

Clyde pushed his sopping hair out of his face, looking as unhappy as the cat. A second later, his bangs flopped back over his eyes. "Aren't all the access ports the same? They all have wires."

"Don't work that way, yeah, yeah," Plucky yelled over the storm. "Each dragon tower runs on its own circuit. That way if the power goes out, it don't affect them all. Found that out when I was doing some repairs on the other side of the city. Trig thinking, whoever done the designs."

They reached the end of the street, turned left, and started down the next block. Kallista looked toward the white tower, which was surrounded by dozens of guards standing at attention around the walls. For a moment she allowed herself to study the faces of the people going through the gate, then forced her attention back to the street.

"Stop," she called. "There's another one."

As Plucky hopped out to check the access port, Angus rubbed his hands together and blew on his fingers. "Not too late to call it off, you know."

"What are you taking about?" Kallista said without meeting his eyes.

"I've seen the way you've been watching the people going in and out of the tower. If it was my dad, I couldn't do it."

Kallista opened her mouth, shut it, and shook her head. Since when did Angus pay attention to anyone but Simoni—and himself, of course?

Angus clutched the controls, seemingly oblivious to the rain dripping down his face. "I didn't agree with what your dad did. Still don't. My father never liked the guy, but he didn't like most people. The thing is, you stuck up for him." He nodded his head. "If you think your dad is in the lab—and I can tell you do—let's leave this electronics stuff to Clyde and Plucky and figure out a way to get your old man out of there before it blows."

Kallista had never heard Angus talk like that before. Honestly, she didn't think he was capable of understanding the emotions of anyone else. But looking at his dark eyes watching her from under his bunched brows, she was sure he meant every word he was saying. He would risk his life to find a way to save her father.

She found it hard to speak for a moment, and she had to swallow to clear her throat of the ball that seemed lodged in it. "Thank you, but we can't take the risk. If we tried to reach the lab and failed, it would put everyone else in danger."

"You're just going to let him die?"

She pressed a hand against her chest, forcing her chin not to tremble. "I don't even know for sure if he is in the lab or the tower. Believe me, I want to make sure he is safe, but I also know I need to make sure everyone else in the city is safe, too. He'd want me to do whatever it takes to stop the monarch."

Plucky came running back to the quad and grabbed her tools. "I found it. Kallista, can you help me set everything up?"

Angus got out of the quad without looking at Kallista. The moment was gone. "I'm going keep a lookout for guards. Clyde, keep that hair out of your face and be ready to drive out of here if there's any trouble."

Clyde rubbed a hand over his face. "I've never driven a quad."

"It's just like driving your dragon," Angus said, starting down the street. "Only it doesn't have wings."

The crawl space under the street was extremely tight, but mostly dry and a little warmer than out in the rain. Plucky pushed a lantern past her head to give them more room to maneuver before unscrewing a metal pipe, exposing a cluster of wires.

"You're sure these go to the white tower?" Kallista asked.

Plucky tapped a code etched into the pipe. "It's this one, no doubt about it. Most buildings only have a central power connection. Lights and such aren't separated out until they reaches the fuse box, yeah, yeah? Only the dragon towers run individual lines to each device." She tapped a red wire. "This is for them stairs. Takes a lot of juice, don't it? White tower is the only one like it. This blue one here is for the windows."

Kallista ran a fingertip along the blue wire. "If we cut the power flow for a second, the windows either open or close. Cut it again and they reverse. But if we cut the power completely, the windows stay open or shut."

"Rum straight," Plucky said. "Figure they can force them open manually. Them dragons is strong, yeah, yeah."

"But by then it will be too late."

Allie squeezed out of Plucky's jacket, looked around, and meowed as if agreeing with the plan.

Plucky pulled a roll of wire from her tool belt. Working carefully, she stripped the insulation back from the blue wire. "This here's the tricky part."

Kallista held her breath as Plucky connected her wire to the circuit and added a cut switch. They couldn't turn off the power without alerting the dragons. One mistake with that much live voltage would fry them both. Allie watched intently, whiskers twitching.

When Plucky finally made the last connection and cut the main wire, they both froze, listening for any sign that things had gone wrong.

"How do things look at the tower?" she called up through the opening.

"Wet," Clyde called back.

"You're a regular dry boots, you is," Plucky said, wiping sweat from her forehead. "Makes me laugh so hard, me braces twist."

Clyde popped his head into the shaft, dripping water all over everything. "That's why you like me."

Kallista looked from Clyde to Plucky. *Did* she like him? How had she missed that?

Plucky blushed. "Is there any hubbub at the tower or ain't there?"

"Nothing more than usual."

Kallista checked her pocket watch: 4:45. Fifteen minutes to go. Trenton and Simoni should be under the lab by now. They reeled extra wire out and ducked under the quad where it wasn't as wet. From there they'd be able to keep an eye on the tower when they pushed the button.

A Ninki Nanka waddled out of the rain, moving down the street. It raised its dark-green nose to the air before heading in their direction.

Clyde backed away, holding his arm in front of Plucky. "You're sure that tree oil worked?"

"Of course," Kallista said, hoping it was true.

The Ninki Nanka stopped a few feet away, then tilted its head to the side. The dragon shouldn't smell anything it would have a problem with. Unless . . .

She turned to Plucky. "Where's Allie?"

Plucky touched her jacket, then looked from the Ninki Nanka to the electrical shaft. She pulled out from under Clyde's arm, crawled to the shaft opening, and slammed the cover shut.

The dragon studied the three of them, flicked the air with its tongue, and continued on its way.

That was *too* close.

A shout came from down the street, followed by a clang and a thud.

Kallista dashed out from under the quad as Angus jogged toward her. One of his jacket sleeves was torn, and a cut dripped blood above one eye.

"What was that?"

"Ran into one of the guards. He'll be fine in a couple of hours."

"Did he recognize you?" Kallista asked.

Angus wiped the cut with the back of his hand, rubbing it off on his pants. "Probably."

That was it, then. There was no turning back now. No matter what happened, they would be on the run.

"It's time," Plucky said.

Kallista checked the clock on the tower down the street. One minute until five.

She looked toward the white tower. She could just make out the white dragon staring through the upper level's open windows. Part of her wanted to push the button now, but there was no way to know exactly when the lab would blow, and she didn't want to take a chance on the dragon escaping.

She shut her eyes, trying to see her father's face. "If you are in there," she whispered quietly, "get out now."

Clock towers all over the city began to chime the hour, and Kallista opened her eyes.

"Push it."

Plucky pressed the button, and they all dropped to the street, waiting for the explosion that would rock the city.

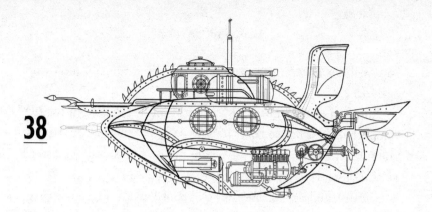

Trenton didn't think they were going to make it.

Things had gone wrong from the beginning. The cargo quads Simoni had hoped to use were under lock and key, so they had to improvise and hook up a heavy-duty trailer to a normal quad. But the quad wasn't built to pull a trailer, so they also had to rig a connection. Even then, the vehicle handled like a one-winged dragon, constantly pulling to the left.

In the warehouse, one of the jacks failed when they were moving the submarine onto the trailer, bending a fin. It took them thirty minutes to get the sub onto the trailer and another forty-five minutes to reach the water without being spotted by any guards. By the time they managed to get the sub into the ocean, and themselves into the sub, the rain and seawater that had come through the hatch was two-inches deep.

Then they launched the sub, and the real problems started.

Waves tossed them about like a giant playing with a toy. Compared to the power of the ocean, the submarine's propellers were about as useful as a pair of oars in a typhoon. Trenton had hoped to escape the turbulence by going deep underwater, but the current version of his periscope only extended six feet, so they couldn't dive much deeper than that.

This close to the surface, they were rocked about so hard that their heads slammed against the vessel's metal walls. It was impossible to keep a steady course, and Simoni was green with seasickness.

With no other choice, Trenton had to take them farther and deeper out to sea than he'd wanted. In the murky depths, the sub's headlamps did little to illuminate the occasional fish or strand of seaweed that floated past.

It was almost 4:30, and they still hadn't made it into the cave.

Studying the speed and compass, Trenton turned their course more to the east.

"Do you have any idea where we are?" Simoni asked.

He looked at the map and checked their speed again. According to the pitmeter log, a device that measured the rotations of the propeller, they should be close to the cliffs, but he had the feeling it wasn't working the way it was supposed to. It was one of the things he'd been hoping to test before taking the sub out for an actual voyage.

"Can you turn on the switch to your right?" he asked. "The one labeled *echo generator*."

Simoni flicked the switch, and immediately a *bloop* filled the submarine, followed a few seconds later by a slightly quieter *bleep*. "What is it?" she asked.

"Something else I haven't had a chance to test."

The *bloop* and *bleep* sounded again, and he tried to time them to see if they were any closer together. "I got the idea from a book about lighthouses. It said they sometimes had bells that rang underwater. Sailors attached horns to the underside of their ships to pick up the sound."

The *bloop, bleep* came again. This time he was almost positive it sounded closer.

"I send a noise out of the front of the sub. It bounces off anything in front of it, and the horns pick up the sound on the way back. I have no idea how well it works, but I'm hoping it will at least warn us when we get close to the cliffs."

For the next few minutes, they listened intently as the echoes sounded slightly closer each time. Soon they were going to have to surface to see where they were. The problem was, Plucky would lock the tower in fifteen minutes. They would have a short window of time after that to blow up the lab.

"Trenton," Simoni said quietly. "I know you don't want to hear this, but once we're inside the cave, I'm going into the lab with you."

"But—"

She cut him off. "Don't even try to argue."

Trenton recognized the look on her face. She had made her decision, and she wasn't going to change her mind. He'd promised Angus that he'd keep Simoni safe, but it was going to be hard when nothing they were doing could be considered *safe*. "We're nearing the cliffs," he said. "We have to surface."

Simoni was quiet for a moment, then she asked, "Are we doing the right thing?"

Trenton craned his neck to look back at her. Her face still looked greenish, but he couldn't tell if it was from the submarine lights or being sick. "Of course. The only way to free the people who have been brainwashed is to destroy the monarch and all of the white dragons. We have to do it, whatever the cost."

"I know." She shook her hair from her face. "I want to tell you something first. I understand that people look at me and see a pretty girl who gets her way by being sweet and agreeable." She gave him a small smile. "The thing is, I *am* that person. I learned early on that if I could make people smile, they'd give me what I wanted. And if things had stayed the way they were in Cove, I might never have changed. Then you showed me the dragon"—she paused—"and I betrayed you."

"You thought you were helping me," Trenton said. The echoes came again, much closer together this time. He started to bring the submarine up. "Check the underwater periscope and tell me as soon as you see anything."

Simoni raised the glass and put it to her eye, but she didn't stop talking. "I *did* think I was helping you, and instead I nearly killed us all. That's when I took a close look at myself. And I didn't like who I saw looking back."

"Let's talk about this later," he said.

The echoes were coming fast now.

She turned the glass left, then right. "The thing I've always admired about you and Kallista is that you don't accept things the way they are. You try to make them better. That's the reason I came on this trip."

Something dark appeared in the sub's lights.

"You never asked me what I do best," she said. "I didn't know myself, until now. But what I do best is—"

Whatever she was going to say was lost when she screamed, "Look out, Trenton! Look out!"

He pulled the submarine up sharply, expecting to see the cliff face. Instead, as he cleared the water, he saw the cave entrance a hundred yards ahead. They were on a perfect course.

Just then, a piercing howl came from outside the sub. The echo system went crazy. *Bloop, bleep, bloop, bleep, bloop—*

Something heavy crashed against the side of the sub, spinning them like a top.

"Back up!" Simoni shouted.

He shoved the sub into reverse when another crash came from the other side. A huge purple limb smashed across the viewports, and he turned to see a monster looking in the window. A birdlike beak punctured the side of the ship, ripping through the metal hull like a drill bit.

It was the dragon he'd seen in the lab—the one with wings that looked like fins. There were dragons that could swim?

A tentacle as thick as a tree smashed across the top of the submarine. Barbs gouged the metal, and the periscope was torn from Simoni's grip. She fell backward, blood gushing from her nose.

There was the sound of tearing metal, and the top of the submarine was gone. Trenton looked up in time to see lightning flash as water began to splash inside. He hit the button to empty the water of the ballast tank. That, and the buoyancy of the ship, might keep them floating for a while, but not long.

Fighting to turn the sub, he saw the cave nearby. If he could get inside, maybe they'd still have a chance before the monster ripped them to pieces.

He pushed the throttle full ahead; a crunching sound came from the propellers. Something hot sprayed over the top of the sub. The vessel pulled from the creature's grip and leaped forward.

A waved pushed them from behind, and they were racing toward the cave. It'd be a tight fit, but maybe they could make it.

They were nearly to the entrance when the water dragon gripped them in its tentacles. It heaved them in the air, and they flew sideways above the water. Metal crunched against rock, and Trenton felt himself falling. Icy darkness closed over him. It took him a moment to realize he was no longer in the submarine.

A wave smashed over him, and saltwater filled his mouth. He choked, coughing and spitting. Pain like fire raced up his ankle as he struggled to stay afloat.

Lights shined down on him from on top of the cliff, and he heard men's voices shouting. For a moment, he thought he saw dozens of purple eyes staring down at him, but that was impossible.

Where was Simoni? He looked for the sub, but saw only pieces of broken wood. The submarine was gone, and so was Simoni.

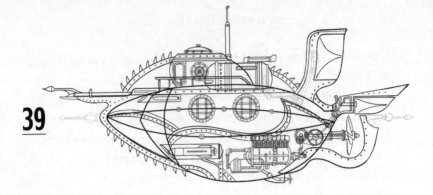

39

What was taking so long? Kallista checked the clock on the tower. It had only been a minute or two since they'd sealed the tower, but it felt much longer. Lights flashed both inside and outside the tower wall. She could hear people shouting but couldn't make out what they were saying.

A roar shook the tower, and a blast of violet light ripped a hole in the door on the top level. The metal bulged outward, and, a second later, the door exploded in a flower of molten steel.

Plucky scratched her head. "That didn't work out so well, yeah, yeah?"

Alarms began to blare across the city. Had Trenton and Simoni been caught? Were they still in the lab? Had the submarine sunk?

Angus jumped into the quad. "Something's happened. We have to get to the tower."

"We can't," Kallista said.

The shutters on the dragon towers were opening across the city, dark shapes soaring in the direction of the white tower. The monarch flew out of the destroyed door, which still glowed orange from the heat of the blast. It flew to the top of the tower, spread its massive wings, and roared.

A blast of purple energy so bright it seemed to illuminate the entire city shot out of its jaws. Lightning crackled out of the clouds, striking a building a mile to their left. Immediately the building burst into flames.

Kallista backed away. Had they really thought they could defeat this dragon?

A quad filled with guards rumbled through the intersection to their right, and Kallista and the others ducked down. As the vehicle raced past, one of the men turned in their direction, and his eyes glowed purple in the darkness.

Clyde gasped. "What was that?"

"Nuts," Plucky whispered. "His eyes looked like someone lit a purple fire in his head, didn't they? Gives me the shivers."

Kallista turned to her three friends. "We have to go to the meeting place."

"Are you kidding?" Angus shouted over the wailing sirens. "Simoni is in trouble. I'm going to help her." He started the quad, but Kallista grabbed his arm.

"How are you going to help her when you don't even know where she is? For all we know, they could be heading to the meeting place right now. We have to stick to the plan."

"She's right," Clyde said. "I want to help them as much as you do, but first we should go to the docks and see if they're there."

Angus jerked his arm away. "All right. But if they hurt her, I swear I'll go into the white tower and—"

A quad came rattling around the corner, and Kallista dove into the seat behind Angus. "Go!" she yelled.

Plucky grabbed the back of the quad and flipped herself into the seat next to Kallista.

Angus gunned the engine as Clyde scrambled to get in. Angus reached out and yanked him into the front seat.

Clyde sighed. "Thanks."

"Just don't fall out," Angus barked.

Slashing rain pelted them, and the quad's metal feet slipped on the wet stones as Angus took a sharp right and an immediate left.

Plucky looked behind them. "Them dirty hog-grubbers is still behind us."

As they came to an intersection, another quad full of guards turned the corner in front of them, and Angus had to go up on the sidewalk to get past.

The guards turned to give chase, and they were so close that Kallista could see the blank expressions on their faces, lit by the purple glow of their eyes.

The purple glint was the same color as the white dragon's eyes. Did that mean it was controlling their minds more directly? Could the monarch see what the guards were seeing? She hoped not or they were doomed.

"Which way?" Angus yelled as they came to a fork.

Gripping the edge of the quad as though his life depended on it—which it probably did—Clyde rose out of his seat. "That way," he shouted, pointing to the left.

Angus turned sharply, grabbing Clyde's arm and pulling him back into his seat.

"They're getting closer," Plucky yelled.

Kallista looked back. The other quads seemed to be more powerful than what they were driving, with extra feet that had better traction on the wet ground.

Angus cursed, and Kallista turned to see a pair of quads blocking the entire street in front of them. There were no side streets and, with two quads behind them, no way to turn back.

At the last second, Angus cut to the right. "Hold on," he shouted as they flew over the edge of a set of concrete stairs. The quad's legs bounded and chattered, unable to get a grip on the uneven surface. They started to flip to the right, and Angus steered into the slide. "Not this time," he muttered.

One of the quads behind them lost control and rolled down the side of a hill, throwing the guards into the air.

At the bottom of the stairs, Angus hit the brakes, and they slammed onto the street so hard that sparks shot from the vehicle's metal feet.

Kallista looked back, hoping the second set of guards had given up, but they were closer than ever. They had to lose the guards before they reached the water.

She reached into her pocket and pulled out one of three smoke bombs she had left. She didn't have a punk to light it, so she climbed back toward the engine and opened the hatch. The flames from the steam engine were just out of reach. She stood on her tiptoes and leaned over as far as she could.

"Hold my legs!" she yelled. Kallista felt Plucky's hands close around her ankles, and she stretched out her arm until the wick of the clay ball touched the flames. The wick hissed, and Kallista handed it back to Plucky.

One of Plucky's hands let go of Kallista's ankle as she took the bomb. A moment later Plucky yelled, "Rust and oil, I missed."

Kallista grabbed the second smoke bomb and lit it.

Plucky took the ball from her hands. A moment passed, then she heard Clyde call, "Good try."

Angus took a turn too fast, and Kallista slammed against the side of the engine compartment. Pain flashed along her arm, and she jerked back from the hot manifold.

"One more try." Holding her breath, she lit the last bomb and handed it to Plucky.

"You can do it!" Clyde yelled.

Kallista wiggled out of the compartment in time to see

Plucky's arm sling forward. The last smoke bomb flew through the air. For a moment, it looked like it was on track to land directly in the guards' laps. Then their vehicle jagged to the left, and the bomb hit the front of the quad. It bounced in the air, spun, hit one of the soldiers in the head, and then dropped inside the car. A cloud of smoke billowed out, and the driver looked down as though trying to find the bomb. As he did, the road veered to the left.

Angus yanked at the controls, barely managing to stay on the road. The guards weren't so lucky. By the time the driver looked up, it was too late to make the turn. There was a shriek of metal on stone, and the quad disappeared. A second later there was loud crash.

"I think that's the last of them," Plucky said.

Angus pulled to the side of the road and wiped his arm across his face. "Now what? I'm completely lost."

"Wait here," Clyde said. He hopped out of the quad and shimmied up a nearby tree with more agility than Kallista expected. He stopped about fifteen feet up and looked around. "There," he called, pointing down and to the right. "I see the rock where we're supposed to meet."

Once he was back in the car, Angus drove the quad quietly down to the shore, keeping one eye up for dragons and one down for guards. At least they didn't have to worry about the Ninki Nankas they passed. The eucalyptus trick was working perfectly.

When they reached the rock, Kallista scanned the beach, hoping Trenton and Simoni were there. But the shore was empty.

Angus leaped out of the quad and ran down into the water until his legs were wet to the knees. He scanned the dark ocean. The wind and rain had finally stopped, and the waves were calm, but there was no sign of the submarine.

He pounded his fists against his thighs. "They aren't here. I told you we should have gone to the tower."

"And died there?" Kallista asked. "How would that have helped Trenton or Simoni?"

"Give them time," Clyde said. "I'm sure they're on their way."

Kallista wasn't so sure. With every minute that slipped past, she became more convinced that something terrible had happened. Some locked windows in the white tower wouldn't generate this kind of response from the guards and the dragons, would it?

For all anyone knew, the storm might have caused the malfunction. But the white dragon hadn't acted as if it was an electrical short, and the guards were obviously searching for someone.

Yet the laboratory hadn't exploded, which left only two possibilities. Either the plan to blow up the generator hadn't worked the way she'd thought it would or the submarine had failed to reach the lab. Trenton and Simoni were dead or captured.

Maybe Angus was right and they should be headed toward the white tower. Right this minute the dragons could be torturing Trenton to get information out of him.

Angus marched back and forth, his feet splashing water with each stomp. "We're wasting time."

"Stick with the plan," she whispered to herself. Then she said it louder for everyone to hear. "Stick with the plan."

Kallista searched the water for any sign of movement, listening for the rumble of the submarine's engine, but there was nothing except the crash of waves and the constant howling of the alarms.

As the minutes crept by, a sense of dread sank deeper and

deeper into her bones. Without warning, the sirens shut off. The silence was almost worse.

Angus continued pacing, smacking his fists against his thighs and muttering to himself until at last he spun around. "You three can stay here. I'm not."

"Where are you going?" Clyde asked. "We need to stick together."

Angus glanced out at the dark ocean. "Simoni is out there somewhere. We're not going to find her standing on the shore." He looked toward the docks. "I'm getting us some transportation."

They'd seen several boats leave the harbor since they arrived, but now, with most of the guards following the white dragon's command, the docks were nearly deserted.

"I'll helps you," Plucky said. "Time to fleece the coup, yeah, yeah."

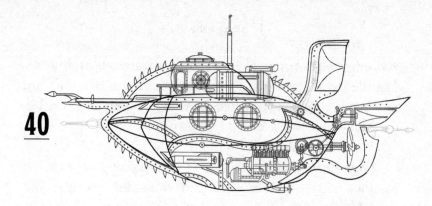

40

Trenton looked desperately around in the darkness as waves tossed him left and right. He'd never had any reason to learn how to swim in Discovery, and despite his thrashing, he kept slipping under the surface, sucking in mouthfuls of saltwater.

A piece of wood from the hull of the submarine slammed against him, and he instinctively reached out to grab it. Clinging to it like a raft, he paddled around the opening of the cave. On top of the cliffs, spotlights panned left and right across the ocean. As one of them passed by, he caught a glimpse of red hair floating on the water.

"Simoni," he called, paddling toward her.

The hair disappeared under the waves, and Trenton released the plank, kicking with his feet and pulling with his hands to propel himself forward. It was too dark to see anything under the water, and he waved his hands, feeling blindly before him. He touched Simoni's arm, but she slipped away from him. He grabbed again, closing his fingers around her wrist.

He kicked to the surface, and a wave threw him toward the shore. Before he could come up for breath, a second wave hit him. His lungs burned, but he refused to let go of Simoni's wrist. A third wave smashed into him, and he thought he was going to drown when his feet suddenly touched ground.

Gasping for air, he pulled Simoni toward him. Her body

was limp, her arms and legs flopping about with each wave. Lightning flashed overhead, revealing her white face. Trenton touched her cheek. Even against his freezing fingers, her skin felt cold.

She wasn't breathing.

Pressing his mouth to her icy lips, he blew air into her lungs. Nothing. He tried again, and again, and again. "Breathe," he whispered.

He'd promised Angus he would take care of her. He'd promised his friends he'd blow up the lab. He'd promised the Runt Patrol he'd get them out of the city. All of those promises—broken. Every plan he'd made had been a failure. He'd pretended to be a leader, but it was all a lie.

Still, he couldn't let Simoni die.

"Breathe!" he shouted through chattering teeth. Pressing his mouth to hers, he blew with all his strength. Her chest rose, lowered, and rose again. This time on its own. She was breathing! He turned her head to the side, and water gushed out of her mouth.

"Simoni, can you hear me?"

Her eyes fluttered open, then shut again.

Propping her against a boulder, he rubbed her hands and arms, trying to warm her.

"Wake up."

Her eyes fluttered again. "Tired."

She was alive. He couldn't believe it. His body shivered until he felt like he would rattle to pieces.

He shook her gently. "It's me. Simoni. Please wake up."

Her eyes opened all the way, and her gaze met his. "Trenton?"

"Oh, thank goodness." He wrapped her arms around her. "I thought you were—"

"Where are we?" She tried to sit up on her own and moaned. She touched her nose and winced. A line of red trickled down her face, and a second cut ran along her hairline. "I think I hit my face on something right before—"

"Who's down there?" a voice shouted.

Trenton turned to see men with lights using ropes to climb down the side of the cliff. A beam of light flashed toward them, and Trenton pulled Simoni behind the boulder.

"We have to get out of here." He tried to stand, but his leg gave out under him. A bolt of pain shot from his ankle to his thigh.

"You're hurt," Simoni said.

He ran his hand down from his calf. "I don't think it's broken."

But even if he could walk, Simoni was barely strong enough to sit up by herself. There was no way he could carry her. And where would they go? The shallow water went all the way to the edge of the cliffs. They couldn't climb up, and the men coming down would be there any minute.

He heard a thunk against the rocks next to him, and a wide plank of wood from the submarine washed ashore. He glanced out to sea. Ships were already on their way around the point. They'd arrive soon after the men on the cliffs did. There was no way he and Simoni could remain out of sight for much longer.

They were trapped.

He pulled the plank toward them. "Help me get you onto this."

Simoni's eyes opened wide with fear.

"I'll hold on to you. We aren't going out any deeper than I can stand. But if we stay here, the guards are going to catch us."

With Simoni's help, Trenton got her up onto the plank. Holding on to the wood and putting most of his weight on his good leg, he was able to wade out to sea until the water came up to his chest. It took him a moment to get his bearings, but once he figured out where they were, he knew the meeting place was somewhere to the northeast.

Could he get the two of them that far? How long would it take? Would the others wait for them or would they assume he and Simoni had been captured? And what about the water dragons? Where there was one, there had to be more. All he could do was head in the right direction and hope for the best.

Glancing over his shoulder, he saw the guards at the water's edge. He hoped they'd see the wreckage of the submarine and assume there were no survivors. Several boats were nearby, but the water was too shallow to let them get close. Their searchlights swung back and forth, but if he stayed in the dark, he didn't think they could see him.

Clinging to the wood, Simoni shivered. The water was cold, but it felt almost warm compared to the night air. "I wish I had something to keep you warm," Trenton said. "I lost my jacket when we crashed.

"I guess we didn't b-blow up the lab," Simoni said.

Trenton nodded. "The plan was a failure."

"We t-tried our b-best. There was n-nothing more we could have done."

"I feel like I should have done more," Trenton said.

"It's o-okay," Simoni said, her teeth chattering. "Just talk to me so I have something to think about."

"All right." Trenton tried to think of something to say, but the only things he could think about were how cold it was, how much he hurt, and that every guard in the city was probably searching for them right now. None of those seemed like good topics of conversation.

What came out of his mouth was not what he'd been

expecting. "I guess you like Angus." As soon as he'd said the words, he wished he could take them back.

Simoni tilted her head, her teeth flashing as she smiled. "I guess you like Kallista."

"Sure," Trenton said. "But not that way."

Simoni gingerly touched the cut on her head. She winced and took her hand away. "What way *do* you like her?"

"I mean, we're friends."

"*Good* friends?" Simoni's eyes flashed.

Trenton was glad for the darkness. "I guess."

"So, do you like her as much as . . . cheese?"

"What kind of question is that?" Trenton said.

Simoni laughed. "I'll take that as a yes. Do you like her as much as ice cream?"

Trenton wrinkled his nose. "Stop talking about food. You're making me hungry."

"How about machines? Do you like her as much as you like working on machines?"

Trenton felt like they were getting into dangerous territory. "Yeah, I guess so."

Simoni shifted on the board to face him. "If you had to ch-choose between being with Kallista but it meant n-never working on machines again, you'd p-pick her?"

"Why are we even talking about this?" Trenton said. How did girls manage to twist your words so easily?

Simoni laughed again. "You brought it up."

"I didn't say anything about Kallista. I asked you if you like Angus." Trenton didn't want to talk about who liked who, but if it would keep the conversation away from Kallista, he was willing to push through. "It's just that you're nice almost all the time. And he's such a . . ."

"A jerk?" Simoni asked. Her expression turned serious. "I don't think people understand Angus the way I do."

The rain had finally stopped, and although the night was still cool, it wasn't so bad without the wind blowing.

"It's hard to understand someone when they're punching you," Trenton said. "Trust me—I've had years of experience."

"I know," Simoni said, looking up at the sky where the clouds were clearing away, revealing a galaxy of sparkling stars. "He can be a jerk. And a bully. But I think it's because he doesn't really understand who he is."

"Yeah, he's dumb too," Trenton said.

Simoni glared at him. "That's not what I mean. As weird as it sounds, Angus spends most of his time thinking about who he can protect—his family, his city, his father's reputation."

"And you. He wants to protect you," Trenton said.

"I think he'd give his life for me," Simoni said softly.

"I think so too," Trenton said.

Simoni nodded. "But what you probably don't know is that he'd give his life for you too. For anyone in our group. He fights hard, he talks hard, and he flies hard because he believes it's the only way to protect the people he loves."

It was all Trenton could do to keep from shaking his head. If she really thought that Angus loved him, she was totally wrong.

Caught up in the conversation, Trenton didn't see the small boat until it was almost on top of them. "Get down," he whispered, uselessly looking for a place to hide.

"Simoni, is that you?"

"Angus?" Simoni sat up, nearly overturning the plank.

The boat floated closer, and Trenton made out four shapes in the darkness.

Angus leaped out of the boat before it had reached them,

plunging waist-deep into the water. "What happened? Are you all right?"

He charged through the water, lifted Simoni from the plank, and held her close in his arms. Then he saw the blood on her face. "What did they do to you?" He glared at Trenton. "You let her get hurt."

"I'm fine," Simoni said. "A sea dragon attacked the submarine, but we're okay."

Trenton waded to the boat as Kallista and Clyde pulled it toward them. He licked his lips. They tasted salty. "We didn't blow up the lab. We were almost to the cave, but we couldn't see where we were going and then a dragon came out of the water and—"

"It's okay," Kallista said. "I'm just glad the two of you are all right. When we didn't see you at the meeting place, we thought you'd been captured—or worse."

"Just a twisted ankle," Trenton said, keeping his weight on his uninjured leg.

"What now?" Clyde asked.

Trenton looked at Kallista. He wanted to be a leader. He wanted to tell everyone he had a new plan that was even better. But he wasn't a great leader, and he didn't have any more plans. He looked at the boat, not even bothering to ask where it came from. Maybe with all the commotion they could make it to Alcatraz. They definitely couldn't go back to the city

"I guess we try to make it to the island, find our dragons, and leave. It's over."

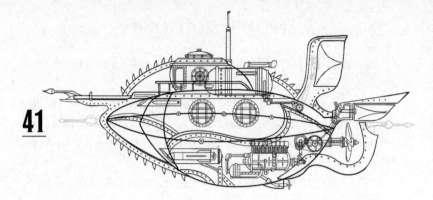

41

The sky was beginning to turn the purplish-pink of dawn when Kallista pulled the boat up to the edge of the island. Nobody spoke. As Clyde and Angus helped Trenton onto shore, he glanced back at the mainland that looked far too close for comfort. There had to be twenty or thirty dragons flying overhead.

"We have to sink the boat," Trenton said. "They probably already know where we are, but it might buy us a few extra minutes."

"What if we need it?" Clyde asked.

"We won't," Kallista said. "We won't be coming back—here or anywhere else near here."

Trenton dropped his head. The truth was sinking in for all of them. They'd failed. Not only was the monarch unharmed, but the lab was still completely functional. Every dragon in the city would be hunting for them now, and going back would only put themselves and their friends on the Runt Patrol in danger.

Clyde found Trenton a stick to use as a cane, and they watched as Angus smashed a sharp rock against the boat until the wood cracked and water began to seep through the hull. Kallista and Simoni pushed the boat deeper into the water. It floated out into the bay, sinking lower and lower until, eventually, it slipped from sight. Trenton thought it was a fitting metaphor for everything they'd tried to do. They'd tried their best, and they had failed.

He didn't realize he was crying until Kallista wiped a tear from his face. "If I hadn't been so stubborn, maybe—"

"No." He shook his head violently. "You aren't going to take the blame for this. None of you are. This is my fault."

Tears leaked from his eyes, and he didn't try to stop them. The only one who wasn't crying was Angus. He stuck out his chin like it was a pickax and he need to break through a vein of coal.

Plucky pushed Allie into Trenton's hands. "Holding something warm and fuzzy is good when yer feeling blue, yeah, yeah."

Trenton tried to say no, but there was something about the soft kitten that made him want to hug it to his chest.

As the six of them hiked slowly to the crumbling garrison, Angus dropped back to walk by Trenton.

"Something you want?" Trenton asked, wondering if Angus was going to slug him for letting Simoni get hurt.

Angus cleared his throat before saying in a soft voice, "We've never gotten along very well."

"You think?" Trenton asked. Angus had terrorized him every year of school. Violence was supposed to be against the law in Cove, but Angus had managed to "accidentally" trip him, hit him, or knock Trenton's lunch out of his hands at least twice a week. It only got worse around fifth grade, when the two of them started competing for Simoni's attention.

Angus shoved his hands in his pockets, looking down at his feet. "You probably don't believe me, but I'm sorry about all the stuff I did."

"You're right," Trenton said. "I don't believe you."

Red creeped up Angus's neck, but it wasn't from anger. "Believe me or don't, but I *am* sorry. I know I'm a bully," Angus said, "but that's kind of the way I was raised. I'm not saying that as an excuse, just that maybe it's part of the reason I did all those things to you."

Trenton looked at him out of the corner of his eye. "Go on."

Angus waved his hand. "What I want to say is that I really appreciate what you did for Simoni last night."

Trenton nodded. "Okay."

Angus cleared his throat, struggling to find the right words. "The thing is, you really stepped up. I'm not much for the whole leader thing, and I know I've given you a lot of trouble on this trip, but I owe you. If you ever need anything from me, anything at all, say the word and I'll drop whatever I'm doing." Angus stuck out his hand. "I promise."

Trenton stared at the outstretched hand in wonder for a minute before gripping it. "You don't owe me anything. I didn't help Simoni because of you. I did it because it was right."

Angus grunted. "Yeah. You always do the right thing." He paused for a moment, then added so quietly Trenton almost couldn't hear it, "Sometimes I wish I was more like that." He gave him a quick nod of his head, then hurried to the front of the group to walk by Simoni.

Trenton hobbled up to walk beside Clyde.

"What was that all about?" Clyde whispered.

"I'm not sure," Trenton said. "I wonder if maybe Angus is actually human after all."

Clyde considered it for a minute, then grinned. "Who would have thought?" He wiped his nose with the back of his hand and asked, "Where will we go from here?"

Trenton sighed. "Back to Discovery, I guess. Regroup. Tell everyone about what is happening here. Hope the white dragon doesn't find us, but prepare a defense just in case it does."

Flying out of Discovery for the first time, Trenton had felt like the world was his. They could go anywhere they wanted, explore anything that seemed interesting. But they weren't exploring anymore. They were running.

He saw Clyde take Plucky's hand as they walked. It made him smile. Maybe something good had come from this disaster.

Trenton moved over to walk by Simoni. Angus had gone ahead to help Kallista clear a path for the others. "Can I ask you something? When we were in the submarine, before the dragon attacked, you were going to tell me what you were best at."

Her hair was plastered to her head from the seawater, her nose was swollen—he was pretty sure it was broken—and her eyes were pink around the edges, but when she smiled, he thought she had never looked more beautiful.

She started to flip back her hair with one hand, realized it was stuck in clumps, and lowered her hand to her side. "It doesn't matter now."

"It does to me," he said.

She wiped her nose, winced, and stuck her hands in her pockets. "I thought—well, I thought maybe I was best at seeing things clearly. I can look at a situation and know what needs to be done. I've always been good at strategy, but I mostly used it back in school to get good grades and make boys like me."

Her face pinked, but she kept going. "Out here, though, I realized I was good at battle plans. I figured out ways to work through the bureaucracy of the city to get what we needed. I always told myself one day I'd see something that needed to be done—something really and truly important—and when that moment came, I wouldn't hesitate to do the right thing. I guess it's too late for that now."

They walked into the building, and for a moment Trenton thought the figures moving in the darkness were guards. Then he realized how small they were. It was Alex and the other members of the Runt Patrol.

"Leaving without saying good-bye?" Alex asked.

Trenton raised his hands. "It's not like that. After the initiation, we followed Kallista's father and discovered a lab . . . Wait, how did you get here?"

"You're not the only ones who can steal a boat," Michael said. "Especially during the kind of confusion that happens when some fools try to seal the monarch in his own tower."

"Where's the submarine?" JoeBob asked.

Trenton couldn't meet his eyes. "Destroyed by an underwater dragon." He shook his head. "I'm really sorry. I ruined everything."

Alex folded his arms across his chest. "What's this about a lab?"

"It's hidden under the white tower," Trenton said. "The only people who go in and out are scientists." Together, he and Kallista explained what they'd discovered about the origin of the dragons, the jewel wasp DNA, and the white dragon's power. The longer they talked, the more amazed Alex and the other members of the Runt Patrol grew.

"The monarch's been controlling our parents' minds the whole time?" Hallie whispered. "It's not that they *want* to serve the dragons. They don't have any choice."

Michael rubbed his temples as if trying to work out a bad headache. "That's why I've felt so strange lately. I'm getting older, so the white dragon is gaining control of my mind. If I stay here much longer, I'll end up a mindless slave like the rest of them."

"But you don't have to," Kallista said. "You can escape. Take your boat and sail north. You'd have a good chance of getting away without anyone seeing you."

"Is that what you're doing?" Alex asked. *"Escaping?"*

"We're *regrouping*," he said, but his voice lacked conviction, and he heard the lie in his words along with everyone else. They weren't strong enough to fight against the monarch and the rest of the dragons in San Francisco. When they left, they wouldn't be coming back.

Alex ran his fingers through his dark hair. "So you're going to abandon us—us and our families. We'll be slaves to the monarch. With all the new white dragons in the lab, it will probably have more control over us than ever."

Trenton clenched his teeth. "What other choice do we have? You should get away too. All of you. Save yourselves while you can."

Angus, who had been following the conversation with an intense concentration, stood up. "No."

"No, what?" Trenton asked.

Angus folded his arms across his broad chest. His hair was a mess. He had cuts and bruises on his arms and face, but he stood staring straight ahead as if dragons would fly around him, as if mountains would move rather than stand in his way. "No, I'm not going with you."

"What do you mean?" Simoni asked. "You can't stay here."

Angus clenched his jaw. "I can't run away. I just can't."

"It's not running away," Trenton said. "We tried and we failed. There's nothing else we can do."

Angus inhaled until it looked as if his chest might burst. When he spoke, it was in a tone of voice Trenton had never heard him use before—as if he'd been holding something inside him for a hundred years and it had finally broken loose.

He held Trenton's gaze. "I've never been as smart as you or Simoni. I wasn't ever going to be a mechanic. I would have been terrible at growing things. I probably would have managed to mess up working in the mines, and that's just digging in the ground. The only thing I've ever been good at is fighting." He stuck out his chin. "And if fighting the dragons means I can protect the people I care about, then that's what I am going to do."

"We fought the dragons," Trenton said. "And we lost."

"No," Angus said. "We haven't lost. Not yet. Not while we still have our dragons, and each other." He turned to Simoni and shrugged his broad shoulders. "I'm sorry. I guess I'm not done fighting for you yet."

Simoni squeezed Angus's hand and smiled at him. "I'll go with you."

Kallista ran her fingers through her hair. "My father is still in the city."

Plucky scuffed a toe across the floor. "I wouldn't mind having a go at them rusty buzzards again if I thought we had a chance."

"But we don't," Clyde said. "We'd be outnumbered at least a hundred to one, maybe two hundred. And that's not even counting the white dragon."

Trenton looked from one person to another. "How many of you want to go back and fight?"

Simoni and Angus raised their hands.

"Who wants to leave?"

Clyde and Plucky raised their hands.

Trenton turned to Kallista. "What about you?"

She thought for a moment before moving to stand with Angus and Simoni. "I can't leave my father alone."

Three to fight, two to leave.

"What do *you* want to do?" Simoni asked.

Trenton started to speak, then stopped. There *was* no good answer. Clyde was right. Fighting the dragons would be beyond difficult, but it would be totally impossible if only part of the group was fighting. They'd been lucky to escape the first time they flew into the city; they wouldn't make it out a second time.

On the other hand, what Angus said made sense. There was a time when you had to do the right thing even if you didn't think there was much chance of success. He glanced toward Alex.

"I can't tell *you* what to do," Alex said. "But we aren't deserting our families."

"Right," JoeBob added.

Hallie lifted her hands. "If there's anything we can do to help you . . ."

The Runt Patrol had helped him every time he asked. Could he really abandon them now?

"What if we *did* have a plan?" he asked. "Some way to trick the dragons or strike an important blow?"

"I'm listening," Clyde said.

"What kind of contrivance you got in mind?" Plucky asked.

Trenton didn't actually *have* a plan. Every angle he considered seemed doomed to fail. It all came down to the white dragon. If they could stop it, free the minds of the adults in the city, then the people would have the free will to make their own choices. Maybe one of them could even get into the lab and destroy the other white dragons before they grew any larger.

But how did you kill something that strong? He thought back to everything he'd seen in the lab. How the scientists had created the white dragon in the first place. Was there some weakness, some flaw, he could exploit?

He'd always thought he was creative—maybe even an inventor—but now that he needed to invent a plan that would make a difference, he couldn't come up with a thing.

He looked out one of the windows at the gray morning fog that engulfed the island, and something clicked in his brain. What looked like fog but wasn't? And why did thinking about fog make him think of Clyde? A hint of an idea danced at the edges of his brain. Something to do with the white dragon's DNA and a comment Simoni had made about—

His mouth dropped open, and all the pieces snapped together into a single, crazy, ingenious, idiotic, amazing plan.

He drew everyone to him. "Okay, people, listen up."

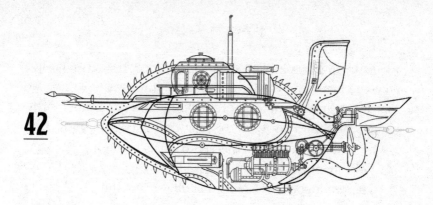

42

Kallista nearly screamed when Trenton told her what he needed. "It's impossible. It took me two weeks to put the first turbo in Ladon. Now you want me to build two—in a *day?*"

"We don't have a day," Trenton said. "I'd say we have maybe three hours—four, tops—before the fog burns off. Once it does, the dragons, the guards, everyone will know where we are."

"*Three* hours?" Kallista gritted her teeth. "I'm a mechanic, not a . . . a whatever it is that could build and install two turbochargers in three hours."

"They don't have to be perfect," Trenton said. "They just need to work once."

"Maybe if we was to—" Plucky began, but Kallista shook her head.

"I'd need at least *ten* trained mechanics to even have a chance."

"I've got nine who are ready to help," Alex said. He rolled up his sleeves and patted his tool belt. "Tell us what you need."

Kallista blew her hair out of her face and shook her head. She pointed her finger at Trenton. "You're crazy."

He grinned at her.

Kallista and Plucky put the Runt Patrol to work immediately, scavenging parts and gathering tools. The sound of hammering and clanging filled the warehouse as Kallista supervised what was going to be a slapdash job that only had a twenty-five percent chance of working. It was difficult to get more than two mechanics inside one of the dragons at the same time; fortunately, the Runt Patrol was used to working in tight spaces.

Simoni, Clyde, and Angus approached Trenton.

"What can we do?" Simoni asked.

Trenton limped outside the building where the sound wasn't as deafening. "Simoni, you're the best strategist in the group. I have the start of a plan, but I need you to refine it. Angus, we'll be lucky to get one shot at the monarch. I want you to take it."

They both nodded.

"What about me?" Clyde asked.

Trenton gripped his friend's arm. "This plan is going to be a long shot at best. Your artistic skills would give it a better chance, but I don't want to pressure you into doing something you don't think you can handle."

"I told you before," Clyde said. "I won't let anyone take what I love away from me. I think my paints are still in Rounder."

Trenton knelt in the dirt and began to draw. It reminded him of the night before they'd discovered the city. He'd drawn his plans in the dirt that time as well, trying to convince Angus his idea was best.

Only this time he wasn't trying to convince anyone of anything. Instead, he showed them what he was thinking and asked for their opinions. This time, instead of leaning against a tree chewing a pine needle, Angus paid close attention.

As Trenton revealed his idea, Simoni's eyes grew wide. "That's brilliant!"

"I have you to thank for it," Trenton said.

Simoni laughed. "I had no idea you'd use it like this, though." She nodded to what Trenton had drawn. "May I?"

"Of course," Trenton said, leaning back.

Simoni erased one of his lines and moved another. "I think if we come in like this, we'll have the best chance of arriving unseen. Once the other dragons realize what we're up to, we'll need a distraction."

"Plucky and I can take care of that," Clyde said.

Angus studied what Simoni had drawn. "We'll need to shoot from here?"

"Yes," Simoni said. "We have to give the white dragon everything we've got the first time."

Angus cracked his knuckles. "I won't miss."

As Angus and Clyde left to prepare for their parts, Simoni smiled at Trenton. "I knew you were the right one to lead us."

"But I'm a terrible leader," Trenton said. "Everything I've tried has failed."

Simoni shook her head. "History doesn't judge leaders on how many times they fall. It judges them on how many times they get up."

• • •

By the time they were ready to leave, the fog was beginning to thin to the west. Another thirty minutes and it would be impossible to approach the white tower unseen.

Everyone was gathered outside the building. Alex and the rest of the Runt Patrol looked exhausted but proud. Trenton buckled himself into his seat on Ladon's back and glanced at his friends already aboard Devastation and Rounder. "Everyone ready?"

"Ready!" the other five called. He barely recognized them. They'd already been beaten up from the night before, but now, with Clyde's assistance, they looked like they'd gone through a meat grinder. Every face had at least one black eye or split lip, and blood dripped from ears and noses. Even the flight jackets and helmets that hadn't taken damage looked burned, torn, and battered.

The mechanical dragons weren't any better. Although they were in perfect flying condition, each had been camouflaged to look like it had taken heavy damage. Trenton knew it was fake, and he still felt nervous taking the machines in the air.

"Good luck," Alex called from where he stood with the other kids.

Graysen raised a fist in the air, and Lizzy shouted, "Before you shoot the monarch, look it in the eye and tell him 'This one's for the Runt Patrol.'"

"Will do," Angus promised.

"You guys better get going before the fog completely clears," Trenton said.

"And miss the fight?" JoeBob shook his head. He pointed to the lighthouse. "We'll be up there watching every minute of the action."

"But if this plan fails, the dragons are going to come straight here. The white dragon could start controlling Alex and Michael any day."

"Then don't fail," Alex said.

Kallista glanced up at the sky. "We need to leave."

"Right." Trenton put his hands to his mouth and called, "On my count—three, two, one."

In single file, the three mechanical dragons raced across the ground and lifted off from Alcatraz Island.

Clyde, wispy hair blowing back from his forehead. Plucky, black hair glistening, shoulders firm—telling the world there wasn't a wall she couldn't scale, a lock she couldn't pick.

Simoni followed close behind, racing Devastation toward the shore until it seemed she and Angus would surely crash into the ocean. Devastation's wings lifted at the last second, and the dragon's metal talons skimmed the water, sending a spray of blue and green into the air.

In the backseat of Devastation, Angus looked like he was heading to a day at the beach. He reached out to catch a handful of Simoni's hair, and his sun-roughed cheeks pulled into a grin as she turned around and laughed with him. He yanked back on the flight stick, and the two of them spiraled high into the air.

Last in the group were Trenton and Kallista. They weren't flashy. They didn't do any tricks. They operated Ladon as only a pair who has spent many hours together could. Two people and one metal dragon functioning as a single, perfectly coordinated whole.

Watching his five friends, the sun glinting off the golden skin of their three dragons, Trenton wondered if this was the last time they would fly together.

He leaned forward and asked Kallista, "Back in Seattle, you told me that sometimes you had to give yourself permission to fail. Is this what you were talking about?"

Kallista smiled back at him, her face a mixture of real bruises and fake. "Flying off on a mission none of us thinks we can complete with equipment that probably doesn't work and is completely untested before fighting hundreds of dragons led by a creature that for all we know is invincible? Yeah, I think this qualifies."

"Just checking," Trenton said.

As they flew into the mist, Devastation took the lead, Ladon dropped behind them, and Rounder took up the rear.

"Stay tight," Simoni called. "We can't afford to lose each other in the fog."

Staying as close to the edge of the fog as they dared, the pilots flew their dragons across the bay, listening for the sound of the crashing waves to guide them along the edge of the cliff. After a few minutes, Simoni called back, "I think we're close."

"Let's find out," Trenton shouted. "Remember to make it look real."

One by one, they flew out of the fog. As soon as they appeared, the first alarms sounded. Guards along the edge of the water shouted to one another. Telescopes reflected sunlight as they turned to track the mechanical dragons. Shutters on the towers began swiveling open, and dragons raced out, heading in their direction.

Trenton cut back the power to his engine and angled Ladon's wings to make it look like he was barely able to stay in the air. They needed to buy a couple of minutes to pull off the plan. He hoped it would work.

The monarch looked out from the top of the white tower, and Trenton and Kallista flew toward him making awkward dives and swoops. Although he didn't look back at the others, Trenton knew his friends were doing the same.

He raised his hands and shouted toward the white tower. "Don't attack us. We give up."

The white dragon stretched out its wings and opened its fanged mouth. "The great adventurers have come to grovel?"

"We surrender," Trenton yelled, not having to fake the fear in his voice. "Our dragons are damaged. I think Simoni is about to pass out from loss of blood. Let us land, and we'll come quietly."

To his right, Simoni dropped toward the ocean. She pulled up, then dropped again, each time edging closer to the tower.

"*Your* dragons?" the monarch said. "Everything in this city is mine—including you. Why should I let you live?"

Trenton circled, waiting for Simoni to get closer to the white dragon. Out of the corner of his eye, he saw Plucky lift a red ball out of a bag on her lap and drop it into Rounder's furnace.

"Please," Trenton called. "We ask for your mercy."

The monarch chuckled. "That is your mistake," it said with a wicked grin. "I don't have any mercy." Nearly twenty dragons had landed at the base of the tower, and at least a hundred more were on the way. The white dragon raised its bearded chin. "Kill them all."

"Go!" Trenton screamed. "Now!"

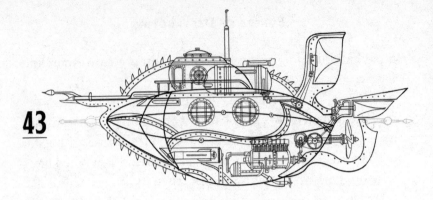

43

Kallista dove toward the dragons that were taking off from the cliff on the monarch's command. Trenton pulled Ladon out of his erratic flopping, spread the dragon's wings, and laid down a stream of fire.

At the same time, Simoni and Angus raced toward the monarch, shooting one fireball after another.

Angus raised both fists above his head, his eyes bright with fury. "This is for my family. And my friends. And every person ever killed or taken captive by a dragon!" The fireballs bounced harmlessly off the white dragon's scales.

Plucky and Clyde flew over the cliff, raining attacks on the dragons below them before soaring toward the city.

"This is for Seattle," Plucky yelled.

About half of the dragons turned to follow Rounder. The others went for Ladon and Devastation.

Kallista and Trenton didn't need to speak. They knew where they were going. Banking right, they soared over the whitecapped waves, drawing as many dragons as they could away from the white tower.

A pack of dragons angled to cut them off.

There was no time to think, only to react.

Simoni and Angus joined the battle hard and fast, fireballs bellowing out of Devastation's mouth as fast as Angus could hit the trigger. They drew the dragons to them like a target and were immediately enveloped in a mass of teeth and claws.

Rounder curved over the city directly into the horde coming toward them. Clyde and Plucky managed to shoot a few fireballs, but they were quickly overwhelmed.

"Turbos," Trenton yelled, although he knew the others couldn't hear him.

A second later, Rounder blasted out of the swarm of dragons like a comet. With the turbos on, smoke boiled out of the back of their steam engine.

Trenton cheered to see that the smoke was a deep red. The iron oxide ball Plucky had dropped into Rounder's furnace had worked. Thick, red smoke filled the air, making it all but impossible to see as Clyde looped around and around. They were no longer attacking, only trying to create as much confusion as possible.

Four dragons swooped toward Ladon, and Trenton had to focus on his own fight.

"Hold on," Kallista said, grabbing the controls.

Trenton swallowed. It was time to try something they'd only talked about doing.

Flying straight toward the dragon swarm, Kallista dropped Ladon's right wing down and pulled his left wing up. Spinning like a corkscrew, they dove into the fray.

Trenton clamped his hand on the fire button as earth and sky rapidly swapped places. Talons slashed around him; fangs bit at metal. Flames, acid, steam, and scales blurred until he had no idea who was attacking whom.

And then, miraculously, they broke out on the other side. When Kallista pulled out of the spin, there was not a single dragon between them and the white tower where the monarch still perched, watching the battle below. They had to draw him out.

"Go!" Trenton screamed.

Kallista didn't need to be told twice. Realizing the tower was unprotected, the dragons behind Ladon screamed with fury and turned to chase them.

Angus and Simoni took down a black dragon with a blast of fire and flew toward the monarch again, but a pair of blue dragons appeared from behind the tower, belching steam.

A trap.

Walls of scalding vapor drove them back, and Simoni headed low over the water to avoid being engulfed. Devastation was only feet above the waves when a hooked purple tentacle reached up and wrapped around the dragon's metal leg.

"No!" Trenton screamed.

He dove down, blasting one fireball after another at the sea dragon. The water boiled, and the creature howled. Simoni dug Devastation's talons into the sea dragon's back, and it released them.

Kallista tried to cut left, but they were surrounded. A green dragon clamped its jaws on Ladon's tail, swinging them through the air. Trenton yanked the tail control left and right, but he couldn't break free.

The green dragon forced them down. Waves rushed up, and Trenton held his hand in front of his face, sure they were about to crash.

A stream of fire blew so close he felt his hair curl from the heat.

He looked up to see Angus grinning at him as Devastation flew past.

The green dragon opened its jaws with a roar, and Trenton pulled up just before Ladon hit the water.

"Take that," Angus shouted.

Trenton leaned close to Kallista, yelling to be heard over the noise of the battle. "We have to get the monarch out of the tower."

Kallista nodded. Ignoring the dragons around them, she raced toward the white tower. When they drew close, Trenton slammed the fire button over and over, blasting the white dragon with everything he had, but the flames didn't appear to have any effect at all.

They were almost to the edge of the cliff. Kallista screamed at the monarch as they flew by. "I know about your laboratory! My father showed me where it was. You might control his mind, but he will never serve you, and neither will I!"

Trenton blasted a fireball that melted a chunk of the tower wall.

Roaring with rage, the monarch shot out a stream of purple energy from its jaws.

Trenton yanked the flight stick backward, and the energy beam passed under them. It hit the water, and the ocean turned purple.

"You will die!" the monarch screeched. Spreading its white wings, it dove out of the tower toward them.

Immediately Kallista hit the turbo button, and they circled toward the dragon. To their right, Simoni and Angus did the same. The engines in both mechanical dragons roared, and black smoke boiled from behind them.

Trenton gritted his teeth. Either his plan would work, or they were all about to die. The idea had come to him when he remembered how Simoni had sedated the wasps back at the campsite with smoke. At least part of the white dragon's power came from the jewel wasp DNA. The question was if the jewel wasp part of it was strong enough to be stupefied by smoke the way the regular wasps were.

Racing at a speed so fast it threatened to tear off their dragons' wings, Kallista and Simoni circled around and around the white dragon. Silver lightning flashed from the sky, and purple energy beams split the air, but Ladon and Devastation were moving so fast it was nearly impossible to hit them.

The dark smoke grew so thick it was hard for Trenton to see what was happening. Peering through the black cloud, he hacked up the sludge coating his throat.

"Something's happening," Kallista yelled. "I think it's working!"

The monarch's purple eyes flashed bright, then dimmed. It wings stuttered.

"More!" Trenton yelled. He flew dangerously close to the white dragon's head. If the monarch chose to shoot one if its energy beams, Trenton, Kallista, and Ladon would be vaporized.

But the monarch didn't attack. Its body shuddered. Its head wobbled. "What . . . are you . . ."

For a moment, it looked like it might to fall into the ocean, but it managed to make it back to the cliff and landed at the base of the tower. Its wings flopped limply open. Its head dropped back against the tower, leaving its chest and neck exposed.

"Now!" Trenton screamed.

As one, both Ladon and Devastation turned to attack. Trenton checked the pressure gauge. It was dangerously high. They had thirty seconds before the engine would explode. They only had time for one shot.

Flying like two arrows shot from the same bow, the mechanical dragons closed in on the monarch. Kallista and Simoni aimed their dragons' heads while Trenton and Angus prepared to fire. When they were nearly at point-blank range, Angus yelled, "This is for the Runt Patrol."

"This is for all the people whose freedom you stole," Trenton said. Then he added quietly, "Especially Kallista's father."

At almost the same time, two massive fireballs exploded out of the mouths of Ladon and Devastation. A pair of dragons who had swooped in to protect the monarch tried to fly away, but the flames turned them to ash in an instant.

Trenton's shot was slightly off, hitting half of the monarch's body and half of the white tower. But Angus's shot was perfect, hitting the dragon directly in its exposed throat.

The huge explosion made the air ripple. Black smoke billowed as the mechanical dragons banked away from the heat. As the fire died away, Trenton swiveled back to see the results. For once he hoped Devastation's name was accurate.

The smoke slowly cleared, revealing the white tower leaning precariously toward the ocean. Standing at its base, though, the monarch appeared undamaged. If anything, the flames seemed to have woken the dragon from its smoke-induced stupor.

The white dragon tilted its head, spread it wings, and laughed. "Did you really think your fire weapons could harm me?"

Trenton's heart sank. He had failed again.

Ladon's engine began to shudder. Trenton glanced at the pressure gauge. The needle was at the far end of the red. They had to shut off the turbo before they exploded. He glanced from the gauge to the broken white tower and the dragon standing beneath it.

He knew what he had to do.

He didn't need to tell Kallista. She reached for the controls. Before she could touch them, a blur of gold flashed past.

Trenton barely had time to see Angus's sunburned face and a hint of streaming red hair.

He saw Angus's jutting chin and heard Simoni's voice: *"He fights hard, he talks hard, and he flies hard because he believes it's the only way to protect the people he loves."*

"No!" Trenton cried.

The monarch's violet eyes opened wide, glowing purple, but its mind control couldn't touch Angus or Simoni.

Instead of going directly for the dragon, Angus flew low over the water, aiming for the cave opening where the water flowed out from the lab. He slowed for a moment and leaned forward as if whispering something to Simoni. As she began to look back, he unclipped Simoni's harness. He slipped one of his arms around her waist and pushed her into the water.

A second later, Devastation hit the rock and disappeared in a ball of flame. The rocky cliff exploded outward, revealing the lab inside. The white tower—already damaged—toppled toward the ocean.

The monarch looked up in terror. Tower, cliff, and dragon disappeared into Devastation's inferno and plunged to the jagged rocks below.

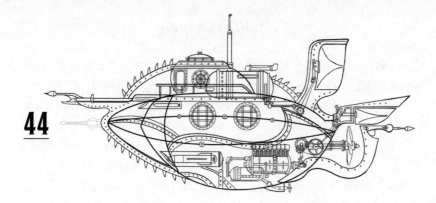

As the water boiled and the dust settled, everything seemed to come to a halt. The dragons continued to circle above the city, but none of them were attacking. It was almost as if they expected the monarch to rise from the debris and tell them what to do.

Kallista half expected that as well. The monarch seemed unstoppable—a perfectly designed creature that would live forever. But looking at the water near the base of the cliff, she could see the white dragon's body crushed beneath tons of rock and dirt. It wasn't moving, and it was clear it never would again.

There was no sign of Angus or Devastation. She tried to tell herself she hadn't seen her friend disappear in a ball of fire, but she knew in her heart that he was gone. She'd thought about doing the same thing—she almost had—but for Angus, there had been no thought, only action. He'd been a bully most of his life, but in the end, he'd sacrificed himself for the good of others.

She switched off Ladon's turbo.

Trenton was the first to come out of his daze. "Simoni!" he shouted. "She's somewhere in the water. We have to find her."

They circled Ladon and searched the choppy ocean. Kallista was afraid Simoni was gone too. Angus had slowed at the last minute, throwing Simoni away from the cliff, where the water was still deep and the debris from the explosion would be unlikely to reach her, but they'd still been moving fast. Too fast? Could she have survived the drop at that speed?

Even this far out, the once blue-green water was turning a sludgy brown from the sudden influx of millions of pounds of rock and dirt. It would be impossible to locate anything in that.

Trenton dropped them so low, Kallista could feel the spray of saltwater against her cheeks. "There!" he shouted, pointing to a small, redheaded figure floating in the water. She was face up, arms spread, but she wasn't moving.

Trenton unsnapped his harness.

"No," Kallista said. "You can't swim, and I can't fly Ladon by myself."

"I have to save her," Trenton growled, jaw set.

"We will."

Kallista circled around, setting them up to make a pass over Simoni's body. "Cut the power back all the way, but don't turn off the engine. Gun it as soon as we have her or we'll end up in the water too."

Trenton dropped the engine speed to idle, putting them into a glide, and Kallista opened Ladon's talons wide. She reversed the dragon's legs so the talons became scoops. It was still going to be tricky, and dangerous, and if it didn't work, she wouldn't be able to keep Trenton from diving over the side, leaving him to drown and her unable to help him.

"Easy," Kallista whispered, her eyes focused on the body that bobbed up and down on the waves. "If we miss her the first time, we can come around for a second try. But if we drop too low . . ."

"I'm not going to miss," Trenton said. "Just be ready to close the talons as soon as we have her."

Kallista chewed her lower lip. If they were off by even a little, Ladon's talons would—

She couldn't let herself think about that. Riding the current like a seabird, they swooped toward the water.

"Here we go," Trenton whispered, feathering the flight control. "I've got you."

The waves lifted Simoni up just as Trenton pushed the flight stick forward, dropping Ladon's legs into the water. "I've got her!" he shouted.

Kallista closed the talons, and Trenton gunned the engine and pulled back on the stick at the same time.

But was it too late?

They tried to pull Ladon up, but he was dropping deeper into the water. First his talon disappeared, then his legs. The water reached all the way to Ladon's belly, and Kallista could feel the waves trying to drag them under.

Trenton yanked back on the flight stick while Kallista jiggled Ladon's wings left and right. A sudden gust of air jerked them free.

They quickly banked and headed back to the city. Kallista spotted a small patch of open grass near where the white tower had once stood and headed for it. Using the same technique they'd used to pick Simoni up, they glided over the area and rolled her onto the grass.

They'd barely landed before Trenton was over the side of the dragon. Gripping the sides of the ladder, he slid to the ground and ran back to where Simoni lay on the grass.

Kallista closed her eyes and held her breath. *Don't let her be dead too.*

"She's breathing!" Trenton shouted a moment later. "Simoni's alive."

Kallista exhaled deeply and shut off Ladon's engine. She was thrilled Simoni was alive and that they'd killed the monarch, but it had come at a high cost. At the thought of Angus, she felt a sob clog her throat. She shook her head. Mourning would have to wait. The battle was far from over. With the monarch dead, the dragons were free to do whatever they wanted. And, more important, had the monarch's death freed the humans' minds or were the effects permanent?

With no one in charge, things could quickly turn into a bloodbath.

As she climbed down the ladder, Clyde and Plucky flew over the park. One of Rounder's legs was completely torn off, and huge rips in the metal fabric on the wings flapped as the dragon came in for a rough landing that churned a deep furrow in the grass and ended with Rounder facedown in the street.

Clyde scrambled down from the dragon. The cuts and bruises on his face and body were no longer fake. He had a deep scratch on one cheek, and the right side of his shirt was soaked with red.

He stumbled to Kallista and grabbed her arm. "Where's Angus?"

Tears welled up in her eyes, and she shook her head.

"No," Clyde sobbed, burying his face in his hands.

The men and women who were standing nearby blinked in dazed surprise, looking around with shocked expressions as if unsure where they were or what they'd been doing.

A shadow passed over the park, and a huge black dragon landed by Rounder.

Plucky, who was climbing down the ladder, jumped the last few feet as the black dragon closed its talons on Rounder and smashed the mechanical dragon to the ground over and over.

"What have you done?" the dragon roared.

Two other dragons landed in the park.

"They have killed the monarch," a golden dragon snarled.

A red dragon blasted the ground with a stream of fire that turned the grass black.

The dragons closed ranks, forcing Kallista, Clyde, and Plucky into a tight circle with Trenton and a still unconscious Simoni at the center.

"How dare you attack our city?" the black dragon roared. "How dare you kill dragons?"

Kallista's heart pounded, but after all they had been through, she wasn't about to back down now. "How dare *you*? Killing humans. Kidnapping them. Forcing them to be your servants without the ability to think for themselves. What gives you the right?"

Trenton, who had been kneeling beside Simoni, stood. "You think you're so powerful? Who do you think created you in the first place? You may be bigger and stronger than we are, but we will never stop fighting."

The black dragon snorted and turned to the red dragon. "Destroy them and hang their bodies in the city as a warning to any other humans who think they can disobey us."

As the red dragon moved forward, a single figure climbed from the hole in the ground where the white tower had stood. His face and hair were blackened with soot, and his left arm hung useless at his side, but Kallista recognized him immediately.

"Dad!"

Leo Babbage stumbled toward the trio of dragons. "Stop! Stop!"

The red dragon paused, glancing toward the black dragon uncertainly.

"Half the laboratory is gone," Kallista's father gasped. He raised his good arm, revealing a small black box with a copper switch set into the top. "If I flip this switch, a series of explosives will destroy the rest of it."

The black dragon tilted its massive head. "We will force the other humans to rebuild it."

"No," Leo said, his breathing pained and shallow.

Kallista saw his right pant leg was slowly turning red. She started toward him, but he shook his head.

He stared the black dragon in the eye. "Without the white dragon, you can no longer control the people of this city. Stand down, and I will preserve the lab—and the documents describing how each dragon is created. Continue to fight, and I'll destroy everything." He shook his head. "No laboratory means no more dragons. Ever."

Was he bluffing? Had he really planted explosives? He'd managed to resist the monarch's mind control enough to lead Kallista to the lab, which meant it wasn't impossible.

Kallista knew one thing for sure. It was never a good idea to underestimate Leo Babbage.

The black dragon ripped a gouge in the earth with one of its talons and fixed its golden eye on the inventor. "Tell me what you have in mind, human."

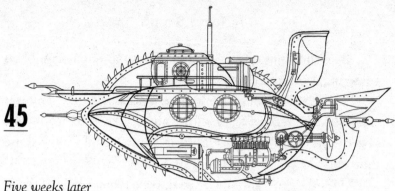

45

Five weeks later

Trenton's father was waiting for him outside the city center—the only building large enough to hold ten dragons at the same time—when Trenton, Kallista, and several members of the Runt Patrol emerged from their latest meeting.

Trenton's parents, along with Angus's, Clyde's, and Simoni's parents had arrived in San Francisco almost a week earlier. Leo had flown the airship to Discovery and back in order to reunite the families.

"Well?" Trenton's father asked. "How did it go?"

Trenton shook his head. "If you'd told me five weeks ago that I'd be negotiating a peace treaty between humans and dragons, I would have thought you were crazy. But I honestly think it might work."

"I'd love to have been in there," his father said. There'd nearly been another battle over who would meet with the dragons to negotiate the peace settlement. The adults of the city felt the children were too young, while the children felt the adults shouldn't be negotiating anything until there was clear proof that their minds weren't still clouded by the monarch's control. And the dragons simply didn't trust anyone.

Ultimately, it came down to the fact that if it hadn't been for the kids, there wouldn't be any peace process to attend.

"I wish . . ." Trenton started, then shook his head.

His father put an arm around Trenton's shoulders. "You wish Angus was there too."

"If it wasn't for him, none of us would be here." Trenton slammed a balled fist against his thigh. "I keep replaying the last battle in my mind. Thinking what I could have done differently."

"It wasn't your fault. I've talked to everyone who was there, and they all agree you did everything you could."

He hadn't done enough. He'd been the leader of the team, and he'd failed to bring one of his friends home. "How do you do it?" he asked, wiping his eyes. "How do you get over losing someone?"

"You don't get over it," his father said. "You only learn to live with it. But time makes it easier."

They walked down the hill toward the house where they were living. It wasn't as big as the mansion on the hill, but that was fine. Trenton liked cozy better anyway. Kallista and her father lived next door.

"Do you think the humans and dragons will reach an agreement soon?" his father asked.

Trenton knew his dad was intentionally changing the subject, and he appreciated the effort. "There's still a lot to figure out. The dragons aren't used to working together. Without a single leader, they spend a lot of time fighting among themselves."

"Like some humans I know," his dad said.

Trenton knew his father was referring to Angus's father, who had organized a group of people who wanted to change Discovery's name back to Cove and seal it up again. This time for good.

He claimed it would only be a matter of time before the

dragons broke the peace treaty, and he planned to reseal the mountain before that could happen.

"Do you really think they'll seal up the city?" Trenton asked.

"I don't know," his father said. "Darrow has taken his son's death hard, and there are a lot of scared people right now. People do crazy things when they're frightened."

Trenton wondered how long it would be before they returned to the lie that the outside world had been destroyed by creativity and change. "It would be like everything we did for the city was for nothing."

His dad patted his shoulder. "I believe calmer voices will win out. It will take time to repair the damage the dragons did when they broke in. The fact that you and your friends have negotiated a peace treaty here may give people enough confidence to wait and see what happens before doing anything rash."

"Leo says he thinks the monarch was controlling the dragons' minds too," Trenton said. "He thinks that's why some of the dragons left the city and others are refusing to obey the truce." There had been several attacks from both dragons and humans, until the peace treaty committee had established a law that said that any human or dragon who attacked the other was permanently banished from the city. Since then, things had been calmer.

"He would know," Dad said. "I wish we could get him involved in politics, but no one can convince him to pull his head out of his books and experiments."

That sounded like Kallista's father all right. Kallista wasn't much better. She spent so much time with her father, Trenton barely saw her these days.

A quad clattered past them, weaving from one side of the street to the other. Jack was driving while Cameron fought to get control of the wheel. Lizzy waved and shouted, "Hi, Trenton."

Trenton waved to his friends and grinned. He'd never seen the Runt Patrol so happy.

"Have the dragons agreed to recognize humans as equals?" his father asked.

"The ones who are staying in the city don't have much choice," Trenton said. "Over the years, they've come to rely on humans and technology for too much. I'd say they've become . . ."

"Domesticated?" his father suggested. "How many dragons are leaving?"

Trenton shook his head. "I'm not sure. They kept close track of the humans, but no one saw a need to count the dragons. The night after the monarch died, every Ninki Nanka in the city disappeared. Some people think they've gone to the forests to hunt, while others think they're living in the sewers, but no one really knows. It's making people nervous."

They passed a family moving beds and furniture into an empty house. With their minds restored, many of the adults had moved out of the dorms and into homes of their own. Families who hadn't lived together for years were being reunited.

"I think we'll get the Great Treaty ratified in the next few days," Trenton said. "We've agreed to create safe zones where dragons and humans can peacefully coexist, rules governing interactions between the two species, and rights for all 'intelligent, free-thinking beings of choice.'

"For now, it will only apply to a few cities. San Francisco, Seattle, and a couple of other cities the dragons destroyed in the past—assuming people want to move back into them. Until we get a better idea of what's happening in the rest of the world, no one feels comfortable making decisions about other areas."

He'd intentionally not mentioned Discovery since Marshall Darrow and his followers wanted nothing to do with a dragon treaty.

They paused outside their house, and Trenton heard Plucky say something that made his mom laugh. He grinned. It was good to hear his mother laughing again. Ever since his parents had decided to make Plucky an official part of the family, his mother was like a new person. She'd stuffed Plucky with every kind of dessert imaginable and sewed new clothes for her. The two of them spent hours playing games, going to the library, and dangling bits of yarn in front of Allie. Plucky was even secretly working on a pair of mechanical leg braces for his mom.

Plucky absorbed the affection like a sponge that had been far too dry for far too long. It really was a perfect match. Mom's attitude had completely turned around. Well, *almost* completely.

"Do you think Mom will ever be okay with machines?" Trenton asked.

"I'm not sure," his father said. "She was getting more comfortable around them, but once she found out technology was responsible for creating the dragons, she swore she'd been right all along. I think part of her still believes machines are an abomination and that mankind will be cursed until we turn away from them."

"Do you think she could be right?" Trenton asked. "I mean technology has been a part of some terrible things. We were almost completely wiped off the face of the Earth because some scientists were trying to create a better weapon."

He'd been struggling with the idea a lot lately. He still loved to build, and the sight of gears and pistons still sent his heart racing. But look what had happened in Seattle. He'd been so excited about creating new inventions that he'd completely overlooked how they might be used. Some days he thought maybe it would be better if he quit building things. Other days he couldn't stop dreaming up new inventions. It was complicated.

His father placed a hand on his shoulder. "I don't think technology by itself is either good or bad. People are the ones who make it that way. You have a talent for inventing, but you're the one who has to decide how you'll use it. Now let's go inside and see what those two are finding so funny."

• • •

Kallista walked into the room to find her father on a ladder directing a group of men as they fed wires into a conduit attached to the ceiling. Unlike the old lab, which had been completely gutted, this room was bright and airy with skylights and windows overlooking the bay. "Looking good, Dad," she called up.

"I never did like that old place," he said. "Too wet and cramped. Besides, it reminded me of one of those novels in the library—*Frankenstein*, I think it was called."

Kallista grinned. She'd picked up the book after her father read it, finishing the novel in a single night. Was he even aware of how closely what he'd been doing with the dragons matched the theme of the story? She doubted it. More likely he'd only skimmed the book to see if there was any actual science he could use.

Like the previous lab, there were giant glass cylinders placed along the walls on one half of the room. They were still growing dragons, but a few species were conspicuously missing, including the white dragons, the sea dragons, and the Ninki Nankas, which her father had refused to create.

It was the other half of the room that caught her attention, though. Here the glass tubes were smaller, and the walls were covered with detailed anatomical breakdowns of each type of dragon.

She walked past a line of workbenches, nodding at how well organized and clean the tools were. She paused to examine some surgical equipment and a set of medical books. This half of the room looked more like a hospital than a workshop.

Curious, she began flipping through a stack of diagrams.

"Ah," her father said, walking up to join her. "You have found my latest work. What do you make of it?"

Kallista looked from the diagrams to the books and equipment. "You're studying the dragons' anatomy. How to keep them healthy."

Leo chuckled. "I like to think of myself as a dragon veterinarian."

"Do you think that's a good idea?" Kallista asked. "Wouldn't it be better if the dragons died out?"

"Perhaps," her father said, not sounding convinced. "Or perhaps we will find other ways to be mutually beneficial to each other." He scratched his head. "Besides, I believe we owe them something."

Kallista wrinkled her forehead. "Why do we owe the dragons anything? Considering how they almost destroyed our species, I'd say *they* owe *us*."

"Come with me," Leo said, walking to the other side of the room. As they passed the glass cylinders, he stopped in front of one of the tiny growing dragons. "When I told you that humans had been replaced on the evolutionary ladder, my mind was being controlled by the white dragon."

"I know," Kallista said. "And I don't blame you."

In the weeks since the monarch had died, her father had explained how he'd succumbed to the dragon's control the first time he'd looked into the creature's eyes. Inside, a part of him knew he was being controlled and had fought against it. But he'd been unable to do or say anything that directly contradicted the monarch's will.

Using what little freedom he still possessed, he did what he could to help Kallista and the others—seeing that the dragons were repaired, pointing Kallista to their location, dropping hints about the lab, and, of course, the night he'd intentionally led her there. These small bits of insurrection took all of his strength and gave him massive headaches, but he'd hoped that her years of playing games with him would lead her to the truth.

"There was some truth in what I said, though. Mankind didn't just invent a weapon, we created a new species with intelligence rivaling our own. The moment we brought this new life into the world, it became our responsibility."

He tapped his chin. "We might hate what we have created, we might wish we could take it back, but if we abandoned responsibility for our actions, if we failed to recognize the right of the 'monsters,' we would be no better than Dr. Frankenstein, would we?"

Kallista grinned. Maybe he understood more of the book than she'd thought. "You're saying now that this species exists, we have no more right to destroy it than they have the right to destroy us?"

"Exactly. For now, I will search for ways to keep the dragons healthy. What happens after that will be up to the next generation. *Your* generation." He tapped her forehead. "I have great confidence in you."

Kallista leaned forward and wrapped her arms around his neck. "I love you, Dad."

He looked surprised for a minute, then hugged her back. "I love you, too. I always have."

"I hate to break up this touching moment," Trenton called.

He was standing inside the lab door with Clyde, Plucky, and Simoni.

"You're out of bed," Kallista said to Simoni.

Simoni nodded. She still looked pale but much better than the last few times Kallista had checked in on her. "I've been needing to get up for a while, but I just couldn't seem to find the strength. Then Trenton showed up and told me about his idea."

"It wasn't my idea," Trenton said. "It was Angus's. I wouldn't have thought of it if you hadn't told me what he said."

"I think it's what he would have wanted," Simoni agreed.

"What idea?" Kallista asked.

"It's a plummy corker, yeah, yeah," Plucky said.

"Amazing," Clyde said. "Tell her, already."

"I will if you'll all stop talking for a second." Trenton took a deep breath and grinned. "Okay, I have this idea for an invention."

Epilogue

Clyde was adding the finishing touches to the paint as people began arriving.

"Quick," Simoni called. "Pull up the cover."

Trenton and Plucky grabbed a pair of handles and began cranking them around and around. Gears turned, winding thick ropes around metal wheels. As the ropes tightened, a large tent-like structure rose from the ground, hiding what was underneath it.

Clyde climbed out from under the edge of the tent, wiping blue paint off his fingers onto his pants.

"Everything ready, yeah, yeah?" Plucky asked.

"Fine, as long as no one touches the wet paint," Clyde said with a grin.

Trenton was glad to see that the two had remained close friends after everything they'd been through on their adventures together. He wondered if maybe that friendship might even grow into something more someday. The idea made him smile.

"How are the hands?" Trenton asked.

Clyde held his arms out straight, fingers extended. The tremors were barely visible. "I told you I wouldn't let anyone take what I love."

"How are *you* doing?" Simoni asked, standing beside Trenton.

"Good, I think." He rubbed the back of his hand across his mouth. "Okay, a little nervous." He studied Simoni. She looked as beautiful as ever. Only someone who had known her as long as he had would notice the dark smudges under her eyes and the fact that she didn't smile nearly as much as she used to.

She hadn't spent much time with Trenton and the others except to help with this project. She'd explained that being around them made the pain of Angus's death too sharp. She hoped one day that wouldn't be the case, but, for now, it was what she needed to do.

"Are you sure you want to do this?" Trenton asked. "If it's too much, you don't have to speak."

The corners of her lips rose, but the smile never reached her eyes. "It's the least I can do. His family is still here?"

Trenton nodded. "They promised to come, but they're leaving as soon as we're done."

Trenton and his friends were standing on a spot near where the white tower had once been. It was close enough to overlook the ocean but far enough away that none of the littlest kids were in any danger of falling off the ragged edge of the cliff.

A crowd of humans and dragons had gathered to see the unveiling of a new invention. There'd been rumors swirling for weeks of what the kids had been working on. Some said it was a new mode of transportation; others said it was a monument. A few thought it might be a weapon. The Runt Patrol put an end to that rumor immediately.

Whatever it was, it was big—at least thirty feet tall and a hundred feet across. It was completely covered by a huge, circular, white-and-red-striped tent.

Trenton, Kallista, Simoni, Clyde, and Plucky stood in front of their invention and looked out over the crowd. Trenton's mother and father were nearby. His father beamed, face alight with curiosity. His mother sat in her wheelchair. She didn't look as thrilled, but at least she had come. Next to them stood

Leo Babbage and Simoni's parents. Clyde's family stood near the front, his sisters waving at Clyde, trying to get his attention.

To their left stood Angus's family.

With his hands shaking, Trenton took a piece of paper from his pocket. He cleared his throat and tried to speak, but found he was too choked up to get the words out. Kallista smacked him on the back—harder than was necessary, he thought—and the people in the audience laughed.

The moment broke the tension, and Trenton found that he could talk.

His eyes blurred as he read the words. He stared at the paper in his hand, then crumpled it up and jammed it into his pocket. He knew what he wanted to say.

"Angus was a stubborn, rust-brained know-it-all. He did what he wanted, when he wanted. But he was one of the greatest people I've ever known."

He paused, and Simoni spoke up. "It is because of his bravery and unwillingness to give up, because of his determination and sacrifice, that we all stand here today. I miss him so much."

Tears streamed down her face, and Trenton put an arm around her shoulders. "It feels like a lifetime ago that Angus accused me of being an inventor. At the time, we both believed that creativity was bad. Since that time, I've wondered if maybe that is true, at least a little." He glanced down at his mother.

Kallista stepped forward.

"Technology can be a terrible thing. Weapons and machines can replace love and human kindness. It is because of technology that millions of people have died. But it can also be a wonderful thing. It can save lives, feed the hungry, and it can even bring new life into the world."

She stepped back, and Trenton took a deep breath.

"Creativity isn't just machines, though. It isn't just

inventing. It's painting and sculpting, writing and music. Creativity is imagining, dreaming about a better world—a world where we can stop fighting and start working together.

"Angus once told me that he admired me for trying to do the right thing. He said he wished he could be more like that. Well, when it counted the most, he did exactly the right thing." He glanced at Simoni, who looked toward Angus's family.

"Right before . . ." Her voice trembled, and she wiped her eyes. "Before Angus saved my life by pushing me off the dragon, he said to me, 'Tell my father I've learned that protecting people is about who you help, not who you hurt.'" She turned and hugged Trenton.

Trenton took a deep breath. "In honor of our good friend, Angus Darrow, who wanted to help people, we have something to donate to the city. Something we hope will bring you joy. I think that if Angus were here today, he'd agree that creativity is a good thing. It can bring joy, and maybe, just maybe, creativity can change the world—for the better."

Together, all five of them reached up and pulled a thick golden rope. The tent fell, revealing a huge, circular, mechanical swing. A much bigger version of the swing Trenton had once built back in the city of Cove to impress Simoni. Only instead of seats, each swing was either a mechanical dragon or a representation of a real one. Flying together, side by side.

Trenton pulled a switch, and the machine started up. Music composed by Plucky's friend Talysa filled the air as the dragons whirled higher and higher. There was an audible gasp from the people watching, then every kid in the audience crowded forward for a chance to ride a dragon.

Trenton looked down to see a girl no older than six with long red hair stare longingly up at the swings. A bigger kid started to push her out of the way, but a muscular boy stepped in, put an arm around her and escorted her to the front of the line.

He glanced at Simoni, who smiled back at him. Together she, Trenton, and Kallista helped the boy and the girl take the first seats on the ride.

Maybe creativity really could change the world.

Acknowledgments

Four years ago, I had lunch with Chris Schoebinger of Shadow Mountain and said, "I have this idea for a book about a boy and a girl who live in a city under a mountain where creativity is against the law. They end up building a giant steam-powered dragon." Chris's eyes lit up, and this series began. I don't remember what we had for lunch, or even where we ate, but I remember how excited we were about the story and the way it would play out.

Since that time, I've been amazed by how many other people have fallen in love with the combination of steampunk and dragons. I've received drawings, book trailers, dragons of all shapes and sizes, and tons of cool steampunk gifts from my readers. But even more than that, I've received so many wonderful messages about my books. It thrills me when I think about all the new friends I've made through this series and all the old friends who started reading my earlier books and came with me on this journey. I hope you'll stay with me wherever the next idea takes us.

I'd also like to recognize some real people who allowed me to use their names for characters in this book. Talysa Sainz was the high bidder in a charity auction that helped raise money to buy books for needy students. Hallie Meredith, Michael Whitlock, and Joey Moore were entered into a contest by their parents. Alex Vaughn is a good friend and fine actor whose plays I have enjoyed, and Graysen, Lizzy, Jack, Asher, and Cameron are my own grandkids, who I stuck in the Runt Patrol because I could.

Special thanks to Cori Bailie, Jackson Porter, and Matt Hayes for their amazing and helpful feedback on the story.

I also want to say thanks to the teachers, the librarians, the bookstore staff members, my friends, my publisher, my agent, my incredibly supportive family, and especially all of you amazing people who put down the remote, turn off the phone, ignore the chores, errands, and all the other things the world has to offer in order to dive into the pages of books. You are the people who change the world.

ACTIVITIES

1. At the end of *Embers of Destruction*, the dragons and humans work to establish a peace treaty. Divide your class, friends, or family into two groups. Half of you will be dragons, and half of you will be humans. See if you can negotiate a set of laws that both groups can agree on.

2. Trenton and Kallista discover that the different species of dragons got their powers from the animal DNA that was used to create them. List three different kinds of animals, like insects, birds, mammals, reptiles, or others. If you combined those three animals into a single dragon, what powers might it have?

3. Angus was known as a bully. Take three examples from this book of his bullying and discuss how he could have handled those situations better. Try role-playing your version with a friend.

4. Kallista, Trenton, and the Runt Patrol try to come up with a plan to stop the dragons. If the Runt Patrol came to you for a plan, what would you do?

DISCUSSION QUESTIONS

1. Simoni tells Trenton he should stop trying to be the best at everything. Do you think that was good advice? Why can trying to be the best at something be good? How can it be bad?

2. The people of San Francisco have enough to eat and houses to live in. To earn this security, they must give up their freedom by serving the dragons. If you had to choose between security or freedom, which would you pick? Why?

3. Simoni says that leaders make those around them better. Can you think of a leader you know who has done this? Are there leaders who did not make those around them better? What did they do differently from each other and how did their leadership end?

4. The people who founded Discovery didn't bring pets (like cats or dogs) into the mountain with them because they only wanted animals that could be used for food. Do you think that was a good or bad decision? Why?

5. Kallista believes her father is right about everything. When he says something she disagrees with, she struggles to decide whether to believe him or not. Has an adult ever said something that you thought was wrong? How did you respond to it?

6. In *Fires of Invention* and *Gears of Revolution*, Trenton and Kallista choose to protect their home and family. In *Embers of Destruction*, they decide to fight for the people of San Francisco. Do you think this is a good or bad decision? Why?